Sweet Grass Memories

The House That Became a Bridge

Jan Morgan

ISBN 978-1-64003-687-1 (Paperback)
ISBN 978-1-64003-688-8 (Digital)

Covenant Books, Inc.
11661 Hwy 707
Murrells Inlet, SC 29576
www.covenantbooks.com

This book is dedicated to the students, families and friends of BridgesWork. Isaac Newton was indeed correct: We build too many walls and not enough bridges.

4/24/2018

Sarah

With sincere gratitude for your support of BridgesWork

Jan Morgan

Contents

Everybody Has a Story

"There is no greater agony than bearing an untold story inside you."

—Maya Angelou, "I Know Why the Caged Bird Sings"

My high school senior English teacher made everybody memorize a quote she particularly fancied. Credited to Mark Twain, it was written on her front blackboard everyday: "Truth is stranger than fiction, but it is because Fiction is obliged to stick to possibilities; Truth isn't." Sadly, I never really gave that quote or most of the others she shared much thought until now, but after the events of the past few years, I believe I have tangible proof that Mark Twain was indeed correct.

I am sixty-six years old, retired, and as far as I know, healthy. What is more important, however, is that I think I finally know what I want to do with my life.

Years ago, if someone had asked me whether or not a story about a despondent old house that seems to communicate with selected individuals; several disenfranchised kids who want to believe in themselves but aren't exactly sure how; a poignant tale of star-crossed love during World War II; and two retired ladies, one black and one white, struggling to unearth their purposes in life before it is too late was more fact than fiction, I clearly would have replied "fiction." The problem is that the story is mine, and it is true.

I've heard others say that life is a circuitous path that most of us journey along, and we don't usually stop to think about whether the route we are following is a predestined one or something that occurs by chance. Statistics might support that assessment, as well as the hypothesis that most of us don't take time to reflect on the impact of every choice we make along the way until we've already made quite a few of them and are in the fall or winter of our years.

Now, on the backside of my youth, I've come to believe that most of the time, things happen for a reason, and people who cross paths usually do not do so by accident. And if that revelation isn't disconcerting enough, I also believe that most of the events in our lives were meant to occur.

Over the last six years, I've taken an unexpected detour along my route that I would never have considered plausible before. By virtue of this I've been drawn headfirst into the lives of people with fetching and exotic names such as Raven, Jalissa, Chanté, Jillian Marie, and Justine.

By the way, there is one more personal revelation that I need to share before I begin this story, and I promise it is a doozy. It took a while for me to accept the fact that I now can hear, and even decipher, the thoughts of a melancholy, old house with a painful past. Even more coincidental may be the fact that since our first encounter (the house and me), I've been pulled back across time and distance to a historic and enchanting southern city that I was moonstruck over during my college days.

The house, myself, and others, have now come together to chart a path for success for several, marginalized children who are living over fifty years later and a thousand miles west of that city by the sea. Truth may indeed be stranger than fiction because, honestly, you just can't make this stuff up.

Chapter 1

A House Is Just a House, Isn't It?

"There are people who, like houses, are beautiful in dilapidation."

—Logan P. Smith

Ever since I was a child, I have had a habit of attributing human attributes to nonhuman entities—the wind talks, the lion is proud, the fox cunning—but when I started "hearing" the thoughts of an old house, my anthropomorphic tendencies advanced to a whole other dimension.

Sometime around 2008, after I had started teaching evening classes at a local university, my twice-weekly route would take me very near an old, rundown mansion just beyond one of the intersections I had to cross. Sometimes, I'd get caught at the traffic light at that corner of Tremont Street and Venture Boulevard, the main artery through town. When that happened, I'd sit for a few moments observing the place from a distance.

I could see tiny Blessing Path and its only structure off to the right of the intersection. I often mused that my focus of attention, the house, must be somewhere between fifty to seventy years old, and I marveled that it was still standing since no one appeared to have lived in it for a very long time. Often I felt I could sense its pain of abandonment and wondered if there had ever been a time when it had felt contented or even loved.

If you had been riding with me then and had paid careful attention, you would have seen a two-story wooden structure with stately entrance columns. Most of the house was festooned with huge areas of peeling paint and voracious, climbing vines. Its extensive front yard and circular driveway were overgrown with an enthusiastic assortment of weeds that put on a show of vividly colored blooms in the spring months. The shingles had been torn from the roof, more than likely the result of the fury of past Texas spring storms. The overall sense of the property was one of desperation.

Quite honestly, most people who passed by this place on a regular basis probably never gave it a second thought, or if they did, it was more than likely one of irritation. Even though the surrounding area was replete with overgrown vacant lots, apartment complexes that could have used a little work, and tired "mom and pop" convenience stores with bars on the windows, the house was probably the most noticeable eyesore in the neighborhood.

Over the years, each time I passed by and took a moment to study the lonely house, I felt sad and empty. Definitely neglected and superficially unappealing, I couldn't help but think that at some point in the past, it had to have been a center of activity and pride. For some reason, I was never able to let it go. Had there been grand plans for it at some time—perhaps a large family home? And if so, how had life gotten in the way of that?

The more I studied the place, the more I decided its overall design was out of place. There simply weren't many two-story houses with tall, paired rectangular windows, broad overhanging eaves, and a big porch with stately columns in our area of Texas. I wondered why someone with an eye for beauty hadn't purchased it for renovation. I decided it had to be the location.

Seasons came and went, and I usually drove by Blessing Path only when going to work, but my infatuation with its only structure never waned. Something compelled me to know more.

Early one spring evening, on a whim, I printed a copy of a photograph I had taken of it some months earlier. Sitting quietly at my desk with a soft breeze drifting through the window, I examined the photograph for what may have been the hundredth time when I noticed something odd. There were tiny carvings on its eaves. I pulled a small magnifying glass out of one of my desk drawers and passed it over the photograph. Looking closely, I was puzzled. The carvings looked surprisingly like tiny pineapples.

Without a second thought, I retrieved my car keys and headed over to Blessing Path to get a closer look. It was that fateful evening that I first saw the kids, and now looking back, I realize that Elisabeth Kubler-Ross was probably correct when she said, "There are no mistakes, no coincidences. All events are blessings given to us to learn from."

Chapter 2

Dealing with the Unexpected

"The best kind of friend is the kind you can sit on a porch with, never say a word, then walk away feeling like it was the best conversation that you ever had."

—Anonymous

There were eight to ten of them sitting on the front porch, and as I considered the unexpected scene confronting me, I realized this was the first time I had ever seen anyone anywhere near the house. There was no posted signage indicating private property, so I had intended to stop and walk around the exterior of the structure to see if I could somehow get a closer look at the carvings.

I also thought the house might have historic significance and wanted to look around to see if I could find something on the property affirming that. As overgrown as the trees and shrubs were, I felt a historic marker could easily be overlooked, and I was eager to walk around the perimeter.

I changed my mind, though, when I saw the kids and decided it would be better to come back at another time when I wouldn't be intruding on their time, and also when I wouldn't need to explain why I was there.

During the weeks that followed, I began to stagger my departure time for work and would always make it a point to drive slowly past the house looking for activity. It was not until I went by another time in the early evening that I saw them again.

Still numbering eight to ten, and across all ages, they appeared comfortable and established sitting on the steps of the dilapidated porch. Their laughter and conversation filled the evening air, and I was able to catch a stray word or two. Still too hesitant to stop, I realized, quite to my chagrin, that I was now becoming as curious about them and their relationship to the house as I was about the structure itself.

It was mid-May before I finally mustered the courage to stop. I pulled into the dusty driveway slowly, stopped the car, and unfastened my seat belt. When I opened the car door, the younger children jumped off the porch and ran in several different directions, but three adolescents remained in place: their demeanors fraught with wariness, bordering on anger.

I don't know why I was concerned, but I was. The last thing I wanted to do was frighten or offend them. I hadn't had the opportunity to interact much with children over the years since I had none of my own, and my career, though in public education, had centered mainly on work with teachers and curriculum. More to the point, however, these children were from a different part of the city and almost of a different world.

I don't know how long I sat there with the car door slightly ajar contemplating what I should do next, but I remember my mind drifting back to something that had happened more than forty years earlier. Buried deeply in the recesses of my memory, I was surprised that I could remember the event with such clarity.

I spent my high school years in the Deep South in the late sixties and had been a participant in events that were no doubt meant to ensure a smooth transition for our society from segregation to integration. Even after all these years, I can still recall the pain, confusion, and awkward moments of that time.

It was my junior year, 1966–1967 as I recall, when I had my first meaningful lesson in discrimination. I was the drum majorette for the "white" high school band in my sleepy, little southern town. One particularly frosty evening in early December, when all the local bands lined up for our annual Christmas parade, I noticed something that I'd never given much thought to before: the band from the "black" high school across town was assigned a slot behind all the other schools.

Since the talk of integration versus segregation was prevalent among the locals at that time, anything illustrating the differences between the two piqued my interest. I looked across the myriad of faces and instruments milling about and finally realized that this had been the order of things for every local parade I could remember. For the first time, I seriously puzzled over why this was the case. I had always thought we were ordered on the parade route alphabetically, but our school name was Stone Church High School and the "black" high school was Forest Ridge.

That year, the prevailing consensus was that our two schools would be combined into one building the next school year. Integration had suddenly become personal, and I couldn't help but wonder what would happen to all of us if that occurred. Standing in the cold night air, my thoughts rambled.

I remembered thinking that having two high schools in the same small town was a bit weird when my parents and I had moved to Stone Church a couple of years before, but my dad told me that it had always been this way around his hometown and not to worry much about it, so I didn't. But as the months passed, it appeared that more and more people, mainly the adults, were worrying about it. What was going to happen?

Familiar with the order of events, I knew that the parade was about to begin since all the directors had left to assume their places on the Main Street reviewing stand to await our processional past the mayor and other city dignitaries. Not the norm in other local towns, Stone Church exercised a different approach. It should be noted, by the way, that this was at the mayor's request. With time running out, I walked briskly to the back of the parade line hoping to talk to the drum major for Forest Ridge High, a.k.a. the "Negro High School."

Almost immediately, I caught a glimpse of him: a tall, lithe, regal-looking guy, who, while jovial and animated, seemed simultaneously relaxed and calm. He was somehow different from most kids

I knew, and for a moment, I was taken aback by the broadest smile and whitest teeth I had ever seen. He looked particularly sharp in his new crimson and gold uniform, and his fuzzy hat caused him to tower over me. I, myself, refused to wear one since it usually messed up my unruly, wavy hair and caused my head to sweat profusely.

We had never met, so initially we engaged in nervous small talk about how cold it was that evening, the new Christmas lights in downtown Stone Church, and which local parades each of our bands had agreed to attend. If he was surprised by my unexpected intrusion into his band's space, he never said.

Realizing that I was about to lose my nerve and that time was running out, I hastily suggested that, in the absence of our directors and recognizing that we played exactly the same arrangements of all the carols, why not combine our two bands? I vividly remembered my ramblings that evening, in particular, my killer point—"After all, Maurice, you definitely have the better percussion section, and we have the better woodwind section."

I talked way too fast and knew it even then, but the minutes continued to tick away so I blurted out my second point before he could decline further conversation. "Besides," I stammered, "I hear that we will all be together in the same building next year so what better way to show our maturity and flexibility than to come up with this gesture on our own?"

Continuing to reminisce, I saw a much younger me smiling lamely in his direction and could still recall the breathlessness I experienced when I finished speaking. This confrontation was a definite stretch for me. Seconds passed as I awaited his response. I had no clue what to expect and hadn't thought about what I would do if he declined my invitation.

Though he waited a little too long to respond for my comfort level, deep down in his soul, there must have been a rebel spirit because his face erupted with one of the most captivating smiles I had ever seen, and he replied simply, "Why not?"

He glanced nervously at his classmates but spoke with deliberate exuberance. While a bit apprehensive about what I had just done, I remember feeling good about it. It crossed my mind that maybe we were about to make a significant, historical statement. I rushed back to the front of the parade line, not quite sure how I would break the news to my band members. Never one to bring attention to myself in church, I was startled to hear myself mumbling "Amen, brother!" to no one in particular.

Thinking back, the turn of events that occurred after our innocent stunt that evening was probably predictable, even probable front-page news fodder in tired, little Stone Church, South Carolina, with its three traffic lights and new, antique street lamps. But it was still an uncomfortable, grown-up history lesson that, in my youthful innocence, was unexpected.

I can still recall the pain, as well as the not-so-easily-disguised twinge of amusement, on my father's face and in his eyes as Maurice and I marched our two bands side by side down Main Street past the local reviewing stand replete with our aghast directors and various city officials.

We continued down the main drag in front of Woolworths and Belk's department store where most of the town's white population had gathered. While the volume and quality of the music coming from our combined effort was impressive, I was still able to perceive the stunned silence of the crowd.

Actually, the only truly positive response we received that fateful evening was from the African-American citizens of Stone Church. Further along the parade route, their passionate, joyful reactions to our gesture restored my confidence in what we had done and to this day remain indelibly etched on my brain. Maybe we were too young or naïve to appreciate the magnitude of our social faux pas then, but even today, especially knowing what I know now, I really believe I would do it again. I don't know about Maurice.

Forcing my mind to fast forward to the present, I mentally returned to the driveway of the mansion on Blessing Path and looked over the steering wheel at three pairs of young, wary eyes. I had no clue how much time had passed since I entered my "reverie" and hadn't considered how peculiar it must look for an older, white lady to be sitting quietly in a car for several minutes with the driver's side door ajar, in front of an old, rundown house they considered theirs.

As if to reinforce my nerve, I muttered to myself, "Well, why did you come here this evening if not to learn more about this place? Maybe these kids can answer your questions, or if not, at least fill in some blanks."

I got out of the car, slowly closed the door, and wondered if I still had that same courageous resolve I had exhibited that cold December evening some fifty years earlier.

Chapter 3

The First Encounter

"Don't settle for average. Bring your best to
the moment. Then, whether it fails or succeeds,
at least you know you gave all you had. We need
to live the best that's in us."

—Angela Bassett

There were three adolescents on the porch, a boy and two girls. The girls were the first to approach me and walked down a few of the porch steps with suspicion clouding their eyes. It was apparent that they were concerned about protecting their space.

"So who are you? Why you here? We never seen you around here before. Where do you stay?"

Their words came fast, and I wasn't certain if they were expecting me to answer or were just hopeful that with that bombardment I would leave. I was momentarily distracted by the fact that the huge columns of the house looked somehow familiar. My mind struggled to recall why that image had caught my attention, but fearing I'd lose the opportunity for conversation, I pushed the distraction aside.

"Hi, I'm Jamie. Do you come here often? Whose house is this? Have you been inside? How many rooms are there?"

Somewhere in my subconscious, I had decided to answer their barrage of questions with an equal number of mine. I had been a high school teacher in several different cultural settings, yet unless

I could catch them off guard in some way, I quickly realized that it would still be easy for them to intimidate me.

Staring at me for a while as if mulling over how to respond the kids seemed particularly invested in this encounter. Eventually, the shorter of the two girls spoke up defiantly, "This house is ours. We come here to talk and hang out. Unless you own it, and come here to tell us to leave, we don't feel much like talkin'."

I was startled by the aggressiveness of her words and tone. "What is your name?" I inquired. "I told you mine."

"Why do you need to know?" she shot back.

"I don't know," I stammered. "I just like putting my friends' faces and names together."

"We're *not* friends," she announced defiantly, "but my name is Jalissa."

I took a moment to look more closely into her flashing, dark eyes. While brooding they may have been her best feature as anyone looking at her face couldn't help but be drawn to them. She was a compelling young woman with a flawless, deep-brown complexion and a determined chin. Her coal, black, wiry hair had a mind of its own and her efforts to tame it seemed fruitless, but even that feature couldn't detract from the passion and fire in her eyes.

As I studied her, she crossed her arms in front of her chest and stared directly into my face. Taken aback by her scorn, I wondered what had caused her to adopt an attitude similar to that of a lioness protecting cubs.

The other girl spoke up next. She was dressed in bright pink athletic shorts that accentuated her long, lanky build and had donned a sparkly purple T-shirt to complement the shorts. It read "Precious and Perfect." Even though I was initially drawn to the cute, flashy attire, it was her arresting smile that held my gaze. Sincere and disarming, she seemed the antithesis of Jalissa.

She approached me openly with an outstretched hand, "Hi, my name is Raven. Don't mind Jalissa, she's okay, but we don't have much trust for strangers who come around here, particularly white people."

What a curious thing to say, I thought to myself and made a mental note to further explore the demographics of the area. Although I'd been in Texas for over forty years, I'd never really concerned myself with the facts and figures about the multitude of people in the metropolitan area. Our lives, while closely intertwined by the ribbons of freeways, were still separated by individual pockets of culture and socioeconomic differences.

I turned back to the conversation and replied timidly, "That's fair, I guess." I hesitated briefly and then added, "I can appreciate your concern, but I'm only interested in the house and don't mean to intrude on you, guys. What can you tell me about it?"

"There's only one guy here," the boy interrupted as he moved closer to the center of our conversation.

Before I could explain that the term was actually a generic one and not intended to offend, he broke in again and blurted out, "You gonna buy it?"

He was smaller and appeared younger than the two girls, but the look in his eyes was remarkably similar to theirs. He was defiant, yet definitely fearful of something and clung to his scooter as if I would grab it and run. Still he edged closer as our conversation continued.

"Do you mean the house?" I inquired and then continued with a smile, "Oh no, I hadn't even thought about buying it. I've just driven by it for years and sometimes feel like it is sending me a message."

"Houses can't talk," he commented disgustedly and turned to the girls with a self-satisfied smirk.

"You don't think so?" I smiled. "Maybe it's been trying to talk to you, too, but you haven't realized it yet."

He didn't answer and appeared confused by my comment. The moment became awkward, as we all stood there wondering what would happen next. I thought his knitted brow and squinty eyes suggested he was trying to decide if inanimate objects might really have the ability to communicate after all. Soon though, after nodding to Jalissa, he backed slowly away from where we were standing, turned his scooter around, and sailed off one side of the porch into the brush.

I learned later that his name was Chanté. Actually, of the three, he may have intrigued me the most because after many similar encounters I realized that no matter when our paths crossed I had no clue what he was thinking at any given moment. Just when I thought I had him figured out, a chameleon-like persona emerged, and I became conscious of the fact that I had been totally off base.

As I became more involved in the lives of these children, some teachers told me Chanté had bad tendencies and would eventually drift to "the other side." My gut told me otherwise, but then what did I know? I was a lady who had worked for most of her career in one of the white, affluent pockets of the metroplex, not in any area remotely similar to this one.

There didn't seem to be much more to say so I thanked the girls for taking time to speak with me, said I was sorry to have disturbed them, and started back to the car. On impulse, I turned back around and asked if I might drop by again. Their eyes met, and I was afraid that I had lost the opportunity to return by forcing the issue.

After what seemed like an eternity, Raven shrugged her shoulders, and Jalissa mumbled, "Whatever."

Chapter 4

Jalissa and Raven

"Oh the innocent girl in her maiden teens
knows perfectly well what everything means."

—D. H. Lawrence

Jalissa and Raven

After that first encounter on those weathered steps, I realized I now had two things that intrigued me. Yes, I was still captivated by the house, but now, contrary to what I had told them that first evening, I was also curious about the kids and their relationship with it.

For the next couple of months, I drove back by in the evenings looking for some activity. When I would see Raven or Jalissa, I would pull into the dusty, weed-infested driveway and wait for an unspoken invitation to stay. I learned early on that fruity cereal bars, icy popsicles, or bags of their favorite brand of spicy chips, Takis, went a long way in encouraging a summons to sit awhile on the porch.

Meeting Jalissa and Raven first was a godsend. Both had matriarchal tendencies and were wise beyond their years. Physically, they were budding adolescents. Emotionally they were seasoned, realistic young women who had dreams of their own but were reluctant to share. It was because of them that the younger kids eventually drifted back to sit with us. Clearly they had long ago learned to take their cues from one or the other of these two. The bond of trust, I sensed, was something remarkable, probably worthy of a graduate study at some university.

For whatever reason, the group came to accept me and even appeared to tolerate my overactive curiosity that summer. We talked about everything from school to sports to clothes and even bullies, cyber and otherwise. Finally one evening as the long, lazy days melted into fall, I asked again about the house. The conversation was abruptly halted as the younger eyes either looked into the distance or toward Raven or Jalissa.

"Ms. Jamie, what do you keep asking about our house?" Jalissa inquired, her prior frustration with me emerging once again.

I paused for a long while and then honestly admitted, "You know, I'm not sure. Do you remember what I said the first time I came here?" I asked.

"Yeah," Chanté laughed as he shoved the last bites of a melting, cherry popsicle into his mouth, "You said something about this old house talkin' to you."

"That's right, Chanté, I did. You have a good memory," I commented softly, adding a smile.

"So what's it say?" he inquired, wiping his red-stained mouth on his shirt while glancing furtively at Jalissa.

After a long pause I continued, "I think it is saying you can make me happy again."

As soon as the words were out of my mouth, Jalissa and Raven abruptly rose from where they were sitting, brushed off their clothes, and as if on cue, began to usher the children down the steps and back across the street to the apartment complex where they lived.

"We need to go get home, Ms. Jamie. See you around."

Later, when I was driving home, I said out loud to no one in particular, "Well, that was a really stupid thing to say. If the kids hadn't already decided you were deranged, that statement probably convinced them."

I recognized then that I had no clue why I said what I did. It was certainly not something I would have shared had I taken time to think about it. I had simply uttered what had been on the tip of my tongue.

Chapter 5

Chanté

"God gives us dreams a size too big so that
we can grow into them."

—Unknown

Chanté Sharing His Dreams

Chanté was into sports and *really* into football. He was small in both stature and weight, had a lean, gangling body with fast feet, and that summer, usually sported medium-length dreadlocks. Most notice-able, however, was his never-failing determination to achieve athletic success. It was unmatched by most kids his age that I knew.

Sometimes when I came by to sit for a while on the porch steps, I would see him across the street in the park hanging out with some much older guys trying to horn in on their basketball games. While they appeared to tolerate him, I was uncomfortable with both the propensity for significant tattoo coverage that I could see, even from a distance, and the language that drifted across from the court. When I obsessed about him trying to mimic what he saw and heard, I'd remind myself that I was not his mother and didn't know the whole story of his reasons for doing what he did.

The differences between the worlds of these delightful children and me were never more evident than during the evenings we sat together on the decaying, weathered porch. Until it got too cold or dark, the girls would usually be sitting out there helping the younger kids with their homework.

"Why isn't Chanté here with you doing homework?" I asked one evening.

"Oh, he don't need to," one of the little ones piped up. "He gonna be a pro-player."

Dreams and drama were abundant on "the porch," and we'd often share every thought with one another. Olympic competitor, movie director, dancer, pro athlete, actress, fireman—the list went on and on, and sometimes fluctuated depending upon what had been discussed at school or seen on television the prior week.

As I listened to their stories and watched the twinkle in most eyes, I was reminded that few dreams become reality without a con-crete plan of action, a lot of hard work, and a strong foundation of support from others. It was becoming painfully apparent that such things were not the norm for the group I had begun to think of as "my kids."

Deep down inside, I think some of the kids already sensed this as well, particularly Raven and Jalissa. I had learned over the last few months that once you knew a little about a child, you could sometimes read the thoughts her eyes conveyed. Maybe that's what it was like as a parent. Having no children of my own, I couldn't be sure.

I usually went home after these evening encounters feeling unsettled and, on more than one occasion, had toyed with the idea of tutoring the kids myself. Over the summer, I had discovered that all of them could use a little academic assistance, but more importantly, my gut told me they also needed someone who would listen and support their dreams as well.

While the current location, a.k.a. our porch, was not feasible on a long-term basis maybe we could find a place in the apartment complex where they all lived that we could use. I made plans to pursue that possibility.

Chapter 6

Jimar

"Things will go wrong at times. You can't always control your attitude, approach, and response. Your options are to complain or to look ahead and figure out how to make the situation better."

—Tony Dungy

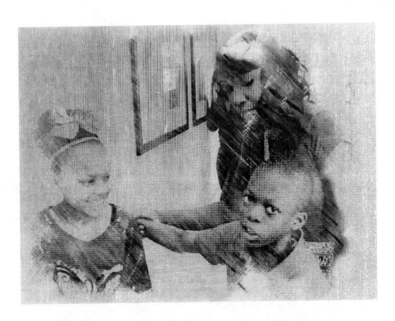

Jimar Being Encouraged to Overcome His Shyness

I remember seeing television commercials as a child about an investment company known as E. F. Hutton. For me the most memorable line in the commercial was "When E. F. Hutton talks, people listen!" So it was with Jimar.

A second-grade student, small in stature, just like Chanté, and particularly stingy with words, Jimar watched me for a long time before he decided to engage in conversation. In fact, I am embarrassed to admit that early on I found it difficult to remember his name since he stayed so much on the fringe of my interaction with the group that usually even his angelic, yet roguish, face was a blur.

Since it was now late fall and cooler than usual in North Texas, "the porch" was not an option for homework or small talk, and it had become a particularly frustrating time for me as I was trying to find another place for us to get together on a regular basis and was not having much luck. I had already expanded my academic assistance idea to include providing one-on-one tutors, and while I had the people, I did not have the place.

My initial visit to the apartment manager to "float" the idea had been less than productive. While not overtly dismissive during our meeting, I sensed from her comments that my project was not a priority. In fairness, I learned later that she was new to the property and had other, more important "fish to fry." In fact, there were rumors that she had been sent there "to clean things up." Even though I could somewhat understand her lack of interest in helping the kids, I left feeling impotent and discouraged. In my "hurry up, find a solution and get it implemented" world I felt I was failing those who had come to mean so much to me. It was at that very moment that Jimar said something profound, and I was reminded of the phrase "out of the mouths of babes."

He had been waiting outside the apartment offices for me the evening I met with the manager because kids were not permitted inside unless accompanied by an adult. As I emerged from the lighted warmth just on the other side of the door, I was surprised to see him standing in the cold, semi-darkness of that early November evening. Never one to remember his coat and gloves, I marveled at the determination he had to have had to wait there for me the twenty or so minutes I was inside. "How had he known I was there anyway, and why had his mama permitted him to do so?" I mused.

His teeth were chattering a bit, and he seemed in a hurry to get his words out. "You gonna get me a tutor?" he blurted out. "My teacher says I need to read better. Jalissa says you gonna help."

I was listening to his ardent plea, still wondering about his mama's level of commitment to her son's well-being, when I recalled that earlier in the week I had shared my thoughts with some of the older kids. Obviously, that information had been passed around, and their trust in me to find a place for them to gather together was never more evident than in Jimar's comments.

In addition, the kids' recognition of what might help them get a leg up on the world was unexpected, and now stared me in the face as never before. I didn't know how to respond and, on impulse, did something that, because of my ingrained public school training, I usually avoided. I dropped down and hugged him fiercely.

I think it felt good and right to both of us because while he pulled back at first, seemingly afraid, he soon melted into my arms and quietly said, "I need just a little help, Ms. Jamie, just a little. Won't take much of anyone's time."

"Okay, Jimar," I mumbled, fighting back my tears. "We'll find you a tutor. We just need to find a place to go first."

He pulled away from my grasp once again, obviously puzzled, but then commented in a small, quiet voice without hesitation, "But, Ms. Jamie, don't you think we could go back to the house that talks to you? Don't you think that would make it happy?"

Chapter 7

Cassandra

"If my mind can conceive it, and my heart
can believe it—then I can achieve it."

—Muhammad Ali

Adia and Cassandra Getting Ready for a Performance

As an engaging and bubbly fourth grader, Cassandra oozed confidence. One of the few children in the group from a two-parent home, she never shied away from participating in whatever game, conversation, activity, or task was front and center. She dreamed about becoming an actress and magically appeared whenever there was mention of a camera or the possibility of random photographs. Much later, she was a star in one or more of our summer afternoon plays.

Her smile was arresting and her femininity delightful. Cassandra was definitely, as I heard one of the other kids say, "a girly girl." If I hadn't known otherwise, because of her air of self-confidence, I would have believed her to be an only child, but as I later learned, she had a little sister who was just as outgoing and equally as determined as Cassandra to develop her own identity.

After my conversation with Jimar, I became even more consumed with how I could positively impact the lives of the children. The holidays were rapidly approaching, and I was seeing them less and less. Without benefit of our Blessing Path porch conversations, I was losing touch with them and felt I needed to do something to reestablish contact.

One afternoon, I drove to the apartment complex and waited for the bus to drop them off. It was a warmer-than-usual December day with bright sunlight and little wind. They erupted from the lumbering, yellow vehicle the minute the door opened and ran across the parking lot to where I stood. There were hugs all around, and I realized just how much I had missed them.

"Ms. Jamie, Ms. Jamie, did you bring us snacks? Are we gonna get tutors? Has the house said anything to you lately? Want to see my report card?"

I hardly knew whom to answer first. Before I could speak, however, all eyes turned toward Cassandra who, while standing in the middle of the throng of backpacks; loosely attached, quilted coats tied around waists; and bright hair bows, put her hands on her hips and matter-of-factly announced, "My daddy says they gonna tear our house down. He says since nobody lives there Ms. Tracy read in the paper that the city says unless someone buys it and fixes it up, it gonna be gone!"

Chapter 8

Sam

"The question is not whether we can afford
to invest in every child;
It is whether we can afford not to."

—Marian Wright Edelman

Cassandra, Sam, Justine, and Raven

I was not prepared for Cassandra's announcement and stood there dumbfounded as the kids' anger and frustration spilled out in word and gesture.

"What's your daddy know?" Chanté shouted. "He ain't nothing but a handy-man 'round here."

Cassandra's eyes welled with tears, but she fiercely defended her father as she raised her voice above the others to say defiantly, "He knows more than you think, and at least he lives with us and works!"

Just as Cassandra's words were out of her mouth, Sam punched Chanté in the back and said, "Shut your mouth!"

Backpacks were immediately thrown to the ground, coats were discarded, and sides were chosen. The fight was on. I knew I should respond and turn this sudden expression of fear and discouragement into a more positive situation, but I never expected to see a fight among these kids and was momentarily frozen.

Jalissa and Raven hurriedly intervened and the situation that appeared to be spiraling into chaos instantly changed. Had I not been there myself to witness it, I wouldn't have believed what happened.

"Stop messin' around," Jalissa raised her voice in controlled anger. "Sam, you can act like a bully at school but not here. Do you understand me? And, Cassandra and Chanté, what is your problem? We are all brothers and sisters, you know that. Stop trash-talking one another."

As Jalissa spoke, Raven moved among the kids, balancing stern looks with supportive hugs. I was mesmerized. Suddenly, the situation that had been out-of-control moments before returned to normal, and it occurred to me that I didn't know many teachers who could have gained control so quickly.

Thinking back it was then that I perceived Sam as yet another enigma, and I found it fascinating that both she and Chanté, the two that challenged me the most, would be engaged in verbal and physical displays of emotion with one another.

Sam was a third-grade student who, in my opinion, had been discarded far too early by many adults. I learned that she was often in trouble at school and, indeed, widely labeled as a bully.

Observing her in the weeks that followed, I saw a fierce loyalty to friends, and an almost desperate need to belong somewhere—anywhere. A tall, spindly kid, with a sharp wit and determined propensity to continually challenge the status quo she didn't seem to know her niché or even care how the prevailing winds blew. She was not a "girly" girl but also definitely not a tomboy either as she appeared to waffle back and forth with each new day and change of outfits.

She was impatient, a quick learner, and a superb reader with much curiosity. But sadly, she lacked the focus and resolve needed to pull everything together. I envisioned her as a burst of potential energy, and without direction maybe even an atomic bomb waiting for a triggering event. As I watched her try to fit in day after day, I had to ask myself what happens to the "Sam's" of the world without a consistent, gentle, nurturing hand?

The compelling nature of Sam's situation became most heart-rending the day she showed me her attempt at original fashion by creating and donning a colorful necktie she had made from an elongated piece of striped ribbon. She looked particularly cute that day, and I wanted her to know that I noticed. "Wow," I commented, "that is really creative. You could start a trend."

"What's a trend?" she asked.

"Something others like and want to copy," I replied with a grin.

Later, when I found the strip of ribbon lying on the windowsill in the room where we had been talking I was profoundly sad. Why had Sam decided to discard her creative accessory, which moments before she had been so proud to wear?

With that incident, I was again reminded that there were more individual holes in the lives of these children than I could ever have imagined, and it was uncomfortably clear that what I was trying to make happen was far more complex than I had earlier perceived.

Not only were my thoughts whirling about the promises I had made to the kids, but I was also dealing with the urgent nudging in my subconscious to save this house on Blessing Path but for what? Lately, I had even started dreaming about it, and that fact alone was unnerving.

Chapter 9

The House and Its History

"A house must be built on solid foundations
if it is to last. The same principle applies to man,
otherwise he too will sink back into the soft ground
and become swallowed up by the world of illusion."

—Sai Baba

Papa and Mama "C"

Over a strong cup of Earl Grey the next morning, I put my concerns about the kids momentarily aside and returned to the pull of 1324 Blessing Path on my life. Quite honestly, though it embarrassed and somewhat alarmed me, I did feel that the house communicated with me in private, quiet moments.

Even more disconcerting was the fact that those episodes had begun to occur with greater frequency and were now laced with a sense of urgency. I had yet to admit this fact to my most trusted friend, my husband, or to anyone else I considered of sound mind and body.

My greatest fear, truth be known, was that if I did break down and share this information the standard southern comment for an individual who is either less than perfect in some way or demonstrating delusional tendencies would be whispered quietly behind my back.

It was that very interesting phrase, with a meaning totally dependent on context that I most vividly remembered overhearing when, as a child, I would eavesdrop on the conversations of my southern born and raised, middle-aged aunts and grandmother. They gathered most summer evenings on Mama C's front porch to string beans or shell peas, drink a little iced sweet tea, and share what was happening in each of their worlds.

While those July evenings were usually sticky and oppressive, their conversations under the Carolina moon were an intoxicating, verbal elixir for a freckle-faced, skinny adolescent who went south each summer to learn a little about family history.

On those rare evenings, when my local cousins went home from our grandparents' house a little early, I would politely ask permission to go into the parlor to read some from one of the books I had brought with me. As an only child and summer visitor, it must have been assumed that I couldn't get into much trouble alone since I was usually permitted to explore places we cousins were never permitted to enter as a group.

The front parlor was a musty room usually off limits to those of us under the age of eighteen since it housed the cherished pump organ and Mama C's prized antique, Victorian settee and matching chairs. The room also contained a couple of ornate cherry end tables that supported fragile lamps with frilly, beaded shades.

The wooden clapboard walls were painted a creamy white and were adorned with several brownish-gray, formal photographs, in which no one smiled. These were hung precariously from single nails. In the sultry, semi-darkness of those evenings, I'd pull a throw pillow off the settee, lie on the area rug just in front of the organ, and half-heartedly read my Nancy Drew mysteries.

Most of the time, I'd have to reread one or more paragraphs since I'd also be straining to hear the gossip about neighbors and church members that drifted through the open windows of the parlor that was fronted by the screened-in porch. "Bless her heart" could be heard on several occasions, and while I wasn't sure the meaning of the phrase, it seemed clear to me, even then, that it wasn't all that complimentary. It was those words that I now feared would be uttered behind my back among my friends and family if they knew what was happening in my life.

Returning to the present, I realized that the more compelling issue I should be thinking about was what the house and the kids had to do with one another. While it hadn't "said" anything specific to me about a particular person or persons, I never returned to the Blessing Path location without now thinking of the children.

Maybe the answer was in the site's history. Did a family with several children live there at one time? Even though I had never been inside, there certainly appeared to be enough rooms to accommodate a large brood.

Weeks earlier, I had tried to research the property by looking online at the website of the Texas General Land Office. I found the collection of over 35 million records dating back to 1720 daunting. With only an address to go on, and I wasn't even sure that had always been the address for this property, I didn't have enough information to know where to begin a reasonable query.

In fact, most of the historical documents I had been sifting through at the state level were based upon genealogical records, and I didn't have a definitive family name to research. I decided then that I might have more luck if I searched local historical documents and artifacts.

When we first met, Reid, my second husband, had reveled in sharing stories about Texas and its people, and he had painted a picture of folks fiercely loyal to their families, their communities, and their state. In addition, his stories suggested that most Texans have at least a working knowledge of the history of the area(s) in which they were born and raised and didn't mind sharing their information with anyone who appeared even remotely interested.

The antique clock chiming insistently above our dining room table caught me off guard, and I realized that more than an hour had slipped by while I, immersed in my thoughts, had been reminiscing.

Immediately after retiring, I had found it difficult to break the old habit of my day revolving around having a definitive place to go every morning and a specific time of departure, so the incessant ticking of the clock had nearly driven me to distraction. Gradually, though, as the months dragged by, I had learned how to quiet my buzzing mind, and now rarely noticed the clock or its sounds.

I sat a while longer, finishing the now lukewarm tea, and thought about where I was being pulled to go. Though still cognizant of the clock I stretched, yawned, and pulled an Afghan throw from the back of the sofa across my legs.

Ever my best friend, Malcolm, Scottish terrier no. 1, noticing movement, raised his head from his bed positioned beside the fireplace. He quickly sensed an opportunity to get more comfortable and jumped onto the sofa to lie on the softer Afghan.

While Fergie, Scottish terrier no. 2, had also had her nap interrupted, after a few seconds, she decided it would require too much effort to get up from her already warm bed and fight for a spot in the crook of my knees. Settling in then, with only Malcolm, my mind drifted back across the years once more.

When I turned fifty, I married Reid, a native Texan. For our honeymoon, we agreed to visit Big Bend National Park, a remote, desolate, yet alluring area of far west Texas. We both had a love for that part of the state though we had been drawn there for totally different reasons.

As a high school science teacher, I had taken students there to participate in summer field studies courses. As a high school football star, my husband, who had grown up in the town of Big Spring, received a scholarship to attend Sul Ross State University in Alpine where he later earned his bachelor of science degree in health, physical education, and biology. After spending four years in far west Texas he, too, was infatuated with the solitude of the desert.

No one who has traveled west of Midland/Odessa or has seen the beautiful work of photographer, Wyman Meinzer, can deny the unique, rugged beauty of that part of the state. But as I later came to appreciate, the most intriguing aspect of the area may be as much the people who call it home as the land itself.

I now believe that those who are born and live in west Texas are sociable, independent, and honorable folks who intuitively grasp the true meaning of family and friendship. They can usually trace their families back several generations and typically share this history through engaging stories.

When I think about some of the more famous people who were either born or grew up in Texas: Dwight Eisenhower, Audie Murphy, Buddy Holly, Sandra Day O'Connor, Willie Nelson, Larry McMurty, and Molly Ivins to name a few, I picture colorful storytellers. Some of their tales, whether in word or song, are steeped in the culture and belief structure of the Lone Star state.

Maybe this propensity of Texans to remember their families through story would be evident in the historical documents of Eden Hill as well. I decided that it might be worth a visit to the local library to find out.

I showered, dressed, and once again disappointed my loyal companions when I promised them a walk tomorrow. "It's the fault of the house," I mumbled as if they had the capacity to understand. They tilted their heads to the left, as Scotties often do, eyed me as I picked up my keys, and then sauntered over to their beds by the fireplace resigned to the fact that this particular morning would unfortunately mean another nap rather than a more intoxicating stroll through the neighborhood.

I, caught up in my own thoughts, opened the garage door and headed out hopeful that I might find some answers.

Chapter 10

What Is It about a Library?

"In a good bookroom you feel in some mysterious way that you are absorbing the wisdom contained in all the books through your skin, without even opening them."

—Mark Twain

I walked into the main lobby of the Eden Hill Library around 10:15 a.m. and stood there for a moment taking everything in. I was embarrassed that even after living ten years in the area, I had never crossed the threshold of this building's front entrance. I read a lot but lately have begun to purchase most of my books online since I've run out of bookcase space in my home office. I tell myself it's faster and more convenient that way, and since I never know when I might want to keep a book, borrowing from a library seems less practical.

The quiet setting only a library can convey enveloped me like a dense fog. Having spent a great deal of my life as a student, it almost felt like coming home, and I realized that I had actually missed the competing, intoxicating aromas of old and new books.

I wandered past the circulation desk, reading rooms, and into the book stacks as my thoughts crisscrossed several decades. I recalled the many late nights I had spent sifting through card catalog drawers at Clemson University's library in the early seventies searching for just the right research article to include in the literature review for my master's thesis. Deep into science at the time I was looking for references regarding the pollination activities of bees and a species of white clover known as *Trifolium repens*. Remembering the computer lab I had passed near the entrance, I smiled to think how much easier it was to research a topic today.

Standing here in present time, light years removed from my college days, I suddenly wondered whether a single person at Clemson had ever opened the bound copy of my thesis that I had been required to provide the library over forty years ago. Is the expediency of research through the internet that we now enjoy worth the sacrifice of never again sitting among all the possibilities and adventures actual books can offer? A cavernous question, I concluded, but decided that, while it was definitely one worth considering, it would have to wait for another time.

I must have looked bewildered because shortly thereafter, a seemingly good-humored and sharply dressed lady came up to greet me. Her nametag simply read "Ms. G—Volunteer" but her smile captivated me. Much later whenever I recall our first meeting I know that, just as Rick had said to Captain Louis Renault in the final lines of the movie *Casablanca*, that moment signaled the beginning of an extraordinary relationship.

She introduced herself as Ms. Grant but said everybody called her "Ms. G." "How may I help you?" she inquired.

I tried to explain the reason for my visit without overly burdening her with the whole story of the house, the kids, and the sense of urgency I was feeling. She listened patiently and then said, "Do I understand that you would like a historical snapshot of the local area and its people?"

"Yes," I said.

"For what time period? That is, how far back would you like to go?" she continued.

I hadn't thought about that. I really didn't know when the house had been built and didn't know enough about architectural trends to even predict a span of years.

When I appeared stumped, she said, "Well, let's begin with when the city was founded and work our way forward. I have a couple of hours free before lunch so maybe I can get you started."

Chapter 11

Ms. G

"The kind of beauty I want most is the hard-to-get kind that comes from within - strength, courage, dignity."

—Ruby Dee

Ms. G

We had worked for about an hour in the apparently seldom-visited local history section when I stopped reading for a moment to steal a glance at my new friend. I estimated her age to be close to mine and marveled at her dedication to the task. The past seemed very important to her.

As we were searching through a few locally published books, she shared that she had come to Texas in 2005 as a result of the dire warnings about Hurricane Katrina. She explained that several of her family members had relocated from their long-established home in the ninth ward of New Orleans to this area just before the horrendous event, but now only she remained.

When I asked how or why she had selected Eden Hill as a destination, she said she didn't really know. "We just piled in our cars with everything we could take and drove west," she mused. "Maybe we simply ran out of gas here or were just too tired to go on."

As I closed the book, I was exploring to pay closer attention to her story she relaxed a bit and gazed into the distance. Her voice became softer as she continued. She shared that her children eventually drifted back to their former jobs and friends in Louisiana, but she, retired and settled, had decided to stay in Texas.

While she acknowledged that she missed her family and the unique culture of New Orleans, she also recognized that they had their own lives to live and would be fine without her daily presence. Hesitating a moment, she peered over her glasses at me and asked somewhat pensively, "Have you ever felt you were supposed to do something, but you haven't quite figured out what it is?" Moments later, she dismissed her own query and immediately followed up with "Listen to me talking this nonsense at my age."

I felt a twinge of déjà vu. Should I tell her my crazy story? What would she think if I told her that I was feeling exactly the same thing, and then there was the part about the house "talking" to me; I kept a picture of it in my purse and could easily use it to share my story and elaborate a bit about what I was experiencing. I really was beginning to feel the need to unburden my thoughts to another adult, and rationalized that what better person than a perfect stranger who seemed especially kind and nonjudgmental.

When I didn't respond right away, she looked at her watch and shared that she needed to hurry out for a quick lunch before another appointment. My window of opportunity was gone, and I couldn't help but think that there must have been a reason why it had evaporated so quickly.

I didn't hear Ms. G mention that she had located a couple of interesting references that I could remain to review and was still lost in thought when once again she reminded me that she would be leaving. Realizing that I had appeared rude, I quickly thanked her for her efforts.

As an afterthought, I asked if we might meet again one day during the next week. She agreed but then remembered that she would not be volunteering the next week after all as she was packing and moving to a new apartment complex. I asked her about the new place, just to be polite, and was appreciably stunned to learn that she would be moving to the apartment complex across Tremont Street from Blessing Path: the apartment complex where the kids lived.

I sat there unable to move. The reoccurring dreams of the house, the mounting coincidences, the continuing pull to make a difference in the lives of the kids, and the sense of urgency I was feeling all seemed to descend upon me like a thick, smothering, wool blanket.

Ms. G was gathering her things together when she glanced across the table and said, "Are you okay? You look pale. Can I get you anything?"

I did indeed feel cool and clammy, and when she commented that my face had drained of color, I stammered that I was fine and made up some nonsense about how it was probably because I hadn't eaten that morning and had a tendency to be hypoglycemic.

Though reluctant, I could tell that she felt the pull of her schedule. She accepted my comments and left the room as I struggled to find the words to say goodbye.

Later that evening, as I sat on the patio with a chilled glass of wine, the faces of my newly found friends and acquaintances kept spiraling through my mind. I thought about my impressions of Ms. G, Jalissa, and Raven, in particular. I decided that, while significantly different in age, they exhibited some of the same characteristics. I didn't know any of them well, but I thought I could sense a desire among all three to do whatever was required to improve their situations and those of the children in their families or close community.

It was a fragile generalization at best, but I was curious if this was a common attribute of successful women who lived in poverty situations. Since Reid was attending a school board meeting and I needed a distraction from the unsettling events of the day anyway, I climbed the stairs to my little nook, turned on the computer, and began to research stories about notable women who had overcome a myriad of obstacles to ultimately succeed.

I plowed through several articles, editorials, and historical excerpts, and found that many referenced African American women. As evening twilight transitioned into complete darkness, I realized that grandmothers and mothers are considered, by African tradition, the custodians of the generations, and one of their most important roles is the maintenance of the culture and stability of the family in order to positively impact the lives of the children.

It was late, and I didn't trust my ability to draw valid conclusions, but as I sat there rereading the last article, I finally admitted to myself that there must be a reason why I, at this stage in my life, was being drawn into the lives of individuals, particularly women and children, so different than me.

Chapter 12

More Faces

"Children's talent to endure stems from their ignorance of alternatives."

—Maya Angelou

Justine with Friends

Just as the world seems to slow down from January into March, so did my interest in the research. I seemed to run into dead ends with every new reference that had originally looked promising. Even with Ms. G's help and dedication, finding something meaningful seemed elusive and hopeless.

In addition, I was missing my conversations with the kids since we had no place to get together. I had not discussed my connection to them or her new apartment complex with Ms. G, so I had no way of knowing if she had met any of my younger friends.

I rationalized that I had not stopped by to see them get off the bus these past few weeks because it had been miserably cold, and I assumed that no one would want to stand around for small talk. Truth be known, I was also afraid I'd see Ms. G and end up having to explain everything.

One day around lunchtime, I decided to take a risk and go by one of the schools some of the kids attended. Having worked with public school administrators all across the area, I knew several in the local district. I reasoned that the principal of the elementary school where most of them were enrolled might be willing to share information about how the kids were doing in general terms. I knew the law and realized that I had no right to inquire about one or more of them individually, but I thought if I shared my story she would understand my need to be reassured about their wellbeing as a group.

It was only when I was signing in at the reception desk that I realized my imposition. No, I did not have an appointment but just wanted to say hello. The curt, measured response of the attentive young woman behind the sliding glass window said it all. The principal was a busy lady, and would I mind waiting just a moment while she checked to see if she was in a meeting or observing a teacher's classroom? "No, of course not," I quietly mumbled.

I stood there trying to decide how to make a graceful, apologetic exit. What was I thinking my mind raced? How could I not remember the pace and challenges of everyday life in a public school? Of course I should have made an appointment, and what was I expecting her to tell me anyway? How awkward!

I caught sight of Cassandra and Sam out of the corner of my eye. They were marching in a controlled, hushed line down the main hall on the way to the cafeteria for lunch. When they saw me, they both squealed, "Ms. Jamie, Ms. Jamie! What are you doing here? Did you come to eat lunch with us? Want to meet our friends?"

Both their teacher and I were caught off guard. It was obvious that students were not permitted to speak while in line, especially to a visitor to the campus, but it was also quite evident that they were delighted to see me. I was secretly pleased.

As I nodded to them and pressed my fingers to my lips indicating they should obey the rules and quietly continue their path to lunch, I turned back to the receptionist and hastily inquired of the policy regarding visitors for lunch. I knew the answer before it could be given and understood the reasoning as well, but I had to ask anyway.

My memory had not failed me. Because I was not an employee of the school district, and also did not have the permission of the parents or guardians to visit their children, I could not make contact with them. It had been a mistake to come, and I was embarrassed at my seeming lack of forethought after so many years in the school business.

Shortly after the kids entered the cafeteria, the principal emerged from the hallway adjacent to the reception desk. No doubt she had been informed of the situation. To her credit, she graciously received me and invited me into the quiet of her office.

We talked for a few minutes about the current state of affairs in public schools, the upcoming high-stakes state assessments, and finally, the joys of retirement. It was definitely small talk and somewhat stilted but still sincere and more friendly than polite. I appreciated her generosity.

After the initial pleasantries, we sat in silence for a few moments, and she glanced over at a clock above her desk. Sensing that her time was limited even before noticing her gesture, I hastily tried to summarize the reasons for my unannounced visit, recap my actions since retirement, and acknowledge that I truly never meant to disrupt the educational day for the children I had come to know and care about.

She listened attentively, smiling and nodding in all the appropriate places. When she thought I had finished speaking, she leaned forward ever so slightly and began, "Jamie, what are your plans for these kids? How did you get to this point with them? How much have you thought about what you can do as one individual to effect change in their lives? It all sounds genuine and is definitely needed, but you and I both know to become a reality there must be a concrete plan that those of us entrusted with their lives and well-being can see, sell and ultimately deliver."

Her eyes were kind and her words laced with empathy. I sat quietly, slightly embarrassed, as she finished. The reason for all of the coincidences was becoming more and more apparent. The issue was not just getting to know the details of these kids' lives or bringing them snacks and having summer porch conversations. It was also not about developing and implementing "feel good" short-term projects like random tutoring sessions.

The compelling point was how could I make a real difference in their beautiful lives. Most importantly, it was time for me to decide just how committed I was going to be to these children. I appreciated her candor more than I believe she realized, apologized for intruding upon her day, and said my goodbyes. Fortunately, I was able to exit the building without seeing any of the children again.

I met the bus later that day intending to apologize to Cassandra and Sam for failing to eat lunch with them and try to explain why. As the students emerged from the bus, it was obvious that there was less enthusiasm for my presence than in previous months. There were still smiles and a few hugs, but the effort seemed lukewarm.

When most of the kids had disembarked, I caught sight of Raven and Jalissa toward the end of the line. I caught up with them to inquire about their day and attempt to reconnect since it had been several weeks since our last visit.

Raven, sometimes the more articulate of the two, spoke first. "Ms. Jamie, where'd you come from? It's good to see you, but it's been awhile. We've been wonderin' where you been."

Rarely one to be anything but positive, I thought I caught a hint of sarcasm in her voice when she continued, "We almost decided that you were the same as everyone else who says they want to do things with us but then nothin' ever comes of it."

Realizing that she had been thinking about this awhile and had more to say I stifled my reply and let her continue. As the three of us walked toward the complex, she began, "Like several churches give us stuff, especially at the beginning of school and at Thanksgiving and Christmas, but we know that usually just makes both them and us feel good a while. Besides, most of us know which places we can go get things without anyone ever finding out we are goin' to more than one. Sometimes our mamas make promises about coming to their services, but we usually don't go back, because it don't seem to matter to them whether we do or not. Don't get me wrong we are grateful, but what happens the next day and the next? Even the lady who brings breakfast and lunch to us in the summer don't come by any other time."

I could tell this was requiring an extreme amount of effort and courage on her part, and I longed to intervene and stop the flood of pain but wisely hesitated.

She paused to catch her breath and then continued almost inaudibly. "Most of us around here have been disappointed a lot when somethin' starts and then don't keep goin'. We thought you had forgot about us and the house. Maybe you never thought about that. After all, we haven't seen you in a while, and no one seems to be doing anything about the signs on our house sayin' it's gonna be sold."

As Raven's words faded into the late afternoon breeze and Jalissa whispered, "Last summer was fun," we drifted slowly apart. There didn't seem to be much more to say then. Both girls hugged me loosely and moved on to catch up with their friends.

I stared across the street at the house with an aching heart. Indeed, there were signs advertising that the property was for sale. I tried to simultaneously process the frustration I had just heard and consider this new development regarding the property on Blessing Path.

Truthfully, all I really wanted to do at that moment was get in my car and drive far away. I needed time for reflection and was scared that I had entered into a situation I was not prepared to confront. Yet, once again, I was not in control of what was about to happen as my attention was immediately diverted to new faces walking toward me.

"Hi, Cassandra, Sam, Jimar." I nodded to each as I called their names. "I am so sorry I missed eating lunch with you today. I had come to see my friend, Dr. Bradley, your principal, and didn't expect to see you. How was school today, anyway, and who are your friends? I'd like to meet them."

Chapter 13

Ms. Tracy

"It's so clear that you have to cherish everyone. I think that's what I get from these older
black women, that every soul is to be cherished,
that every flower is to bloom."

—Alice Walker

Ms. Tracy and Jessamy

It was Jimar who spoke first. He grinned and began to recite the greeting I had tried to teach the kids over the months, "Good afternoon, Ms. Jamie. How are you today? It is good to see you. May I have a snack?"

Everyone giggled at his singsong rendition of my attempt to get the kids to ask politely for a snack. But a clap of thunder changed our focus immediately and everyone looked up at the sky in unison. It was spring in Texas and severe weather was more often the norm rather than the exception. I momentarily lamented that I had failed to check the forecast for that afternoon—something that was usually a standard task for me March through June. In fact, I sometimes built my schedule around the severe weather forecasts and whether or not I would be able to find a convenient location to secure my car to prevent hail damage.

The sky was indeed angry and ominous as we turned to run for the closest sheltered area. We gathered at the entrance to the office complex. When we reached the front door, no one went inside, but instead huddled under the overhang.

Jimar attempting to divert our attention from the coming storm, smiled his crooked grin, looked up at me with his twinkling, mischievous eyes, and once again melted my heart. "How'd I do a minute ago?" he inquired. We all laughed and some of the tension dissipated into the wind of the coming storm.

"It was perfect, Jimar," I said and then continued, "You remembered every part of it, but unfortunately I left the snacks in the car. Besides, I think we should all head home right away, don't you?"

About that time, the door to the office opened, and I saw a woman I had not yet met standing in the entrance. The wind had picked up and the sky was darkening rapidly.

Obviously concerned about the approaching storm, she indicated that we all should come inside immediately.

Remembering that the policy of the complex was that no children were allowed in the office area without a parent or guardian, I again chastised myself for the lack of attention to the weather conditions. Why had I not noticed the impending storm and encouraged the children to go on home before now? What kind of headaches had my inattentiveness created for the staff and the families of each child standing in the vestibule with us?

I learned later that the lady's name was Tracy, otherwise known as "Ms. Tracy" to the kids. She ushered us into a room just down the hall from the reception area. It was adorned with chairs, a white board, toys, and a bookcase filled with a myriad of games and books of all shapes and sizes. I stared at the area, recalling my conversation with the apartment manager months earlier. I puzzled over her earlier lack of enthusiasm for my tutoring program proposal since the primary reason she had offered for not being able to support it had been a lack of appropriate facilities.

I turned back to Tracy and apologized for distracting the children. Searching for a way to make amends, I asked if I might help her contact the families of the kids to let them know where we were.

She shot me an incredulous look and said, "Seriously, are you for real?"

I was surprised and confused. "Yes, ma'am," I said. "I'll be glad to help get them home since I think it is my fault that they lingered after the bus left."

As the kids, seemingly familiar with the area, started to pull games and books off of shelves, she softened her tone, smiled at me, and said, "You aren't very familiar with this complex and its residents, are you?"

"No," I said. "I actually met many of these kids last summer when I started visiting them on the porch of the old house that is listed for sale across the street. I came in here in late November to talk with someone about the possibility of implementing a structured tutoring program, but there didn't seem to be any interest. I never inquired further about the tutoring program but have tried to keep in contact with the kids over the past few months."

I studied her carefully as she stood there trying to decide how to tactfully respond to me. Unless I had misread her facial expressions, it appeared that she had flinched ever so slightly at the mention of my prior visit.

Here was yet another elegant black woman to cross my path. She was smartly dressed, articulate, and because of her actions in the past few minutes, I surmised organized and caring. It was obvious that the children knew who she was and felt safe and happy in her presence.

She didn't mince any words when she finally responded. "What exactly is your interest in these children?"

Again, just as with that first encounter with Jalissa, I sensed a protective presence. I tried to lighten the mood by saying, with all the sincerity I could muster, "How much time do you have?"

I don't know why or how but with a flash of lightning and another deep rumble of thunder, we seemed to connect. She smiled, her eyes reflecting the warmth of her words and responded, "Let's take care of these kids first."

I watched as she methodically, and with obvious love and affection, arranged to get each and every child to his or her place of residence after the brunt of the storm. She seemed to know every family's situation intimately. As I listened, I realized that many went home to empty apartments every day so she had them use their own cell phones or provide her with a work number for their mamas to let all know their child's location, and reassure them that we would see that each child got home safely after the storm had passed.

For the children who did have someone waiting for them at home, she had each one call and tell the parent or guardian where he or she was. The parent was given the option of coming to get the child immediately, or we agreed to monitor their activities until the storm had safely abated, and we could permit them to walk home as usual. Most wanted us to keep the children in the office area, as they had no transportation available to pick them up in the driving rain.

I realized then how truly confining it was for many of the residents living here. Without a way to get around, it was no wonder that these kids had not seen much of the world outside Oak Lakes Apartments.

I played games and did homework with those that remained behind while Tracy returned to the reception area. The storm raged on, but I was elated and enthralled with the opportunities afforded me quite by chance that afternoon. The kids I knew from last summer relaxed and began to talk as if we were again "on our porch." The new faces observed us curiously.

Chapter 14

Amber

"If I had influence with the good fairy who is supposed to preside over the christening of all children, I should ask that her gift to each child in the world be a sense of wonder so indestructible that it would last throughout life."

—Rachel Carson

Amber

After the day of the storm Ms. Tracy let us gather together in the classroom around the corner from the reception area for an hour or so one or two days a week. I sensed that she was taking a significant risk at opening the doors to us, but we both tacitly agreed to operate from the philosophy of asking forgiveness rather than permission if ever confronted.

I never inquired about why I hadn't seen her earlier or how she managed to accomplish what I had not been able to do myself, but I noticed that the manager's car was never around on the days we agreed to meet the bus and escort the kids inside through a back door by the workout room.

As the weeks passed, more and more children began to join our throng. I became fearful that we were living on borrowed time and was also concerned that by including so many more I could possibly miss something of significance in the lives of the original "porch crew."

The new kids entered into our midst tentatively, and I watched closely as their wary eyes would dart fervently around the room looking for something familiar and safe that first day they slipped inside. Most came at the urging of a friend who had been before, and while the afternoon snacks continued to be a huge draw, I sensed through cautious first hugs and their eventual willingness to talk, that we were filling a void.

Some of the regulars, Jalissa, Raven, and Cassandra, started organizing the kids into reading groups each day to help me out, but I soon realized that I would need additional adult assistance to make a real difference. I wasn't ready to confront the manager again, especially now that I had serendipitously started a program on property without her knowledge and approval.

However, without coming out in the open and asking permission to continue what had already been started, I wouldn't be able to invite others in to help. Both Tracy and I realized that the situation could not continue, but most days, I pushed those thoughts aside as every moment we had to read, talk and laugh was more than the kids had had yesterday or the day before.

I noticed that a few third- and fourth-grade students came regularly and seemed to press forward with greater urgency than the others. One day, Amber, a quiet, disciplined eleven-year-old, proudly shared a comment a teacher had written on her report card. "Dependable" was all it said, but Amber could not have been more overjoyed. With five children in her family, to include an older sister in junior high, and three younger brothers and sisters, she walked a fine line in her public persona between that of adult or child.

When her older sister is present she relaxes and behaves as a child. Yet in the forty or so minutes before Jessamy, her older sister, gets home from school, Amber is tasked with assuming responsibility for the younger siblings and ultimately must play the role of parent without having had the opportunity to acquire the needed wisdom and experience. Informally she is in apprenticeship with Raven and Jalissa, and while no one but me seems to find that unusual, what I observe I find quite extraordinary.

It is during these episodes of accountability and responsibility that she exhibits one of the most engaging countenances I have ever seen. Still a child, she obviously weighs every decision and action between what her heart draws her to do and what her head compels her to do. Throughout this process, every thought, question, and trepidation she experiences is visible in her eyes and on her face. The pursed lips, the knitted brow, the raised eyebrows, with accompanying hands on hips, all speak volumes as she considers her decisions.

Daily she sways back and forth between adult and childlike behaviors, yet in the end, I have never seen her waiver from the path the significant adults in her life must expect her to follow. The child ultimately always succumbs to the adult, and I wonder what is lost in the process?

One day, just as we were beginning our reading time together I noticed Amber, Sam, and Cassandra peering out one of the front windows of the room we use for our reading lessons. While I couldn't hear their comments, I sensed apprehension and mistrust as they gestured toward the three or four people walking around the house across the street. I walked up to the window and peered out. "What do you think is happening over there?" I asked casually.

"Don't you care 'bout it no more, Ms. Jamie?" Sam shot back at me with undisguised annoyance.

"Of course I do," I replied, "but I haven't been able to learn much about the house even though I have tried."

Amber spoke up immediately in uncharacteristic anger, "Well, don't ask nobody who don't live around here bout it 'cause they don't tell you the truth."

This was the first time since my encounter on the porch so many months before that I had any reason to believe my initial gut reaction about a possible history between the kids and the house could be correct. I tried to choose my words carefully so as not to lose the opportunity.

"Why do you say that, Amber?" I inquired. My words seemed to fall at my feet because both Sam and Cassandra remained quiet and peered nervously across the room at Jalissa who was handing out bags of chips to some of the kids who had just come in.

Amber, tears welling in her eyes, followed Sam and Cassandra's gaze and then blurted out "Guess you should ask Jalissa 'bout that."

As I had come to know her a little better over the past weeks, I had noticed that Amber had no compunction about reporting incidents of lying and coercion among her peers or even, occasionally, by the adults who crossed her path.

She told me one day that, in her opinion, one of the greatest sins a person could commit was lying and that lying was as serious as stealing or killing. When I asked her about the difference between "little white lies" and "big black ones," she stared back at me and said forcefully, without hesitation, "Nothing!"

Chapter 15

Justine

"No one has yet fully realized the wealth of sympathy, kindness and generosity hidden in the soul of a child. The effort of every true education should be to unlock that treasure."

—Emma Goldman

Justine

Unable to compose herself, Amber walked quickly away from the window and ran out the door of the room. I was trying to decide how to respond when, Justine, another new face, approached me tentatively.

Shy, thin, and desperately in need of some individual attention, she bravely began, "Ms. Jamie, where do you stay?"

Puzzled by the question and torn between missing a moment to connect with Justine or comforting Amber, I responded, somewhat distracted, "Well, I live close to here in Beddington. Why do you ask?"

She glanced back and forth between Jalissa and me, still at opposite sides of the room, and then nervously began. "A long time ago, some other white lady come up on our porch and asked us a lot of questions about the house. We said we liked hangin' out there and asked if it was her house. She said no but told us that it didn't belong to nobody else around here either and belonged to somebody far away. Jalissa asked her what was gonna happen to it. She said nothing and that everything was gonna be fine and told us that we shouldn't worry none about it."

Taking a breath, she pushed herself to share her most pressing question, "We believed her, but Jalissa made us promise not to say nothin' to nobody about the lady or what she told us about the house. Then you came along and started asking a lot of questions about it, too, and now there is a 'For Sale' sign over there. Do you know that lady?"

When I had first met Justine, I decided she was another child with too many issues for me, by myself, to be able to address effectively. A child who had yet to decide to take pains with her appearance, she often pouted and was loud and insolent when she didn't get her way. On more than one occasion, we had to send her home after a tantrum.

She was self-conscious about her physical features as well, and I learned that in addition to an orthodontist, she also needed glasses. Yet setting all those issues aside, Justine, just like Sam, desperately needed a niche and direction. A couple of weeks earlier, I had begun to spend extra time working with her in reading and had seen some rays of light. I rationalized that much of her behavior was in self-defense and could be addressed with a little attention and genuine praise.

Her willingness to open up to me confirmed my gut feeling. This child was salvageable, and more importantly, she was reaching out in trust and faith. I looked into her expectant eyes and said, "Let's talk to Jalissa about this situation. No, I do not know the lady you are talking about, but let's try to find out what is going on. I like a good mystery, don't you?"

Chapter 16

The Visitor

"With time, grief has a way of slipping
down in the crevices of your heart. It never really
leaves; it just makes room for more."

—Nancy B. Brewer, *Beyond Sandy Ridge*

My conversations with Amber and Justine confirmed what I had
learned long ago about the difference in dialogue between adult
and child and adult and adult. Children, for the most part, believe
and, take to the bank, what is said to them—literally. Whoever told
them not to worry about the house meant well but obviously did
not understand the dynamics of a promise to a child who lives in a
marginalized, yet hopeful world.

I wanted to keep my promise to Justine so as we were finishing
the tutoring session for the day, I asked Jalissa if she could stay a bit
longer to talk with Justine and me. She looked puzzled but agreed.

About that time, Jessamy came into the room with Amber in
tow. While her eyes were red and puffy, it was clear that Amber had
had time to reflect upon her outburst and had returned for a specific
purpose. She glanced up at her big sister, uttered a poignant sigh and,
as if on cue, began to apologize for running out of the room and leaving us to watch over her younger brothers and sister. Jessamy placed
a hand on her sister's shoulder, and Amber fervently promised that
would never happen again.

With anxious eyes, she looked up into Jessamy's face awaiting a response that would signify her sister's approval of her pronouncement.

"Okay. You did good," Jessamy began with a softer than normal tone. "Now take everybody home and start dinner. I'll be there soon."

Wanting a moment alone with her, I walked Amber to the outside door, hugged her fiercely, and shared that I was about to talk with Jalissa about the house.

Her eyes fluttered as she responded, "Really, Ms. Jamie? Will you tell me all about it tomorrow?"

"Of course!" I commented and waited for a few minutes watching her gather the brood and skip home with the little ones close behind dragging their backpacks and coats.

After all of the kids who had shown up for our afternoon session left for home Jalissa, Jessamy, Justine, and I worked in silence picking up stray crayons, granola bar wrappers, empty chip bags, and game pieces. We were just finishing our routine by stacking the plastic chairs against the wall when Ms. Tracy came in to tell us that the office would be closing in a few minutes.

I could tell she was curious as to why the three girls had stayed behind when everyone else had gone. We typically tried to get all of the kids out of the area thirty or so minutes prior to the closing of the office in the event one of the management staff members returned to the property for an update of the day's events.

I was summarizing, as best I could, the conversations of the afternoon when, without saying a word, Tracy glanced at her watch and then walked over to the wall and removed five of the chairs we had just stacked on top of one another from their assigned storage places. She placed them in the middle of the room, uttered a huge sigh, and said, "It's time we talk."

The incredible narrative unfolded piece by piece in what seemed like a developing storyline for a movie. I listened as my newly found friends shared their individual stories of how they came to visit the old house.

Justine, still too young to truly understand, said the least, but her desire to be part of the moment was genuine and compelling. It was clear that she considered it her responsibility to save the house from some unknown fate.

Undoubtedly, there were things Tracy and I would discuss later, as adults, but I learned enough that afternoon to know that the house had a mysterious past, and that all of the kids, seemingly regardless of age, who lived in the Oak Lakes apartments were inexplicably drawn to it.

I also learned that the city of Eden Hill had been trying to determine how to deal with the property for as many years as Tracy could recall, but each time, there appeared to be resolution on the horizon either a contract of sale fell through or something else occurred to prevent the recommended action.

The most promising information gleaned that late afternoon, however, was shared as an afterthought and nearly left out of the conversation all together. Jalissa told us that she remembered speaking with the white lady who visited the house a year or so before me. "She talked funny, Ms. Jamie, and asked us strange questions."

I tried not to appear overly eager as I challenged her for more details. "What do you mean when you say 'she talked funny'? What kinds of things did she say?" I inquired.

Jalissa pondered my questions earnestly, and I could feel her reaching deeply into her memory for answers. "Well, she said 'ya'll' a lot, talked real slow, called a storm a cloud, and asked me where my people was from. Then she asked if I had ever heard anybody speak 'Gulaa' or something like that, or if I knew about the story of the pineapples. She made us go out into the yard and look up at the top of the house. She pointed to the little pineapples up there and told us they were very special. We hadn't seen them before, and it made us feel really weird."

Eagerly wanting to be part of the conversation, Justine interrupted, "Yea, I remember that. She acted spaced out."

I sat upright, startled. Probing a bit more forcefully than intended, I inquired, "Did you say Gullah and pineapples? Did she explain why she mentioned those things to you?"

"No," Jalissa stammered as if she had missed something important and by doing so had upset me in the process.

Recognizing my impertinence, I quickly added, "It's okay, Jalissa, you didn't do anything wrong I was just surprised because those are things I know about from home and remember from when I was in college."

"Oh, okay," she relaxed and then continued, "Right before she left, she said we should call her Ms. Blessing. I asked her if the street was named for her and she smiled and said, 'No, not me, but somebody very special.' As she walked away, she looked like she was gonna cry, but she smiled and told us to not to worry about anything and asked that we take care of the house as best we could, visit it every chance we got, and keep it in our prayers at night. That way everything would be all right."

"That's why when you came, Ms. Jamie, we got scared all over again. You asked a lot of questions, and then all of a sudden, the house was for sale. Do you know what's happenin'? Is somebody gonna tear it down like Cassandra's daddy says?"

While the details she shared were definitely more than enough to fill in several of the blanks in my search and should have satisfied me, I watched her glance nervously at Justine and Jessamy and, unexpectedly, felt a gnawing sensation in the pit of my stomach that there was something she had purposefully left out.

With everyone else looking on, I moved my chair closer to hers, gently cupped my hand around her chin and raised her eyes to mine. Taking a chance and hoping I could find just the right words to elicit a response I inquired, "Jalissa, is there anything else you want to tell me? Right now I feel like you are scared about something and not certain that you should say anything more, but what if I told you that in my heart, I believe there is a reason you should, and also a reason why our paths crossed so many months ago that neither of us may understand now but will later. Am I making any sense?"

She nodded tentatively as all of us waited for her to speak.

Seconds passed, and I could hear the ticking of the clock we'd just put up in the study area to remind the kids when they needed to head home after tutoring time. The tension in the air was palatable, and I felt beads of perspiration begin to form in the small of my back.

I was about to remove my hand from her chin and back away, when Jalissa sighed heavily and then revealed what she and the kids had kept secret from the adults in their lives for so long. "There is one more thing, Ms. Jamie. The last thing she asked was whether or not the house talked to any of us."

I must have gasped audibly because I could feel everyone's eyes on me. Now I understood why my comment that very first day had unnerved and frightened them so.

I wasn't sure what to say, but as Tracy looked on apprehensively, I promised Jalissa, Justine, and Jessamy that everything was okay, and that we would do all we could to save the house and secure its continued presence in their lives.

Before the girls left that evening, we all hugged one another tightly, and as I watched them go their separate ways toward home, I sent up a short prayer asking God to help me do everything in my power to fulfill that promise.

Chapter 17

Eden Hill

> "This town of churches and dreams; this
> town I thought I would lose myself in, with its
> backward ways and winding roads leading to
> nowhere; but, I found myself instead."
>
> —Kellie Elmore, "Magic in the Backyard"
> (excerpt from *American Honey*)

Now that I had a definitive name to use, I contacted Ms. G and we renewed our search in earnest for documents that might reference the name Blessing. Searching through local historical records, Ms. G discovered that a building permit had been issued to Thomas Abraham Eden and Jillian Marie Blessing in May 1950 to build a structure on a large tract of land that we learned encompassed what is now 1324 Blessing Path.

Earlier in our research, we had become familiar with the story of the founding of Eden Hill. In 1888, Abraham Eden and Josie Moore Lee, apparently Thomas's great-grandparents, had purchased a sizable tract of land southwest of what is now the intersection of Main Street and Venture Parkway. They built a home and dairy farm.

In April 1890, the local town council petitioned the Tibold County Commissioners Court to create a road from Beddington, then a small community about four miles west of the Eden land, to the Devonshire-Tibold County line at Mud Creek. Mr. Eden requested that the road pass by his newly built country store on the

71

edge of his property in Tibold County. The court ordered the road established and appointed a jury, including Eden, to lay it out.

The structures at the edge of the Eden property eventually expanded to include a small school and community hall. The hall burned down in the early 1900s, but the Eden family continued to remain active in community affairs across many generations. After several years, local residents decided to honor the young man whose arrival and whose faith in the community seemed to coincide with the end of hard times. They named their community, Eden Hill, for him.

With Jalissa's revelations, we now knew that the names Eden and Blessing were intertwined and connected to the property we were researching. However, we still didn't know anything about prior generations of the Blessing family. We could find no record of the name Blessing in any other Eden Hill records. Even more intriguing for me was why did the mysterious stranger make reference to things I automatically associated with the state I called home, South Carolina?

Chapter 18

So What Do You Want to Do with Your Life?

"If you don't design your own life plan, chances are you will fall into someone else's plan. And guess what they have planned for you? Not much."

—Jim Rohn

Just prior to my sophomore year in high school, my parents made a life-altering decision when the strip mining company for which my dad worked decided to move its business far back into the mountains of my mother's beloved home state, West Virginia. While the move would indeed increase business and production opportunities for the company, the area was remote and desolate. Of particular concern for my mother was the fact that the graduation class of the local high school for that year totaled six.

After what must have been a series of gut-retching, late-night discussions, my parents agreed to quit their jobs in the city where both my mother and I had been born and return to Dad's tiny home-town in South Carolina. I assume they reasoned that it would be easier for both to acquire new jobs in a location with family ties. As the place I visited every summer and thought of as a second home, I was thrilled with the idea and never considered the impact the move would have on my parents' then vibrant lives.

Although she tried her best my mother was never quite the same person after the summer of that move. The cultures were very different in the two states, and she didn't possess the same adaptive capacity of my father. Her ginger hair, vivacious spirit, and adventuresome Irish nature did not quite match the genteel appearance and quiet, submissive countenance of the local women.

She never seemed to establish the close friendships I remembered from her life before in the mountains where we both had been born and reared. While she did find a job as a bookkeeper in the local bank, she no longer engaged in the variety of outside activities she had previously enjoyed in her far away hometown.

I particularly remember that she stopped indulging her passion of shopping for "glad rags," the affectionate term she used for leisure clothing. There weren't any boutiques in our new, little town so the kinds of things she took pleasure in finding and purchasing were few and far between. She'd usually comment that it didn't matter much since there were no places that were appropriate for wearing the colorful frocks anyway. Unknown to me then, it was a trying time for both of my parents as they attempted to start over.

For Dad, who had left South Carolina years earlier to find a job in the Detroit automobile industry where his uncle was a plant supervisor, going home was merely a bump in the road. Often described as easygoing and jovial, he had a knack for accepting life's twists and turns and getting on with business.

In my adolescent memory, the prime example of his ability to adjust and survive was the story of his trek to Michigan after his army discharge at the end of World War II. Traveling north, he and his best friend, Ned, had stopped at an inn in northern West Virginia to stay the night.

My mother, a beautiful, independent redhead was home from New York for a visit and had stopped by briefly to see her sister, the inn's proprietor. Since it was a weekday night and all the rooms were booked with Highway 50 business travelers, the staff was very busy.

My mother, never one to shy away from work, pitched in to help tend bar and serve drinks.

Years later, my maternal grandmother and my mother's two sisters never tired of telling me the story of how the trip to Michigan never materialized for my father since he spent the better part of three months following that fateful night at the Log Cabin Inn convincing my mother to marry him.

After we moved to South Carolina, if the weather was nice, my dad's whole family, to include brothers, sisters, children, and grandchildren, would gather in Mama and Papa C's front yard on Sunday afternoons after church services and lunch. Depending on the time of year, we would sit on colorful metal lawn chairs and blankets laid out on the grass to share a little watermelon, pecan pie, or a freshly baked coconut cake and conversation.

Once we felt we could slip away without being noticed those of us older cousins would hurry to our secret place in the pasture to talk about our dreams, and try to outdo one other with predictions of where we would go and what we would do once we were able to leave Stone Church.

Jackson was going to be a journalist and would attend the University of South Carolina. Jane would study piano at Winthrop, while Thomas and Richard, younger and still undecided, just made fun of the rest of us. Actually, Thomas thought he might be a race car driver since he didn't see college as the right place for him. Richard, now that I think back, never actually committed to anything.

All I could think of to say at the time was that I loved animals, loved the beach, and wanted to be known for doing something different. I think it was the part about wanting to be known for doing something different that made them roll their eyes. I knew, even then, that I would always be their weird, distant cousin. While nothing was ever decided during those conversations, it was a dreamy, magical time for us all.

Chapter 19

Watermelon, Spanish Moss, and Pineapples

"There was a land of Cavaliers and Cotton Fields called the Old South. Here in this pretty world, Gallantry took its last bow. Here was the last ever to be seen of Knights and their Ladies Fair, of Master and of Slave. Look for it only in books, for it is no more than a dream remembered, a Civilization gone with the wind."

—Prologue, *Gone With The Wind*

South Carolina Barrier Islands

Like many of the students of my era, I gave no practical consideration to the selection of a major or a college. It was just expected that I would go on to some institute of higher learning after graduating from high school, and preferably, it would be one in South Carolina since money was tight and the tuition would be less.

Early in my junior year, our high school counselors began to conference with each of us about what we would do after graduation. I waffled between becoming a veterinarian or an animal behaviorist. Practicality was never part of the equation.

One Friday evening in late November, I was brooding over not having a date while channel surfing the television in the den when I came across one of the programs in the Jacques Cousteau series. I was immediately smitten and sat there envisioning myself in a wet suit helping Jacques and his sons with their research.

Just like that my major was decided. I would be a marine biologist, and since the only college in South Carolina at the time to offer such a program was a small, private school known as The College of Charleston (C of C), the location for my post–high school studies was determined as well.

My first visit to the Holy City, as Charleston was often called because of its proclivity for churches, was the Saturday my father and, Jimmy, a maternal cousin, dropped me off for my freshman year. Quite coincidentally, that weekend was also the occasion of a surprise visit from one of my mother's sisters' families on their return trip to West Virginia from a vacation in Florida.

My mother was visibly torn. How could she accompany me to Charleston the momentous occasion of dropping your only child at college for the first time while accommodating her family's rare visit as well? Dad, ever the peace-maker, suggested that we make it an adventure for him, Jimmy and me while mom entertained Aunt Ruth and the rest of the clan. He reasoned that there would be time for mother to visit me at school prior to the Thanksgiving break when I would come home.

I could see the sadness in her eyes as we packed the car, and she lamented not being able to meet my roommate or make certain the bedspread and decorative throw pillows were just the right colors. When we were saying goodbye to everyone she rushed back into the house to get the camera she had purchased for me to use to take pictures of my dorm room.

She passed it to me through a passenger window of the packed car and squeezed my hand tightly. I smiled broadly and told her I loved her and was sorry she wasn't going with me.

She murmured, "I love you too" while I earnestly promised that I'd start snapping pictures immediately once we got to the college.

For all that, like most kids leaving home for the first time, as we waved goodbye to those standing on that black top driveway and drove away, I experienced my first palatable sensation of freedom, and the promise to send several pictures of my new life away from Stone Church evaporated ever so slightly.

Chapter 20

Charleston, My Charleston

"Charleston is an extraordinary place. There is a deep connection between the residents and nearly three hundred and fifty years of history, and those ties between life and the distant past are strengthened by the occasional glimpse beyond the veil."

—James Caskey, *Charleston's Ghosts: Hauntings in the Holy City*

I don't know which enchanted me the most, the live oaks with their cascading Spanish moss, the pastel colors of the houses of Rainbow Row or the fascinating, high-spirited ladies who were busily weaving baskets in the marketplace near the old harbor. But as each day of that first week melted into another, I found myself less and less interested in the activities of orientation and matriculation for school than in the attributes of my new, citified environment.

I remember being overjoyed to learn that my roommate, Gracie, had graduated from the prestigious, private girls' school in Charleston, Ashley Hall, and was eager to share everything about the city and its fascinating ways of life that she had learned over the years. Luckily, she saw me as a sort of immigrant roommate who had a great deal to learn about the "real" South Carolina and subsequently decided that it was her duty to educate me.

One August afternoon, after class, I decided to continue the walking tour of the city I had initiated almost immediately after Dad and Jimmy had left to return to Stone Church. I had begun to use the camera to take pictures of the city rather than my dorm and wanted to venture further away from campus to capture more images. I had never lived in an urban setting and found the ability to get around on foot exhilarating.

Eager to explore every aspect of the city, especially the old waterfront area, I walked several blocks to East Bay Street and the water's edge. Wandering along the Battery with its elegant, majestic homes, and then down East Bay past enticing restaurants and unique shops I found the area to be so intoxicating that I had difficulty making progress amid the cobblestoned streets.

The magnetism of the myriad sites, sounds, and aromas drifting from each of the alleyways and courtyards was difficult to resist. I felt like a voyeur as I tried to peer discretely through wrought-iron gates into fragrant, peaceful gardens, and each time I stopped to do so, I could almost hear my mother chastising me for snooping.

Many of the houses were long and skinny and appeared wrongly situated on the street since the actual front door to the house was inside the fence and gate that fronted the street. An excerpt from an essay, "The Charleston Single House" by Bernard Herman, that I later found in the Charleston Public Library best described the style:

"The Charleston Single House was a creative response to the increasing scarcity of space in the city and was designed to mitigate the unpleasantness of hot, humid summers. With its narrow side directly on the street, the rectangular house with two rooms in each story grew tall to raise the main entertaining room to the level of the prevailing breeze that passed through a side piazza. As a free-standing house communicating more with a side garden than with the street the Single House offered a masterful but still vernacular solution to the residential problems of achieving comfort, privacy, and propriety."

As captivating as the architecture and East Bay Street sites were for me, I was actually more interested in something else. Gracie had spent hours telling me about one of the more popular attractions of the city. There were older, black ladies who spent their days sewing baskets down in the marketplace by the water, and I was determined to make it there to observe that tradition before it became too dark to find my way back to the C of C. Hurrying on, I recalled fragments of our conversation the night before and reminded myself that if I really wanted to see them today, I had limited time for exploration along the way.

We were rearranging the furniture in our tiny dorm room for possibly the third time when Gracie began the story about how West African slaves had brought the sewing process to the coastal area during the height of the plantation era. The baskets, used mainly in the rice cultivation process to separate the rice seed from its chaff, a process known as winnowing, also doubled as a way to collect and carry vegetables and fruit back to the house.

She shared that the weaving process, a traditional art form, had been passed down from generation to generation, and the baskets were and still are sewn with several types of materials to include sweet grass, bulrush, pine needles, and saw palmetto fronds.

When we took a break to survey our arrangement, she began rummaging through a box of books she'd yet to unpack. Muttering that she had a botany book somewhere that explained all about the grasses of the marsh and tidal regions she continued, "We call all baskets 'sweet grass' today, but most of the earlier ones were made primarily of the stronger bulrush or black rush material."

She grinned as she located the book and sat down on the floor to thumb through its pages. When she found the information she wanted, she motioned for me to sit beside her and then continued her story by reading from the text, "Appropriately categorized as needle rush or black rush, bulrush is indigenous to the Carolina marsh area, too, but it is tougher than sweet grass and, as a result, rougher on the hands and more difficult to bind tightly. Many of the Gullah ladies use bulrush alternately with sweet grass and add it to baskets for strength."

Later that evening, as we collapsed on our beds, she continued to share what she knew about the history and process of basket making in the area. For some reason, it was clearly a part of low country history that she wanted me to understand.

Even in the semi-darkness, I could see her slurping the Diet Coke she'd retrieved from our tiny refrigerator. After a big gulp, she picked up the story she had begun earlier. "It was only at the beginning of the twentieth century that the ancestors of slaves began to make 'show baskets,' which used sweet grass. One of my teachers told us that it was because the descendants of many of the slave families needed income in the aftermath of hurricanes and boll weevil infestations.

"Until my junior year when my Botany and South Carolina History teachers collaborated on a unit about the low country, I never knew there were so many types of grasses around here. We visited Boone Hall Plantation on a field trip and saw a display that explained everything about making the baskets," she continued, "I remember being fascinated that sweet grass usually grows in tufts behind the second dune line from the ocean, or you can sometimes find it along the boundaries between the marsh and the woods. It's pliable so it does well in the more intricate designs and once dried, it is a pale green to straw colored."

Trying to appear interested and keep myself awake I asked, "Why is it called sweet grass?"

In the moonlight, I could see her propping up her pillows to get more comfortable, "Well, I think it's because it has a sweet scent like fresh hay. It's hard to find much of it along the low-country coast now because of increasing development of all the islands. You'll see, though, when you go to the market, that it is still highly prized for use in the sewing of the baskets that bear its name."

"Why do they use pine needles?" I questioned. "They seem so brittle to me."

"The long leaf pine needles are red and make a great contrast color for the yellow of the sweet grass. They really make the baskets stand out. Sometimes even saw palmetto fronds are used to bind everything together in an unusual design."

I thought she might be drifting off to sleep when I heard, "Jamie, you know what the most interestingly thing of all is for me?"

Without waiting for my response, she began to bear her soul, "It's not really the baskets themselves, though they are pretty, but it's learning about how tough and creative the people were. Today, the women do most of the sewing, but during the slave days, large baskets for the field were made by men, while smaller baskets used in the home were sewn by the women or older slaves who were no longer able to work in the fields."

I sat up to hear more as she continued, "Someday you need to take one of the rice cultivation tours. The lives of the slaves were really awful, Jamie, really awful. Most people don't understand the half of it. Cultivating the rice was a horrible ordeal.

"Legally, the slaves couldn't marry one another either, but they still wanted some sort of ceremony. It was called 'jumping the broom.' But there were no guarantees that a family, once formed, could stay together. Many times wives were taken from husbands, or husbands from wives, or children from their parents if the plantation owners needed to trade or sell them. Slaves were pieces of property just like a horse or mule. That's a part of my history that I'm not proud of, but I make myself study it because it helps me understand everything indigenous to my sweet South Carolina low country."

Maybe it was listening to a living history story the likes of which I had never known existed in the twilight of that stifling evening, or maybe it was Gracie's fervent, impassioned love of the low country that pulled me so strongly toward that market that day. I wasn't sure, but I did know that there was almost nothing that could keep me from going there.

Chapter 21

The Gullah Ladies

"My grandmother has only a third grade education, but she could read and held her head high. She was a proud American, but Gullah was her native tongue."

—Mary Ravenell, teacher

A sweet grass basket weaver in the old market

When I arrived at the market, there were several ladies working on their intricate creations. I wandered aimlessly for the better part of an hour walking slowly past their carefully staged displays laid out on quilts or blankets covering the cool cement floor. Good-humored, jovial, and attired in brightly colored stripped and floral fabrics, they appeared as close as sorority sisters and conversed in a strange, intriguing language that was fringed with spurts of uninhibited laughter.

As they chuckled and talked with one another, I watched their nimble fingers work a tool that Gracie had called a sewing bone through the fine, delicate grass strands. It was like watching a virtuoso piano concert. Their fingers seemed to intuitively know how to combine all the different reeds into a concerto of woven patterns.

Using a combined vocabulary of English and words of African origin, these enchanting ladies introduced me to yet another reason why the Carolina coast can tug at one's soul. The Gullah language they were using, as I later learned, arose independently in Georgia and South Carolina in the centuries just prior to the 1900s. I also learned that "Gullah" was the term used to describe both the dialect and culture of West African black people in the area. The word itself may have come about as a derivation of one of the countries of their origin, *Angola*: Angola, Gola, Gullah.

The minutes rushed by, and the late August afternoon sky was transformed into a soft, grayish evening light. Against my better judgment, I hung out beyond the time I had established for myself to start back across the city. I continued to watch them practice their craft and strained to understand their exuberant conversations. I was almost without a will of my own as I was inextricably drawn to this time and these powerful women like nothing I had ever experienced before.

Just before I knew, I absolutely had to leave I caught a glimpse of a very large pineapple that was made from the same materials as the baskets. It belonged to Ms. Beatrice, whom I later learned was one of the regular weavers in the market. The woven fruit was the centerpiece of her advertising display and definitely unique among all of her other creations.

Trying to avoid demonstrating my ignorance all afternoon, I had refrained from asking a lot of questions. But as she was packing up her varied array of baskets, I was drawn to the uniqueness of that piece. I moved closer to where she was working and without thinking demonstrated what I later came to realize was embarrassing impertinence. "Why did you sew that huge pineapple rather than another beautiful basket?" I questioned. "Aren't the grasses you use difficult to find?"

"Shuh, gal, why you ax'me squeschen?" she replied shortly. "Da'dey sweetn is onuhrubble in Chaa'staun."

I didn't want to admit I had no clue what she was saying so instead, so I simply smiled sweetly, mumbled "thank you, ma'am," and retreated quickly into the night air. Several times, I nearly lost my footing on the cobblestoned streets as I rushed back to campus.

I managed to walk through the front archway of the stone gate opening onto campus before the streets were completely dark. Feeling more than a little unsettled, I hurried into the college library just prior to the last call for dinner. I wanted to research the possible significance of the pineapple to Charleston. There were several versions of legends associated with the fruit that were specific to the Charleston area. However, the prevailing consensus was that the pineapple was a symbol of hospitality not only in Charleston but also throughout northern port cities and the south in general.

One story even suggested that when sailors returned to Charleston from their travels they would often bring tropical fruit home with them. Pineapples were sometimes placed on the front gate to signal that the man of the house was home and the family was ready to accept visitors.

Chapter 22

Officer Steve

"Coincidence is God's way of remaining anonymous."

—Albert Einstein, *The World as I See It*

Reid and Officer Steve working with some of our boys

After finding the information about the building permit further researching the name Blessing in local records had proven unproductive until Ms. G, as a last resort, decided to search birth and death records beginning with 1950. While we had found no prior reference for a marriage license, documents revealed that Thomas and Jillian Blessing Eden had welcomed a son, Matthew Abraham Eden, into the world in August 1951.

Sadly, however, the records also indicated that Jillian Blessing Eden, his devoted mother, had died the winter of 1953. While the information the records revealed was substantial, the missing details, in my opinion, were the most crucial piece to understanding the whole story. We were once again at a dead end. Tired, defeated, and wanting time to think about our next move, Ms. G and I agreed we'd let the matter rest a bit.

As the library was closing, we decided that early the next morning we would go in separate directions. I would make another call to the real estate company that listed the property to obtain an update on its status, while she would continue to search old newspaper files for any reference to the family name, the property itself, or the recorded social events of Eden Hill in the early 1950s.

Driving home, my spirit was at an all-time low. For a very long time, I had been neglecting the other important aspects of my life: especially my husband, our home, and of course, our resident Scotties, with little to show for my efforts. Maybe all my friends had been right. What was I doing obsessing about an old, abandoned house and a bunch of kids whom I kept disappointing?

I was seriously toying with finally abandoning the whole thing when I received a text from Reid suggesting we meet for dinner at one of our favorite little cafés in a neighboring town. Eagerly accepting the invitation, I texted him back while stopped at a traffic light. I then tried to determine the best way to get there avoiding the maze of highway construction projects and significant afternoon traffic headaches that currently consumed our metropolitan area.

Navigating the detours and road closures, it took me over forty-five minutes to drive ten miles, and as the welcoming red awning and flowery pots of the café's cool patio came into view, I realized that Reid had arrived long before me. I drove slowly past *The Tuscan Glass* on Main Street looking for the closest parking place when I saw him raise a glass of what I knew was my favorite variety of white wine. Because I had recently purchased a shiny, new Acura that had yet to acquire its first scratch, it took me more time than I would have liked to park; yet another delay. As quickly as I could, I hurriedly crossed Main Street and practically sprinted past the boutiques and novelty shops to where he was seated.

I could see him from a distance and, as always, marveled at how well he was dressed. In fact, the first time my southern cousins met him, they were disappointed that he didn't own a pair of cowboy boots, a bolo tie, or a huge belt buckle but instead typically donned designer shirts, pressed pants, and shined shoes. He had left our house around six thirty that morning so I didn't see the pale pink Daniel Cremieux shirt, lightly starched and pressed khaki pants, and shined leather loafers that he was wearing.

I mused that had I known we would be going out for dinner, I might have selected something other than my blue-jean, three-quarter pants, favorite Clemson T-shirt, and comfortable Clark's sandals as the attire for the day. I made a mental note to keep an extra outfit in the car for just such spontaneous occasions should one ever occur again.

He stood when I arrived at the patio table and lightly kissed my cheek. "Long day?" he inquired.

I took a sip of the chilled wine he handed me and challenged myself to refrain from launching into my litany of disappointments. I willed myself, instead, to listen to comments about his day. It had been a very long time since I had intentionally focused on something other than my world, the kids, or the house.

"Probably no longer than yours," I began. "How is the new school project coming along?"

He twirled his empty glass between the thumb and forefinger of his right hand, offered a crooked grin, and said, "Do you really want to know all the gory, construction details?"

Shortly after retiring my highly respected and successful husband had been asked to return to his former school district to manage several new bond construction projects. One of his most significant strengths has always been recognizing how to effectively communicate with people at all levels to include both management and laborers.

Obviously, this skill still serves him well as he was invited back to work in what I've come to learn is a challenging arena. I was pleased to realize that he continues to enjoy the respect of colleagues and contractors alike and is relishing his latest challenge.

"No," I honestly confessed, "but I'm certain you are equally uninterested in my library research issues." I hesitated ever so slightly and then continued, "Driving over here, I realized that I rarely give you or anyone else the opportunity to say much lately."

Before he could respond, I took a deep breath and then blurted out the rest of what was on my mind, "In fact, after today, I think I am going to give up on this whole thing so we can get back to normal."

The evening breeze warm, dry, and sparsely apportioned across the colorful patio, seemed to swallow my words, and I thought that perhaps he hadn't heard me. I don't know exactly what I expected at this point, but it certainly wasn't silence.

Without acknowledging my last comment, Reid managed to get the waitresses' attention and ordered us two more glasses of the featured Sauvignon Blanc. I sat in silence nervously awaiting his response.

A few moments later, as our waitress came through the front doors of the restaurant to bring our wine, so did a noisy party of "thirty-something" folks. One, a burly, muscled guy, nodded a greeting in our direction. He smiled and tipped his cowboy hat politely.

Reid caught his glance and acknowledged the gesture. They stared curiously at one another for a few moments. "Coach Mo?" the burly guy commented, almost inaudibly.

Hesitantly Reid replied with a questioning voice, "Yes, may I help you?"

One never knows when his past will surface unexpectedly. And so it was that with friends, family, and complete strangers looking on, my husband and one of his former students, hugged fervently, reconnected on several emotional levels, and remarked more than once about the coincidence of this chance meeting.

Officer Steve, as we later affectionately named him, had played high school football for my husband, a.k.a. Coach Mo, and while I had always envisioned Reid as a powerful teacher and mentor in his earlier years, I never expected to meet one of his former students and players.

As dusk faded into the gray of twilight, we sat together with Steve and his wife, Karen, sharing tales of dreams both realized and unrealized, stories about past football moments, and tidbits regarding what both Steve and Reid knew of the current lives of former players.

The most significant juncture, however, may have been when, after we'd been talking for a while, Steve looked straight at me and said with more openness than I imagined possible from a stranger, "If it had not been for your husband, I would not be where I am today."

He went on to tell me that the man I loved had believed in him when no one else would. In short, he made the point that without Reid's influence he would have wandered aimlessly as an adolescent and never realized his potential. With those few words, I was reminded of what had drawn me to the wonderful man I had married several years before.

The wine and beer were flowing freely, and we were becoming far too sentimental, so on the spur of the moment, since their friends had long since moved on, Reid suggested that Steve and Karen join us for dinner on the back patio of the café. They accepted, and we moved to another table, and what we thought would be lighter conversation.

After we ordered dinner, we talked haphazardly about children, grandchildren, and our current lives and professions. At some point, Steve told us that he was working as a police officer for Eden Hill. I tried not to read too much into his revelation, but as he went on to lament that while he liked the job, it was often a difficult one emotionally, I began to feel that familiar, prickly sensation of déjà vu.

Lately, he continued, he had had occasion to serve more than the typical number of warrants to residents of local apartment complexes. Casually I inquired about the names of the complexes he visited. While Reid looked on with a knowing smile, Steve shared that the most frequently visited facility on his list was the Oak Lakes Apartments.

It was late, we had finished dinner, and everyone else was ready to head home. But something compelled me to spill my mysterious story to these quasi-strangers and try once again to find the common thread among all the coincidences surrounding the house, the kids, and my life.

I hurriedly shared a couple of stories about the kids I knew at Oak Lakes and winced internally as kindly eyes drifted beyond me to the lighted clock on the wall behind the bar. Despite their waning interest, I persevered.

When I got to the part about the old house across the street from Oak Lakes, Steve interrupted me, "You've been to the house? Do you know, Ms. Blessing, the lady from South Carolina?"

"No," I commented with hushed yearning, "no, I don't. I've heard of her though. Do you know her?"

Steve was about to comment when I leaned over the table and interrupted, "Okay. I've never told anyone this before, not even Reid, but maybe you are the person and tonight is the right time . . . that house on Blessing Path talks to me, I swear."

It was done. I had said it aloud, and maybe by doing so admitted my lunacy, but while no one commented further that evening, we all sensed that additional conversation was definitely warranted, and the urgency of the timeline I had in my head suggested sooner rather than later. Before we left the restaurant, Steve and I exchanged email addresses and cell phone numbers.

We said our goodbyes, reveled in the significance of the evening one last time and made plans to connect soon. Reid walked me to my car, and when we reached the TL, his eyes surveyed the vacant parking spaces and sidewalks on Main Street. Apparently satisfied that the area was safe, he inquired about my ability to drive home. When he was convinced that I was sober enough to operate a motor vehicle, he reached for my hand and asked, "Are you still thinking about abandoning this whole thing?" I caught the softness in his voice and sensed protection and warmth in his words.

It was late and quiet for a downtown street. Thin, cottony clouds drifted across a particularly brilliant half-moon when I replied, "I guess not, but, Reid, I'm scared all of a sudden, and don't know what to do. What's happening here?"

He pulled me into his arms and commented, "Honestly, I don't know, but I think it might be time to consider letting go, and letting God have this."

It was a few moments before I responded. "For some reason, I think He already does."

Smiling, he brushed a kiss across my lips and said, "You may be right. See you at home in a few minutes, drive carefully, and stop worrying."

Chapter 23

The End and the Beginning of the Mystery

"The possession of knowledge does not kill the sense of wonder and mystery. There is always more mystery."

—Anais Nin

Miss Charlotte Blessing

I slept fitfully and felt more than a little unsettled as night faded into the gray light of early dawn. I keep both my iPad and phone by the bed and around 4:00 a.m. was awake enough to catch the familiar dinging sound that signaled a new text message.

Apparently, equally as disturbed, the message was from Steve asking if we might meet at a local Starbucks prior to his 8:00 a.m. shift. I eagerly agreed and finally was able to drift off, but by six thirty, I had showered, dressed, and arrived at Starbucks.

Earlier, as I left the semi-darkness of our bedroom, I gently patted the heads of my favorite canines haphazardly stretched out on the top of the covers and kissed the forehead of my unbelievably supportive husband. When he appeared slightly coherent, I asked him if he'd take care of the typical morning chores while I rushed out to learn more about Ms. Blessing. He mumbled agreement, and as the three of them settled in for an extra half hour of sleep, I slipped out through the kitchen to the garage, made my way to Starbucks, and ordered a steaming venti hot green tea with two Splendas. I always forget to put packets of my sweeteners of choice, Stevia or Truvia, in my purse.

Minutes passed, and I waited with great anticipation. Until now, I hadn't permitted my logical mind to chew much on the recent events. I found it disconcerting to really think about was happening in my life and brooded whether or not I was prepared to handle what might occur.

My morning devotional lay open before me when Steve walked through the door. Our eyes met, and it was clear that we both realized this situation might be bigger than either of us had perceived. He walked to the counter and ordered coffee before approaching the quiet spot in an out-of-the-way corner I had selected for our conversation.

For a brief moment, we surveyed each other as if we were meeting for the first time. Commenting simultaneously, "You go first," we both laughed. Steve pulled out a chair, glanced quickly at his watch, and soon began to share what he knew of the story that eventually would unite both of us in a common mission.

He had met Ms. Blessing months earlier when one afternoon, as he was routinely delivering a warrant to an Oak Lakes residence, he caught sight of her. The sky was darkening as he left the complex, and he noticed a solitary figure standing in the dusty driveway of the Blessing Path house.

It was a cool, blustery day, and he was intrigued and somewhat bothered by the appearance of an older white woman standing alone at the vacant house with no apparent means of transportation. As he drove out the main gate of the complex, he became more alarmed, not only because her tiny, fragile figure seemed inappropriately dressed for the day's weather, but also because she appeared disoriented and confused.

He turned into the circular driveway and stopped. When she didn't turn to acknowledge the car, he opened the door, got out, and asked if she needed assistance. She turned to face him as he spoke, and through the wire-rimmed glasses perched on her nose, he could tell that she had been crying.

"Pardon me, young man, but what did you say?" she asked.

He particularly remembered those exact words because they were uttered so softly and were so slowly drawn out. "The first word that came to mind when I saw her was genteel," he recalled, "and I decided she probably wasn't from around here."

Taking a sip of coffee, his words kept flowing, "I asked again if I could be of assistance and she turned back to the house before saying anything. I gave her a minute or so to answer and took the opportunity to observe her a little more closely. It was like going back in time. She appeared to be around eighty years old and was wearing what my mother used to call a shirtwaist dress with a flowery print, nylon stockings, and heels. She also had a tiny little hat with a veil sitting squarely atop her silver hair and her hands were sleeved in white gloves.

"When she turned around the second time, she appeared more composed and politely thanked me for stopping by. She asked if I might be so kind as to call her a taxi as she was finished with her business and wanted to return to her hotel. She mumbled that she had no use for portable phones and never carried one. She also mentioned that it would be awhile before the car she had ordered would return for her as previously arranged.

"Concerned for her safety, I told her that I would be glad to give her a ride to wherever she needed to go. Again, I remember her comment because it was the first time I had ever heard a particular phrase she later used quite frequently. She said, 'Well, I do declare aren't you just the nicest young man! I'd be very proud to ride in your police car, but only if you will permit me to compensate you for your trouble.'"

I interrupted Steve almost immediately and commented, "My dad's sisters used to say 'I do declare' a lot, but I think I heard it the most during the time I lived in Charleston."

"Charleston?" he commented. "You lived in Charleston, South Carolina?"

"Yes," I said. "Is that significant?"

"Well maybe so . . ." he mused. "This is really unbelievable. You see, Ms. Blessing is from Charleston."

There it was, yet another coincidence. Seconds ticked audibly from a clock hanging nearby, and I wasn't sure how to respond.

Suddenly, a picture of the house crossed my mind. "Of course!" I almost uttered aloud. I saw its stately columns, the rectangular floor-to-ceiling windows, and the huge veranda. The house was from Charleston.

Should I encourage Steve to continue his story or share some of mine with him? I had waited so long to learn something, actually anything, about Jillian Blessing that I loathed to wait a second more. I shared this thought aloud, and Steve suggested that he might have a solution.

"I have an idea," he said, "but I need to tell you a bit more about that day first."

Dawn brightened into full morning, I retrieved a second cup of tea, and he continued, "As it turned out, I didn't just take Ms. Blessing back to the hotel. Something compelled me to befriend her, so I called Karen and asked if I might bring someone home for dinner. Though a little surprised she said 'certainly' but inquired who it was. I laughed and said 'An old lady . . . I'll explain later.'

"It took some time to convince Ms. Blessing to come for dinner, but she finally agreed. The only condition she imposed was that she would need time to change before going to our home so I should come back to get her after she had the chance to freshen up."

Steve took a sip of his second cup of coffee and hurried on, "I picked her up around six to take her to our house. I went inside the hotel lobby to greet her, and when she stepped off the elevator, I noticed that she was wearing a velvet green dress with a strand of pearls around her neck and a delicate black lace shawl across her shoulders. She had removed her hat and gloves but was definitely still formally attired.

"We walked slowly to the car with her arm on mine. I struggled with the moment and couldn't figure out what to say. It didn't seem to matter as she was tight lipped and silent herself.

"After she established herself in the backseat, the silence continued. I started to think it had been a bad idea to invite a stranger into our home, even a seemingly harmless, old lady. I shouldn't have worried, though, because once we arrived at the house and their eyes met, she and Karen bonded immediately. Looking back, both Karen and I agree that it was one of the most incredible evenings of our lives.

"Since our dinner had a few more minutes in the oven before it would be ready we settled in the living room. She selected our only upright chair, a Queen Anne, and made herself comfortable. I noticed that she took great pains to keep her tiny purse in the middle of her lap.

"When Karen asked if she might get her something to drink, I observed her eyes scanning the walls and fireplace mantle of the room as if looking for something in particular. She politely declined the offer for a glass of water or wine and then asked about where we grew up, if our families were from Texas and what it was like to live in such a dry, dusty place.

"Karen did most of the talking, and eventually, Ms. Blessing seemed to relax a bit and asked if the offer for a small glass of white wine was still available. I poured her a glass of Pinot Grigio as she and Karen continued their conversation.

"At some point, she inquired about the absence of children's pictures in our home. Though a personal question we were comfortable sharing that we hadn't been married very long but eventually hoped to have a large family. The answer seemed to please her, and by the time we moved to the dinner table she had relaxed and apparently made up her mind to share some of her own fascinating story.

"It was as if she had been waiting a long time to do so because she barely ate a bite throughout the meal and talked on and on about the connection of her family to Eden Hill. She told us she had come to try to decide whether or not the family should finally sell the property on Blessing Path."

I was enthralled with the story but couldn't help but stop it momentarily to remark about his propensity for detail.

He smiled, saying, "A policeman's curse," and then continued, "Ms. Blessing told us that while the property belonged to her nephew, Matthew, he had never returned to Texas after the death of his father, Thomas Eden.

"It turns out that Matthew was sent to Charleston, as a child, to live with the Blessing family. Ms. Blessing, or Charlotte as she requested we address her, was Matthew's aunt and her sister, Jillian, had been Thomas Eden's wife and Matthew's mother."

Attempting to gauge my response to the idea of Matthew being sent to Charleston as a small child Steve momentarily paused his story. When I motioned for him to continue, he concluded, "I found it strange that a father would send his son so far away but didn't want to appear impudent by sharing my thoughts. I knew there would be an explanation for that event and decided that Charlotte would share it when she was ready."

Then leaving me hanging, Steve smiled and said, "Okay, that should be enough to wet your appetite. Now let me get to that solution I brought up earlier. I think for you to fully comprehend the Blessing-Eden story you should go back to the beginning."

A bit exasperated, I raised my voice ever so slightly and interrupted, "Well, that's what I have been trying to do for months, but I haven't been able to find out what or where that is. Ms. G, an Eden Hill library volunteer, and I have been searching through all kinds of local historical records to no avail. I don't know where else to look. The real question it seems to me is what additional ideas do you have to offer about where we should look next?"

Obviously enjoying my exasperation and clearly cognizant of my tone of impatience, Steve asked, "What about thumbing through an old diary or reading letters from that time? Stories are a great way to learn about the past."

"Great," I chimed in, "but unless you know where to find those kinds of things, in my opinion, we are still standing on square one."

Waiting a moment to make certain I was ready for the magnitude of what he was about to say, he drained his coffee and then shared, "Actually, I do know where to look."

Chapter 24

Jillian and Thomas

"And think not you can direct the course of love, for love, if it finds you worthy, directs your course."

—Khalil Gibran

Jillian and Thomas
(pictured in the middle with friends from his squadron)

To say I was stunned by Steve's announcement would be a significant understatement. Yet even after all of these months of dead ends and disappointments, all I could think of to say that morning in Starbucks was, "What? Where?"

Grinning with delight, like a child who just shared a secret, he continued, "Charlotte stayed longer in Eden Hill than I think she had intended and during that time was a guest in our home on several occasions. Karen, whose favorite book and movie has always been *Gone With the Wind*, had begun to again read about the city of Charleston and its history. With each visit, she would beg Charlotte to tell her stories about the people, their traditions and their culture, and would sit for hours listening as Charlotte described her childhood, her educational experiences, the allure of the city, and the families who lived around her home and out on the islands.

"One evening, as it was growing late, Karen asked Charlotte to suggest a good southern love story, other than *Gone With The Wind*, that she might read that would exemplify the lives of the local people while also painting a picture of the city and its intoxicating nature. For a moment, we both thought she hadn't heard the question and was about to doze off. Her head dropped to her chest and she folded her tiny, delicate hands in her lap.

"After a while, she reached down beside her chair and retrieved a black leather briefcase that she had brought with her that evening. Earlier, when she had arrived, I had found this new item a curious addition to her attire, but I long ago learned that Charlotte usually had a reason for her seeming idiosyncrasies and that, in time, I would learn their significance if she meant for me to do so.

"Snapping open the lid, she pulled a tiny, tattered, leather book and a thick stack of envelopes bound by a brilliant crimson ribbon out of the case. With tears welling in her eyes, she extended a quivering hand toward Karen and offered, 'This is the best love story you will ever read. I've never shared it with anyone but now may be the right time. The real reason I made this last trip to Texas was to decide if it needed to be shared with the townspeople of Thomas and Matthew's birthplace. I'm not certain that history will treat either of them fairly without knowing the whole story.'"

Steve's emotions seemed to get the better of him as he made every effort to finish the story, "I tried to hide the fact that I was on the verge of crying like a baby and glanced over at my wife to gauge her reaction. I was relieved to see that she was teary eyed as well."

"Karen stood and crossed the room to embrace Charlotte. She knelt down in front of her chair, looked her directly in the eyes, and softly asked if she was certain that she wanted to share such meaningful and private things.

"Charlotte's voice became stronger then and without hesitating she told Karen that Thomas and Jillian's writings were meant to be read by others as their story exemplifies the words our Lord gave to us so long ago in the book of Corinthians, the thirteenth chapter and the thirteenth verse. To be certain we remembered the words she whispered them aloud, 'And now these three remain: faith, hope and love. But the greatest of these is love.'

"Karen accepted the letters and the diary. A bit later, just when Charlotte was about to leave she inquired what the family might like us to do with them.

"Peering over her tiny, wire-rimmed spectacles, this gentle lady who had kept such a powerful story deeply embedded in her heart for so many years shared that she, and mind you she emphasized that she was speaking for herself alone, would like us to help her find a way to get both the diary and the letters into the hands of someone who would not only share the story but would also find a way to preserve the house as well. She was adamant that the house was a very integral part of Thomas and Jillian's history and should not be forgotten.

"It was her final thought that evening, though, that stayed with me, and now, after meeting you, seems surreal. She was walking down our front steps on the way to my car when she turned around and spoke from her heart with the words, 'Actually, after this visit, I'm afraid even the house has given up the fight to live on.'

"Ms. Blessing stayed on a couple more weeks as Karen tried to find someone associated with the local historical society to meet her and hear the story. Unfortunately, we learned that the couple that had been instrumental in creating the society in Eden Hill had both recently passed away, and without their strong passion for the organization and its projects, the work of the group was in limbo and disarray.

"We put the letters and diary in a safe place while Ms. Blessing, sharing that she was exhausted, decided to go home. After she returned to Charleston, we talked quite often by phone and urged her to pursue the process there. Several times we offered to return the precious documents. She was adamant, however, that we keep them and continue to search for just the right person in Eden Hill since this was where Thomas and Jillian were happiest, and this is where the house still remains."

It was nearly time for his 8:00 a.m. shift when Steve and I finally said goodbye and left to go our separate ways. We both agreed that inextricably, we'd been united in an unimaginable quest to determine the fate of an old house.

Chapter 25

Faith, Hope, and Love in the 1940s and 1950s

"When you put faith, hope and love together
you can raise positive kids in a negative world."

—Zig Ziglar

I met Karen for lunch soon after my Starbuck's epiphany with Steve. She was gracious and kind but appropriately apprehensive of my intentions regarding the letters and the diary. We spent a great deal of time discussing life's twists and turns, especially across the past months, and as she intently questioned me, I tried to be as candid and transparent as I had ever been with someone who was practically a stranger. While our husbands knew one another, we did not, and I sensed and appreciated her desire to protect the precious information with which she had been entrusted.

While I found myself impatient to acquire the letters, I was also fascinated and intrigued by Karen's admiration and respect for a lady she had only recently met. I also reveled in the stories she shared about their time together in Texas. It was clear she was drawn to Ms. Blessing in a very compelling way.

As our conversation was drawing to a close, I sensed that she was not ready to share her treasures with me. Then she startled me by saying, "Steve tells me you are from South Carolina and lived in Charleston for a time."

"Yes," I smiled and continued, "as a matter of fact, it is my favorite city in all the world."

She studied me for a while and then commented, "I have shared as much of your story as I knew before today with Ms. Blessing, and she would like to meet you. Would it be possible for the two of us to travel to Charleston in the near future to talk with her and Matthew?"

Startled by her matter-of-fact announcement, I mumbled, "Why would she want to meet me?"

Karen grinned and then commented, "Well, I think it was when Steve told her that you said the house talked to you that she was hooked."

We spoke further about the significance of the story that was unfolding in our midst and began a serious discussion about the possibility of a trip to Charleston. Worried that I wouldn't be able to read the diary or the letters until I had Ms. Blessing's approval and remembering the realtor's sign at the house I agreed that we should go fairly soon.

All the talk about the city had caused me to recall the smell of the salt marshes, and I tingled with excitement at the possibility of again seeing them in person. Karen agreed to telephone Ms. Blessing that evening and get back to me with possible dates for our visit.

After saying goodbye to Karen, I still had some time before I needed to be on campus to teach my evening course. I decided to run over to the library to catch up with Ms. G and share my news.

When I arrived, she was busy helping an elderly gentleman learn how to navigate the internet. Her patience with people of all walks of life and all ages never ceased to make me smile. She was indeed a treasure, and as she stood over the frail, yet eager man, I was reminded of a Martin Luther King quote I had read somewhere long ago . . .

"Everybody can be great . . . because anybody can serve. You don't have to have a college degree to serve. You don't have to make your subject and verb agree to serve. You only need a heart full of grace. A soul generated by love."

I walked by their location in the computer center, and she nodded in my direction. Holding up five fingers, she gestured that that I should give her five minutes to wrap up her conversation there. I was glad for the brief respite because had I faced her at that moment I probably would have ended up falling into an abyss of emotion before adequately explaining the events of the past couple of days.

I composed myself by milling about the featured books section. Several titles intrigued me, and I again chastised myself for not setting aside some dedicated, quiet time to stop by here more often. To settle in among the precious gifts of someone else's thoughts that had been converted into the printed word seemed especially irresistible right now. When she walked up, Ms. G caught me browsing through a new release entitled *High Price* by Dr. Carl Hart.

"That's a good one," she remarked, "maybe something all educators should read. Actually maybe something you, in particular, should read."

"You've already read it?" I asked.

"Yes, it's about a young black man who grew up in what I'd call the 'Hood' and became a neuroscientist who primarily studies drug addiction. As a kid, basketball was all that kept him in school. Know anyone like that?"

Her words were challenging as she peered at me over her glasses. I felt a shiver run down my spine because it seemed that her comment probed a little deeper than that of a casual remark.

I couldn't read her steely, charcoal eyes, but began to think it certain that she had met some of the kids at Oak Lakes and maybe even had learned of my connection to them. Since I didn't have time to launch into our past and current associations, I simply said, "Well, as a high school teacher, I knew a lot of kids who didn't come to school just for science class."

She smiled, as if she had expected me to be evasive, and then switched topics revealing that she had some news for me. "Let's go into Conference Room A. I found something in the old newspaper clippings we might be able to use."

I followed her uneven gait into the conference room, observing that time and gravity were generally not advocates for our generation. The furniture behind the glass windows was typical for most areas set aside for private conversations in public places.

I glanced across a spacious table of cherry veneer and six large, mid-back, black leather chairs. We sat down facing one another across the width of the table, and Ms. G began excitedly. "Oh my, I should have asked before we sat down. Would you like a bottle of water or a soft drink?"

"No, thanks." I said, "I just finished a large Diet Coke."

I'm not certain what I said mattered anyway because she was preoccupied busily spreading photocopies of the newspaper clippings she had removed from a manila file across the table top. I noticed that she handled each page gingerly as if it were a fragile treasure and suddenly felt a surge of tenderness for this gentle lady. Perhaps, God does, indeed, place very special people in our paths at just the right time to help us in our quest to make a difference.

When she looked up, I saw that her hair was slightly unkempt and not as neatly styled as usual. In addition, her glasses were somewhat ajar on her nose. Her voice quivered with anticipation as she spoke, "I was thinking about world events when I started going back through the microfiche documents we have. The library managed to salvage two to three readers for historical document research so, while tedious, I managed to work fairly quickly through the filmed entries of the local newspapers. While the resolution quality varied, I did find some very interesting articles."

She slid a copy of the first of several articles across the table to me. The title, *Local Man Enlists*, was not very eye-catching and caused me to speculate about the experience level of the copy editor. As I scanned the article, however, I became almost feverish.

Dated June 15, 1942, the words jumped out at me, and I read them aloud:

"Thomas Eden enlisted in the Army Air Force earlier this month and has departed Eden Hill for Charleston, S.C. He is scheduled to spend several weeks in that southeastern port city where he will begin an intensive training program to become a fighter pilot."

There were more details about Thomas Eden's life and family, but it was those first two sentences that captured my attention.

Before showing me the other two articles, Ms. G watched me closely to gauge my reaction. Silently recalling what I had learned since our last conversation, I mumbled, "This is unbelievable."

"I don't think news of a patriotic, young man enlisting in WWII is unbelievable," she quickly retorted, sounding rather perturbed with my answer, but then she appeared to catch herself and enthusiastically continued, "When I found it, though, I couldn't help but think it was fortunate that a clipping I would consider rather insignificant existed at all, but then I came across this second one."

Dismissing the first brief article, she pushed a second photocopy into my hands. The words of its title stared back at me like a cold, formal diagnosis of a terminal disease, and I felt a lump forming in my throat as if the person I was reading about was a close family member. The article, though short, was dated August 27, 1944, and its message dire and chilling:

Local USAAF Pilot Wounded in France
By Hank Fullen

Naples, Italy - While the details of his condition are unknown Second Lieutenant Thomas Eden is reported to have been wounded during heavy fighting in the area of Sainte-Maxime, France. Sainte-Maxime is located on the French Riviera in southeastern France approximately 90 kilometers from Nice and 130 kilometers from Marseille. Thomas had been participating in Operation Dragoon. The family has learned that Thomas will be returned to the states aboard the hospital ship, *Marigold*, and receive continuing medical attention in Charleston, S.C. before coming home. There were no details regarding the extent of his injuries.

"Was there any information in later stories about what happened to Thomas after he returned to Charleston?" I inquired with a hint of nausea beginning in my stomach.

"No, not about his injuries or recovery. But I found two more entries about Thomas both dated several years later that should relieve your anxiety," Ms. G interjected. "This time the articles were posted on the social page of the *Eden Hill Gazette*."

I quickly noted that the first was dated September 25, 1950, and the second July 4, 1951. Both were of a considerably different tenor than the first two.

Local Hero and New Bride Plan to Build Eden
Hill's First Mansion
September 25, 1950
By Mary Ann Jackson

Eden Hill – Thomas Eden looked on today as local contractors broke ground for the construction of his new home on a tract of five acres given to him as a wedding gift by his father, Blake. Thomas explained to this reporter that to entice his new bride to leave her revered homeland of South Carolina, he had worked with an architect to carefully design and draw the blueprints for their new home to capture the unique attributes of both Texas and Charleston architecture.

The young Mr. Eden continued, "Jillian has grown up living in a beautiful Charleston Single House, but I couldn't really envision that style of home with its side garden and piazzas here in Texas, especially since it would be difficult to maintain the lush gardens in our drier, less humid climate. I also told Jillian that we'd have trouble convincing our neighbors that the door to access the piazza was not the actual door to the house. In Charleston if that outside door is open the family is usually home to callers even if the real door to the house is closed. Do you really think Texans would come into a person's private garden without an invitation?" he grinned."

Smiling broadly, he continued, "I did manage, though, to work in some fairly noteworthy features of southern plantations that should help her feel at home. I'm certain our friends and neighbors will be curious about them, but I believe it is the people who come by who will definitely appreciate the unique mix of southern and western cultures we'll try to establish. By the way, keep watch as we are planning a real, housewarming party once the house is completed and Jillian finally comes home to Texas."

Eden Hill Grand Home Open House
July 4, 1951
By Mary Ann Jackson

Eden Hill – As if the celebration of our country's independence was not enough to warrant a citywide party, the residents of our entire town received personal invitations to drop by, Sweet Grass Memories, the name Thomas and Jillian Blessing Eden have given to their new home, to celebrate the holiday in style.

Those who visited the Edens were treated to a local Fourth of July celebration of immense proportions. Opening their home to everyone in town it was clear that this couple plans to be an integral part of the community right from the start.

The afternoon included tours of the house, historical talks about its special features, and finally a gigantic backyard barbecue replete with tiny American flags, picnic tables covered in red and white checkered cloths, and lots of aromatic, smoky chunks of juicy, charred meat.

Huge platters of brisket, sausage, ribs, and cabrito were delivered to every table as well as over flowing casseroles of baked beans, gigantic bowls of cool, creamy Cole Slaw and gallons of sweet tea.

At the request of Jillian, Thomas also sheepishly encouraged our community residents, cowboys and townspeople alike, to try a famous specialty in the coastal areas of S.C. known as a Low Country Boil. The one pot dish is composed of secretly seasoned shrimp, newly shucked corn on the cob, Andouille sausage, and red-skinned potatoes. It is typically served on a newspaper-covered picnic table, eaten with one's fingers, and shared with family and friends alike.

While we all laughed at the combination of recipes, politely tasted the Low Country boil specialty, and quietly gossiped about the steps Thomas and Jillian must have taken to get fresh shrimp from South Carolina to Texas, we were touched and enamored with our new residents, and the things they had done to let us know that they sincerely desired to become part of the local community.

As the fireworks Thomas had arranged faded into the evening sky, and we finished off the last of the pecan pies and peach cobblers, we realized that there was little food, either Texas or South Carolina style left to give away. Regrettably, we said our goodbyes and profusely thanked this young, loving couple for one of the greatest events Eden Hill had ever experienced.

After reading both clippings, I smiled in spite of myself and realized just how much I continued to yearn for and treasure my South Carolina roots. Gazing out the small window of the conference room into a peaceful courtyard, I found myself wishing that I had known Jillian and Thomas personally and imagined what it might have been like to be part of their lives so many years ago.

I envisioned a scene with Jillian and I sitting on a peaceful, fragrant piazza engaged in quiet conversation about the similarities between us. I couldn't help but feel that both of us had desired to make a connection between our two most beloved states.

Still sitting across the table from Ms. G I realized that, while I had briefly succumbed to the unfolding story and escaped into my private reverie of home, she, unaware of my newly discovered information, patiently awaited my response. Her work was profound and exciting, and after all we'd been through, she was as animated and excited as I felt weary and drained. I could see twinges of eagerness in her older, yet luminous eyes.

I looked up and finally admitted to myself that I owed it to her to share everything—all that I had recently discovered—and all the other stuff I had kept hidden.

I broke the silence, "Ms. G, how much time do you have? There is a lot I need to tell you."

After a few moments, her rich, velvet voice floated across the table to where I was sitting, "Girl, how much time do you need? We started this journey together, and, since I assume you know something I don't and want to share, we gonna finish it together!"

Listening to her comments, I wondered if she knew anything about the Gullah people and the culture of Charleston. Her words, though strong and determined, flowed gently across my conflicted soul as a salve one might spread gingerly over a tender wound.

The sensation conjured up several stories I had heard while still in Charleston about how the spiritual power of the benevolent Gullah people could overcome trouble, even evil. There were probably such legends and stories of people around the New Orleans area as well so maybe that was the reason I sensed similar understandings in Ms. G.

I was still musing about the Gullah people when someone knocked on the door to inquire how much longer we would be using the conference room. As Ms. G walked over to respond I noticed the striking blue, silk scarf tied around her neck. It caught my attention because it was not a typical fashion accessory for her and also because of its unusual color—a painter's attempt to marry the hues of sea and sky into one color on his palette.

The color tugged at my memory for a while, and then I knew. It mirrored "haint" blue; the color the Gullah people would sometimes use to paint their porches to ward off evil spirits.

I rose to finish our conversation just as she returned to the table and suggested that we meet for an extended, quiet dinner early that evening at the location of her choice. Without asking for further explanation, she smiled an upbeat smile and answered me with a single word. "Absolutely!"

We selected a tiny, family-owned Mediterranean restaurant where we could talk privately for as long as needed and agreed to meet at six o'clock. It was only during my drive home that I remembered my five thirty class and realized I'd screwed up. I knew that I owed it to Ms. G to bring resolution to the situation as soon as possible, but what about my commitment to my students?

It was already 5:00 p.m. when I opened the garage door, left the TL in the driveway, and hurried up the stairs to my computer. I quickly developed an online assignment for the course, emailed it to everyone in the class and then texted each student with my apologies feigning an emergency that needed my immediate attention.

I tried not to think about my lack of ethical behavior as I walked back downstairs to sit for a few moments on our patio. Clearly, consumed by this situation, I was neglecting my students and life in general. This was not who I wanted to be and yet, somehow it seemed "right" . . . a following of a much larger purpose. My devil's advocate propensity simultaneously pointed out that I was clearly adept at rationalizing most anything.

It has always amazed me that dogs appear able to sense human moods. Today, the resident Scotties had apparently decided not to be their usual boisterous and cantankerous selves, at least for a while.

As I sat quietly on our back patio, their almond-shaped eyes stared directly into mine, and their sighs were audible as they stretched prone, back legs flat against the cool, gray slate of the floor while I sat on the settee just above them. I wondered what we would have said to one another were we actually capable of having a conversation.

With the patio door slightly ajar, I caught the faint beeping of our alarm system signaling that the garage to kitchen door had been opened. Reid was home. He walked outside to say hello, and we exchanged comments and pleasantries about our respective day's events. I didn't share the whole story with him because the recollections about the Gullah people and my connection with Ms. G needed more time for explanation than I had to give at the moment.

He seemed to understand about the need for a private dinner between Ms. G and myself but was more than a little surprised that I was skipping a class. After changing clothes, he busied himself with his craft projects in the garage. Shortly thereafter, I rinsed my face with cool water and left home determined to share everything that Ms. G needed to know to bring resolution to this mystery and maybe get my life back to normal.

Though the restaurant was almost empty when I arrived, I requested a table outside. It was a hot, muggy evening, even sitting in the shade, but as I wiped my face with the soft linen napkin at my place, I decided that it was tolerable enough to remain on the patio.

It had seemed too dark and cold inside for the tenor of the conversation we needed to have. I wanted us to "feel" as well as share the words of the history we had uncovered and the people we were about to discuss. In my mind, all that translated into heat, humidity, and personal sacrifice: true Charleston attributes. Also, while I knew it silly, my gut told me Ms. G, being from New Orleans, would understand.

Chapter 26

The Truth Shall Set You Free

> "Truth is by nature self-evident. As soon as you remove the cobwebs of ignorance that surround it, it shines clear."
>
> —Mahatma Gandhi

Always punctual, I could see Ms. G walking from the parking lot to the restaurant just as my watch registered 6:00 p.m. When she came closer, I realized that she was not alone, and my heart leapt into my throat as if I was a kid who had been caught doing something that would warrant a trip to the principal's office.

While they were unable to see me, I had full view of Ms. G and her companion through the boxwood hedges surrounding the patio. Tracy looked as elegant as ever, and she and Ms. G were engaged in the friendly, comfortable banter of good friends.

My lack of candor over these past months now caused an eruption of acid reflux into my throat. While never meaning harm, I now realized how terribly foolish and shortsighted I had been. It was time to pay the piper, and I hoped that their forgiving nature for adults was as obvious and accessible as it had always appeared to be for children.

I stood tentatively to greet them. Their smiles were warm and accepting while mine nervous and hollow. As the distance between us narrowed, I sensed that they recognized my embarrassment. They walked through the gate onto the patio, and we hugged one another as if nothing was amiss.

"So," I offered nervously, not really knowing where to begin, "who should go first?"

Ms. G smiled broadly and interjected, "Well, how about everyone sitting down and ordering a round of drinks before we start talking? I don't know about you two, but I could use a little liquid refreshment."

Tracy agreed, so we called a waiter to the table to take our drink orders. Once that business had been addressed, I stared into their eyes and said sheepishly, "Okay, what do you already know, and what do I need to otherwise confess?"

Both laughed uproariously with obvious delight before Ms. G commented, "Oh, Ms. Jamie, relax, we know where your heart is, and we've just been waitin' for you to realize the power of pulling us all together to achieve the dream we all share for our kids."

I relaxed and lamented, "I should have known you two would connect, but honestly, I was too selfish to introduce you. Can you ever forgive me? You both know me well enough to realize that these kids have become very special to me and for some crazy reason I feared that sharing them with the two of you, because you understand and love children so unconditionally, would diminish my contact. I now realize how wrong and misguided that logic really was."

Neither Ms. G nor Tracy responded right away, and I, ever the pessimist, imagined all sorts of negative outcomes. But as I studied their faces I realized that I was the one with the problem, not them. There are "larger than life" individuals everywhere, even today. We just have to look for them and trust that they are genuine in their intended actions.

"Ms. Jamie, you don't give yourself much credit," Tracy commented as she tilted her head slightly and then added, "If these kids didn't trust you and believe that you love and care about them, they wouldn't come around when you appear. Surely you've realized by now that they have an uncanny ability to sniff out insincerity. That's pretty much been enough for us, besides we've gotten to know you as well."

The waiter brought our drinks, and when he walked away, Ms. G softly added, "Don't you think there is enough empty space in their hearts for more than one person, especially a star team like us, to work magic?"

And with those words it was done. From that point on, we tacitly agreed to work as a team, and the past transgressions any one of us had inadvertently committed were forgiven and forgotten.

We filled our plates with square after square of soft, warm pita bread stuffed with some of the best hummus, baba ghanoosh, and tzatziki in the city. Taking our time munching on these delicacies, we took turns sharing everything we knew about the kids, the house, and its history. To say my news about the letters and diary was the highlight of the evening would be a noteworthy understatement, and the significance of the chance meeting between Officer Steve and Reid that I recounted was lost on no one.

While none of us voiced our thoughts out loud I think it was safe to say that Ms. G and Tracy now realized, just as Steve and I had, that this story was bigger than anything we could have imagined and clearly under the direction of a higher power. Preparing for my next conversation with Karen and recognizing that time was of the essence, I was eager to know what Ms. G and Ms. Tracy thought about the proposed trip to Charleston.

"So knowing what we all know now and desperate to know more about the information in the diary and the letters, am I the best person to go? There are several of us Ms. Blessing might like to meet, and you both know the children's circumstances much better than me. How should we handle it?"

Ever the pensive, wise member of our little triad Ms. G reflected aloud, "Bear with me for a moment as I think about this. Let's talk about the house first. Who among us can truly say we have heard its call?" We all three sat there for a moment thinking about the significance of her question.

Tracy began, "Well, I'm disappointed to admit that I can't really say it has been me, although I have had some of the kids share that they can actually hear its words. In truth, it all sounds pretty far-fetched as far as I'm concerned, but after the last few weeks I'm willing to believe anything is possible."

After Tracy responded, and since Ms. G had been the one to ask the question, both sets of eyes now turned to me, and I realized that I had to share the one thing that made me most uneasy.

I sighed and began, "Well, for a long time, I have felt funny around the house. Actually I even started dreaming about it several months ago when I first sat on the porch with the kids. I even asked them if they had ever heard its words. No one answered me, but I sensed that at least some had an idea of what I was suggesting."

"Later, I took several pictures of its facade that I studied in great detail, and, while I was never certain why I felt drawn to it, I never seemed able to escape it either. So yes, I guess you could say I believe it communicates with me. For some reason, I sense that the house has decided I can save it and in doing so contribute to something universally good. I know it all sounds ridiculous, but there it is. I've stopped trying to deny what I know I've heard and feel."

We sipped our drinks simultaneously almost as if hoping that by doing so we could usher a sense of reality back into the moment. Sensing a lull in conversation, the waiter approached our table. Ms. G waved him off and then commented, "Ms. Jamie, my gut tells me that while we all have a significant part to play in this story, it is you who have the juju to pull all the pieces together. Forgive me for the nonsense you may perceive I am about say, but please listen and take heed.

"First of all, for whatever reason, the house does communicate with selected people and has somehow become comfortable with and trusts you. Secondly, you understand and love the culture and history of Charleston where the Blessing family has its roots. I know enough to respect and honor the pull of history on our lives.

"Every bit as curious and significant is the fact that the meeting with Office Steve was not an accident, and you have obviously been selected to unite others to make a difference in the lives of the children in our area."

She hesitated only slightly before finishing, "Finally, Ms. Blessing asked specifically for you to come. So I recommend that you go with Officer's Steve's wife, her trusted friend, and pull it all together."

With those words, she was done. Tracy and I sat quietly respecting her directive and its significance. While we all had very important parts to play in this story, I was to be the point person with the Blessing family and the link to South Carolina. She concluded by commenting, "As always, we will be here for both you and the kids. Funny, but I think I now finally know why I didn't go home to New Orleans after all."

With that decision, my mind and heart surged once more at the thought of returning to the Holy City after such a prolonged absence. I could almost smell the salt marshes and sensed that I had been charged with a very significant task.

Even though I was not alone, for a moment my mind followed yet another detour and I sat there marveling at how my life was unfolding. I felt so differently now than when I had first retired. God was indeed good and abundantly evident in His blessings as He worked to unite the best attributes of my past and present lives into one. I also decided that He (or She) probably had a very dry sense of humor as well.

Chapter 27

Going Home with and to Friends

"Yes'm, old friends is always best, 'less you can catch a new one that's fit to make an old one out of."

—Sarah Orne Jewett

A fragrant magnolia blossom

Reid was deep into a documentary on the History Channel when I arrived home, but he looked up long enough to share that Karen had called asking that I call her no matter the time this evening. The dogs acknowledged my presence as well, but only barely.

I decided to make the call from the bedroom since it was quieter there, and I wouldn't disturb Reid. I stretched out on the bed as the phone was ringing, feeling better than I had in months. Karen picked up on the second ring, "Hi, Jamie, I was hoping this call was from you."

Changing the audio to speaker so that I could lie flat, I responded, "I trust it's not too late. Reid said for me to call no matter the time. I was actually eating dinner with Ms. G from the library and another friend. Honestly, Karen, the coincidences keep continuing."

She interrupted, "Well, I'd really like to hear more but first let me tell you about the conversation I had with Charlotte earlier this evening. Apparently, she is feeling some sense of urgency about our visit, and while she didn't elaborate on the details, she asked if we might come to Charleston this weekend. Could you do that?"

My concrete sequential mind began trying to process what she was saying. It was already Wednesday, and there were so many details to consider.

"Jamie, are you there?" Karen continued.

"Yes," I responded, "but putting all the details of a trip like this together in one day sounds a bit hasty. I mean shouldn't we take time to consider options regarding where we stay and then decide if we need to rent a car? Also, what airline would offer us the best deal and schedule?"

I sat upright on the bed and couldn't believe the hesitation in my voice since less than an hour ago, I was reminiscing about the marsh mud of the Santee, Ashley, and Cooper tidal rivers. Karen's comments, however, had caught me off guard.

"Well, here's the thing," Karen persisted. "Ms. Blessing indicated that if we would agree to come on Friday, she would have Matthew's secretary make all the arrangements and email them to us. She wants to pay for everything and will leave the airline return ticket option open as she believes we might decide to stay awhile."

I didn't respond right away but finally found voice enough to ask what I feared to be the most obvious question, "Is she ill?"

"I don't know. She sounded strong enough on the phone, but something is definitely propelling her to act quickly. I told her I would talk with you tonight and then call her back as soon as we had decided. What do you think we should do?" Karen's voice registered the same uneasiness as mine, and I didn't think that either of us was prepared for this turn of events.

"How do you feel about letting her pay for everything? I mean, why do you think she would offer to do that?" I questioned.

After a while Karen simply said, "I think she is just ready for this story to end, and I believe she is hopeful that you are the one to write the last chapter."

We talked only a few more minutes tentatively agreeing to accept Ms. Blessing's generosity and make preparations to leave on Friday. After we hung up, I lay there staring up at the ceiling and trying to decide just how to explain this new twist to everyone involved but, most importantly, to Reid. He was an extremely patient man, but I figured that even he had his limits. Besides, I was going to have to interrupt the History Channel presentation, and that wouldn't be a good start.

Chapter 28

Once a Coach Always a Coach

"Players respond to coaches who really have
their best interests at heart."

—Mike Singletary

Reid a.k.a. "Coach Mo"

Since I had never played a competitive sport in my middle or high school years, I had really never had a "coach" in the truest sense of the word. Other than an eighth-grade Algebra teacher who offered extra points on our grade if we came to his basketball games, my first real experience with athletic coaches occurred when I started my own teaching career. In my first assignment I became part of a high school science department where many of the teachers were also responsible for coaching one or more sports.

I found most of them to be enigmas. During the first few months of school, I realized that they were passionate, almost frenzied, about their sport but not necessarily so about their academic responsibilities.

It wasn't until many years later, after Reid and I had met, that I began to understand why. He explained that it was actually an economic thing since most of the time if a coach didn't win on the field or the court he or she didn't keep a job no matter how fantastic the individual was as a classroom teacher.

But the student/coach thing was really much more complicated than that, as anyone who has ever known an awesome coach can tell you, and it was partly this attribute that had drawn me to Reid in the first place. It is the unwavering desire to help someone be the best he or she could be, and my husband was a master at that.

I walked into the den after my conversation with Karen with terribly conflicted emotions. Excitement, trepidation, an exhilarating sense of purpose, and even a twinge of selfishness were all there, but so too was fear: fear of losing what mattered most to me if I continued this seemingly ill-conceived endeavor.

Yes, we had talked about the events and coincidences in my life since I had retired and yes, he had been supportive, kind, and loving, but what if this turn of events constituted the proverbial line in the sand? What if I sensed that I needed to make a choice, even if he didn't specifically ask for me to do so? What was this trip to Charleston going to commit me to do, and how would that impact our relationship and future?

He must have sensed my unease because without a word, the prized remote was accessed, and there was silence in the room. After all the months of superficial conversations, I sat down across from the one who supported me the most and finally shared my profound embarrassment about the end days of my career.

I admitted that my life had been defined by my work, and that I had always been extremely proud of the workaholic persona and numerous positive accolades I'd received. However, during my last year of employment, my confidence was shaken, and I began to question if the significant number of episodes of prior, positive feedback had really been authentic.

My supervisor at the time appeared disingenuous, and I, intensely hurt, lost all will for positive confrontation, even at the risk of never knowing why I had lost favor. On the cusp of retirement, I took the plunge, turned in "my papers," and began to think there was nothing meaningful left for me to do.

Late into the night, as we talked about my pain and the subsequent surreal events of the past year, I came to understand and appreciate even more the man I had married. I realized then that he had always sensed my restlessness and sadness but had staunchly believed I would find my way back. Now I was beginning to believe it as well.

Later, turning out the lamp beside our bed, I couldn't help but smile when I realized that I finally had my own personal "coach."

Chapter 29

Meeting George and My Return to the Holy City

"Charleston has a landscape that encourages intimacy and partisanship. I have heard it said that an inoculation to the sights and smells of the Carolina low country is an almost irreversible antidote to the charms of other landscapes, other alien geographies. You can be moved profoundly by other vistas, by other oceans, by soaring mountain ranges, but you can never be seduced. You can forsake the low country, renounce it for other climates but you can never completely escape the sensuous, semitropical pull of Charleston and her marshes."

—Pat Conroy, *The Lords of Discipline*

Historic Downtown Charleston and St. Philip's Episcopal Church

We said our goodbyes to Reid and Steve early Friday morning, made our way through security to the assigned gate, and walked down the jet way to board a Delta flight for Atlanta. Ms. Blessing had requested first-class seats for us on the first leg of the trip, and while we were still a bit uncomfortable with the financial arrangements, Karen and I were determined to be gracious recipients of her gift.

Neither of us said much during that first flight, but I did notice Karen checking and rechecking her bag to make certain both the letters and the diary were still safely tucked inside. She had refused to store it in the overhead compartment and instead kept it cached snuggly beneath the seat in front of her.

Since it was easily accessible, I toyed with the idea of asking if I might begin reading either the letters or the diary but thought better of it as I glanced over at her trying to get settled in her seat. She seemed anxious and distracted, and I didn't want to cause any additional stress by putting her in a position of making a decision she might later regret. As I drifted off to sleep, I remember thinking it coincidental, though, that the bag with our treasures was resplendent with pink, blue, and crimson hearts.

Our plane from Atlanta to Charleston was much smaller and overhead bin space was limited. When we walked out to the tarmac to board, Karen was asked to place her carefully guarded bag on the luggage cart for storage in the cargo section of the plane. She hesitated, but I continued approaching the steps of the plane figuring that she didn't need my assistance.

A few minutes later, she joined me with the bag in tow. "Okay," I commented. "How did you manage that?"

She buckled her seat belt, smiled smugly, and said, "Items that may be of interest to the Charleston Historical Society apparently are afforded special dispensation."

A car and driver awaited us when we arrived in Charleston. Holding a sign that simply said "Ms. Karen and Ms. Jamie" the driver, a charming, elderly gentleman named George, couldn't have been more accommodating. Actually, seeing him in crisp, formal attire caused me to have a momentary flashback to the character Morgan Freeman portrayed in the movie *Driving Miss Daisy*.

We collected our luggage and walked out to the car. The humidity was as stifling as I remembered, and I glanced over to see Karen perspiring like crazy. I struggled with how to describe the oppressiveness of the low country to one who has never been there before. To me, it was a natural thing: something to expect and deal with. Oh yeah, I was back.

Beginning the short drive into the city, George chatted almost nonstop about our trip, the weather, the low country, and its people. "Never been to Texas," he shared, "but I've heard it's terrible hot and dry out there. Do you have a lot of dust? Can't handle dust. I need my salt marshes and water standing alongside the roadsides to feel comfortable . . . um, hum, yes, I do."

Obviously expecting no response, he nodded his head and continued, "Mr. Matthew, well, he don't say much about his time out there, and Ms. Charlotte don't take no pictures when she goes."

"Then you'll just need to come see for yourself, George," I interrupted.

"Oh no, Ms. Jamie, I never was much for airplanes and these old legs can't drive that far anymore. Besides, I'm happy right here in my city, yes, ma'am, I am, and if I was a bettin' man I'd say there probably ain't no place to sample a good low country boil in Texas and there probably ain't no benne wafers neither. Nope, couldn't stay there, even for a while, no, ma'am."

We rode quietly for a few miles when I thought I could just make out the steeples of the three sister churches I'd come to know so well: St. Matthews, St. Michaels, and St. Philips. Lost in a momentary reverie, I caught only the last words of Karen's query of George, "And where are we staying?"

"Well, Ms. Karen, you see, I was hopin' you wouldn't ask me that question before we got to the city."

Somewhat uncomfortably, he continued, "She, uh, gave me strict orders to bring you straight to the main house. Now, I take it you know Ms. Charlotte well enough to know one don't typically argue with her so I said, 'Yes, ma'am, right away!' Truth be known, you better get ready 'cause she's had rooms gussied up for you. No guest of the Blessing family has ever stayed in a hotel. No way, no, ma'am!"

We were stunned by George's revelation, but with no apparent options sat mute. I did manage to ask the address of the house, however. "It's on Legare Street, Ms. Jamie. You ever hear of it?"

My mind struggled to recall the history and geography of the city. Running parallel to Meeting and East Bay Legare stretches from Broad Street to the Battery. It is in the prestigious "South of Broad" district, and if my memory from all the walking tours I took served me well it was called Johnson's Street, for Sir Nathaniel Johnson, Governor of the Province in the early 1700s.

Later, it was named for Solomon Legare, a prosperous Huguenot silversmith who owned considerable real estate at the Legare and Tradd streets intersection. I toyed with explaining the significance of the address to Karen before we arrived, but there wasn't time.

Getting out of the car, I realized that the house was one of the finest examples of the Charleston single house that I had ever seen.

It was a three-story red brick structure rising above a high basement. The narrow street side door was exceptionally tall and painted in what I imagined was "Charleston Green."

Local legend is that "Charleston Green," a green so deep it looks black, came about after the Civil War when Union troops sent buckets of black paint to help rebuild the city. The residents of the Holy City could not bear the thought of their houses being painted government-issued black so they tinted the paint with yellow and green, creating a greenish black hue. The color still exists today.

Visitors to the house walk up four curved steps from the sidewalk to the street door's landing. The door is framed by a creamy white wooden encasement with a delicate transom. There is an entrance into the side garden as well. Matching brick pillars, each adorned with a large stone rendition of a pineapple, guarded the path, which is accessed through an ornate, black wrought iron gate.

When we arrived, the garden was resplendent in summer brilliance with crimson camellias, white gardenias, and purple crepe myrtles. We walked through the gate along a winding cobblestoned path to an inviting first floor piazza reminiscent of a time gone by.

There were two sitting areas on the main level piazza. To the left of the door to the interior of the house were two Charleston rockers separated by a naturally colored wicker table supporting a huge Boston fern. To the right sat a white wicker settee with plush, flowered pillows and cushions. A matching rocker, chair, and coffee table surrounding a braided oval, hemp rug completed the ensemble. It looked like an inviting place to read or simply sit quietly with a cool drink, maybe a mint julep or tonic and gin. The lush, full foxtail ferns sitting atop pillars on either side of the settee enhanced its allure.

Ms. Blessing, wearing a soft, white, gauzy dress and delicate sandals, met us at the door to the house and hugged Karen tightly. She turned to me after a moment and warmly clasped my hands in hers.

I studied her features as best I could. Though both Steve and Karen had described her to me, and I expected the epitome of an older, southern lady I was still surprised by her delicate countenance. Despite that she looked strong and determined with no evidence of the advanced illness I had earlier feared.

133

I had worried about how she would respond to me. Yet even as her eyes, steel blue and fierce, stared intently into mine, her first words were soft and warm, "Welcome back to Charleston, Ms. Jamie. I hope your trip was not too stressful. I've heard so much about you that I can't wait to talk quietly about your time here so many years past. I believe there is much we have to say to one another as it seems we have a southern bond that cannot be explained to those who do not know Charleston in their hearts."

I chose my words carefully, "Ms. Blessing, thank you for inviting me. Even though I wasn't born here, I have always felt drawn to this city, and, in my heart, it now seems like I have finally come home with a purpose. Thank you for the opportunity."

She studied my face as if searching for verification of the sincerity of my words, but suddenly, she abruptly changed her focus and commented, "My, my, where are my manners? Please come inside, ladies, less this heat and humidity render you incapable of rational thought."

She opened the screened door to the house and ushered us inside. "Now I know you didn't expect to stay in our home, but neither Matthew nor I will hear of anything else. No guest of our family has ever stayed in a public establishment and never will as long as I am alive."

With that statement and George's profuse nodding, as he carried our luggage up the steps of the piazza and into the house, we knew it was decided. My eyes adjusted to the dimmed lighting of the interior. The mahogany windowsills and doors, floating cypress paneling, and exquisite, interior shutters all caught my attention simultaneously. I glanced over at Karen to see if she had picked up on these features as well.

I struggled to recall what I had learned about the history of these houses and intuitively knew that the integrity of the original features and plan of this house had been retained in every way possible. Even the gleaming, wooden floors oozed historical significance and serenity. I caught myself thinking that given the opportunity I would, without hesitation, stay here forever.

Ms. Blessing called for a housemaid to show us to our rooms on the third floor. While we were waiting for Nancie to come from the kitchen Charlotte indicated that Matthew would be home for drinks at 5:30 p.m. sharp with dinner served at six o'clock. She gently reminded us that dinner in this household continued to be a formal affair. Gloves, however, were no longer required. We were to meet for drinks in the drawing room on this floor and proceed to dinner in the dining room immediately across the entrance foyer from there.

With no elevator in the house, we climbed the two flights of stairs to our rooms with Ms. Nancie. I was glad I had packed only one piece of luggage since neither Karen nor I would permit George to carry our bags any further.

After we had been shown the location of the linens, how to operate the faucets in each bathroom and the controls for the air conditioning system, Karen and I thanked our delightful hostess and began to explore the third floor of the house on our own. Its beauty and simplicity were beguiling.

Just as the entryway on the first floor each of our rooms had the same polished wooden floors and exquisite area rugs. My room was painted a soft eggshell blue with white three-inch baseboard crown molding and a matching fireplace mantle. Both were probably a combination of wood and plaster.

While a small bedside table and delicate lamp had been placed beside the bed to provide a reading light, I also noticed a gorgeous, yet unpretentious, chandelier encased in an ornate plaster medallion towering above. The bed itself was a stunning high poster affair with a matching lace coverlet and canopy. I was relieved to note the wooden steps at its side since the mattress was quite high off the floor. Karen's room was almost the mirror image of mine but painted a canary yellow.

We sat in the small sitting area in my room to share our first impressions and decide how we would proceed. "Did you bring gloves or a dress of any kind?" Karen inquired.

"No, I laughed, I don't even own a pair of evening gloves and haven't since I was in high school and bought a pair for prom! I did bring one skirt though, as an afterthought, but that's it. Guess I'll wear it tonight."

Changing the focus of our discussion, I continued, "Actually, I'm more curious about Matthew right now than Charleston social protocol. What do you think about researching him before dinner? I'll bet there are several local references on the internet, and my iPad has its own Wi-Fi connection."

As she thought about it, Karen mused, "Well, he is an unknown in this equation, so I think it might enable us to have a more informed perspective when we sit down for drinks. We'll probably get the gist of the situation regarding the house tonight, don't you think?"

Chapter 30

Matthew

"You gain strength, and courage, and confidence by each experience in which you really stop to look fear in the face . . . we must do that which we think we cannot."

—Eleanor Roosevelt

Matthew surrounded by our kids

After texting Reid to let him know we had arrived safely, I called Ms. G to check on the kids. I also wanted to review what we had learned about Matthew from our earlier research. I realized it wasn't much even before I called, and she confirmed what I had remembered. The only reliable details we had were that he was born in Eden Hill in 1951 and that his mother had passed away in 1953. We also knew that sometime during his childhood Matthew had come to live with the Blessing family in Charleston.

"How is everyone doing?" I asked.

I could hear her chuckling on the other end of the line. "Ms. Jamie you only been gone one day! We're all good, but the kids did ask about where you were when they came around for lunch today. I told them you'd gone to meet Ms. Blessing and figure out what to do about the house. They had a thousand more questions, but I suggested that we just wait and see what happens."

"By the way, the complex may get assigned yet another manager. Ms. Clark, she was gone today, and her office is cleaned out."

I could hardly contain the curiosity in my voice, "Really? Do we know why?"

Ms. G continued, "No, but Tracy and I took advantage of the situation, and we set up play time and games for the little ones. With the complex pool still closed there's not much for them to do with their time."

"What about Raven, Jalissa, Jessamy, and the other older kids? Were they there? What are they doing with their days?" I questioned.

I could sense the hesitation in Ms. G's words as she quietly continued, "No, Ms. Jamie, I haven't seen them in a while. I suspect, though, that unless one or more of they mamas has them babysitting they not doing much but flirtin' with trouble. We need a place for them, Ms. Jamie, we really do, and Tracy and I are prayin' for you to make it happen."

I asked Ms. G to tell the kids how much I missed them and let them know that I would be home soon. We said our goodbyes, and I promised to check in every day. After I hung up I relayed the whole story to Karen.

"Well," she said, "I guess we need to get busy."

While the internet is often a less than reliable source for desired information, Karen and I took a chance and plugged in Matthew's full name. I don't know why Ms. G and I hadn't done this earlier, but I guess we felt there might be more pertinent information in the local records.

The Charleston Post and Courier ended up being our best source when researching local records for Matthew. Matthew Abraham Eden had apparently been a busy guy if the information we found was to be believed.

Specific references for a Matthew Abraham Eden of Charleston, SC, began with several articles describing his lucrative medical practice in obstetrics and gynecology in Charleston in the mid-eighties. Apparently, Matthew was a respected physician and citizen of the city. Other citations, however, highlighted a different facet of his life. Matthew was also widely known for his philanthropic endeavors.

It was almost time to dress for dinner when Karen and I came upon our first picture, and it was a surprising one. In an article highlighting his unceasing generosity and emotional support for programs that addressed the needs of disenfranchised children, Matthew appeared in a posed shot with the mayor and representatives of the local city council and school board.

Everyone, except Matthew, was standing either adjacent to or behind an enlarged poster of a check made out to a home for abused children in downtown Charleston. Matthew was seated in front of the poster and to the left. The surprise was neither the amount of the donation he had made, nor that he was the only person seated. The surprise was that he was in a wheelchair.

I knew we should be dressing for dinner, but with this new revelation I wasn't ready to interrupt our research just yet. "Did Ms. Blessing ever say much about Matthew's childhood? I mean, did she say anything about an injury or illness? Do you know where he went to school, was he an athlete?"

Karen continued to study the picture then shook her head, "No, nothing, and now that I think about it, her only mention of Matthew was that after his mother passed away his father felt he would have a better life with the Blessing family and sent him to Charleston to live."

"Quite honestly, although Steve and I thought that tragic, we both could see how a single father in those days might feel a child could be better raised in a household with a woman's touch. We never questioned Charlotte further because she is an intensely private person, and we didn't want to pry any deeper into her affairs."

I switched off my iPad. "Well, at least we won't be shocked to see Matthew in a wheel chair this evening, that is, if he still uses one. I'm glad we know a little more about him now, perhaps, that will help break the ice."

I glanced at the clock on the night stand, "Oh my, look at the time do you plan to take a shower?"

"Definitely," Karen replied as she stretched and then lifted her long, blonde hair off her neck. "I didn't realize how humid it would be here."

"Well, while the shower will feel great, unfortunately, it's not going to help much with that sticky feeling you're experiencing. You'll feel as damp fifteen minutes after drying off as you did fifteen minutes before enjoying the steamy, warm water."

As she walked out of my room, her voice trailed off down the hall, "Great, thanks for the encouraging words. Let's just hope my outfit will be appropriate for dinner. If we stay very long, I'll definitely need to do some shopping!"

At five twenty, following one last look in the mirror in the hall, we made our way down the two flights of stairs to the drawing room. As we descended to the first landing, we simultaneously held up crossed fingers like a couple of kids.

Chapter 31

A Sense of Urgency

"I have been impressed with the urgency of doing. Knowing is not enough; we must apply. Being willing is not enough; we must do."

—Leonardo da Vinci

Ms. Blessing was waiting for us at the bottom of the staircase and smiled as we descended the last few steps. Apparently our outfits met her approval, "I trust you had a restful afternoon and found everything you needed in your rooms?" she queried.

We glanced quickly at one another, and Karen replied, "Oh yes, thank you. Everything was wonderful. Our rooms are exquisite and very accommodating."

"Excellent. Now come and meet Matthew. He has just arrived."

We followed Charlotte through wide, polished double doors into a large and comfortably apportioned living area. Matthew was seated in an elegant overstuffed chair to our right engaged in conversation on his cell phone. He acknowledged our presence and raised a finger as if to say, "one minute, please."

I was barely able to grasp the warmth and comfort of the room before Charlotte motioned for us to turn around. Wanting to avoid an awkward moment and also permit Matthew some privacy, Charlotte ushered us back into the entrance foyer and began to tell us a little about the house. "What do either of you know about the Charleston single house?" she began.

"Just that each floor is rectangular, typically two rooms wide with the narrower side facing the street," I commented. "There are many explanations for the design, but I think the main reason was to attract prevailing breezes through the piazza windows."

"You remember your history very well, Ms. Jamie," Charlotte smiled.

"The Charleston Single House is found exclusively on our peninsula and was built throughout the 1700 and 1800s. It has been suggested that at its peak, it dominated the city with around four thousand single houses in existence. Today that figure is estimated to be much less than that maybe somewhere in the neighborhood of 2,500."

I glanced over at Karen. Realizing that many people are not into history or architecture, I was afraid she would not find this conversational detour of any interest. I wanted her to understand why I felt knowing about the culture and history of this city was important in our quest to benefit the children of Eden Hill but wasn't sure how to go about doing so.

As Charlotte continued talking, however, I realized that I shouldn't have worried. No one understood the significance of Charleston history and culture on Sweet Grass Memories better than she.

"We are not certain of the precise details of the story of this house, however, we believe it was built around 1795. Our great grandfather, an architect, was fascinated by historic structures and purchased it around 1875. At that time, it was in a terrible condition, as was much of the city after the Civil War. Most of its interior had been destroyed or damaged, and the exterior had suffered the loss of the piazzas. He and our grandfather spent a great deal of time researching the history of the unique features of the single house and then began a slow restoration process that took many years." Her words continued as if she was delivering a fervent sermon defending her beloved city.

"The War of Northern Aggression, as many Charleston families of the time called the American Civil War, was devastating. In fact, when General Sherman toured the city in 1865, he is credited with proclaiming that 'Anyone who is not satisfied with war should go to Charleston, and he will pray louder and deeper than ever that, the country, in its long future be spared any more war.'"

"Charleston suffered great destruction prior to Sherman's visit so in reality no one needed to worry about the city when he finally did arrive here. The Yankees, however, hated our city, and considered it the place that started the secession and later the war. In 1864, Charleston had more than twelve thousand rounds fired upon it over 209 days. Sherman knew to destroy it would be pointless. He is said to have mused that if he destroyed railroad lines and took Columbia 'Charleston would fall on itself.'

"As a result, General Sherman did not destroy Charleston but instead marched from Savannah to Columbia and burned that city in 1865. There are numerous stories as to why. Some say he had a girlfriend in Charleston. Others say he had a soft spot for the city since he had spent several years here stationed at Fort Moultrie. Sadly, Charleston, anticipating a great battle, had sent many of its historic treasures to Columbia for safety.

"To this day, however, Charleston considers Sherman the personification of the war."

As we stood there in that foyer listening to her impassioned description of her family's association with this city, I sensed the depth of Charlotte's love for both Charleston and her family. I also sensed something else. She knew that Matthew's father had felt the same way about Texas and had deeply loved her sister, Jillian, as well. It was apparent that she believed family dreams and homes were inherently linked and therein lay the problem for Jillian and Thomas.

Before we could say anything more, Matthew called to us from the drawing room. We walked back through those richly, lacquered doors to find him standing alongside the chair with the help of a cane.

"Welcome to our home, ladies. I trust my aunt has already made you feel comfortable," he smiled.

Both Karen and I responded simultaneously, "Oh yes, thank you."

He walked slowly to the enclosed bar on the other side of the room and asked, "May I get you a drink—a glass of wine, a tonic and gin, mint julep, bourbon, scotch? You will find we have most anything you might like."

Both of us selected a glass of wine, and when we were all comfortably settled with our drinks, Matthew began. "Ladies, you will find I am a man of few words and don't usually succumb to emotionally laden or impulsive decisions. That being said, my aunt has done her best over the years to remind me that relationships are the key to life's most treasured memories and, thus, should be considered as an integral part of every decision. I try to listen to her words, since I learned long ago that they are usually laced with profound wisdom."

Charlotte seemed to blush with the compliment as Matthew continued. "Ms. Romero, while I know more about you than I do about Ms. Malone, I have learned that both of you are connected in some way to the house in Eden Hill. I hope over the next few days to hear the story Charlotte has brought you here to share because, quite frankly, it is only because she has urged me to do so that I have agreed to postpone accepting an offer from a development company to purchase the house and land on Blessing Path until after your visit. Thus, the fate of the place rests in your hands."

With those remarks, Matthew took a sip of his tonic and gin and watched us closely for a response. Neither Karen nor I was prepared for the bluntness or immediacy of his words, and apparently, neither was Charlotte.

Nevertheless, she sat with downcast eyes for only a moment. Sighing heavily, her voice firm but quiet, she lifted her head and began, "Yes, ladies, one of the reasons you are here is to help our family finally determine the fate of Sweet Grass Memories." Her voice gained strength as she continued.

"However, as I have always known in my heart, a house is not simply a possession, it is an extension of a family and the wellspring of human development and interaction. It is where we learn right from wrong, develop our values, and find a sense of purpose."

It was as if the impassioned story she had begun in the foyer was being continued, but this time I felt the message was more for Matthew's benefit than either Karen or me.

"Consider this house on Legare and its history. What if my great-grandfather had not seen its potential for happiness and, yes, even influence? Without his passion, we certainly wouldn't be having this conversation now."

"Sweet Grass Memories represents the soul of what is left of Jillian and Thomas's story. I cannot and will not agree to its destruction without first seriously considering whether or not the series of events since their deaths have been more than mere coincidence. In addition, I feel I must ask all of us to carefully consider whether or not the house still has a destiny to fulfill."

I wasn't sure I was capable of grasping the significance of her words just yet, and certainly wasn't ready to review them in terms of the last few months of my life. I couldn't look at Karen, and instead, took a sip of wine.

Matthew stood, reached for his cane, and walked to one of the piazza windows. After a few moments of staring into the garden, he remarked, "I apologize profusely, ladies. In my haste to bring closure to the situation with the property, I have obviously forgotten every rule of etiquette and, more importantly, kindness that I have ever been taught. I imagine my impudence is the result of my professional propensity to achieve immediate solutions for my patients."

Continuing to gaze out the enlarged, rectangular windows of the gorgeous, historic room he persisted. "Sometimes the only real fool is an old fool. Our story, as tragic and beautiful as it truly is, in my opinion, is just that, our story. However, Charlotte reminds me that I have failed to consider that it may also have a broader, more valuable interpretation."

"While the house in Texas holds nothing but painful memories for me, even I find the coincidences Charlotte references more than a little disquieting. Once we have had the opportunity to talk candidly, I hope you will be able to understand the pain of my heart and forgive me my indiscretions."

I think that both Karen and I sensed the sincerity of Matthew's words, but before we could comment, it was Charlotte who interjected much needed levity into the conversation. "Well, Matthew, you certainly haven't lost the knack for getting down to brass tacks and sometimes that causes me to question your bedside manner. I always did feel you missed your calling by not choosing law school after graduating from the University of South Carolina."

She rose from her seat. "Now, let's put serious conversation aside for the remainder of the evening and enjoy the lovely dinner I had envisioned by getting to know more about one another over the southern specialties Mamie has prepared."

We transitioned into the dining room where the mood was decidedly different. The room was the quintessence of subdued elegance and the meal a welcomed diversion.

Matthew, as it turns out, was an excellent host and skilled conversationalist guiding us through a myriad of topics to include classic and contemporary literature, gourmet cooking, Charleston history and culture, and stories of the local theatre productions.

Around 8:00 p.m., as we were served a dessert of lemon buttermilk pie, the earlier tension that had erupted in the drawing room finally evaporated into the delightful aroma of toasted Southern pecan coffee.

Chapter 32

The Cicadas
and a Message from George

"Letters are among the most significant
memorial a person can leave behind them."

—Johann Wolfgang von Goethe

Before climbing the stairs at evening's end, I asked Charlotte if I might sit for a moment on the first floor piazza. I desperately needed some time alone to think about the direction I felt being pulled to go and reflect upon the prior conversation with Ms. G.

Matthew's startling pronouncement didn't help either. It was like pouring gasoline on an already smoldering fire. Before calling Reid to share the events of the day I had to better know my own heart. Karen was fine going up alone and said good night from the landing.

I opened then slowly guided the screen door back into the door-frame to prevent startling anyone and made my way to the larger sitting area. Sinking deeply into the cushions of the settee I began listening to the song of the cicadas. Some cultures regard these insects as powerful symbols of rebirth. I wondered about the symbolism of hearing their song tonight.

I didn't expect to see anyone and was startled to hear the garden gate creak open followed by the sound of footsteps on the cobble-stone path. "Hello? Who's there?" I inquired nervously.

"Ms. Jamie, zat you? I'm so sorry, ma'am, I didn't expect nobody outside and was just makin' certain things are all locked up tight. I'll come back later."

I recognized the voice as George's and was relieved. "No, it's okay, George, really. I just thought I'd sit out here a moment before going to bed. I'm not sure I could get to sleep right away anyway. I still can't believe I'm here."

I could just make out his silhouette in the moonlight. "How long since you been back, Ms. Jamie?"

Looking up at the sky, I mused, "I don't know, maybe forty-five years? Guess it's changed a lot, huh?"

"Depends upon what you mean by change, Ms. Jamie, yep, sure does."

He walked up the first couple of steps of the piazza toward me. "Some things never change and shouldn't."

He paused a moment and then added, "You read those letters right soon now, ya hear? You've come home for a reason, and I think Ms. Jillian will 'splain it to you real clear, yep, sure do."

He turned and walked back toward the side entrance to the garden without hurrying.

"George?" my voice trailed after him. "Do you live here . . . in the house?"

"Have a good night, Ms. Jamie, I'll see you after breakfast."

And with that, I heard the street side gate open and close once more. I felt a momentary chill and pulled my sweater closer around my shoulders.

The letters, what was so special about them and what did they have to do with me? Had Karen read them, and what did George know about the Eden-Blessing story, the house, the letters, or me? Why would he mention them?

I was now certain Ms. Blessing had a plan that definitely included me, but what it was, and how many people knew about it continued to remain elusive.

Chapter 33

A New Insight into the Word "Transient"

"I always tell my kids if you lay down, people will step over you. But if you keep scrambling, if you keep going, someone will always, always give you a hand. Always. But you gotta keep dancing, you got keep your feet moving."

—Morgan Freeman

Abeo and Adia

I needed to talk with someone, but I've always had this hang-up about disappointing Reid, and I didn't want him to hear the doubt and apprehension I knew would be apparent in my choice of words and my voice. More importantly, I felt that I needed to speak with someone who had faced the same emotions I was feeling. I needed Ms. G's insightfulness.

The phone rang several times, and I decided that she had already gone to bed. Just as I was about to hang up, I heard "Hello, Ms. Jamie, I recognized your number. What's goin' on?"

Relieved to know she had picked up the call I uttered, "Oh, Ms. G, it is so good to hear your voice! I was afraid that you had already gone to bed. Thank you so much for answering."

She responded in the patient, easy manner that I recognized as so representative of whom she was and what she had seen. "Everythin' okay there? You sound a bit discombobulated."

"Well, things started off a bit uncomfortably this evening when we met Matthew," I began and then proceeded to tell her everything about the past few hours. I tried not to skip any details.

She listened attentively, I thought, even though I couldn't see her expressions through the phone, and I sensed that she was concerned. When I was finished, I waited for her say the words that I hoped would bring me peace.

I could hear the ticking of the mantle clock as I sat on the edge of the bed, wondering if she was still on the line. Was it that I was extremely impatient or was everyone bent on taking his or her own, sweet time to have a conversation with me lately? "Ms. G? Are you still there?"

"Yes, Ms. Jamie, I am," she answered softly. "But before I share my thoughts 'bout your evenin's events, I have some news I wanted you to hear before you got back home. Actually even though I hesitated to answer the phone, I'm glad you called tonight as me and Tracy been wonderin' how to tell you."

Now I was alarmed. Standing up, I paced around the room talking much too fast and a bit too loudly. "What is it? Is someone sick? Did something happen to the house? Are all the kids okay?"

"Everyone is fine, Ms. Jamie, just fine, but something has happened that will make you sad."

I could hear her take a deep breath before she continued. "This kind of thing is commonplace among our families, but you ain't never experienced it that I know of, and I don't know quite how to help you get past it just yet. Tracy and me been wonderin' for a while now how long it was gonna be before it happened with one of your kids."

It was now my turn to be quiet, and as my mind imagined all sorts of terrible scenarios, it was almost as if Ms. G could sense my musings.

"Ms. Jamie, nobody in a bad way, it's not like that, but one of your first families is movin' away in two weeks. Movin' to another city altogether. Don't know that you've ever thought about it, but it's how we have come to be referred to as a 'transient population' by schools and businesses."

"Nobody who comes to Oak Lakes or moves into most any other section 8 property, for that matter, ever stays too long. The grass is always greener somewhere else or the 'move-in specials' down the road too good to pass up, or we lost this job and can't stay around here or we go live with somebody who has a car or access to more government assistance . . . on and on. The reasons are endless."

I sank into the overstuffed chair near the fireplace, "Who is leaving, Ms. G?"

It took a while for her to answer perhaps because she had sensed the truly special bond I had developed with the kids she was going to tell me about. "It's Abeo, Adia, and Ahadi, Ms. Jamie. I know your heart will be achin', and I am truly sorry."

My eyes welled with tears, maybe because I was already emotionally overwhelmed.

"Ms. G, thank you, maybe we can talk more tomorrow, I'm just really spent now. What happens, though, if we get the house and then lose the kids? I truly never considered that. Oh my God, how much of a factor is this?"

"Well, possibly a huge one, Ms. Jamie, but before you sink any deeper into your hole of doubt and despair, just remember this, for every child that leaves, a new one comes, and the more lives we can touch the more good we can do. Do you hear me now?"

Smiling, crying, and blowing my nose all at once I said, "Oh yes, ma'am, yes, I do."

After a moment, I quickly added, "Ms. G, I love both you and Tracy like the sisters I never had. Does that make any sense? I haven't offended you, have I?"

"Ms. Jamie, go to bed now, you getting way too sentimental, ya hear?"

Grinning, I said, "Yes, I'm prone to do that. Thank you for telling me about the kids, by the way."

"You welcome, sister, hurry home. We got big work to do," came the reply.

I lay down across my soft, lacy coverlet and cried openly. I cried without caring about who might hear me . . . Abeo, Adia, and Ahadi. My dreams were most vivid of each of them as they had been permanent fixtures from the beginning of my days on the porch, and I had always imagined seeing them into high school and perhaps, adulthood.

Adia had an arresting smile and infectious laughter with the most pronounced dimples of any child I had ever seen. And Ahadi, sweet, silent Ahadi, sincerely struggled to be all that we wanted him to be, all that he instinctively sensed he could be with someone's patient hand guiding him.

But it was Abeo, an introspective, caring young woman who constantly hungered for knowledge, acknowledgment, and guidance, who captured my heart at an unimaginable depth from the very first time I met her. While she rarely spoke in those early days she never missed an opportunity to sit quietly by my side and drink in everything I, or any one in our group, had to share. It was as if the phrase "fill my cup" had been coined especially for her.

It was a slow process for one so shy but her hugs gradually progressed from limp and soft to firm and joyous across the span of our first few months. Yet, the moment that sealed our connection was the day she slipped me a note she had obviously taken much time to write. She exited the room as I was opening it:

Ms. Jamie and Mr. Reid,

Everything changed because of you! Thank you for everything. You have opened me to the perfect road. You have changed my life.

Love you, Abeo

The anguish I was feeling now, as I considered the possibility of losing touch with her forever, both discouraged and surprised me. I lay there listening to the silence a very long time.

Chapter 34

Matthew, Me, and BFF

"If you would convince others, you must be open to conviction yourself."

—Lord Chesterfield

I waited until morning light to call Reid and wandered quietly among the solitude of the piazza garden as we talked. I felt his support and love through the phone as I relayed the details of the previous day's events. His silence when I relayed the news about Abeo, Adia, and Ahadi told me that he felt the pain of loss as much I did.

He didn't seem that surprised about a potential buyer for the property or Matthew's bluntness, but he was as intrigued as I about the references to Jillian's letters, and I promised to share their content as soon as I was able to read them.

As we ended our conversation, I asked if he might stop by Oak Lakes and take pizza to the kids that evening. I gave him Ms. G's number and suggested that if he bought the pizza and took it to the complex, she would make it happen.

I could almost see his crooked grin as he responded, "Yes, ma'am, let me get right on that." Then he hesitated and said, "We all miss you, you know, not just the kids, but me and even the Scotties. Hurry home soon."

After we hung up I plopped down again on the comfortable piazza settee. Twisting my wedding ring on my left hand I wondered why was I running around the country following the trail of a mystery with so many blessings right in my own back yard? Deep in thought I barely heard the screen door open.

Charlotte emerged carrying a tray with a colorful, ceramic pot trailing steam from its spout, an assortment of teas and sweeteners, slices of lemon and lime and three cups. She carefully placed it on the table in front of the settee.

"I thought I might find you out here." she began. "Karen came down earlier and secured a pot of coffee and a cup. She has gone back up for a shower. Did you sleep well?"

"Actually, yes and no," I commented. "But please know it had nothing to do with our wonderful accommodations. It's just that Matthew's words yesterday evening, my memories of this city, and my continuing reoccurring thoughts of our kids in Eden Hill kept interrupting my ability to fall into a deep sleep. I apologize."

"And why would you apologize, child? I do declare if I am reading the situation correctly you are at a precipice of a life-changing event so uneasiness should be expected."

She poured two cups of the steaming water, offered me a selection of teas and continued. "I have asked George to give Karen a tour of the city this morning, and while I know you would revel in accompanying her, Matthew has agreed to sit with us and talk about the group of children you affectionately refer to as 'the porch crew'; your relationship, however strange, with Sweet Grass Memories; and your dreams for the property."

"By the way, I have asked Mamie to just leave the breakfast entrees on the sideboard in the dining room. We will need to help ourselves this morning."

Startled I ignored the breakfast information and replied, "Ms. Blessing, with all due respect, I haven't really formulated any plans for the property. My husband and I have never discussed its acquisition and, quite honestly, financially we are not in a position to continue such a conversation."

Never looking up from her tea and never acknowledging my comments she continued, "Spend some time this morning telling us stories about the children you have come to know at Oak Lakes, and share with Matthew the pull of the house for you. The rest will come."

With that, she looked deeply into my eyes and inquired, "Do I understand correctly that you are able to hear its thoughts?"

I sat pensively for only a moment, looked down at my lap, and then replied softly. "Yes, I think I can."

"And what does it say?" she pressed.

Until this point in time, I hadn't permitted myself to seriously consider what I sensed I was hearing, but at Ms. Blessing's urging I shared. "Well, I hear many things but the predominate phrase of late is something like: I can help you help the children. Give me a chance."

"Have you let yourself think about what that means?" she inquired.

"No, and quite honestly, I'm still struggling with the fact that many people think I'm demented for suggesting that a house actually communicates with me. I have always made decisions based primarily on facts not feelings. This whole situation has turned my way of thinking, specifically, and my life, in general, upside down, and I have no clue what I should do at this point."

Sipping her tea, she gazed into the garden and whispered, "Many don't have our gift, child. Be patient with them and good will come. Once you read the letters, your path will be clear."

There it was yet again another reference to the letters.

Karen emerged from the house just as our conversation drifted into a lull. She walked onto the piazza in a colorful outfit of jeans and a stylish, pink T-shirt. She carried a light sweater over her arm and was wearing fashionable but comfortable sandals. She smiled as she looked over at us and inquired of me, "Are you going with George and me to see the city?"

"No." I smiled. "I think I will stay here and talk with Matthew and Charlotte awhile. George will probably be a better guide than me any way since I have been away a very long time. Just make certain he shows you my old alma mater, the College of Charleston, and its historic cistern."

"Absolutely!" she grinned.

I hadn't heard the creaking of the street gate as it opened and closed, but at that moment, George walked along the cobblestone path to the piazza steps.

"Yes, ma'am, I'll be the best guide you could ask for! I thought I'd also show her the sites along East Bay and the marketplace first. My days runnin' around there 'bout made me an expert! She may even want to purchase a sweet grass basket and sample some benne wafers."

"Y'all want us back here for lunch or may I take Ms. Karen to Magnolia's, the Peninsula Grill, or High Cotton?"

Ms. Blessing smiled at his impudence and said, "Now, George, just how do you plan to pay for such an extravagance? By the way, I don't think High Cotton or the Peninsula grill is open for lunch. Magnolia's is a good choice but often crowded because of its location. Other options might be Husk or Slightly North of Broad."

"Okay, we'll be fine. By the way, I have my means, Ms. Charlotte, yes, I do. Should you like to join us, just give me a call on that little phone thing you gave me. We'd love to have you accompany us for a bite."

"Well, perhaps, George, perhaps, but if you do not hear from us continue on. We will reconnect a bit later today. Take an umbrella now. Ms. Karen probably isn't accustomed to our late afternoon clouds."

"Yes, ma'am, always keep one in the boot, yes, I do."

And with that, both he and Karen walked down the path and through the garden door to the awaiting car. I could hear that his "guided tour" had already started. I smiled and had a fleeting thought that George might just be considered more "family" than employee at this point.

Shortly after Karen and George had gone Matthew emerged from the house. I took a moment to observe him more closely in morning's light. We were born at about the same time so I envisioned his age to be about sixty give or take a year. He was definitely middle-aged with thinning hair and a slight paunch. He wore attractive gold, wire-rimmed glasses and had kind eyes.

Since it was a Saturday, I was surprised to see that he appeared to be dressed for an appointment in the city or for work. But then I remembered that he was a physician and might have hospital rounds to make this morning. Still walking with his cane, he approached me warmly and without the sense of urgency evident yesterday evening.

"Did you sleep well, Ms. Malone?"

"As well as could be expected, Mr. Eden," I replied.

He laughed. "We're being awfully formal, aren't we? Why don't you call me Matthew, and I will call you Jamie. Would that be okay?"

I relaxed and said, "Of course."

Charlotte made herself comfortable in the rocker, Matthew settled in the matching chair, and I maintained my spot on the comfortable settee. Matthew poured himself a cup of tea, added sugar, real sugar, and a lemon.

Not really knowing where to begin I was relieved when he started our conversation with a funny story about his first year at Porter Gaud. The fact that he had been born in Texas had been tough for some of his classmates to grasp. After his first week there, fresh from a visit to his dad's ranch, he was ready to go back to Texas and thought Charleston a snobby place.

I laughed and subsequently shared a story about Gracie, my college roommate, who had attended Ashley Hall. After several weeks of living together I affectionately referred to her as "blamelessly snobby" since her only frame of reference seemed to be Charleston and the low country.

We both leaned forward into the center space of the sitting area and continued sharing stories about our younger years and potential plans for growing older. Even though he had had a privileged past, attended Porter Gaud and the University of South Carolina, and I had had a struggling past attending a small public school high school and the College of Charleston on a government loan, we came to realize that we had much in common.

The fate of the Eden Hill kids and house became secondary for a while as we navigated the uncharted territory that stretches between two individuals who have limited time to get to know one another but a distinct purpose for doing so.

Matthew had contracted polio in 1952 when he was about a year old, and he recounted that while his case had been mild and he had recovered, his mother, a devoted nurse, had not fared well. Apparently, already frail, she had been weakened by her constant devotion to the families, especially the children, in Eden Hill and the surrounding communities during the epidemic. She eventually came down with pneumonia and succumbed to its ravages in 1953.

Even though Matthew suffers from a condition known as PPS, post-polio syndrome, today he considers himself fortunate. While I had no recollection of the seriousness and pain of the illness, I could vaguely remember lining up for the sugar cube vaccine some years later.

We continued to talk and were surprised to note that both of us were only children. But that was where our stories diverged. I grew up in a home with both parents but didn't know whom I was supposed to be or what I was supposed to do with my life.

He grew up with neither parent in his daily life and felt abandoned, yet somehow knew early on that he wanted to work in the field of medicine and with children. He had been born in Texas but ended up in South Carolina.

While not born in South Carolina, my life had been shaped indelibly by my years there, but I had ended up in Texas. Now, both in our sixties our paths had crossed, and as we sat here in the midst of a city, we both loved I think we finally realized that like it or not there was probably a reason this was so.

We continued sitting and talking on the piazza for the greater part of the morning. Around ten thirty after we had transitioned to iced tea, Matthew said, "So tell me about the kids you met on the porch of Sweet Grass Memories."

I noticed that it was the first time he had referred to the house by its given name and was encouraged. I then repeated the phrase I had uttered to Tracy so long ago, "How much time do you have?"

He smiled and said, "Well, since Charlotte, my task master, is sitting right here, I guess I have as long as you need."

Charlotte chuckled, shook her head, but did not disagree with his description of her.

And with that invitation, I described each eventful coincidence that had brought me in contact with the house, and every child I had come to know over the past year. I started with Jalissa, Raven, and Chanté but also described Justine, Amber, Cassandra, Jessamy, and the others.

I tried to explain the complex relationships I sensed among all of them, told him of the pain I felt when observing Sam, and shared the ardent plea and profound observation of Jimar that cold November evening. I finally told them about Adia, Ahadi and Abeo. Both he and Charlotte listened intently, but while Charlotte occasionally touched a delicate, lace handkerchief to her eyes I could sense no emotional response to my words from Matthew.

Morning progressed to early afternoon, and Matthew excused himself for a moment to make a telephone call. In Matthew's absence, Ms. Blessing suggested we move to a small table in the kitchen alcove for lunch. It was there we resumed our conversation, if one could call it that.

I didn't seem able to stop my filibuster-like soliloquy, and Matthew began to show interest in what I had to say. Occasionally, he would interrupt with a question or interject thoughts of his own, but most of the time both he and Ms. Blessing just let me ramble on.

I shared my struggles to find a comfortable place to continue to interact with the kids and discussed the uniqueness of the team of people who had been drawn together. Reid, Ms. G, Ms. Tracy, Officer Steve, and Karen had all become blessings in the lives of these children. I finally ended by relating the concerns Ms. G had shared with me over the telephone the afternoon before. "These kids are adrift, Matthew," was my final comment.

I thought I had nothing more to say and glanced at my watch. Quite embarrassed, I spoke once again.

"I apologize that I have dominated the conversation for so long. I've never really had the opportunity to share the story of the house and its kids with someone who has never met any of the real players. I regret that I don't have a concrete plan of action but would be willing to consider any ideas you and Charlotte might have to make a difference in their lives."

As I finished, Charlotte got up from the table and made her way to the front door to welcome George and Karen back from their day in the city. I could just make out their laughter and some conversation from the entrance foyer when Matthew spoke. It was apparent he was not ready to conclude our conversation.

"Charlotte has long believed the house has supernatural powers and can, in her words, 'talk' or at least share thoughts with certain people. What is your opinion of that?"

I knew this question would probably come up. I sat silently for a moment and then began. "Matthew, my hope is that even as I act upon my father's words, that honestly is the best path, I will still be able to maintain a modicum of credibility with you."

"I related to Charlotte earlier today that I am still struggling with the fact that many people think I'm mad as a hatter for suggesting that the house actually communicates with me. Actually, I, myself, find that disconcerting as well. I have always made decisions based primarily on facts not feelings, and this is a very difficult issue for me to reconcile."

"That being said, I must tell you that I will no longer dismiss something an individual, particularly one I trust, believes just because I am unable to rationalize it cognitively. So yes, I believe the house communicates with selected individuals. Even some of the kids will tell you that they think it speaks to them as well."

Removing his glasses from his nose Matthew rubbed his eyes, looked up at the ceiling and then persisted, "So, the house speaks to you, am I correct?"

"Yes," I said simply.

"And what's the last thing you can recall that it has said?" he inquired.

"Curious, but Charlotte asked me almost the same thing this morning. While I don't necessarily hear words most of the time, I feel I am able to discern thoughts, and the latest one has to do with the fact that the house feels like it can help me help the children and wants a chance to do so."

"Have you read my mother's letters, Jamie?"

"No, Matthew, I have not, but interestingly enough you are the third person in twenty-four hours to reference them, and I must admit that with your permission, I am eager to do so. I can't explain why, and please forgive my impertinence, but I feel like your mother and I might have been good friends had we known one another."

Before he replied, Matthew secured his cane and got up from the table. "I'll see that Charlotte gets the letters to you this evening. Please read them, Jamie, all of them, as you are the first person outside my family who I believe may be able to understand the heavenliness that was Jillian Marie Blessing Eden, my mother, the nurse and the woman."

He was walking out of the kitchen when he seemed to catch himself. He turned to me and finalized our conversation with the following. "By the way, for what's it is worth, yes, I believe you two would have been close friends, potentially even soul mates. What is it kids text today? BFF?"

As those words settled between us, I heard his cane and footsteps advance across the wooden floor as he continued into the drawing room and slowly closed the door.

Chapter 35

Why Should the Past Matter?

"When I was young I was sure of everything;
in a few years, having been mistaken a thousand
times, I was not half so sure of most things as I
was before; at present, I am hardly sure of anything but what God has revealed to me."

—John Wesley

The College of Charleston

I didn't know what to do first. I sensed that the kitchen staff had been patiently awaiting our exit so that they could get about the business of preparing dinner, so I figured I needed to leave. I also wanted to reconnect with Karen and hear about her day in the city with George but wasn't sure where she was. Finally, I desperately wanted the opportunity to read the letters and didn't know how to go about ensuring I was given access to them tonight.

I stood up and walked toward the dining room. I had decided to go out to my safe place, the piazza, once again and process all that had been said. As I opened the screen door, I saw Karen, Charlotte, and George sitting around the table with a pitcher of tea. George rose from his seat and said, "Well, there you are Ms. Jamie! We was just talkin' 'bout your school! Now when did you go there?"

I smiled broadly at George as Charlotte poured me a glass of icy, sweet tea with lime, and Karen made place on the settee for me.

"Oh my, George, if I tell you I'll have to reveal my true age," I teased. "Actually I was there 1968 through 1971."

Everyone waited as I got settled. George then continued the conversation. "Ms. Jamie, that means you was in Charleston in 1969. Am I correct?"

"Well, yes," but there is obviously a more pointed question you want to ask," I challenged.

George paused and then shared his real reasons for the query. "Ms. Blessing, forgive me up front, but you know how I like to study our history. Ms. Jamie, you lived close to the Medical University when you stayed in the C of C girls' dorm, didn't you? Do you remember the strike of the Medical University employees that year?"

I didn't have to struggle much to recall the time because, just like my earlier venture into integration issues as a high school student, I'd overstepped my boundaries on several occasions while in college—this being one of the first times. While I had not been as committed as the Freedom Riders in the fifties, I had come to think of myself as somewhat of a closet Civil Rights champion in the late sixties and did a lot of idealistic, but stupid stuff in those years.

I had been in Charleston during the hospital strike but didn't exercise a whole lot of good judgment at the time, so I pondered how much I should reveal. Something momentous had occurred in the city that year; something that would become one of the triggers for our nation's transformation.

"Yes, I was around but very young and naïve. What do you know about it?"

While Karen and Charlotte looked on with obvious interest, George shared that his niece had been employed at the Medical University of South Carolina (MUSC) during those years.

"What did she do for the university?" I asked.

Proudly he continued, "She was hired as an LPN, Ms. Jamie, and had come back to Charleston after graduatin' from Goldwaite Memorial Hospital in San Francisco. The South Carolina Boards didn't recognize her full degree in nursing so they would only let her work as an LPN, but my murruh and her grumma, Beatrice, wanted her home and home she came."

The story was obviously one of significance for the family and his words flowed passionately.

"After she was here awhile, she began to open up 'bout the workin' conditions before the strike. She told us how the black and white nurses didn't get paid the same wages, and she shared stories 'bout how the black nurses was harassed."

"We got uneasy and wanted her to quit but she told us about the support from Coretta Scott King, Ralph Abernathy, and Andrew Young of the Southern Christian Leadership Conference. She wanted to be part of the movement with Ms. Mary Moultrie. Were you there when the march happened?"

George had tossed the ball into my court, and I was unnerved thinking about how I should proceed. While never limiting myself to either a liberal or conservative label, I felt I faced a dilemma here. I didn't think it really mattered what I did back then, but I also didn't want to give the Blessing family reason to question whether or not they could trust my judgment. There was too much at stake since I felt Matthew somehow might be on the verge of considering other plans for the house and ultimately our kids.

I'm not certain why, but I chose to lie that evening. Without thinking it through, I had become involved with a group of impassioned students who participated in a rally for the hospital workers in 1969 and had barely escaped being discovered. I had been foolish and shortsighted at the time, never recounted the situation to my parents, and could have cost myself the governmental financial support I relied on to stay in school.

"Your niece was involved in an extremely important and historical event, George," I replied trying to sound sincere. "I admire her courage and wish I had known her. I do remember that the college cancelled classes for a couple of days during the rally so I went home with a friend from Summerville until things quieted down. Remind me about what happened."

Maybe I manufactured the disappointment in his voice as George commented, "Yes, um, she sure was a brave one. I guess you all can research the history of the event without me ramblin' on, but it taught my family a lot about trust and love, yes, it did."

To his credit, George let the story drop, and I was left with the gnawing feeling that by not following my gut reaction and being completely honest I had disappointed George. But who besides me really knew the facts of that event so long ago.

It was Charlotte who brought us back. "Well, this historical conversation is most entertaining, but I must see about dinner. Ladies, we will plan to meet in the drawing room again at five thirty so that will permit you some time to freshen up. George, are you going to Mt. Pleasant this evening?"

George stood up gingerly and nodded, "Yes, ma'am, gonna see the new babies and go to their baptisms tomorrow morning."

Charlotte rose from her spot in the rocker as well, brushed off her dress, and clasped his hands.

"How delightful and what a family celebration! Now the twins are both boys, right? And they are the children of one of your grand-nieces correct?"

George beamed, "Yes, ma'am! Gonna be a celebration for sure. Ms. Beatrice is directin' everything so you know it gonna be done right. By the way, I'll be home a little later than usual tomorrow so I hope you won't be needin' me."

"Oh, I do declare George you worry about things as much as me. No, no, we will be fine, just give your family our regards and enjoy yourself."

Karen and I were collecting glasses and placing them on the tray to be returned to the dining room as George said his goodbyes, and Charlotte began walking toward the front door. Suddenly she stopped and called after him. "George, George, oh my, where is my mind, please come into the kitchen I have some things for you to take to each of those beautiful babies, and I nearly let you leave without them."

The screen door slammed behind her as she hurried into the house still mumbling about being absent-minded.

George made his was down the steps of the piazza and around to the back of the house. "I'm comin, Ms. Charlotte, I'm comin" was all he said.

Karen and I collected the glasses, pitcher, and related items and placed them on the tray. "We need to talk," I whispered. "I can't wait to hear all about your tour, and I need to tell you about my conversation with Matthew."

"Definitely," she replied. "I'll run these things into the kitchen and meet you upstairs: your room or mine?"

"I think yours is cooler so let's try that." I held the door for her and hurried up the steps.

Chapter 36

Jillian

"There are many Beths in the world, shy and quiet, sitting in corners till needed, and living for others so cheerfully that no one sees the sacrifices till the little cricket on the hearth stops chirping, and the sweet, sunshiny presence vanishes, leaving silence and shadow behind."

—Little Women

Ms. Jillian Marie Blessing Eden

We both started talking at once. But as Karen threw herself across the bed and began to ramble on excitedly she quickly outpaced me.

"Oh, Jamie, I can see why you love this city, it is so captivating. I didn't want to stop for lunch and the carriage tour we drew was along the Battery, which would have been my pick anyway."

"George was as good a guide as any of the professionals, and his stories made everything real. Did you know his grandmother, aunties, and mother were all basket weavers and speak Gullah? As a matter of fact—"

"Whoa, slow down," I said, as I interrupted her exuberant description of her afternoon.

"I want to hear every detail, I promise, but I have to ask you a couple of questions first."

"Okay, shoot," she replied.

"Do you still have the letters and the diary?"

She sat upright as she said, "Actually, no. This morning when I went down to get some coffee Charlotte asked me if I would mind returning them to her. You were in the garden, on the phone, I think, so I rushed back upstairs to get them and since I didn't see you alone again until now, I didn't think to mention it. Why?"

"Well, like everything else surrounding this mystery it's a long story, but George, Charlotte, and Matthew all three brought them up to me in separate conversations in the last twenty-four hours. Apparently, all of them think I should read the letters, which brings me to my second question. Have you read either them or the diary?"

Karen smiled. "I was wondering when you were going to get around to asking me that. Steve and I talked a long time before deciding what to do. Even though Charlotte had given us permission to do so, I felt strange, like it would be an invasion of privacy, if we did. So initially we just stored them with important papers in our home safe waiting for the time when she would ask for them to be returned."

"When we would talk by phone, she never inquired if we had read them, and we never volunteered that we hadn't. One night, not long ago, after yet another disappointing report from us that we really hadn't found anyone who seemed interested in the house, its history or Thomas and Jillian's story, I felt her frustration peak and sadness seemed to envelope every word.

"It was then that I decided maybe if I knew something of the story I could do a better job of selling it. Trying to decide whether to begin with either the letters or the diary was difficult, but two things helped me make my decision. First of all, the letters seemed much more fragile than the diary and secondly, I was still very reluctant to intrude on what I felt would be very private conversations between a husband and wife. For some reason I felt reading the diary entries would be less intrusive. Funny, huh. Maybe, it's a girl thing."

Karen stood and walked over to the window beside the fireplace. She pulled the delicate lace curtains aside, peered out at the garden, and continued, "I never told Steve, but one night when he worked a late shift, I unlocked the safe, pulled out the diary and settled down to read. I justified my actions by telling myself that I would read only enough to give me a feel for why Charlotte thought the story worthy of being made public."

Returning to her spot on the bed she kicked off her sandals, stretched out, pulled a pillow from the headboard area and with her head now propped up at foot of the bed she gazed across the room at me perched in a chair by the fireplace.

She picked up where she had left off. "I was hooked from the beginning and was still reading three hours later when I heard Steve come through the garage. I decided to keep my secret a little longer and quickly returned the diary to the safe. I couldn't get back to our bedroom before he came into the house so I met him in the living room, which was an unusual thing for me to do at that late hour. Since the safe is stored in the closet of the room we've made into an office, I made up a story about researching sites for kitchen renovations. He was satisfied with that since we'd been talking about the project for weeks."

"Jillian's entries started when she decided to go to nursing school. Apparently that hadn't been a popular decision with her family, particularly her father. Tensions became even more pronounced when after finishing school she announced she would be joining the Army Nurse Corps."

"She met Thomas when she was stationed aboard the hospital ship *Marigold* and he, wounded in France, was being transported back to Charleston. She made daily entries as she monitored Thomas's recovery on the journey. It became clear through her words that she was falling in love with him. The diary chronicled a three-year period, and as I continued to read, it became clear that both Jillian and Thomas faced some unfathomable decisions during that time."

"Devoted to nursing and her beloved home, Thomas's request for her to marry him and come to Texas to live was bittersweet for Jillian. She clearly loved him deeply and wanted to be with him, but she had never lived anywhere but Charleston and leaving both her family and her beloved city behind seemed, through her words, almost more than she could grasp."

"To her credit, however, she could sense his equally passionate devotion to his family and home state. In fact her descriptions of Thomas's thoughts were almost more compelling than hers. As I continued to read her daily entries I not only saw the printed words but felt her associated pain."

"At some point, a compromise must have occurred because the diary, with a significant lag in entries picked up in earnest around March 1950, and on July 13, 1950, Jillian and Thomas were married in St. Michael's Church in Charleston."

I stopped Karen momentarily. "What was the date again?"

"The thirteenth of July 1950, if I remember the entry correctly. Why, is that significant?" she asked.

"I'm not sure," I answered, but "here's the thing . . . it was the day I was born."

"Oh my," Karen responded.

We sat for a moment, each of us deep in our own thoughts.

"Jamie?" Karen teased. "Are you sure you're not related to the Blessing family in some way?"

I was grateful for the levity. "I don't think so, but I do believe Ms. Charlotte has a definite plan she wants put into place, and she's obviously written in a part for me."

Karen then digressed, "By the way, how was the conversation with Matthew this morning?"

"Long, good, revealing, and actually a welcome release for both of us, I think. Matthew is a complex person with what I sense to be a giving, good heart. However, the house and his days in Texas are like a wound that has never healed."

I switched positions in the big, overstuffed chair and then continued, "I've noticed that it is very difficult for him to refer to the house as anything but the 'property in Texas' or the 'Blessing Path structure.' He did though, at one point in our conversation, actually refer to it by its name. Funny, but he also commented that he thought his mother and I would have been BFF."

I watched as Karen raised her eyebrows and chuckled at my last comment. "Really?"

"Yea, really, and he also said that he would see to it that I had the letters tonight."

Even though we had much more to say, exhaustion was suddenly a palatable companion for both of us. Yawning we decided to spend some quiet time alone. Karen was going to call Steve, and I also wanted to talk with Reid to fill him in and check on the kids. I walked down the hall and opened the door to my bedroom with a thousand competing thoughts running through my mind.

Closing the door, I kicked off my shoes and was walking toward the center of the room, seriously contemplating a short nap, when I saw them. The diary and the letters, still bound with the beautiful crimson ribbon, were lying in the middle of the bed atop the lace coverlet. As surprised as I was to see them, it was what was positioned just to their left that caused me to gasp. An intricately carved wooden box encircled with the same type of crimson ribbon also awaited my attention.

I stood staring at my newly found treasures for a moment thinking I was imagining what I was seeing. I hadn't heard anyone climb the stairs nor walk down the hall. But nevertheless, there they were. I walked over to the bed, sat just on its edge, and picked up the visible stack of envelopes first. After gently untying the ribbon, I thumbed through the collection, looking at the postmarks and addresses. They were organized chronologically and the authors only two—Thomas and Jillian.

Assuming that the box contained a similar cache, I removed its ribbon. Inside I found several more carefully preserved envelopes. However, the addressees were different. While all appeared to have been penned by Jillian, the recipients were Charlotte and Matthew, not Thomas. Was this why Matthew had encouraged me to read "all" the letters? He must have known that I had assumed the letters to be between his mother and father only.

Anxious to start reading right away, I glanced at the clock on the mantle and was dismayed to see that there was no time to do so now. Reluctantly, I began dressing for dinner thinking about how I might graciously excuse myself a little early. Karen knocked on my door just as I was applying the last touches of my makeup.

Chapter 37

Anticipation

"Of all the hardships a person had to face, none was more punishing than the simple act of waiting."

—Khaled Hosseini, *A Thousand Splendid Suns*

Dinner was again a delightful affair, but I was preoccupied with my awaiting reading material and not very responsive. While we all did our best to contribute to the conversation, I think each of us sensed the need for individual reflection after the events of the day.

I was able to briefly share the news of my treasures with Karen as we adjourned to the piazza for dessert and coffee. She grinned, indicated a real interest in knowing more about the additional letters, and gave me a "thumbs up" as support.

We seated ourselves in full view of the luxurious garden while Charlotte and Matthew continued their gracious hospitality by sharing lovely stories about the city and its inhabitants, both past and present. Matthew had requested preparation of a very special local dessert for the evening and seemed quite interested in our thoughts regarding the combination of ingredients and their different textures. The Chocolate Praline Soufflé and samplings of local coffees were delivered to the piazza and comments about the local recipe momentarily consumed our conversation.

Not long after, as evening fully descended, and we finished the coffee and slices of sumptuous treat, we all politely took leave of one another. Charlotte offered that she would be leaving for services at St. Michael's around 10:30 a.m. the next morning if either of us would like to accompany her. Both Karen and I indicated we would be delighted to do so. Neither of us inquired whether or not Matthew would go along.

When I moved to ascend the stairs for the evening, Charlotte asked if I might like a pot of tea delivered to my room. It was obvious she was keenly aware of what would consume my next few hours. I graciously accepted and began my trek up the stairs.

Matthew was walking into the drawing room when I glanced back at the first floor. Out of the corner of my eye, I thought I saw a hint of trepidation on his face as he looked up at me, but I couldn't be certain.

"Good night, Jamie," was all he said but then, as if an afterthought, added, "May you have an enlightening evening."

Chapter 38

The Letters: Part 1

"There are two ways of spreading light: to
be the candle or the mirror that reflects it."

—Edith Wharton

The Early Letters

I called Reid before settling in with the letters. I was in such a hurry
to explain all that had transpired that day and begin my evening of

reading that I was slow to realize he was able to hear the impatience in my voice.

"Whoa, slow down a little," he began. "It sounds like the events of today are far too complex for a late night conversation. I really do want to know everything, but why don't we wait until we have more time to talk and you have additional insight into our main cast of characters. It seems that several people believe the answer for all of us lies in the penned words that rest patiently in your presence."

"I miss you," was all I could say.

"And I you," he replied.

"Reid, I can't help but think if you were here you'd know exactly what to do."

I could hear him chuckling on the other end of the line. "Well, I'm not sure about that, but I think I would have enjoyed returning to Charleston with you."

"Then come, now!" I blurted out.

There was a pause and then his gentle words flowed through my iPhone.

"No, thank you for letting me know how much you would like me to be there—that means a lot—but somehow I feel like this is your story, and it needs to be handled by you alone."

I didn't pursue the issue any further because deep down inside I agreed.

After a few more minutes of small talk about the dogs, the weather, and the happenings at Oak Lakes, we said our goodbyes using the words of love we always share whether near or far from one another.

As we hung up, I felt as lonely as I had ever felt in my life and more than a little wary of what might be about to occur. The trepidation I thought I had seen in Matthew's face earlier in the evening had now settled firmly upon my own heart.

Glancing at the clock on the mantle I noted the time, 9:30 p.m. I poured a cup of tea, gently extracted the first letter from its envelope at the top of the stack and moved to the bed to read.

As a child, I had always found it easier to do my homework or settle in with a good book spread out atop my bed surrounded by pillows and fluffy throws or quilts. So there was never a question in my mind where I would choose to get to know Jillian and Thomas.

The first letter was from Jillian to Thomas. She wrote in a cursive style with elegant penmanship. But even though her pen strokes were flowing, the overall effect was one of clean, confident lines that made her sentences easy to read.

I imagined her as a very organized and methodical woman yet one who also had a natural empathy for others, particularly those less fortunate. Her tone was conversational, and, at least in the beginning, rarely intimate as she shared what was happening in her life each day.

Thomas's letters were written in cursive as well, but his handwriting was more upright and his vocabulary less flowery. He shared wonderful stories about the town of Eden Hill, its people and the Texas landscape, and I was momentarily reminded of my earlier hunch that the history of Eden Hill might best be transmitted through story.

As he wrote, he referenced several books that he must have sent periodically to accompany his letters. In particular, he was interested that Jillian read Audie Murphy's 1949 autobiography *To Hell and Back*. The most decorated soldier of World War II Murphy had been born in Kingston, Hunt County, Texas. Thomas felt that Audie Murphy represented what was best about the Texas spirit. Murphy was awarded thirty-three US medals, including three Purple Hearts and one Medal of Honor, and it was obvious Thomas was proud of his Texas roots.

My tea grew cold as I opened and read letter after letter without ceasing. Jillian and Thomas's words were humbling and gracefully laced with emotion. As I slowly read each page line by line, I had no problem understanding why Charlotte had envisioned these letters being included as part of an exhibit focusing on the struggles of true love during times of war and strife.

It was warm that night, and I stopped for a moment to dig through my purse for a tissue to wipe my face and glasses. As always the Charleston humidity colored every event, and I thought about Karen's request of Charlotte for another love story that might parallel that of *Gone With the Wind*. While Rhett and Scarlet were undeniably different than Thomas and Jillian, the anguish of war they all faced, their love of their homeland and their struggles with a passionate relationship seemed somehow astonishingly parallel.

Almost every letter began with a poignant story about each of their attempts to get their respective lives back together after experiencing the horrors they had witnessed. Jillian talked about her frustration with her inability to convince her father that women had a place in world events.

Thomas struggled with his inability to integrate his new respect for and understanding of all peoples of the world into the life of an ordinary Texas rancher.

Then, usually suddenly and without transition, they would move into the realm of their own personal relationship sometimes using the eloquent phrases of seasoned poets or storytellers, while often just simply sharing their private, intimate feelings. I found myself so captivated by their struggles that I yearned to know them personally.

With each line both of them penned I learned a great deal about the myriad effects of war on the human spirit. I also developed a new respect for the beauty and art of letter writing and wondered if it would survive in today's highly technological world.

Sometimes I smiled, even laughed out loud, and on more than one occasion had to remind myself that regrettably these two very special people were no longer living, and I'd never have the chance to meet them.

The clock ticked on, but I was unable to stop intruding on their pain of separation, their indecision about how to proceed and their fierce, also competing, love for their respective homes and one another. I kept reading letter after letter addicted to their words.

Around 2:00 a.m., I arose from my spot on the bed and walked to the window. Needing a break from the intensity of emotion I was feeling, I gazed out into the night sky. The moon was full and the garden almost totally bathed in its light.

My personal story had begun to intrude on their story, and I realized I was having difficulty separating the two—Texas and South Carolina, Jillian and Thomas, Jamie and her past and present

Succumbing to weariness, I opened the window for a breath of air before brushing my teeth and forcing myself to lie down and wait for the morning's light. The slight breeze was refreshing, and I decided to leave the window slightly ajar while I slept. Just as I turned away from it, I thought I saw a figure in the garden. He tipped his hat to me and walked away. I couldn't be certain but the person looked an awful lot like George.

I realized then that I could either keep trying on my own to rationalize what was happening or simply ask God for guidance and let go. I forgot about brushing my teeth and lay down yearning for moment of peace. I was in the middle of a prayer for a little direction when I must have drifted off.

Chapter 39

Timeless Wisdom

"Whatever we are waiting for—peace of mind, contentment, grace, the inner awareness of simple abundance—it will surely come to us, but only when we are ready to receive it with an open and grateful heart."

—Sarah Ban Breathnach

I slept fitfully and sat up around 6:00 a.m. bathed in light perspiration with the sheets tangled around my legs. The day was dawning hot and sultry, but my thoughts were not on the weather.

I decided I needed more than the slight breeze wafting through my bedroom window for relief so I brushed my teeth, and dressed quickly in a pair of shorts, tank top and running shoes. Without regard for Sunday social norms, I tiptoed down the stairs, opened the front door and walked through the garden and out on to the street.

It was a quiet time, and, as I jogged along the narrow sidewalks of Legare, I recalled the freedom I had first come to appreciate years earlier each time I explored this city on my own. I don't know how far I ran or the direction I chose to follow but at some point, out of breath, I simply stopped and listened to the sounds of the morning.

All of the cities' church bells were ringing in joyous unison. Regardless of the events of the world that the major networks would report today, something profound was about to happen in Charleston, South Carolina. I could feel it.

Walking home, I peered into the shops along the way searching for a clock. Discovering that I had been gone a little over an hour, I stepped up my pace and came upon the garden door in record time. I was surprised to see George. He had brought the car around to the street and was lovingly polishing the hood.

"Mornin', Ms. Jamie, you been out for a run?"

Breathing at a pace that usually deters conversation I struggled to reply. "Well, I wouldn't quite call it a run, more like a fast-paced walk, but yes, I have been out awhile now."

He stopped what he was doing and glanced over at me, "Sleep well?"

"Maybe I should ask you the same question," I grinned.

Noticing me trying to wipe the perspiration off my face with an already wet hand, he handed me a clean white towel from a stack he'd placed on the sidewalk. "Fair enough, yes, ma'am, fair enough," he chuckled.

"How was your family celebration, by the way? I thought you were going to stay in Mt. Pleasant for the baptisms today?"

"Oh, I'll go back, Ms. Jamie, yes, I will, but the real ceremony won't be until 'bout 2:00 after church so I got time to get back."

"Why, didn't you stay though? I thought you were going to?"

He stared at me for a moment and then responded, "Ms. Jamie, you look like you could use a drink of cool water, and the household ain't quite ready for the day just yet so would you like to see my place? It's just out back. Several years ago, Mr. Matthew was gracious enough to rent me the carriage house. I thought you might enjoy seein' another piece of Charlston's history."

Sensing this wasn't just about a cool drink of water, I followed George through the garden door and walked along a narrow path behind the house to the quaint cottage he called home. The structure originally built to house horse-drawn carriages, as the name implies, was now a two-car garage with an attached small apartment for George.

It appeared to have been recently remodeled, and if his enthusiastic description of its amenities was any indication of his satisfaction, it suited him perfectly. The roof was supported by two, evenly, spaced pillars. And I noticed that the apartment had its own little porch and garden.

"Now, Ms. Jamie, you just have a seat here on my little porch while I go in and get you some cool water." George opened the screen door and went inside while I busied myself admiring his tiny, but well cared for, garden.

I could hear him whistling and stepped back up onto the porch commenting, "You sound very happy this morning, sir, I imagine this weekend has been very special for you."

I walked to the edge of the door to catch his reply just as the rays of the sun were beginning to peek through the live oaks and illuminate his sitting room. Through the screen, I could see the entire room and its contents.

Sparsely furnished but tidy, I was admiring George's obvious contentment with the simple pleasures of life when my eyes came to rest on one particular item. Positioned on a circular table, just to the right of the sofa, sat a beautifully woven Sweet Grass pineapple.

Approaching the door from my left George walked into the room. "Got your water and a few pieces of watermelon, Ms. Jamie, both should taste real good on this sticky mornin'."

I backed away from the screen door as he pushed it open with his foot. He placed a tray with a bowl of bright red watermelon chunks and two glasses of water on a little table and gestured for me to sit in one of two colorful, vintage metal chairs.

He sat across from me and pulled a couple of napkins out of his pocket. "I thought I heard you ax'me a question while I was in the kitchen, but I couldn't quite make it out, Ms. Jamie."

Accepting the napkin he offered, I replied, "Oh, I was just commenting about your whistling. You seem so happy."

Chuckling he said, "I'm always happy, Ms. Jamie, can't be no other way since I'm so blessed, umm, umm, yes, ma'am, so blessed."

We sat for a moment each savoring the cool chunks of fruit. George seemed content with the silence, but I, impatient as ever, spoke up. "When I was standing by the door I couldn't help but notice how cozy your little sitting area is. How long have you lived here?"

"'Bout ten years give or take one, I suspect. Moved here after I retired to help Ms. Charlotte get round mostly."

I don't know why, but I was surprised to learn that he had had another job. "Oh, I didn't know this was a second career. What did you do before working for the Blessing family?"

"Well, I watched over horses and mules mostly. Good company they are. My daddy was a farmer over on James Island. I grew up around all kinds of animals, and we always had one or more mules or horses on the farm. After school I worked as a barn manager, horse trainer and city guide for several different carriage companies. I always loved history, kept my eyes and ears open growin' up, and had a knack for tellin' a good story. Besides, I knew just 'bout every street and alley in the city and beyond since I'd spend most weekends in the marketplace with Ms. Beatrice, my grandmother."

"Where did you go to school?" I asked.

I caught him taking a swig of water, but he soon replied, "I'd done a little work for a vet when I was in high school, and he helped me get into a veterinary tech program in Georgia. With a little tutorin'

I passed the entrance exams and stayed about a year. I learned enough about large animals to become pretty good at takin' care of 'em."

"So you didn't finish?"

"No, no ma'am, I didn't. The Lord had other plans for me so back to the low country I come. Never regretted it, not a minute. I just wanted to care for animals, not do lab tests and such. Besides my daddy took sick, and I was needed here to take care of the younger ones."

We sat a few minutes more in silence. "You be goin to services this morning, Ms. Jamie? If so, you might wanna get on back to the house. Ms. Blessing always gets to the church early. She don't cotton much to people being late especially when goin' to the Lord's house."

I stood and gulped down what was left of my water. Not knowing quite how to respond, I commented, "Thanks, I've really enjoyed getting to know you a little better." I stepped off the porch and started back to the house. He was just about to carry the tray through the screen door when I added, "George?"

"Yes 'em?"

"Where did you get the Sweet Grass pineapple in your living room?"

His voice trailed off, but I still was able to catch his words, "Now that's another story, Ms. Jamie. We'll get to it when you're ready to talk about the letters . . . all of 'em."

The letters, there it was again, another reference. Hearing voices in the kitchen but nowhere else, I quickly climbed the stairs musing about whether or not the outfit I had worn our first evening here would be appropriate for church.

I nearly ran into Karen at the top of the last landing. She looked fresh and rested in contrast to my sweaty, disheveled appearance. "Oh, there you are." She smiled. "I knocked on your door, but when I got no answer I figured you might be sleeping in. What time did you get to bed anyway?"

"I think around two o'clock but sleep was hard to come by. I tossed and turned a lot, so I got up early and went out for a run/walk. We really need to talk."

"I agree," Karen added. "Are you going to church?"

I chuckled. "Yes, if I can get ready in time! Hold the carriage, please!"

Ms. Blessing, Karen and I arrived at St. Michael's with minimal time to spare, and I couldn't help but notice George's amused grin as I had run from the house at just the last minute to get into the car to leave.

The service was traditional and cerebral, and it was clear the Blessing family had an established place in this church. As we exited the service, Charlotte remarked, "Jillian is buried in the area, did you know that?"

Neither Karen nor I were aware of that fact, and I wondered if that information was embedded in the letters I had yet to read. When we didn't respond, she continued her query, "Would you like to see her grave site?"

"Yes, very much," I spoke up and was now quite curious about how, if she passed away in Texas, her home at the time, she ended up in Charleston.

Thinking she might have a final resting place near the church, I was surprised when Charlotte directed us to get into the car. When we had settled inside, Charlotte asked George to take us north on Meeting Street.

"What do you know of Charleston history and its proclivity for historic cemeteries," she inquired as the spectacular, new Arthur Ravenel Bridge came into sight.

"Not enough I think," I replied.

As Karen sat quietly, and I tried to understand the significance of this short venture away from the main part of the city and the peninsula, Charlotte smiled and continued. "My sister was a many-faceted person, ladies, and surprised all of us when she indicated that she wanted to be buried in the Magnolia Cemetery.

"The Magnolia Cemetery, once a rice plantation, is the oldest public cemetery in Charleston and was founded in the mid-1800s on the banks of the Cooper River. It is listed on National Register of Historic Places and is the final resting place for generations of Southern leaders.

"Her request was a simple one, actually, and her written words were clear. She shared that she desired to lie among those who participated in the history of her homeland, as well as be near the sweet smell of the salt marshes and the waters of the low country. While it took some persuasion of the local authorities my father and I were able to grant one of her last requests."

I didn't inquire further but was very curious about what Thomas's thoughts had been regarding that request.

Later after walking among the history, solitude and peace of the gravesites of Magnolia Cemetery, we started our return to the house. Driving along George, whom I now regarded as our local historian, reminded us of the significance of both St. Michael's and the sacred place we had just visited. "Several confederate officers are buried at Magnolia as well as the last commander and crew of the CSS Hunley. If you study the register you will see that the list also includes several governors, judges, congressmen, authors and artists.

"St. Michaels is just as famous. Its steeple is almost two hundred feet above street level and can be seen in many of the old photos of Charleston during the Civil War. It may be just legend but some say that the clock in the tower has kept the time in Charleston since 1764 and probably helped Mr. George Washington get to service on time when he worshipped there in May 1791. Some people even say that General Robert E. Lee worshipped in the same pew as Mr. Washington in the 1860s.

"The old church has had several bells. As a boy, I heard that all of 'em were made in England before 1800. To keep 'em safe they was sent to Columbia during the Civil War but ended up gettin' cracked in a fire there in 1865. Remnants of those bells was salvaged from the fire and sent back to England to be fixed. They still ring even today.

"Some folks even tell that after the Civil War the bell ringer was a black man, and he played several wonderful melodies like 'Home Again' and 'Auld Land Syne' (Brown 2008). Even the pulpit you all saw this mornin' is the original one just like all the stained glass windows."

As we continued our drive back to the Legare house, George shared more stories about the history of Charleston. I listened with one ear since my mind kept going back to Magnolia Cemetery. I wondered why Thomas agreed to have Jillian buried there. I didn't inquire because the information hadn't been offered. Besides, it was a public cemetery and fit her request for a final resting place perfectly. There was one more curious thing though.

George had gone ahead of us as we entered the cemetery and hung back as we departed. Noticing his deliberate behavior, I glanced back as we were walking away. He said he just wanted to clean off Jillian's headstone a bit, but I couldn't help but notice that when he thought we were out of sight, he retrieved something from his jacket pocket and placed it gently on her headstone.

After the service and visit to the cemetery, I felt an even greater sense of urgency to complete my assigned task of reading all of the letters as soon as possible. We returned to house around twelve thirty in the afternoon, and I excused myself to freshen up before a light lunch.

Chapter 40

The Letters: Part II

"I can imagine in years to come that my papers and memorabilia, my journals and letters, will find themselves always in the company of people who care about many of the things I do."

—Alice Walker

Remi

After lunch, I practically sprinted up the stairs to my room. Karen, sensing my need to immerse myself in the second cache of letters, asked if she might visit a local museum or go back to further explore some of the shops downtown that afternoon. Ms. Blessing appeared pleased at the request, and since George had returned to Mt. Pleasant for his family celebration, she arranged for a taxi to take Karen downtown. We had not seen Matthew all morning, and he did not join us for lunch.

Not even stopping to change clothes I kicked off my shoes, retrieved the prized box, and threw myself on the bed I had hastily made earlier in the day. Again, using the postmarks and now recognizing the distinct handwriting, I noted that the first few letters were from Jillian to Charlotte. The first one, dated August 22, 1944, was apparently written aboard the hospital ship *Marigold*:

> August 22, 1944
> My dearest sister,
>
> I am writing this at a very late hour but for the last week or so sleep has been elusive, and I feel that, perhaps, putting pen to paper might help me rest. While I never know what will be acceptable to the censors I must share what's on my heart so please bear with me as there may be gaps in what I say and the meaning be unclear.
>
> There are so many heartbreaking stories in every day's events that I long for an opportunity to just sit on the piazza and "talk" with you, my best friend, about what I am seeing. Since we cannot yet be together, this medium of communication must suffice.
>
> Charlotte, life is very different here than what I had expected when I committed to be an army nurse and certainly light years away from what we have experienced in our beloved, sheltered city. Sometimes, though don't let on to any-

one there, I wish I had heeded our father's advice as I am sadder now than I have ever been in my life. I thought I was prepared for what I now see, but realize that I clearly was not.

We picked up several wounded American soldiers this past week, and while I feel adequately prepared to deal with most of their physical wounds, I am totally at a loss to know how to provide appropriate comfort for their mental anguish.

I see the fear in all their eyes not only because of their wounds, but also because they now have firsthand experience and appreciation of the cruelty and inhumanity so prevalent in our world today. They come into this conflict so young and full of life, so American actually, that I fear most were not prepared to cope with the reality that is war. But then, who would be?

Many try to mask their fearfulness with humor, but late at night, when I drift by their bunks to check on their conditions, I can sense their loneliness and trepidation. Many cry silently and, embarrassed, attempt to hide that emotion in their pillows. I, in response, try to engage them in conversation about their homes and families, and it is only then that I may see a glimmer of hope or a smile. How I ache for each one.

Realizing that you have always known me better than I know myself I must confess something and ask for your opinion. I, too, am lonely and searching for some sense of normalcy and hope. I do not want to give up and come home (especially since father would believe that if I did so he was correct in assuming that he is better equipped to determine the course of my life than

I), but I teeter on the edge of despair many days, especially during the night hours.

We, as nurses, know that we must maintain a positive spirit and have bonded with one another but, quite honestly, I don't think any one of us is ever 100 percent truthful about the depth of our own feelings for fear of being considered incapable of handling the job we have been assigned to do.

As a result, I have fallen prey to the unthinkable and must confide in someone about my situation. From our first days of training, we, as student army nurses, were cautioned about the myriad of problems associated with developing close friendships with patients—not only for the patient's sake but also for our own.

While the advice is definitely sound, I now know that the extenuating circumstances we face on a mission of this kind can change the human dynamics of any situation and cloud judgment. I don't think I realized what a profound effect the loneliness and close proximity to death would have on me personally.

Without a truly trusted friend among my colleagues, I now find myself sharing more of my innermost feelings than I probably should with a particular, wounded pilot. Believe it or not, he is not a Southerner, per se, but a "Texan," as he is fond of telling me, and his love for his heritage and home land is worn on his sleeve and in his heart, very similarly to what we have always felt and professed for Charleston.

Maybe that's what drew me to him in the first place. We began by sharing stories of our respective homes, customs, and landscape, and it soon became clear that each of us took pleasure in trying to convince the other that our home was the more beautiful, enchanting and worthy of recognition. I particularly revel is telling him stories about Remi as he currently has no canine friend with which to counter.

I find that I look for excuses to visit his ward and recognize that the time spent in conversation with him now represents the best part of each of my days. I am intrigued, captivated, and spell-bound with his stories and try to remember all the book titles he encourages me to read to help support his case that Texas is the only place in the world to live. Since I know this is very dangerous territory you must know why I can only share these thoughts with you. Can you imagine father's ideas on the subject? What would you do were you in my situation?

Well, there it is, probably more than you cared to read so I will end for now. Please write as soon as you receive this letter and continue to keep me, this ship, its dedicated servants and all the men and women serving our proud country in your thoughts and prayers for it is obvious that without divine intervention we may surely descend further into the hell which is war.

Give my love to all and take Remi for a long walk along Folly Beach or the Isle of Palms for me. How I wish you could capture and bottle the sweet smell of the salt marshes . . .

Your loving sister,
Jillian

I read the letter twice then laid it aside. The words affected me deeply, but I wasn't certain if it was because of the vividness of Jillian's description of human pain and emotion, or if I could actually imagine myself feeling and reacting the same way given the situation.

Either way, the impact was visceral. While curious about how Charlotte would respond, I wasn't certain I wanted to know anything more about the war and its wretchedness.

Carefully returning the first letter to the box, I remembered that both George and Matthew had urged me to read all of them so I opened the next yellowed envelope in the stack and extracted the second letter.

It was dated December 21, 1944.

> December 21, 1944
> Dearest Charlotte,
>
> I was thrilled to receive your letter dated November 2 and rushed to my bunk to read it. Everyone on the ship eagerly awaits mail call, and we all have come to respect the moments of privacy receiving a letter affords. Luckily, I had a break in my duties and didn't have to wait to open it.
>
> I wish we could have spent more time together when I was in Charleston some weeks ago, but actually, based upon our orders, I feel that I was lucky to have seen you at all. As I write now we are continuing on our way to yet another location.
>
> Your stories of home never cease to make me smile, and I reread each and every one of them several times trying to visualize myself there with you. I was particularly pleased with your news about President Roosevelt's Proclamation 2629. Several times I have tried to imagine the activities of Thursday, November 23 at the house, at St. Michaels, and within the city. Requesting that Americans observe a Day of National

Thanksgiving was a gesture of grace and reflection that I believe was both needed and welcomed throughout the nation.

Charlotte, I haven't had the chance to properly thank you for the kindness and wisdom you have shared with both Thomas and me over the past few weeks. Obviously, when I wrote to you earlier I was distraught, fearful, and confused. Your methodical, yet caring, analysis of our situation when we talked in Charleston did a great deal to help me think more clearly. I agree with your idea that we look upon the passage of time as more a friend than an enemy, and believe it is the right thing to do at the moment. Thomas is in the process of healing, and I am continuing my duties with a renewed spirit of dedication. Given the situation, I feel we both have been given a gift of time for reflection.

Always remember, dear sister, that nurturing relationships among family and friends is second only to the nurturing of our faith in God in significance. I trust that you continue to keep both close in your heart and paramount in your decisions as always.

I will keenly miss spending the holiday season with everyone at home but am more at peace with my mission than ever before. I am also able to see that there is much for me to do in my current role to celebrate and share the spirit that is Christmas.

Give my love to all, especially Remi. I do so miss his gentle nudging of my hand to prompt a daily walk. Is he doing that to you now? I miss him so. By the way when I talk about him with those aboard the ship and explain that he is a Boykin Spaniel and that his name is short for

Remington, I have to also share his picture and the history of the breed. It's just another way of fondly remembering home while attempting to encourage a smile from a wounded soldier.

I will close now by wishing you a blessed holiday with perfect weather for enjoying a glass or two of Pousse-Rapiere on the piazza before dinner. I will miss sitting down to the table to enjoy the cornbread and sausage stuffing as well as Mamie's famous fried-green tomato and shrimp salad.

By the way, will she still be able to make buttermilk ice cream to go with the sweet-potato pie this year? I guess I must be really hungry or maybe that's just homesickness talking. How I miss my Charleston and family . . .

Much love,
Jillian

As the ship continued in its contribution to the war effort, the letters to Charlotte from Jillian throughout the remainder of 1944 and into 1945 were equally as soulful. It became very clear that she was falling deeply in love with Thomas who offered her possibilities for a life she frankly had not considered and deep down inside wasn't certain she wanted. It was also clear that she had regained her strength of purpose and was more at peace with herself than ever before.

A gap in correspondence ensued between the sisters until after Jillian and Thomas married in 1950, and she moved to Eden Hill. One must assume that was because Jillian had returned from the war to her life in the Holy City. Only the diary entries might be able to piece together that time frame between her return to South Carolina and her departure for Texas and her life with Thomas.

The next cache of letters chronicled her arrival in Texas and were full of humor, excerpts of her missteps as a Texas rancher's wife, work on the house itself, and finally preparations for the open house in honor of Sweet Grass Memories July 4, 1951.

They were joyous and filled with exquisite details of the local culture and people who welcomed her to her new home. It seemed obvious that she was happy, learning how to balance her past and present lives, and was confident that her decision to follow Thomas had been the correct one.

In particular, a letter dated January 5, 1951, seemed to illustrate the pinnacle of her happiness:

> January 5, 1951
> Charlotte,
>
> Happy New Year to all! It seems that each time I write I choose to do so at a late hour, but that fact alone must convey that all of my days are full, and my happiness is assured.
>
> Lately, every day is a delightful adventure, and I cannot tell you how many times I have wished you were here to help me oversee and accomplish the tasks associated with the completion of our new home. The weather has finally begun to turn much cooler and, as a result, we are working furiously to complete the construction of Sweet Grass Memories as soon as possible but definitely before the first of June. We plan to introduce her to the community July 4 and there is still much to do between now and then.
>
> Because Thomas has encouraged me to do so, I have begun to think about what information I want to share regarding our Charleston heritage and customs with my newly found Texas family and friends at that event. I plan to introduce the house with stories about what some of the aspects of its design mean, but there is such a similarity between our two cultures with respect to love of

family and pride of our heritage that I am reticent to say a great deal for fear of offending anyone.

Certainly, I don't want to appear to suggest that our way of life at home is any better than what I find here. Balance is the key, I think, so I'm going to try to encourage Thomas to banter about with me about the aspects of the house that respect Texas tradition and design as well.

Quite honestly, I believe that God must surely have had a long-range plan when he united Thomas and me. Thomas has taken great pains to incorporate the best aspects of both Charleston and western architectural features in the design of the house, but we now realize that our real mission is to let the community know we believe that differences should be celebrated and embraced. We hope the house, in its uniqueness, will simply be a catalyst for that message.

Since I last wrote I have begun to volunteer a couple of days a week at a small hospital in the area. This helps me keep my skills sharpened and also gives me the opportunity to meet several people from the area other than the people who attend the churches we have visited.

Notice that I used the word "churches" in a plural form. Thomas was raised in one of the local Baptist churches, and the number of Episcopal churches in the area is very small. So we continue to talk about how to best worship as a couple and visit other denominations.

Clearly, the Eden family is well known and respected in the community and, as a result of our church visits and my volunteering effort I have subsequently been invited to events with other women in the area. I am learning a great deal!

As I typically do, I can see that I have written far too much, and thus, will bring this letter to a close. Before I do, however, I have a curious thing to ask of you. Recently, I had something happen that caused me to recall a conversation we had several years ago when we were both much younger and still dreaming about our futures.

If I remember correctly, we were wondering if either of us would ever live anywhere other than Charleston, and at some point in the conversation, you were very adamant that you wanted the two of us to agree that, if possible, our home on Legare would always remain in our family.

At the time, I found that a very curious thing to say, and when I asked you why it mattered, you simply said, "That's because it is what the house wants." Charlotte, please don't think me mad when I ask this next question but how did you know that was "what the house wanted?" Did you ever feel like you could "hear" its thoughts?

The reason I ask is that for some strange reason, I am beginning to feel that our new house is trying to communicate with me. It's probably just because I have invested so much of myself in it and want it to serve as a bridge from my past to present that I am thinking these crazy thoughts. Since you are much more intuitive than I, any thoughts on what you think this might mean would be helpful.

Oh, one more thing . . . I haven't made a big deal about it and don't know for certain so don't tell anyone else in the family *but*, I think I may be pregnant! Again, share my love with all.

Your loving sister,
Jillian

The remaining letters from Jillian to Charlotte occurred almost monthly between 1951 and 1953. They chronicled family, community, and world events and clearly illustrated the strength of the bond between the sisters. Jillian adjusted well and established herself as an integral part of the community. She and Thomas were more in love than ever and with the birth of Matthew in August of 1951 the family appeared well on its way to an idyllic life. As I did when reading the letters between Thomas and Jillian, I found myself pulled into their daily routines, their struggles and their moments of triumph and joy.

Chapter 41

When Hard Times Come

"Our vision is so limited we can hardly imagine a love that does not show itself in protection from suffering.... The love of God did not protect His own Son.... He will not necessarily protect us - not from anything it takes to make us like His Son. A lot of hammering and chiseling and purifying by fire will have to go into the process."

—Elisabeth Elliot

During the summer of 1952, the tenor of the letters changed. Both Jillian and Charlotte acknowledged with some trepidation the developing polio epidemic in the country. Their mounting fears darkly colored their written words, and as I read I became fearful, along with them, of what might be happening.

Jillian's letters to Charlotte detailed baby Matthew's illness, the ultimate diagnosis of polio and her helpless descent into despair. Excerpts from her letters shared the following . . .

We admitted over two hundred suspected cases of polio to our local hospital this last month and many of the victims are children. The symptoms appear the same as for any viral infection with headache, fever, nausea, and vomiting.

However, this virus appears much more contagious than the common cold. Kids of all ages, just like Matthew, first develop a sore throat and a fever and shortly thereafter their condition degenerates. Some even complain of a stiff neck or legs.

As parents, we are all questioning how we might have contributed to a child's contracting the disease, and as an epidemic of fear spreads, many of us keep our children at home in virtual isolation. Public parks, swimming pools, movie theatres, etc., have all been closed and both adults and children are terrified.

At the hospital, we provide patients with bed rest, plenty of fluids, a nutritious diet, pain medication, and continual monitoring for any signs of worsening conditions. Some larger hospitals in the area have portable ventilators to support breathing (we call them iron lungs) when the infection appears acute. Apparently, the virus attacks the body's nervous system and can paralyze the muscles used for breathing.

Because we still cannot pinpoint exactly how the disease is transmitted everyone is chilled to his or her marrow, and our treatment options cannot cope with the number of people we see each day. Matthew is young and his symptoms appear mild thus we believe because of our close observation and his isolation, we have caught his illness early enough to make a difference. He is being treated in a larger hospital in Dallas, and we will visit him daily there until we believe his disease can run its course. After just bringing him into the world I cannot imagine losing him to such a wretched disease.

The letters continued between Jillian and Charlotte but were fewer in number that the previous two years. Matthew did indeed improve, and while he had some residual effects of the viral infection that clearly had remained with him into adulthood, he survived. Unfortunately, the story took a decidedly different and unexpected turn for his mother, Jillian.

Jillian was relentless and fearless as she struggled to help those inflicted with the horrendous disease in her community. Once Matthew was admitted for extensive, quality care, she wrote passionately about her return to her local hospital to lend a hand.

Her letters continued to update Charlotte regarding the extent of the disease in Eden Hill as she explained the ways in which she and Thomas supported the local community in its time of need. They provided tangible support such as food and transportation for afflicted families as well as emotional support in the form of supportive notes, visits and even prayer breakfasts at their home. In essence both were dedicated caregivers.

Unfortunately, while an informed and giving individual, Jillian was also quite fragile and had spread herself too thinly. Contracting pneumonia, she was not able to recover and passed away in the summer of 1953.

Oddly enough, she must have realized her fate because before succumbing to the disease, she wrote a series of letters to Matthew chronicling her early life; her passionate love for the city of her birth and its history; her ardent love for his father; her surprise that she had come to love Texas and especially, Sweet Grass Memories, almost as much as Charleston; and finally she shared her dreams and aspirations for him and his future.

Knowing her fate, I found it extremely difficult to read the last letters in the stack that I had spread before me on the coverlet of the bed. Several times I actually stopped reading and simply lay quietly. At some point I heard a soft knock at my door. Glancing at the clock on the mantle I realized that I had been reading for over four hours, and it was close to time to go down for dinner.

The evening shadows were gliding across my room as I opened the door to Karen. When she saw my face, her expression changed immediately from a cheerful smile to concerned wariness. I have never been very adept at hiding my emotions, and my red nose, swollen eyes, and splotchy complexion communicated everything about my state of mind without an uttered word.

"Is it the letters?" she asked tentatively.

I nodded affirmatively and then quickly added, "I am such a sentimentalist and these last letters from Jillian to Matthew seem almost too private and raw for eyes other than theirs. I am humbled and actually embarrassed by what I am reading."

Karen was concerned but her expression was puzzled, "But Matthew encouraged you to read them, didn't he? He had to know what was in them and must have had a reason for wanting you to do so. Have you finished reading all of them? Have you found the connection between them and our current situation?"

"No, I still have one final letter from Jillian to Matthew to read, but I am almost dreading doing so." Changing the subject, I continued, "What should I do about dinner? Obviously, my emotional reaction to the letters is pretty obvious, and I don't know that I'm prepared to face either Charlotte or Matthew just yet."

"Well, my thoughts are that you'll have to face them at some point and I'm fairly certain that knowing the content of the letters they would expect your reaction to be what it is. Then there is the other matter about when we plan to go home and what we are planning to do with all of the information we have uncovered here."

Hearing Karen refer to the present, and our need to think about going home to address the issue that caused us to make this trip in the first place brought me out of my reverie. I couldn't hide in this room and muse about the past any longer—no matter how much I was pulled to do so. It was time to find out why Charlotte was so intent on me knowing about the past and also learn what Matthew had decided to do with the house and property.

"Okay, I'll dress quickly and meet you downstairs," I responded, "but I want to at least glance at the last letter before coming down so that I will have read everything before confronting either Matthew or Charlotte. I may be a little late. Please share that I would like all of you to go into dinner without me if I am not down by the time you are ready."

Karen smiled knowingly, and I felt the warmth of understanding only the relationship of a good friend provides. She responded softly, "Okay," and hesitating only a moment added, "I had a wonderful time today continuing to explore your city. I would love for Steve to see it. Maybe we could all four come back sometime?"

"I'd like that very much," I said as she stepped back into the hall and turned to go down the stairs. "See you in a bit."

Glancing back at the bed and my stack of letters I sighed heavily. Knowing I had limited time I crossed the room and picked up the last one. I was startled to notice that while I was able to recognize that the handwriting was definitely Jillian's, it appeared to be shaky and less flowing.

I don't know how much time passed. While my intent had been to simply scan the pages for clues to the story's ending, I ended up so caught up in what I could only assume were the last words of Jillian to her son that I read each page multiple times.

Here it was—the final piece in the puzzle. The piece that when you find it you feel both a sense of accomplishment, and also a slight sense of despair that the adventure is over.

I sat as if in a trance as I pondered the coincidences that had occurred over the past few months and what could/should occur. Suddenly an absurd idea crossed my mind, and I couldn't help but smile. Perhaps Jillian was still around and determined to impact the fate of Sweet Grass Memories. What if all the things I thought of as coincidences were simply steps she was directing to seal the fate of the house she loved.

I wondered if she could see me now, and if she felt any sense of peace that someone, a stranger who cared about the house, now knew its story. What were these thoughts? Was I losing my mind? I wondered.

I couldn't imagine what Matthew must have gone through reading the words of a mother he could not have known very well, and for the first time, I puzzled over how old he might have been when he first saw them. Even though I had not known her, the wretchedness I felt as I read her carefully selected and penned thoughts was almost overwhelming. Did he feel the same way?

"My dearest son, how I will miss being there to watch over you when you are in pain, when you are frustrated or frightened, and when you bubble over with happiness and glee. My only comfort is in knowing that you have a wise and loving father in Texas, as well as a loving and extended family in South Carolina to always guide you along life's path.

"I know the spot where I will lay to rest is in the low country and while it is not representative of your true home, it is mine, and I hope you will find it in yourself to respect my decision and visit often to listen to the wind and the water and talk with me.

"I have one final request, Matthew, and, this is not only the most difficult but also the most important one I leave for you and your father, as I believe it represents my legacy. I beg you to honor what I am about to ask as your father's grief will try to override what I want and loving him you will want to ignore my desires.

"I am certain that neither you nor your devoted father will be able to understand the request because neither of you have been touched by the Gullah influence that enveloped me as a child. I can only hope that in your love for me and your respect for my wishes you will strive to learn more about the mystery that brings me such peace and thus, be willing to honor the request. If you have any doubts please talk with George's mother, Indigo, as she, my true soul mate, can convey the significance.

"Since I am about to die and we will no longer be able to live as a family in our special place, Sweet Grass Memories, I want you to leave it as it is. I have already shared this with your father, but I am not sure he is committed to doing so.

"As you grow, please visit it from time to time, embrace its magic and listen for its words *but* under no circumstances sell it or tear it down. Trust me that someday someone will come along and fulfill the destiny that I believe is inherent in its creation and that is to participate in the growth and development of children and families who are desperately striving to be all that they can be.

"I cannot provide you with the exact date and time this will occur, but I believe with all my heart and soul that Charlotte and my Gullah family will know."

As I read and reread each page, I realized why everyone had been so intent on me reading all the letters. How many years had passed since Jillian had written these words, almost sixty? Sixty years is a terribly long time for Matthew and Thomas to wait for resolution of Jillian's request.

Their pain must have been unfathomable. I now understood Matthew's impatience and bitterness. The house had been like an albatross around his neck.

Chapter 42

Knowing All the Facts Doesn't Necessarily Make Things Easier

"To state the facts frankly is not to despair the future nor indict the past. The prudent heir takes careful inventory of his legacies and gives a faithful accounting to those whom he owes an obligation of trust."

—John F. Kennedy

I made my way quietly down the two sets of stairs to the first floor, although I'm not certain why I took such great pains to be silent. It wasn't as if it was late and others were sleeping. Perhaps, it was a feeble attempt to demonstrate some form of respect for the incredible story I now knew.

Voices drifted from the piazza into the foyer. Karen was sharing an amusing story about her day's activities. Pushing open the screened door I called out "hello" so as not to startle anyone.

Matthew stood and approached me as I stepped out into the heavy, fragrant night air. I was grateful for the gift of darkness since a reapplication of make-up had done little to mask my still splotchy complexion. I also had to resort to wearing glasses since my swollen eyes would not accept contacts.

Not knowing how or where to begin I was relieved when Charlotte asked if I would like her to go into the kitchen and retrieve the plate that had been prepared for me earlier in the evening. It was as if she sensed my need for a moment of transition before gathering my thoughts and attempting to speak.

"Oh no, thank you, Charlotte, actually I am not very hungry."

The quiet of the moment approached intolerability as Matthew guided me to my favorite spot on the settee. "Are you okay, Jamie?"

"Yes, I am fine, thank you for asking," I replied quietly. Then taking a deep breath directed my next comments to everyone on the piazza, "I am sorry to have missed dinner, but as you have all probably surmised, I spent the last hours reading Jillian's letters. I hardly know what to say at this point but while clearly overwhelmed I want to share that I am also deeply humbled by your trust in me to read something as private as the words in Jillian's letters and simultaneously attempt to interpret their applicability to today's situation."

When no one responded, I continued, "After nearly sixty years, I sense that at least some of you believe I am the one: the one Jillian references in her last letter and the one who is supposed to help the house fulfill its destiny."

I let the words settle among us before continuing, "I feel a great personal responsibility to make everything right. Right for the kids, for you as a family, for Jillian and yes, even for the house. I know that Karen and I should return to Texas as soon as possible since we all have lives to resume. Equally as important, we owe those who await our return and believe we have their best interests at heart some sort of closure. But now that I know so much more than before, instead of this situation being easier it has become much more difficult."

When no one spoke up, I gazed out into the garden and continued thinking aloud, "I actually don't know what I expected the results of this visit would be. At one point I thought we might be able to convince Matthew to sell the property to an organization that would build a community center for the kids of Oak Lakes as well as those who live in other apartment complexes in the area. But that would have meant tearing the house down, and doing so is unacceptable to me on so many levels, not the least of which is the fact that the kids would not approve.

"Now that I have come here as your guest and read the letters, I realize that neither Charlotte nor Jillian would have endorsed that option. Finally, if that was the outcome, there would be no way to know if Reid and I would continue to have any further contact with the kids, and that isn't what I want either.

"Secondly, knowing that none of us who are closest to the situation and the children could afford to purchase, let alone renovate, the property to make our dreams a reality, I pondered whether or not we could attract enough serious investors to make it happen. But even I know that this approach, iffy at best, would require more time, expertise and money than we have, and since there is already an offer on the table for the property I cannot imagine Matthew being amenable to such a suggestion."

My words drifted off into the night air and still no one said anything. It was when I despaired that I had obviously missed something significant or lost the possibility of any sort of solution that Matthew responded, "Let's regroup tomorrow. Perhaps it is finally time for me to seriously consider what is written in mother's letters. Until now I never thought of her comments as anything but absurd, yet ironically I never could bring myself to follow-through with any prior sale of the property either."

No one commented regarding Matthew's reference to his mother's letters, and I was uneasy. Did he truly believe Jillian's words so many years prior were germane to the current situation or was he simply humoring Charlotte one last time?

I wanted the kids to have a place to learn and grow, I wanted to save "their house," and yes, I could finally admit I wanted to be part of the process. But, was I really the link between the past and future that Jillian had referenced.

Chapter 43

Retracing Steps

"Again, you cannot connect the dots looking forward; you can only connect them looking backward. So you have to trust that the dots will somehow connect in your future. You have to trust in something – your gut, destiny, life, karma whatever. This approach has never let me down, and it has made all the difference in my life.

—Steve Jobs

Market Hall

Unsettled and desperately in need of sleep, I was relieved by Matthew's suggestion. Morning wasn't that far away and waiting might actually result in clearer thinking for us all. There might still be time to draft some sort of plan we all could buy into allowing Karen and I to get home to Texas in a day or two.

Just as I had done Sunday with Monday morning's light, I arose early and went out into the streets of the city. Realizing this could be our last day here and that I had yet to spend any significant time outside the house, I wanted a few minutes alone with my city.

I have never been able to explain the pull of this place on my soul. From the first day I arrived for college in 1968 until now, the sensation has been the same. Maybe this is why I have loved Pat Conroy's books. His words have always been able to create vivid pictures in my mind's eye that represent exactly what I feel about the low country in general and, Charleston, in particular.

One of my favorites of his quotes, *"Walking in the streets of Charleston in late afternoons of August was like walking through gauze or inhaling damaged silk"* floated across my mind as I, already perspiring, walked past the colorful homes with fragrant gardens and inhaled the sweet scent of the Noisette rose shrubs which bloom profusely in spring and summer.

Just like everything else in Charleston, the Noisette roses have a rich history. Most any reference to the flower will point out that the Noisette brothers, one in Paris and one in Charleston, were the nurserymen responsible for bringing the flower to the United States in the early 1800s. Philippe received an "Old Blush" China rose from his brother, Louis in Paris and eventually gave the plant to his neighbor, John Champney. On John's farm the "Old Blush" crossed with the white musk rose. The hybrid became popular and remains throughout the city to this day.

I uttered a small prayer asking God for the grace to accept whatever decisions were made today concerning Sweet Grass Memories. Musing about the looming decisions and reflecting upon the events and people of the past three days I felt the urge to visit the old Marketplace.

It was a Monday morning so things would be bustling, and I wanted to hear and feel the vibrant spirit of this low country icon before going home. I walked north to Broad Street and turned left toward Meeting.

The city was lazy in the morning's sweltering grasp, and traffic so light that I was able to concentrate on the historic landmarks I remembered from my college days rather than worrying about where I walked.

I hurried past the majestic Market Hall that houses the Daughters of the Confederacy Museum to the vendor area that stretches from Meeting to East Bay Street. As I came closer, I realized it didn't look the same as I remembered. It was cleaner, brighter, and more tourist friendly. I don't know why, but I was disappointed. What is it that causes us to expect some things to stay the same even as we accept that others change?

Swallowing my dismay, I aimlessly roamed through the open-aired buildings and, much to my surprise, began to marvel at the variety of vendors and offerings. There were still low country natives offering candied pecans, benne wafers, and other local, tasty delicacies. Even the street artists had managed to maintain prominent locations to display their colorful watercolor prints of the city and the sea. But in addition, there were now enclosed art galleries, local jewelry shops, leather and woodwork displays, and even a Christmas store.

I didn't have to search for long before I came upon a few sweet grass artists. While scattered among the various stalls, rather that seated all together as I remembered in years past, I sensed the same contentment in each of their beautiful faces and felt the same joy I had experienced that first August afternoon so many years ago.

"Some things just don't change now do they, Ms. Jamie?"

Startled, I turned to see George standing just behind me. "George, what are you doing here? How did you know where I was?"

Before he had time to respond, I quickly continued, "Oh no, is someone looking for me? I should have left note, I didn't think . . ."

My voice trailed off as he assured me, "Now, calm down, Ms. Jamie, everything is fine. I don't believe anyone is looking for you, at least no one has contacted me 'bout where you might be, and as to why I am here, well, occasionally when Ms. Charlotte don't need me I come by to catch up with friends from the outer islands, visit the old horses and drivers, and partake of some benne wafers. Actually maybe the more interesting question is why are you here?" He smiled timidly.

"Well, I went out for a while this morning just like yesterday, but when I realized, we might be leaving soon, I decided to come back down here and absorb the spirit of the market one more time."

I stood for a moment gazing into his kindly face when the frustration and fear I had successfully held just at bay since the weekend began to bubble over, "I thought my life was going along fairly well in Texas, but why all of a sudden did I meet these kids and get caught up in the spell of Sweet Grass Memories?"

"I'm too old for this, George!"

My annoyance and anxiety continued to erupt in words, "And what is it about this place anyway? Why do I feel a need to continue to come back? It isn't my home any longer, and it's not like I know anyone here. Yet standing right here, right now fills an abyss in my soul. It's almost as if I am addicted to each and every nuance the city exudes. I feel such peace when I am here, but at the same time that feeling is almost suffocating." My voice trailed off.

He stared at me for a while with knowing eyes, then smiled and said, "Ms. Jamie, with your permission I'd like to take you to visit with someone who might just be able to 'splain everything."

I glanced down at my gym shorts, t-shirt and tennis shoes. Embarrassed and self-conscious about my appearance, as well as worried about what everyone at the Legare House might be thinking about my abrupt departure and prolonged absence, I was about to decline.

Sensing my reluctance George added, "I'll call Ms. Charlotte and let her know you are with me and, by the way, just to let you know murruh don't judge nobody by their clothes, she just listens to the music of they soul."

Chapter 44

Indigo and Jilo Circa the 1950s

"Some white people hate black people, and some white people love black people, some black people hate white people, and some black people love white people. So you see it's not an issue of black and white, it's an issue of Lovers and Haters'"

—Eden Ahbe

The morning was spectacular, and the Ashley River particularly fragrant, as we started across the bridge to James Island. I asked George to turn off the air-conditioning in the car, and I lowered my window to let the scented breeze blow across my face.

I was enjoying the moment when I remembered Saturday's conversation on the piazza, "I thought your family lived in Mt. Pleasant, George. Why are we heading across the Ashley?"

"My sister lives in Mt. Pleasant, Ms. Jamie, but murruh has never left Jim Isle even though the big, gated resorts and subdevelopments just keep on risin' up. She live out near Wappoo Creek. We figure someday she may have to leave, but right now, she hangin' on to the old place.

"Do you know much 'bout dis island, Ms. Jamie? Been in the news 'round here a lot the last few years since the town of James Island been fightin' the city of Chaa'stun to become incorporated. Took four tries but eventually Jim Isle won. Lot's of history here too . . . the first shot of dey Civil War was fired at Fort Sumter just off dey island's eastern tip, and it's been said that there was almost twenty plantations that worked slaves way back when. Even Samuel Smalls, the man who the opera *Porgy and Bess* is based, is buried in the cemetery beside the Presbyterian Church."

Actually, I didn't know much about the history or current events of any of the outer islands because while it seemed so much apart of my soul, other than the occasional Dorthea Benton Frank, Anne Rivers Siddons or Karen White novels I rarely read about Charleston any more. When I moved to Texas, I immersed myself in my work and never looked back, at least until now.

The truly remarkable part of all this is that since I've been in Texas over half my life both places pull at my psyche equally, and I wondered if this was similar to what Jillian experienced when she moved from the Palmetto state to the Lone Star state.

"Tell me about your mother, George. Will she be okay with you bringing a stranger to her house, especially an unannounced one?"

While he focused on the road, never glancing over at me, I could still see the smile form on his face. "She is a special lady, Ms. Jamie, she really is. You probably didn't know that my Grumma,

Beatrice, cooked for the Blessing family for many years and would take my Murruh to work with her when she weren't in school. My Murruh played with Ms. Jillian and Ms. Charlotte. But it was Ms. Jillian that she cottoned to."

"Your mama knew Ms. Jillian? Did they grow up together?"

"Yes 'um they did, and it was almost like they was one person sometimes. Grumma tells stories about how they used to finish one another's sentences and know if they other was sick. Sometimes momma, Ms. Blessing, would allow Ms. Jillian to go down to the Market with Murruh and Grumma to shop."

"Ms. Charlotte never wanted to go, but Ms. Jillian longed to see everything part of the city. Them were real special days. Murruh and Jillian would walk around the stalls seein' and talkin' to all the folks while Grumma would pick out the fresh fruit and vegetables for they meals."

"Murruh told me that the best thing was tastin' everything that was there. I think grumma would have been upset had she knowed her old friends was slippin' the girls everything from candied pecans and benne wafers to slices of peaches and watermelon. But it was them juicy chunks of pineapple that become Ms. Jillian's favorite."

"Murruh recalled when she first tasted of them. It was one hot August day while Grumma was concentratin' on getting the best price for a cantaloupe. The girls snuck off to another fruit stand and Grumma caught them all sticky and giggling as they tried to stuff chunks of pineapple in they mouths before Grumma could find them."

"From that day on, Grumma always took a pineapple home every time they visited the market. Everyone knowed that they pineapple was just for Ms. Jillian, especially after she learned 'bout its old legend. She'd tell Murruh, 'My house gonna always have pineapples in it, I promise!'"

Now some of the references to the Gullah people in Jillian's last letter to Matthew made sense.

George got quiet as we turned off Folly Road onto the Maybank Highway. Shortly he slowed and turned down a narrow, unmarked, sand and gravel mix road. "Murruh likes her privacy and still lives on the creek. Subdivisions all 'round but the developers know there won't be no sale of this property until she's gone. Besides, Murruh knows people at the Penn Center on St. Helena so our family gonna do all right."

I wasn't familiar with the role of the Penn Center in local issues so I kept quiet.

We bumped slowly along amid thick brush and tall, spindly trees with low hanging Spanish moss until we came to a broad clearing not far from the creek's edge. The quiet of the marsh, as well as its oppressive humidity, settled over us.

I caught a whiff of decomposed detritus that is characteristic of the area and promptly forget everything else. My earlier frustrations quietly retreated into the recesses of my memories.

I breathed in deeply and could see a classic low country house in the distance. It rested on red brick pilings and had a weathered tin roof and peeling wooden siding. Simple in its design, it oozed peace, tranquility, and contentment. A front porch with a few wicker chairs and a worn, woven grass rug greeted us as George stopped the car at the steps and turned off the engine. I felt as if someone had slipped me a tranquilizer and wasn't sure I could open the car door and move forward.

Ms. Indigo's Cottage

I followed his lead as George emerged from the car. I opened the passenger side door and heard him call out, "Murrah, it's George, just come by to let you seddown with one of Ms. Jillian's fr'en'."

Hearing the reference to Jillian, I shot George a look of incredulousness over the top of the car. What was he doing? I wasn't a friend of Jillian's! I never knew her. She lived decades before me...

We stood by the car doors for what seemed like an eternity, and I wondered why George hesitated to walk up to the porch. This was his childhood home, I reasoned, so why did he hang back?

After a while, a colorfully adorned figure appeared behind the screened door. "George? My, my I didn't 'spect to see you this mornin', but eb'nso I am t'engkful that the Mastuh brought you to me 'round sunhigh! Bring dat gal up on dis do'step. I bin waitin' a long time for dis' day."

George looked over at me and motioned toward the steps. Smiling he said, "It's time, Ms. Jamie, are you ready?"

"Ready for what, George? What is going on?"

Smiling he said, "Ms. Jillian's message, Ms. Jamie, my Murruh know it by heart."

While not my intention, I realized then that I was drawn to this house, this place even more than the city of Charleston itself. The pull was without sensibility and very strong, and somehow, I knew in my heart that what I was about to hear would complement the letters and provide the last piece of the puzzle that would finally reveal why I was here; why the house had found me.

It had never occurred to me that I would meet someone, other than Jillian's family, who had known her. While I had found George to be a mysterious player in this story from that first day during our drive from the airport, I had always felt his presence, while overwhelmingly comforting and never sinister, was somewhat secondary. Nevertheless, I couldn't quite figure out why I had never doubted that he knew more than he let on. His appearance at the most unexpected times was definitely eerie, but yet it was those visits that reassured me somehow.

I walked up the steps to the porch and raised my eyes to a face of pure serenity. Its overall appearance exuded mystery, but it was also layered with kindness like soft icing that has been lovingly applied to a recently baked cake. I studied her and tried not to appear too inquisitive.

Somehow I knew that she was an integral piece of this puzzle and had waited a very long time, just like Charlotte, Thomas, and Matthew to finally bring the story of Sweet Grass Memories to the conclusion Jillian needed to enable eternal rest. Before she even acknowledged me I sensed that this radiant and knowing Gullah lady would touch my soul.

George introduced us telling me that his mother, Indigo, had been named for one of the cash crops of South Carolina's low country past. She smiled patiently as he shared his obvious pride in her and her life.

Indigo, I recalled, was the name Jillian used when identifying her soul mate for Matthew. As George continued to tell me about his mother, I sensed that she was a content woman full of earned wisdom in her advanced age. Her exotic dress, calming presence and spiritual aura made me think that she probably owed as much or more of her commanding presence to her African roots rather than her American. I yearned to know as much as she did and wondered if, even as a child, Jillian ever felt the same.

Chapter 45

Another Porch . . . Another Conversation

"God will not permit any troubles to come upon us, unless he has a specific plan by which great blessing can come out of the difficulty."

—Peter Marshall

Indigo motioned for me to sit in one of the wicker chairs beside the rocker she had settled into just to the left of the front door. She adjusted a cushion or two and without looking up said, "George, go een and git us some of the sweet'n tea I jis mak."

As George walked away, her eyes fell on me, and with a soft, knowing smile she invited me to bear my soul, "I got all teday, chil', and my h'aa't has longed ta hear yo story 'cross many years," she quietly said.

I was hard-pressed to explain how I could understand her message without truly knowing the Gullah dialect. But I began once again to tell the story slowly at first, and then without ceasing. I went all the way back to the beginning explaining how lost I had felt after retiring. I described as many of the kids as I could for Indigo.

This time my words were more fervent than the day before when I had sat on the Legare piazza with Matthew and Charlotte. My aching heart was more in control and if asked today to explain why that occurred, I could not.

She sat quietly, nodded occasionally, and smiled often, especially when I shared stories about Amber, Justine and Sam. I even thought I saw the shimmer of a tear or two running down her soft cheeks when I described both my conversation with Jimar that cold November evening and the still raw pain of knowing we would lose contact with Abeo.

But it was when I talked about the house, and how I thought I could read its thoughts that her demeanor shifted. Though she lay back against the old cushions of the rocker, closed her eyes and began to nod she seemed to intently focus on my words. When I stopped talking, thinking she might have fallen asleep, she vigorously motioned for me to continue. I glanced over at George, who had long before rejoined us with the tea, and held up my hands as if seeking his guidance. He nodded affirmatively that I should go on.

"I think I'm supposed to do something for both the house and kids, Ms. Indigo, but I don't know why or what that is. I want to help them achieve a better life but making occasional appearances in their lives is not the answer. They need consistency, mentoring and love," I whispered, my voice losing its ability to project.

As for the house, I can't stand to see it continue to further decay day after day. I don't have the money to pay Matthew what it is worth, but I can't seem to just walk away from it either. I have been astounded by the string of coincidences that continues to thread all of the puzzle pieces together, but I always come back to the same two nagging questions, "Why me, and what am I supposed to do with what I know?" I stopped talking and swallowed a sip of tea. It was cool with just a hint of lime that soothed my throat.

Indigo opened her eyes and glanced over at me. "Which que-schun you t'ink moris impo'tant, chil'?"

Without much thought, I knew immediately the one that bothered me the most so I answered her straightaway, "It's the 'Why me' question."

"Yaas, yaas . . . Do you believe Gawd lubs an' bress all 'he chils'?"

"Yes, ma'am I do," I stammered.

She closed her eyes once again and began to rock slowly back and forth causing the floorboards of the ancient porch just beneath us to creak and groan rhythmically. A gentle breeze encouraged the Spanish moss dangling from the stately live oak just to the left of the porch to sway back and forth.

I was hungry to hear her response, but if I had learned anything at all these past few months it was the gift of patience so I waited. Sitting there, with only my own thoughts as a companion, I willed my mind to focus on the sound and smell of the breeze as it rustled the tree leaves and branches. I marveled that the Gullah people seemed instinctively able to appreciate the significance of using all of their senses to perceive a situation. I tried to do likewise.

A cloud moved over the sun. Ms. Indigo leaned forward, took both of my hands, and wrapped all ten of her long, delicate fingers around them up to my wrists.

As she did so, she shared a message I was never to forget. "You paa't of a plan, chil, and the plan be big, tetch many and be 'round for a long time."

"I see it first when Ms. Jilo move to Texas, but it be fuzzy. Then when Mr. Matthew took sick it come agin in a dream, and this time I could see 'e bettuh. Finally, when Ms. Jilo pass'um, I see her house huggin some chilun and a lady. The lady, though, 'e be somehow know'um to me."

"Ms. Jilo, b'fo' 'e pass'um, write and ax'me to pray haa'd for an ansuh. 'E knew 'e was gonna die, but the house be talkin to her too, and 'e duh not want to die. It wantuh be a place Ms. Jilo's spirit live on. Ms. Jilo, she see the vision, but 'e mek me prommus to mek sure I see it too so that I could keep prayin hard Mr. Matthew 'e would someday understand."

"George, 'e take me to speak with Ms. Jilo a week or so ago. 'e knew una was comin, chil, and ax'me to see una to 'splain. Ms. Jilo say that the chillun and the house need each other, and una chil, una need dem too. Dis is de Mastuh's plan. Una be 'e cyaa'pentuh. Mr. Matthew, 'e finally know'um dat too. 'E take a long while, but 'e now understand."

I sat there trying to digest what I had just heard. If I interpreted the Gullah language Indigo was using correctly she was saying that God loves and blesses all his children. She also told me that I was part of a plan, and that the plan was big, would touch many, and be around for a long time.

She shared that she had first seen the plan when Jillian (Jilo) moved to Texas, but it wasn't clear. She saw it again when Matthew became ill and finally when Jillian passed away. She said that when Jillian passed away she saw a house, ostensibly, Sweet Grass Memories, hugging children and a grown lady. The lady, she implied, was some-one known to her family from the past.

She also related that Jillian, before she died, wrote to Indigo and asked her to pray hard for an answer about what should happen next. Apparently the house had communicated with Ms. Jillian that it did not want to die and wanted to be the place where Ms. Jillian's leg-acy lived on. Indigo was asked to keep praying that Matthew would somehow, someday understand.

Finally, more recently, George was enlisted to take Indigo to Jillian's grave to hear an urgent message. Jillian seemed to know that the time for resolution was near. She knew I was coming to South Carolina and wanted to make certain Indigo had an opportunity to fill in all of the blanks in the story for me. The message was that the children of Eden Hill and I needed one another. It is part of the Master's plan for me to become a carpenter. She said that Matthew now knows all of this as well.

While her eyes were still closed, Indigo had stopped the gentle rocking. Tentatively I asked, "Ms. Indigo, I still have a question."

"Yaas, chil?"

"Do you have any idea why I seemed familiar to you?"

Opening her eyes, she studied my face a while before smiling and answering, "Yaas, 'em I duh," she twinkled. "Attuhw'ile I pull it all tuhgedduh. When you ax' George 'bout the pineapple murruh made, I knowed."

"Eb'n though una not bawn n Chaa'stun, chil, yo soul rests yuh, jis like Ms. Jilo's. My Murruh, Beatrice, sensed dat and knew we all meet again someday when 'e see una so many years ago down at de market."

"Una see, I give Ms. Jilo an' Mr. Thomas dat pineapple dat you puzzled 'bout so long go when una first come to Chaa'stun as a wed'n' gift. Ms. Charlotte brought 'e home to me when 'e pass'um. I decided dat 'e b'long with the fambly but dey want us to keep 'e. Somehow then I know'um 'e needed to 'ay wid George. Noe I know dat was becus una would come home and see it."

I wasn't sure there was anything more to say since we'd stayed so long into the afternoon, and she appeared tired. Could it really be true that there was a connection between my life as a college student in Charleston in the late 1960s and this unfolding story today? Did I now have the answer to my connection to the house that I had so longed to discover?

As overwhelming as what I had just heard was, I somehow sensed that Ms. Indigo was not quite finished with me. As the mid-day brightness gave way to afternoon clouds she continued speaking.

Her final words, however, seemed more as a life lesson for all of us rather than just a message for me. It was her reference to God's plan that said it all.

"Ms. Jilo, 'e an I both knowed 'e be dainjus for her to leave the low country eb'nso 'e love dat boy so fierce her h'aa't was already gone'way. Our eyes tell each other the truth, but we 'gree to never speak of 'e."

"My'own h'aa't be hebby ever since I leggo my tittuh . . . but 'e was Gawd's plan for her and now tis your paa't to trabble. De ribbuh flows on and 'e is at peace. I sattify my part of the plan and was true to my tittuh and my Gawd. Noe, I can go home too." She closed her eyes again and began to hum quietly. Much more weary than when we had arrived earlier in the day it was obvious that our conversation had drained her.

I sat there as if in a trance, and could only watch as George smiled, lifted his mother off her feet with a powerful hug, and gently walked her into the house. I wanted to say something, maybe thank her, express how deeply her story had affected me, anything, but I didn't know how or even if I should.

After a while, when George didn't return, I made my way down to the banks of the creek. The fishermen were coming in. Odd, I thought, it seemed so early and yet the sun was dipping close to the horizon, and the tide was rising. I plodded along the water's edge as a few fiddler crabs scurried into the marsh grasses. The myriad of bird species nesting in the area noisily squabbled with one another.

It struck me as ironic that while I had just experienced the closure of one life story simultaneously the marsh was experiencing a continuation and rebirth. Then again perhaps that was what was happening with me as well. I looked up at a dazzling cerulean sky and thanked God for his infinite wisdom and love.

Eventually, I made my way back to the house. Through the tall grasses, I could see George sitting alone on the front steps. I was surprised to realize that I neither worried about having been gone too long, nor causing him unnecessary stress.

I also wasn't concerned about the fact that we had been away all day. Maybe I was closer to understanding the Gullah perspective on life than I realized. I closed my eyes and breathed my first calming breath in a very long time. This gentle culture had taught me many things.

When I rounded the corner by the house he stood up, and we walked back to the car together without speaking. It wasn't until we neared the city that he finally broke the silence. "Thank you, Ms. Jamie. You brought murruh full circle today and ensured her peace."

"Is she okay, George?" I ventured, "I have been so worried and wanted to let her know how much she meant to me, but I didn't know what to do or say or how to share my feelings. She seemed so frail and sad."

Much to my astonishment, he threw his head back and laughed uproariously. "Oh, Ms. Jamie, just when I dink you may be part Gullah after all, you come back Buckruh."

I didn't know whether to be flattered or offended, "What is Buckruh, George?"

"White, Ms. Jamie, it's a white person's way of thinkin." He smiled.

"Okay, I get the meaning of the word, but how does what I just ask you make me 'white'?" I puzzled.

His response softened as he continued, "I'm not certain you truly understand what's happened today, Ms. Jamie, but that's okay, because if I was you and had been raised only Buckruh, I wouldn't either. You represent somethin, I ain't never seen before, and I'm not sure anyone who don't know about the Gullah people or wasn't on murruh's porch today could understand."

"Murruh says you been chosen, and because you listened and didn't ignore the call there's a lot more that's gonna be axed of you. We, as a Gullah people, are only your messengers but we understand what has happened. Gawd now done sent you a job to do; one Ms. Jillian set in motion years ago and, while we don't, Buckruh people may sees you 'as touched' if you share what you've learned."

"Well, that's just great," I mumbled, remembering, I had a lot of people to whom I owed an explanation of this whole story. "You mean they may say, Well 'bless her heart' behind my back?"

Puzzled he looked over at me and said, "I'm sorry, what'd you say?"

When I added, "Oh never mind, I was just talking to myself," he gently continued. "Well, it gonna be up to you, but sometimes I have found the less we say the better."

Traffic had picked up, and as we crawled along, we had time to talk about many of the events of the past days.

"Ms. Jamie, to answer your queschen, murruh is doin good and 'cause of you, she be finally at peace. Along the years sometimes her faith would wobble and she bin worryin' for a long time dat 'e would pass on before 'e could keep her promuss to Ms. Jillian. Teday was what she bin waitin' for and you mek dat happen."

"No, George, actually, I think you did. Have you known the whole story all along?"

He grinned once again. "Yaa, pretty much, but I really didn't b'leew 'e 'til I see you at the airport. I'm 'barassed to say I doubted my murruh. Just didn't seem possible in teday's world . . . but there was sump'n 'bout you, Ms. Jamie, sump'n dat mek me feel de story was true."

As I listened, I realized that since we had visited his mama George had drifted back into the Gullah dialect, ever so slightly mixing the words from both of his worlds. We were a couple of streets away from Legare when I finally brought up my lie.

"One more thing, George, you couldn't have known anything about my college days at the College of Charleston when you told us about your niece's experiences at the Medical University that afternoon on the piazza so why bring it up?"

Again, I caught him in a smile, "I was fishin. While I knew you had a role to play in 'dis story I still weren't convinced it could be as positubble and powerful as murrah and grumma b'leew. I think even Ms. Charlotte had her doubts even though 'e, of all folks, wanted to believe so much in you and de possibilities. Me, well, I was just tryin to figure out how you felt about black people even then and what you might have been willin to do."

"So were you disappointed in my answer? Did you know I was lying?"

Almost back to the gate on Legare, he pulled over and stopped the car. Turning to face me he said, "Yaa, I was disappointed in your answer and well, okay, I hoped you had lied. But then I decided you was scared and didn't know how any of us would react. I reckoned I'd figure out who you really was another way and, as it turns out today I think I did."

"You are one smart cookie, Mr. George. Yes, you are," was all I said as I exited the car and prepared to face Karen and the Blessing family.

"Call me if you need me, Ms. Jamie," he responded and drove away to enter the property through another entrance.

Chapter 46

Where is Home Anyway?

> "I have learned that if you must leave a place that you have lived in and loved and where all your yesteryears are buried deep, leave it any way except a slow way, leave it the fastest way you can. Never turn back and never believe that an hour you remember is a better hour because it is dead. Passed years seem safe ones, vanquished ones, while the future lives in a cloud, formidable from a distance."

> —Beryl Markham, *West with the Night*

I walked through the garden door, along the now familiar pathway and up the piazza steps. The house was silent as I opened the screen and entered the coolness of the polished foyer. "Hello?" I called out, but no one responded.

It was early evening prior to dinner, so I really didn't expect anyone to be downstairs. I hurried up the steps to the third floor and knocked on Karen's door. My old apprehensions, those that had momentarily dissipated out by Wappoo Creek, suddenly resurfaced, and I was relieved when she opened the door offering a caring smile.

She broke the tension of the moment with "I'll bet you've had an interesting day!"

I asked if I might come in and she hugged me in response. Without waiting for further comment I crossed the door's threshold and retreated to her bedroom window. While gazing out into the now familiar, tranquil garden I began to share the events of the last few hours before she had a chance to decline the offer to listen.

I left nothing out hoping that I would be able to gauge the over-all response of those I would speak with at home by Karen's reaction. She stood beside me most of the time I rambled on but then, close to the end, when I shared the details of my walk along the creek she sat down near the fireplace and looked away from my face.

When I finally finished, she spoke softly but with courage and resolve, "I never expected anything like this, Jamie . . . I mean anything this far-fetched and supernatural. I'm sorry but I have to ask. Do you believe it? Truly? I mean this place is enchanting, and one can get caught up in the history and the mystery of its streets, alleys, cemeteries and culture. But do you really think that God, or Jillian, through God, is directing the course of events for the house, the kids, even you?"

I didn't need to think about my response. "Yes," I commented firmly, "I do, because I am finally at peace after all these months of turmoil. I can even say that I am comfortable relying on Matthew to determine the fate of the house and its potential impact on all of us."

I thought I caught a glimpse of support, even admiration in her eyes, and I knew it was time to go home, home to Texas. Our journey to Charleston was at an end, and there was work to be done more than a thousand miles away with Sweet Grass Memories and the beautiful children of Eden Hill.

I yearned to see and hug, not only the kids, but also Reid, my Scotties, Ms. G. and Ms. Tracy. I also longed to be back in the midst of the spirit that was Texas. It had been there all along; the realization that Texas was now my home. I just needed Charleston to remind me there can be more than one place in this world that brings peace to one's soul.

Coming back to reality, I commented. "I haven't eaten today and am looking forward to dinner. What kind of reception do you think I will receive?"

Karen smiled and said, "Well, since you are the one with the intuitive Gullah characteristics, I figured you would already know, but FYI, actually, for the first time, what I heard and saw today may indicate that Charlotte and Matthew are on the same page."

Chapter 47

Home Is Where the Love Is

"Home wasn't a set house, or a single town
on a map. It was wherever the people who loved
you were, whenever you were together. Not a
place, but a moment, and then another, building
on each other like bricks to create a solid shelter
that you take with you for your entire life, wherever you may go."

—Sarah Dessen, *What Happened to Goodbye*

Karen was right. When I came down the stairs to dinner that evening, it was as if everyone had been brought into the inner circle.
Both Charlotte and Matthew were aware that I had spent the better
part of the day on James Island with Ms. Indigo and George, and
neither seemed to need an explanation of what I had learned while
there. Conversation at dinner was decidedly off the subject, and our
time together that hour was casual, relaxed and friendly.

When Charlotte requested coffee, dessert, and/or after dinner
drinks be served on the piazza I knew a decision was imminent. To
steel myself I requested a glass of wine. Matthew smiled and ordered
a brandy. Neither of us requested dessert.

We walked into the night air together, and I felt no apprehension. What would be would be. When everyone was settled in his or
her favorite place on the piazza for what might be the final time, I
looked up to catch a glimpse of George standing in the garden.

Matthew, seeing him as well, smiled warmly and motioned that he join us on the piazza. Assuming a place just behind Ms. Charlotte's rocker George nodded to me as Matthew began to speak.

"It's time I finally speak candidly about my mother's wishes for Sweet Grass Memories and my repeated efforts to sabotage her request. Interestingly enough it is also worthy of note that my mother has apparently selected the audience to hear my final comments. I find this to be a perfect example of poetic justice, and from what others have told me quite representative of her unique sense of humor."

"Years ago, when I first read her letters I was extremely angry and particularly childish in my responses. Not only was I devastated by her death and what I believed, at the time, to be my father's abandonment, but I also felt it ludicrous that she had requested, and my father had agreed, that I, as the sole heir to the property be bound by the directive that it be maintained as is until someone came along and agreed to develop the current house as a place for children to learn and grow."

"After father's death, I repeatedly ignored her wishes and put the house up for sale multiple times. While every sale appeared promising at first to either the broker, sales representative, potential buyer, or yes, even me, for various reasons none of them ever materialized and I, never wanting to maintain contact with what I saw as a very painful connection to my past refused to visit the house. While I did continue to maintain its upkeep I felt demoralized, defeated and increasingly enraged."

"It was this last sales opportunity that caused Aunt Charlotte to get involved. While those sitting here know the explicit details, I believe that we are where we are tonight because it was she who realized time was running out to make my mother's wishes a reality and, as a result, fate finally intervened."

"I am humbled and awed by what has transpired. I have no rational explanation for the sequence of events that has occurred this weekend but accept them for what they appear to be, an example of God's grace and goodness manifested for those in need."

Matthew then turned to face me, "Jamie, I would like to sell you and Reid personally or better yet sell a 501(c)(3) entity of your choice the Sweet Grass Memories property for the sum of $1 with the condition that you (a) agree to support initial renovations by the Blessing family to develop the facility as a place that will address the myriad of educational, vocational, and spiritual needs of marginalized children in the area, and (b) agree to maintain the house and adjacent property as a beacon for children's development as long as it stands, and you are able to do so."

"The acreage we own west of the property will be sold to the current interested developers to begin a Habitat for Humanity community. I have contacted them about this arrangement, and they have provided me with a verbal agreement to split the property for sale. Our lawyers will work through the details this coming week. In addition, they will be putting you in touch with the local Habitat foundation in your area so that you might be able to work in partnership with their organization to benefit your, uh, our children."

Charlotte was the first to speak, "I do declare Matthew you definitely know how to make an old lady cry."

I imagined I saw tears in the eyes of most everyone else present as well, but the darkness of that sweltering July evening kept me from knowing for certain.

Our quest to find a way to make a difference for the kids was finished, and the solution better than I could ever have imagined. It was the best of times and yet, for me, a sad time as well. I was going back to Texas to live out the dream of a special, Charleston lady, but I was once again leaving behind a piece of my heart in the Holy City.

Chapter 48

The Plan: Part 1

> "Without leaps of imagination, or dream-
> ing, we lose the excitement of possibilities.
> Dreaming, after all, is a form of planning."
>
> —Gloria Steinem

Before going down to dinner Monday evening, Karen and I had already agreed to leave as soon as possible on Tuesday no matter the outcome of the evening's conversation. Anticipating our decision, Matthew had asked his secretary to research possible flights for us and tentatively booked one for early Tuesday afternoon. There was still a great deal to do, but much of it could be handled via phone or email.

After saying good night to everyone, Karen and I climbed the stairs together, hugged each other like high school BFFs, and agreed to go for one final walk through the city the next morning. I opened the door to the room I had begun to think of as my special refuge, retrieved my phone from my bag, and threw myself across the bed to call Reid. When the call connected, I was still frantically trying to decide where to begin, but then realized that it didn't really matter after all because when I heard his voice all I could do was sob.

"Jamie, is that you? Are you okay?" his alarmed voice flowed through the line momentarily startling me.

"Oh, Reid, I'm so sorry. Yes, I am fine and everything's good. I just am filled with emotion right now."

Relieved he chuckled and said, "Obviously!"

Holding the phone between my shoulder and head, I grabbed a tissue and was blowing my nose when he continued, "Well . . . I love you too. By the way, can you still remember your address or should we begin shipping your stuff east? The dogs are rather enjoying the extra space on the bed I might add."

"Okay. I deserved that but don't tease me, please? I have so much to tell you, and it's so unbelievable—like stuff out of a movie—but first, we are coming home tomorrow. Want me to send you the flight info by text or give it to you now?"

"No pencil or paper handy," he commented. "Just text. Do you know about what time you will land?"

I looked at the itinerary Matthew had given us and said, "Somewhere around 5:00 p.m., I think. It's a Delta flight."

I paused a moment, took a deep breath, and then began, "Reid, are you sitting down?"

"Yes, why? Should I be standing to hear what you are about to say?" he continued teasing me.

"Just listen, okay, you are in this as much as me now."

We talked for over an hour, or maybe I should say I talked and Reid listened, occasionally asking questions for clarification. When I finally finished I thought our connection had been lost because there was silence on the other end of the line.

"Reid, are you still there?"

"Yes, sug, I am here. You really know how to overwhelm a guy, don't you? This is a lot to think about. There are extraneous issues I know you will think about when you come down off of the cloud you are riding right now but owning another property, considering insurance and renovation costs . . ."

"But Reid, Matthew said the Blessing family will pay for all of the renovation," I interrupted, impatience coloring my words.

"I know that's what he said, Jamie, but we're going to need our own lawyer, I think. It's not that I don't trust Matthew, but this is uncharted territory for us, and we need guidance."

I was disappointed in his apparent lack of enthusiasm even though I could understand and appreciate his logic, but I knew enough to let things be for now. Whenever he called me "Jamie" in a conversation, things got serious, and because he rarely made any decision on impulse I knew he needed time to process all the nuances of an endeavor this monumental.

I also knew his heart was in the right place, and that he loved these kids as much as I did. But over the years, I had come to respect and appreciate one overarching aspect of his character. He loved his family more that anything in the world and ensuring our health and wellbeing, as well as that of his children and grandchildren, was his number one priority.

We stopped talking about the house and the weekend a few minutes before saying goodbye, and he made me laugh describing the antics of the dogs in my absence. We both were excited to see one another the next day and the enthusiasm was evident in our voices. We said goodbye in our usual way, and I clicked the end call button.

I purposefully hadn't asked Reid about calling Ms. G because I knew he would have advised against it. He was cautious about getting people's hopes up before anything had been decided, but my gut told me that after all we had been through she and Ms. Tracy should know about the events of the weekend as well.

It was late, but I remembered she was a night owl so I scrolled down my recently called contact list, selected her name and touched the number. She picked up on the second ring. "Well, well, if it isn't Ms. Scarlett O'Hara on the line."

"Oh, not you too, Ms. G, I just talked with Reid and all he did was be sarcastic," I lamented.

I felt her smile as she continued, "Just teasin with you, Jamie. I really am glad you called. The kids ask me every day whether or not I have heard from you, and Tracy and me have been on pins and needles to find out what's goin' on.

"By the way, a sold sign went up on the house today, and I thought the kids were gonna have heart attacks. Know anything about that? When are you coming home, by the way? What should I tell them all tomorrow when they run me down for about the one hundredth time?"

"Oh my," I said, "I didn't expect things would happen so quickly. I'll have to rethink how much to share with the kids. It's been an unbelievable four days, Ms. G, and it would take a couple of hours for me to explain everything but suffice to say I think we have a plan that is the best it could be. Matthew has agreed to sell me, or a 501(c)(3) organization of my choice, the house for $1. He also says the Blessing family will pay for the entire restoration."

"There is one condition, however. We must agree that the house will always be used *only* to help children find their ways academically, vocationally and spiritually. If we ever depart from that agreement, the house will revert back to the Blessing family. Oh, and one more thing, the property to the west of the house will be sold to a developer who plans to build Habitat for Humanity houses."

Just as with my conversation with Reid, there was dead silence on the other end of the line when I finished talking. "Ms. G? Are you still there?" More silence . . . "Ms. G?"

"I'm here, Jamie, I'm here. I was just saying a grateful prayer to God. I am truly humbled by what has happened . . . truly humbled," she murmured.

"Well, dear friend, when you hear the whole story you will come awfully close to thinking you are in a dream. Karen certainly didn't believe what happened. But there isn't time to do justice to it tonight so I'll wait. By the way, we will be home tomorrow around 5:00 p.m. so maybe we can all get together Thursday evening at our special place. What do you think?"

"Definitely, count me in, and I'll check with Tracy," she commented and then as an afterthought, "Before we hang up what you want me to tell the kids about the house?"

I thought about it a moment. How could I be evasive enough so as not to disappoint them if something happened, but also give them reason to celebrate and be happy after all this time of tension and waiting? God only knew how important it was to not be yet another example of people they couldn't trust.

That's when it came to me. "Ask them if they believe that God answers prayers. When they say yes, just tell them that He answered ours, and I will explain everything when I get home."

"And you sometimes wonder if you are supposed to be in their lives, Ms. Jamie . . . what more proof do you need? See you real soon. Godspeed."

I pushed the "end" button a second time and lay back on the bed. I don't remember falling asleep but didn't open my eyes again until morning light was streaming through the garden window.

Chapter 49

The Plan: Part II

"When women come together with a collective intention, magic happens."

—Phylicia Rashad

Philip Simmon's Harp of David Gate

With morning's early light, I knocked on Karen's door just as she was walking out to meet me. We made our way quietly down the steps and out the door for one last moment with the city. Our pace was hurried at first, but when we realized we were not "power walking" and couldn't keep up a conversation at the rate we were going we laughed out loud, slowed down and began to enjoy our time together.

"Have you packed?" Karen inquired.

"No, actually I had planned on doing it last night so that the morning wouldn't be so hurried, but I made a couple of phone calls and then fell asleep," I lamented. "Have you?"

"No, but then neither of us have a lot of stuff so I don't think it will take long," she replied.

"Jamie, I've been meaning to tell you how much I've enjoyed getting to know you and being part of this adventure. I apologize for being such a doubting Thomas last night, but honestly, if I hadn't been here and seen the whole story unfold I would have believed you made it up."

I glanced over at her and said, "Thanks but there's no need to apologize. If it weren't me who was experiencing this I'd feel exactly the same way. Now, I know why people say 'truth is stranger than fiction.' I think even Reid had trouble grasping the magnitude of what's happened. He got very quiet on the phone last night, and I could almost see the wheels turning in his brain. He started talking about insurance, contracts, the fact that we will probably need a lawyer, and on and on. I guess that's what I appreciate about him, he definitely is the realist in our house."

"Steve was a bit overwhelmed as well. He said he might call Reid today and see if he wanted to talk."

Taking a deep breath, she hesitated only slightly before continuing, "Jamie, I hope you know we both believe in what you two are doing and would like to continue to help anyway we can. Who knows, Steve might be able to get some of the kids interested in another side of law enforcement!"

With that we both smiled and tacitly agreed to wait until we got home, or at least on the plane, before sharing any more dreams and plans for Sweet Grass Memories.

As we passed by, one of the gated entrances to a cozy, private courtyard, I stopped Karen and asked, "Did George tell you anything about the blacksmith who designed and molded many of the iron gates in the city?"

She looked puzzled and commented, "No, not that I recall."

I grinned and said, "Well, well, then I may be one up on the guy! Philip Simmons, America's oldest living blacksmith, is an artist whose work is displayed not only in Charleston but also in Columbia, the South Carolina capital, and in Washington, DC. I believe he has designed several fences, balcony and window grills that are still displayed all across the country."

"My favorites are his harp, heart and egret designs that are so prevalent here in Charleston. Interestingly enough when he was thirteen years old Mr. Philip Simmons apprenticed with a Mr. Peter Simmons to whom he was not related. Peter Simmons was a former slave."

We walked on in leisurely conversation until we both knew it was time to go back.

"I have mixed feelings about leaving here," Karen suddenly confided.

I pulled out my phone as she spoke, and I know for a moment she thought me rude. "I want to share a quote with you," I apologized, "But I can't remember it exactly so I have to look it up."

When I found it I read aloud: "*Once you have traveled, the voyage never ends, but is played out over and over again in the quietest chambers. The mind can never break off from the journey.*" I read it a second time, and we both considered the words as they applied to each of us personally.

"Let me guess the author," she smirked, and as if on cue, we both said aloud "Pat Conroy."

We arrived back at the house just as Matthew was leaving for his office. He stopped his car and walked back to the front gate to greet us, "Ah, there you both are. I thought maybe you had gone out for one last walk. Since I am seeing you now I will not come to the airport to see you off. I hope that will be okay."

Karen was the first to respond, "Oh, absolutely, Matthew, we cannot thank you enough for your hospitality, and your willingness to open your heart and embrace the unusual situation we brought you to consider."

"Well, let's just say mother must have finally decided she needed to take desperate measures to get my attention," he smiled and then turned to face me.

"Jamie, I hardly know what to say. I only wish you and my mother had had the opportunity to know one another. I sense that you, she, and Indigo might have formed a triumvirate as powerful as that of Julius Caesar, Pompey and Crassus and, as a result, I believe you would have done great things for this world."

I could think of no appropriate response but simply grasped his hand and said "Thank you."

After a moment, I added, "Will we see you in Eden Hill any time soon?"

"Just like my mother and aunt, you don't miss a beat, do you?" he grinned. "Actually, yes, I will need to come to Texas in the next month or so to close on both properties, discuss the renovation ideas with you and see about setting up an account for your expenses."

"Jamie, I am certain you, and probably Reid, are a bit apprehensive about the responsibilities you now must earnestly consider. Please believe me when I say I understand. I have a lawyer I trust implicitly in your area, and I have asked Charlotte to give you his card. You may seriously want to explore setting up a 501(c)(3) non-profit for the endeavor you are about to embark upon."

"Funny, you should bring it up, but I actually had a dream about that very thing last night."

Both Matthew and Karen eyed me with disbelief. "Oh really?" He smiled.

"Yep," I quipped. "And I already know our name, "We'll call it BridgesWork because when one builds bridges she does God's work."

Matthew shook his head, hugged us both, and as he walked back to his car, I thought I heard him mumble "Amazing."

Chapter 50

Loose Ends

"Ends are not bad things, they just mean that something else is about to begin. And there are many things that don't really end, anyway, they just begin again in a new way."

—C. Joy Bell

I packed and lay back against my historic four-poster bed one last time before meeting Karen in the hallway. When the time came, we pulled our luggage down the stairs to the first floor to begin the process of saying goodbye to the house on Legare and its charismatic inhabitants.

Ms. Charlotte was waiting at the bottom of the stairs as we descended. When we approached each other it was as if none of us knew the other or what to say after the monumental and mystifying events of the past few days. A layer of formality seemed to envelope us all.

Her appearance that morning was actually an enigma. While her overall countenance appeared relaxed and at peace, her eyes reflected a deep, soulful weariness that suggested she was in need of rest and solitude.

She had done her best to not only bring the story to a fitting conclusion but also represent the history and hospitality of a famous, old southern city in its most favorable and alluring light. She had accomplished both with style and grace, and I imagined her sleeping long hours after our departure.

We gazed into each other's eyes without saying much, but we all knew that while our days together had been a blessing, and the three of us had accomplished what we had set out to do, it was time to move on. At that moment the specifics of the future were actually secondary.

Charlotte hugged us both tightly as if she believed we might never meet again. "Jillian came to me last night," she said, "I was afraid at first, but her smile was soft and through her tears she shared that she was finally at peace. I thought I saw Thomas in the background as well but couldn't be certain."

Turning to me she whispered, "Jaime, Indigo told you everything, didn't she?"

Her voice trailed off, "Somehow I sense she was more of a sister to Jillian than I . . ."

"No, Charlotte, no, I don't see it that way," I quickly countered. "She just filled another niche in Jillian's soul, one that you weren't able to see. You were all sisters in the truest sense of the word."

She smiled then, grateful for my words, I think, and we hugged each other tightly once again for what I feared might truly be the last time.

Attempting to lighten the mood, I said, "Okay! When the house is finished we are going to have one momentous dedication for Sweet Grass Memories and BridgesWork! We expect you as a Guest of Honor, Ms. Charlotte, will you come, please?"

Karen took her hand and continued, "Oh my yes, Charlotte, we will need your expertise in guiding the preparation of the food for the reception, in orchestrating the presentation regarding the story of the house as well as the story of Jillian, Thomas and Matthew. You know only women can pull this off and the two of us are relying on you!"

I caught a glimpse of what Karen later told me was reminiscent of the old twinkle in her eye and she said, "Well, my, my, I do declare, it sounds as if this could be one of the premier social events of the year for Eden Hill. Do you really think the town is ready for the required protocol?"

All three of us dissolved into laughter just as George opened the screen door saying, "Ladies, I'm afraid it's time to go."

We stood there not wanting the moment to end, and I couldn't help but wonder what happens to each of us when we come to a point when we aren't quite sure whether or not we can trust that the things we plan and hope for will continue as we currently envision. Is this simply a consequence of aging or does everybody, regardless of age, experience it?

All of us to the person Charlotte, Karen, myself and, even George, were momentarily absorbed in our own, private thoughts. What if we never saw one another again? What if our plans never come to fruition?

Then, as if on cue, all of us reverted back to mechanical behavior. George fiddled with our bags, and both Karen and I busied ourselves searching for itineraries and boarding passes.

Finally, we looked at each other one last time. "Thank you, Ms. Charlotte, for so much more than I can put into words," I stammered.

Karen also struggled to express her feelings, and we walked down the piazza steps feeling inadequate.

As I went through the gate I called back, "See you soon and this next time it will be in Texas!" silently praying my words would become reality.

We drove to the airport in silence, and I couldn't help but recall how different this same trip had been five days earlier.

Finally I had to say something. "Hey, George?"

Yes'um, Ms. Jamie?"

"Just thought you should know that you missed a big attraction when you were giving Ms. Karen a tour."

I saw his brow knit as I gazed into the rear view mirror of the car. "Really now, and what be that?" he puzzled.

"Well, you never showed her the artistry of Mr. Philip Simmons's gates, now did you?" I grinned.

His smile broadened and he chuckled out loud. "Okay, Ms. Jamie, okay, but when you come on back you and me we will have 'e history competition, yes, we will and who do you think gonna win? Hum?"

I saw Karen dab a tissue to her eye but still smile as she gazed out the passenger side window. Listening to George respond and watching her reaction I knew she would come back. Charleston has that effect on sensitive souls.

We arrived at the terminal and began preparing for departure. When George had closed the trunk lid and there was nothing left to say I faced him uneasily. Karen had said her goodbyes and gone ahead inside.

"Well, here we are again, George," I stammered. Suddenly, I realized that I didn't know his last name and was embarrassed to acknowledge that fact.

"Don't really matter now, does it, Ms. Jamie?" he responded. "After all, I dunno yours neither, and you don't know Ms. Indigo's or Ms. Beatrice's . . ."

"Speaking of names, George, why did Ms. Indigo refer to Ms. Jillian as Ms. Jilo?"

"Jilo be an African name, Ms. Jamie. Actually, it'd probably be your name as well."

"Really, why?"

"Well, might be best if you look it up and tell me!" he chuckled.

Time was running out, and we stood there a moment not wanting to let go. I started to walk away and then remembered one more thing. Turning back to face George, I asked one final question, "When we visited Jillian's grave on Sunday I thought I saw you place something on the headstone. Was I right?"

His eyes seemed to take on a faraway look as he replied, "Yes, ma'am, I did, for murrah."

I raised my eyebrows, intrigued, but before I could say anything else he continued, "Now, tellin' what it was will be between you and her."

His voice softened, "You ought to study a little Gullah tradition anyway."

"George?"

"Ms. Jamie, you got to go now!" he replied curtly.

"I'll never forget you—really. You have taught me so much already and yet, I know there is much more out there for me to learn.

Will I be okay, do you think?" I thought aloud. "You know I can't let these kids down, but I am worried I won't be able to figure out everything."

"Oh, I figure you gonna be okay, Ms. Jamie. You got one special angel who gonna make certain you don't fall down. Besides, I'll be 'round, surely I will."

"Even in Texas?" I questioned.

"Yes'um, I 'spose even in Texas," were his final words.

Chapter 51

Just the House and Me

"I think houses live their own lives along a
time stream that is different from the ones upon
which their owners float, one that's slower. In a
house, especially an old one, the past is closer."

—Stephen King, *Bag of Bones*

We may not have followed the formal protocol for most real estate transactions, but Matthew had provided me with a key to the front door of *Sweet Grass Memories* the day I left Charleston for home. Since I didn't use it until after the closing I had plenty of time to think about the first time I would cross its threshold as one of the new owners. I didn't want ceremony, and I didn't want company.

Reid seemed to understand my need to visit alone without requiring an explanation, and we tacitly agreed that we would arrange another time for all of us: Ms. G, Ms. Tracy, Steve, Karen, the entire "porch crew," all of us, to go in together. We would make it a celebration for the kids and arrange all the publicity we could to honor and recognize both their dreams and those of Jillian.

I didn't pick a particular day or time for just me and the house. I figured that I'd know when I should go and, as it turned out, I did.

Early one morning just as our faithful cardinal pair signaled the beginning of a new day, I got up, washed my face, brushed my teeth, hastily dressed and drove to Blessing Way: no makeup, no special clothes, no planning.

The sun was peeking just above the eastern horizon, and I could see that it was about to become one of those never to be taken lightly azure blue, Texas days. I pulled into the driveway just as I had done a hundred times before, but this morning was different. It was quiet, peaceful, and somehow perfect—no traffic sounds, no sirens, and no loud music jamming from car radios streaming by. All I could hear was the soft, faint cooing of a dove.

I got out of the car and walked up to the house. My legs felt heavy, almost like lead. I couldn't decide if I wanted to rush to open the door or sit a moment on those now familiar steps reminiscing about all that had transpired over the past months.

I realized then that I was afraid, but afraid of what? Afraid that I wasn't up to the monumental task that I sensed lay ahead, afraid of disappointing someone, afraid of what I might "hear" the house say? We hadn't communicated since before my trip to Charleston though I thought I could now perceive an aura of peace surrounding her.

I stopped just short of the veranda and glanced up at the roof. Catching sight of Jillian's tiny pineapples, I smiled in spite of my increasing apprehension, and remembered George's explanation of why pineapples had meant so much to her. I walked up the steps to the massive front door.

Leaning against one of the stately pillars, I bent over and brushed off a spot on the creaking boards of the veranda. I promised myself that I'd sit just a minute, and plopping down, I made a mental note that they would need to be replaced. Sitting there, looking around, I also decided that the rose bushes at each corner of the steps were struggling to survive and needed attention as well. I thought about whom Reid, and I knew who could teach the kids about landscape architecture and plant care while simultaneously addressing our plans for improvement. The wheels were already turning.

The breeze picked up, the sun rose higher, and I fumbled in my jeans' pocket for the key Matthew had given me in Charleston. It was time to go in. The realtor's lock box had been removed, and for a fleeting instant, I wondered if the key I had in my hand would still work. Thinking that I should have brought along the other ones we received at closing I realized it was too late to worry about that now.

I stood and walked up to the door marveling that both it and the windows were still intact. I recalled that Matthew had paid someone to check on the house periodically, but it still surprised me that it seemed to have survived significant vandalism over the years. I pushed the key into the lock. It turned easily, and the wind helped me with the door.

I knew the house would reflect abandonment, but I wasn't prepared for the magnitude of neglect that confronted me. Everywhere I looked there was evidence of nature's intrusion. Dust blanketed all surfaces like a heavy layer of ash and billowed with the incoming wind from the open door. It was obvious that no one had ventured inside for a very long time, as there was not a visible footprint anywhere to be seen.

Spiders hanging from their carefully constructed, intricate webs swayed in the breeze and scampered hurriedly upward as if annoyed by my intrusion. The air was musty, even choking. Narrow shafts of light streamed through the slats of the slightly ajar shutters, and there was absolute silence. I felt the dust tickling my nose, and, being allergy prone, considered opening all the windows to prevent me from experiencing a sneezing frenzy.

Yet gazing beyond the effects of time and neglect, I sensed that I was being offered a private invitation to delve into the houses' soul; an opportunity to possibly learn more about the past dreams that had been whispered within these walls so long ago before both our lives changed, and before the world of today intruded. Airing out the house, while tempting, maybe should wait a bit as it could serve as a distraction on so many levels.

I looked around the first floor. I was standing in an open area, rather like a foyer, that flowed into an expansive room at the back of the house. The floors appeared to be wide planked heart of pine, but with the heavy layer of dust it was difficult to tell how well they had weathered the passage of time. The ceiling looked to be constructed of hand-planed tongue-and-groove planks of an unknown wood that had been painted white. The walls of the entry way were covered in peeling wallpaper, and the baseboards and plaster crown molding of the foyer were also a fading white hue.

From where I stood, I could see straight through the house to a beautifully ornate back door. Just off center, to my right, was the beginning of a winding staircase leading to the second floor. Though not meant to be the centerpiece of the foyer it was still a majestic statement with dark wooden steps encased in wooden pin topped balusters that had been painted white just like the baseboards and crown molding.

I walked slowly into the foyer and stopped a moment to gently examine the wallpaper. I couldn't be certain with the dim lighting, but it appeared to be an intricate gray pattern with delicate white lilies. It was peeling in several spots, but I could still sense the welcoming effect this entrance must have provided guests. I made a mental note to ask if there had been any pictures taken of the house interior when Thomas and Jillian had lived here that had survived. I wanted to see the combined effect of the furnishings and the interior design.

Just beyond the staircase, on both sides of the foyer, were doublewide entrances into two uniquely decorated, stately rooms one on each side facing the front veranda. Above the doors were stunning, geometrically paned glass transoms. In addition, both entrances were encased with intricate millwork that had been painted a stark white.

The past and present coalesced in my head as I struggled to recall what I had learned from a course on traditional plantation house interiors that I had taken the summer between my sophomore and junior years of college. I remembered that the diversity of plantation styles had surprised me.

In Virginia, many of the preserved plantation homes date to the Revolutionary period and reflect the Federalist influence with dark woods. While in South Carolina and Georgia the interiors are lighter and more airy, bridging the gap between the darker woods such as mahogany and cherry to the north and the French Caribbean style of Louisiana homes with lighter wood floors, painted crisp white ceilings and trim.

I walked slowly around the perimeter of both rooms. While similar in dimensions, one could have been a living or sitting room, and the other a dining area.

The first room was painted a sage green color with now dulled, peeling white trim. The louvered shutters on both of the large floor-to-ceiling windows were in remarkably good condition and painted white as well. Since the house faced to the east the windows must have invited in spring and fall breezes while at the same time encouraged the warmth of the sun on a winter morning.

The second room's color palette, however, caught me by surprise. The walls were painted a light creamy brown, almost cocoa, and they were adorned with stark white plaster crown molding as a contrast. There were two floor-to-ceiling windows in this room as well, and both were encased in the same style white, louvered wooden shutters as in the living room.

The effect seemed fairly mundane until I glanced to the floor. The baseboard looked as if it had been painted a dark color, almost black. Thinking I was mistaken, I bent down to wipe a bit of dust from a section.

I realized, then, the depth of the love Thomas must have had for Jillian. Sweet Grass Memories was a painstakingly constructed low country architectural treasure in the middle of Texas. Its dining room had been painted to replicate the one in Drayton Hall, the only plantation house on the Ashley River that survives today. The numerous windows in the room, as well as ample wall space to strategically place reflective mirrors to capture and reflect light, was a replication of the efforts of early plantation owners to use available natural lighting.

As I continued to walk the perimeter of the room, I discovered a second opening and came across a louvered double pocket door. When I slid one side open, I expected to enter the kitchen but instead stepped into a tiny, rectangular shaped area that revealed an exterior door, bookcases, a hearth, but no windows.

The room was similar to something we might call a mudroom today. Yet in an interior corner, it had a magnificent old stone fireplace and hearth. The stones of the fireplace and hearth were of different colors, shapes and sizes and appeared to have been carefully stacked one upon another.

I wanted to run my fingers across them to see if their surfaces might be smooth like river rock but, even though I knew better, I was afraid that if I disturbed any one of them the structure would crumble. I decided that this room had to have been Thomas' idea as there was more of a Western than Southern flair.

Doing research on older homes some weeks later, I learned that many had "warming rooms" that were used as a family entrance to the house as well as a place to gather during very cold winters. The walls of this cozy retreat spot were lined with rich, dark wooden cabinets and bookshelves. Standing there I could envision Jillian seated here in front of a blazing fire on cold, winter days with a good book open on her lap.

After a few moments, I pushed through a second set of pocket doors into the kitchen. Because of the danger of spontaneous fires from open hearths, original plantation homes generally had a separate structure that was used to prepare and cook food. The main house usually had a butler pantry at the back of the house where the food that had been prepared in the kitchen was re-plated and delivered to the dining room.

As time passed and stoves replaced open fires for cooking, kitchens were added to the main home at the very back of the house and were adjoined to the Butler Pantries. Sweet Grass Memories was no exception, as its kitchen window looked out over an expansive back meadow.

It was evident that Thomas had taken great pains to replicate some of the older structural features Jillian would cherish and, at the same time, include some of the more modern conveniences of the era. The main rooms of the first floor mirrored nineteenth century historical architecture. The kitchen and bathrooms, however, were purposefully modernized.

The kitchen had a black and white checkered floor tile pattern with electric and gas connections for a refrigerator and stove and plumbing for hot and cold water pipes. The deep, porcelain sink was embedded in built-in cabinets and the entire room, including the walls and cabinets, was painted a creamy white. I backed up and subsequently surveyed a large, efficiently designed cooking and plating area that must have been state of the art for its time. I could almost hear the laughter and conversation that must have flowed from this room as well as smell the aromas of the sensuous meals that were prepared. This was a gathering place for family and friends.

Just to the right of the kitchen with access through both the kitchen and the foyer, was a large open space. The "great room," as I named it, appeared to be have been used as a library or study area. It was warm, expansive, welcoming and possibly exquisite when furnished.

The walls were again painted a creamy white and were lined with richly carved, natural wood bookcases just as in the warming room. With the exception of the kitchen, just as in the other parts of the house, the floor was heart of pine.

The baseboard in this room had been left a natural wood finish, and there was a second large, rustic, stone fireplace on the back wall. Next to the fireplace was an ornate exterior door that led outside to another expansive veranda. Once again, this room with its rustic, prairie nature seemed more western than low country in design.

As I completed my downstairs tour of the house I discovered a quaint, tiny powder room just to the north of the great room that looked as if it had been lifted from a log cabin. Thomas must have considered the possibility of many guests when designing the house, as half baths didn't strike me as commonplace in the 1950s.

Sometime later, I drifted back into the foyer and climbed the winding staircase to the second floor. From the middle of the landing at the top I could see several doorways and assumed that they all led to different bedrooms.

From the moment I had entered the house I had felt safe, comfortable, and welcomed. It was at this point, however, that I thought I might not be alone. I glanced ahead of me and realized that the French doors to the tiny second floor balcony above the front door were ajar. Both the brilliant rays of morning sun and a cool breeze streamed through the opening and surrounded me almost immediately. I was puzzled. I hadn't seen any open doors or windows upon arriving at the property earlier in the morning and wondered if I had just missed this one because it was on the second floor.

I crossed the landing and walked toward the northernmost side of the house. Everything was as dusty and undisturbed on this level as below. The first room I entered was small and cozy with beautifully shuttered windows, an ornate medallion ceiling fixture and a small fireplace. The walls were again covered in a subdued, flowery wallpaper pattern that seemed a bit out of place for an upstairs bedroom. Sometimes plantations included small sitting rooms on the second floor for the comfort and privacy of the immediate family so I decided that this might have been the purpose for the room I had just entered.

Earlier, before arriving at the house, I had promised myself that I would take my time and slowly meander through each room. I hadn't had a problem downstairs but up here, all of a sudden, I struggled. Standing in the sitting room something pulled at me to move on quickly. Without hesitating I walked directly to the eastern most room on the northern side of the house.

Stepping across the threshold, I was immersed in a warm wave of conflicting emotions that ranged from quiet joy to smothering sadness. The room was quite large with the ceiling and walls painted a soft eggshell blue. It had broad, white plaster crown molding, and a subtle, yet beautifully mantled white fireplace. For some reason I liked being here.

I glanced down to see the same wide planked heart of pine flooring that was so prevalent downstairs and felt as if I had been here before. Standing there, I recalled the Blessing home on Legare. Suddenly, I realized that this room was an exact replica of the one I had stayed in while in Charleston and imagined it with intricately hand-carved rosewood furniture, sumptuous draperies, and delicate, thick bedding adorning an ornate canopy poster bed similar to what I had enjoyed back in July. I knew this had to have been Jillian and Thomas's retreat as it was light, airy and spacious. Though not set apart from the remaining rooms on this floor, it was also private in its own way.

I was remembering that eventful weekend in Charleston when I thought I heard a voice. It was whispery and definitely that of a woman. Joyful and titillating, I could actually make out individual words this time, not just vague thoughts. Though I didn't hear complete sentences, the words were distinct: "happy, fulfilled, future, and children."

A moment later, I detected laughter that was spontaneous, bubbly, and infectious. I smiled and began to giggle. Sliding down a wall to a sitting position on the floor, I leaned back and sighed.

I felt at home in this old house and resonated with more purpose than I had ever known before. The room filled with sunlight, and with the windows closed and locked, it grew warmer, but I didn't want to leave. I closed my eyes and was in a reverie of sorts.

I'm not certain how much time passed or whether or not I fell asleep, but at some point, I opened my eyes. I glanced up to see an image of Ms. Indigo sitting directly across from me. She was dressed differently than the day we had met in South Carolina, but she was again sitting on her porch rocking slowly back and forth. Her eyes were closed, and she appeared to have been waiting for me.

The rocker stopped, she blinked open her eyes and smiled. We gazed at each other for a few moments, and then she repeated what she had said to me so many weeks earlier, "Ms. Jilo say that the chillun and the house need each other, and, una chil, una need dem too. Dis is de Mastuh's plan. Una be 'e cyaa'pentuh. After coming home are you ready now?"

I didn't say a word but nodded affirmatively. She smiled and closed her eyes as if satisfied. After a while the image faded into the air, and once again I was alone.

I stood up, dusted off my jeans, and walked out of the room. I strolled over to close and latch the balcony doors. As I did, I glanced directly across the hall into a third room. It was painted all around as a floor to ceiling mural.

Each wall depicted a light blue sky with puffy clouds that melted into a deeper blue ocean. A cheerful boat with white billowing sails was crossing tall waves and was painted on one wall. A red and white lighthouse beckoned from a sandy shore on a second. On the third, I saw a shiny, silver bridge connecting a desolate, urban coastline with a lush island paradise.

I realized that his must have been Matthew's room, and stole a second glance at the scene with the bridge. The symbolism appeared clear, and I decided that nothing in my life was a coincidence any more.

Just to the left of Matthew's room was a bathroom and beyond that another possible bedroom. I made a mental note to talk with Reid and Steve about whether or not we would need to do any major renovations on this floor to accommodate the myriad of plans we had discussed to provide the kids a welcoming place of refuge and learning.

I walked back down stairs to the front door. As I retraced my footprints across the pristine dusty layer of the floor, I realized that both Sweet Grass Memories and myself would probably never again be the same as before. I thought I could finally sense contentment, satisfaction, and peace for both of us.

260

Chapter 52

Suhailah and the Shells

"It's no small thing, when they, who are so
fresh from God, love us."

—Charles Dickens

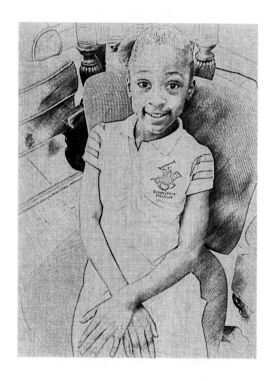

Suhailah

After checking the inside perimeter of the first floor one more time, I reluctantly closed all the shutters and walked outside onto the decaying boards of the front veranda. I was already thinking about schedules, and how quickly I could coordinate a time when Reid, Steve, Karen, and I could do a walk through. I closed and locked the door then turned toward the steps to leave.

The members of the original "porch crew" are never far from my heart, and while I haven't mentioned little Ms. Suhailah in a while she was and continues to be a very special child with her own unique message.

Petite, always positive, and maybe the most sincere and kind-hearted of our kids, she never draws attention to herself, yet is always present and eager. Seeing her leaning against one of the columns in the bright sun I now realized that she was the epitome of what I hoped for in all our children—inquisitiveness, integrity, kindness, and most of all, optimism and expectation.

The youngest sister of Jessamy and Amber she was often dismissed and rarely offered the opportunity to share her thoughts. Perhaps that was because of her place in the hierarchy of children in the family, or because her voice was as tiny as her stature. Seeing her here, by herself, unexpectedly that morning I knew there was yet another lesson to come for me. I was unable to resist her dimpled, infectious smile.

She looked up when I turned away from the door and said, "Hey, Ms. Jamie, I saw your car and decided you must be inside."

"Hey, Suhailah," I replied. "I am very glad to see you, but I must admit I'm surprised. Why aren't you in school today?" I bent down and hugged her as I took a seat on the steps.

"What's the house like inside?" she inquired with a grin, ignoring my question.

"Well"—I smiled—"actually it's really neat, but, no more information until you answer my question about school."

She looked down at the steps and murmured, "I missed the bus, and there's nobody to take me so I'm just hangin' out today."

"Did anyone else miss the bus?" I inquired. She shook her head no.

"Uhm, since Jessamy, Amber, and your little brother made it to the bus on time, I must ask what happened to you?" I challenged, refusing to let her explanation pass.

She struggled with her answer, "It was my turn to be last in the bathroom and everybody was runnin' late. Amber's hair didn't do good, and Jessamy broke up with her boyfriend and needed to talk by herself on her phone so she stayed in there for a long time," she hesitated momentarily and then added, "Ms. Jamie, I was afraid I'd get my math benchmark score too."

"Is that the real reason why you drug your feet and didn't go? Do you think you did badly on the test?" I continued.

"Yes, ma'am," she confided, "I don't want to disappoint nobody." My heart ached for her, and I glanced back at front door realizing that while I probably didn't need a reminder, here was another one as to why this house had a purpose.

Minutes dragged by as we sat there quietly letting the sun and soft breeze surround us. "Ms. Jamie, do you trust me to tell the truth?" she asked pensively. Her face grimaced and was full of anticipation as she waited for my answer.

Taken aback I replied, "Yes, Suhailah, I do."

She stood up, took my hand, and guided me down the steps of the front porch. "Well then I have a secret ain't nobody has ever seen. According to Ms. G you now own the house so you better see it."

We walked through the knee-high grasses and goatheads, a type of sticker I'd only seen in Texas, to the back veranda. I was glad I had worn jeans and lamented that removing the ones hitching a ride on my socks and pants legs would be painful.

When we reached a corner of the steps at the back veranda she stopped, bent down and examined an area that appeared to have recently been disturbed. I didn't kneel down with her but bent over puzzled as she dug down into the cool, soft earth with her hands.

Eventually, after some effort, she uncovered and pulled to the surface an old mason jar filled with seashells of all different shapes and sizes. The band was screwed down and pressed firmly against a separate disc-shaped lid covering the rim of the jar. Both were rusted, but from what I could see, the shells within their glass encasement were polished and exquisite.

Suhailah picked up the jar with both hands, gingerly wiped the dirt away and while passing the treasure between them wiped her hands, one at a time, on her jeans. With extreme pride, she handed it to me watching my face for a reaction.

I took it from her, screwed open the band and dumped a few shells into the palm of my right hand. I picked three or four out of the pile and could actually feel the grit of the sand adhering to their surfaces. Eventually I lifted the jar to my face and thought I smelled the saltiness of the sea.

I suggested we sit on the back veranda and talk about her treasure so we moved to the steps, brushed off a place for us both, and sat down. I carefully laid some of the different shells just above us on the wooden slats of the porch. While I had collected many shells along the South Carolina coast across the years, I rarely found any that were complete and unblemished in some way. Most of those in this collection were perfect.

There were several small shiny, circular oyster shells scattered among larger brown and white Atlantic scallops and giant Atlantic cockles. In addition, there were numerous darker, eastern oyster shell halves, spotted cardita shells, and beautiful Sharks' Eye Moons. I noticed several more smaller examples, but by far, the most stunning was a complete Knobbed Welk.

I pulled the shells out of the jar one by one and shared the names I could remember with Suhailah. I kept emphasizing what a treasure she had found. As we continued to examine them together, I asked the pressing questions that were running through my mind. How and when did she find the jar? How long had she had it and what would she like to do with it?

She began, "Ms. Jamie, do you think I might have been supposed to see you today? I mean, I found this jar a long time ago 'cause I fell over the rock at the edge of these porch steps when I was runnin' around one day a long time ago. I looked around, and nobody seen me so I sat there and wiped off my bloody knee. I didn't want nobody to make fun of me."

"The big rock was all by itself by the edge of the porch. Since I didn't see no other rocks around I figured someone put it here for a reason. I dug around it one time after everyone had gone home and saw something shiny. It was the top of the jar. I was scared but I pulled it out of the ground anyway. I'd never seen anything like it before and thought it was a secret treasure."

"When Ms. Blessing was here that time I sneaked over, dug it up and showed to her. She cried when she seen it and said it were special, she told me that I should keep it safe. I didn't know how to do that so I just left it buried here. I was afraid to show it to Jessamy or Amber 'cause I thought they might take it somewhere else. I check on it all the time, and I decided since I had found it, it was mine, but now I don't know."

"I even looked up pictures of the shapes of the shells when I went to the library one time. Aren't they beautiful? Have you ever seen anything like them before? I thought a long time about keeping them a secret but decided they belonged to the house."

"Since you now own it, I decided they were probably yours now." She hesitated and then concluded with her best grin, "But you know what I'd really like to do?"

I shook my head, and she winked at me as she said, "Put them back on their beach one by one! I never saw an ocean before or been to a beach. You think we maybe could go someday?"

Chapter 53

Those First Days

"Almost all of your life is lived by the seat of your pants, one unexpected event crashing into another, with no pattern or reason, and then you finally reach a point, around my age, where you spend more time than ever looking back. Why did this happen? Look where that led. You see the shape of things."

—Ron Perlman

Robert a.k.a. "Cookie Man"

The months after my first private moments with the house and special conversation with Sahailah passed with lightning speed, and though I agonized about every detail and, especially every decision, George was right, I haven't tripped and fallen, at least not yet.

The papers have been signed, a 501(c)(3) application has been filed with the IRS, BridgesWork is now an official corporation, and we've begun to discuss how our day-to-day operations will be handled. Matthew has been to visit a couple of times and with each visit we are finally learning a little more about the remarkable man who was his father; but that's another story.

The plans for the Open House event are underway and both Ms. Charlotte and George have agreed to attend. Ms. Indigo, however, remains noncommittal but according to George, smiles every time the subject is brought up.

Ms. G has "retired" from her part-time job at the library and for now is working alongside Karen and me to decorate and furnish each of the rooms. She and I are especially enjoying working with the librarians to choose the books and other reference materials for the room that will become the library/reference room.

Once the house is finished, Ms. G will move in to manage the day-to-day operations and monitor the kids' activities. By the way, Ms. Tracy is now managing the Oak Lakes apartment community, and I'm pleased to report business is booming.

Steve has become our business/political advocate and, in his spare time, is working alongside Reid and our BridgesWork Board of Directors to determine the types of programs we want to make available for the kids. Reid spends most of his days right now watching over the contractors and trying to keep me from getting ahead of myself. He is thoroughly enjoying himself.

I won't deny that there are days, several of them, when I ask myself if I'd do it all again given the chance. When that happens, all I have to do is go by and watch the house slowly regain her old beauty or recall the events at the airport the day we came home.

Our journey back had been uneventful and quieter than I think we had expected since both Karen and I seemed content to get lost in our own thoughts. I couldn't wrap my mind around what the next steps should be and had begun to think Reid's apprehension had merit.

We landed on time and the plane was taxiing toward the gate when Karen asked the inescapable question, "So how will we share everything that has happened the last few days? Where do we start?"

Gazing at the back of the seat in front of me I was about to say, "I honestly don't know" when Ms. Indigo's words flooded back into my head . . . "Dis is de Mastuh's plan. Una be 'e cyaa'pentuh."

Smiling it was then that I figured out the perfect response. "I think I'll tell the kids, and yes, everyone else as well, that we have been blessed to receive an invitation to participate in an exquisite plan, and, with every step of the journey, if we accept the offer, we will learn to be some of best carpenters we could ever be."

Karen smiled back, and as she took my hand, she said, "Perfect." We pulled our luggage out of the overhead bins and walked with fresh energy to the main terminal to meet Reid and Steve.

There are a few times in each of our lives when we probably wish there had been a camera crew nearby with the ability to capture certain events in slow motion so that every day we could relive over and over the infinite joy we experienced in that single moment. Such was that day.

It was little Robert whom I saw first. Affectionately known as "Cookie Man" because he could down more cookies than anyone else we knew, Robert represented the epitome of childhood innocence, and his contagious smile never ceased to melt my heart. He broke from Ms. G's corral of kids just as we came through the revolving door into the luggage claim area and ran with abandon headfirst into me. Had I not dropped my luggage we would have both ended up in an embarrassing pile on the floor. Dropping her bags as well Karen burst into laughter and grabbed both of us in her arms.

I looked over Robert's head just in time to see Ms. G, Ms. Tracy and especially my whole "porch crew" rushing toward us.

"How on earth did you all get here?" I exclaimed, but since pandemonium was in full swing, I don't think anyone heard me.

Actually, it didn't matter anyway. The exhilaration of that moment was what counted. Looking down at the emotion evident on those triumphant faces and feeling my heart swell with profound joy I knew that Jillian had waited for just the right person, especially when I saw Abeo standing patiently on the fringe of the group. Our eyes met, and I knew instinctively that no span of miles would ever separate our hearts.

"Welcome home, Ms. Jamie," I heard Tracy say just above the noise and gleeful squealing.

"It's ours, ain't it, Ms. Jamie! It's ours," Jessamy shouted. And, Ms. G, well, I think it was her voice that kept repeating, "Praise the Lord . . . Praise the Lord."

Out of the corner of my eye, I caught my coach's grin just off to the left. He was standing next to Steve, and both were shaking their heads.

He walked over to the throng of bodies, leaned in and kissed me on the cheek. "Appears as if somebody spilled the beans."

Looking as sheepishly as I could in that situation, I could only say, "I tried to tell Karen you would advise against it, but she couldn't help herself."

Chapter 54

If You Build It They Will Come

"When you have a dream that you can't let go of, trust your instincts and pursue it. But remember: Real dreams take work, they take patience, and sometimes they require you to dig down very deep. Be sure that you are willing to do that."

—Harvey MacKay

Time passes, things change, and I'm not certain any of us are really prepared for what might occur. Sometimes it isn't quite what we expected. Such was the case with *Sweet Grass Memories.*

As excited and motivated as we all were that hot August morning in 2011 when we picked up the paint brushes and began the first of many renovation projects I don't think any of us, especially the kids, realized what an arduous process it would be.

Expecting instant gratification, almost to the child, each one gave up at one point or another, wandered off in disappointment and eventually sat at one of the picnic tables in the small park across the street either pouting or seething in anger.

My dismay was almost palatable, but instead of immediately confronting them we all decided to wait awhile to react. It was obvious that they were still interested in the house, but something was keeping them away.

Still trying to internalize the Gullah philosophy of life, I willed myself to be patient, hoping one of us would be able to figure out why. I was even a little perturbed with the house, as she was offering no clue either.

One particularly warm afternoon in early September I was alone at the house. The contractors had left for the day, and I used their absence as an opportunity to study the progress we were making without worrying about interrupting their work.

Troubled by the architect's drawings I was upstairs in what was once Jillian and Thomas' bedroom trying to decide why I didn't think the design as depicted on paper transformed one of the most important rooms in the house into the quiet, inviting library I was envisioning.

Hearing footsteps in the downstairs foyer I got up off the floor and walked to the landing. "Ms. G, is that you?" I called out.

Obviously responding to my voice Suhailah had slowly started up the stairs. "Hello, Ms. Jamie." She beamed when she saw me on the upstairs landing.

Delighted to see her I rushed down the few remaining steps and hugged her tightly. Seeing her backpack, I realized she had just arrived home from school.

"Suhailah, what a sweet surprise! Is anyone else with you?" I inquired.

"No, ma'am," she responded. "Just me. I been wantin' to come by, but we all been afraid to. Don't seem like this our house anymore."

I was startled by her comments but something told me not to pursue the reasons for them just yet. "Well, that's not true, but we'll talk about that later. Now, how about being the first one to see the changes in the house? Can you stay a few minute?" I asked.

She nodded affirmatively, and we walked hand in hand through every room. I tried to help her visualize how each one was to be used for all of our programs but it was too much for her to internalize. Just the size of the house alone was overwhelming. Having lived in a small, nine hundred square foot apartment all her life *Sweet Grass Memories* seemed like a mansion.

We returned to the stairwell and sat for a moment. "Thank you, Ms. Jamie, for showin' me around. When you think we can come back? Is there something we can do to help?" she questioned then continued, "Remember when we picked out the color of the living room and started painting? That was so much fun."

I did remember that summer day, and then recalled that since there had been a number of skilled renovation projects that needed to be completed before we could tackle the projects the kids could actually help do, we had stopped involving them. It had always been my intention to explain the situation to them, but when they stopped coming around I became so consumed with the house itself that I never got around to it.

Now I realized that we had misinterpreted their absence. We had not considered the fact that the appearance of strangers, contractors, landscape architects, inspectors, etc., may have sent a different message than we had anticipated.

"Well, how about telling everybody that we'll do a better job of keeping you all informed from now on, and that we'll let you know when the people working on the big stuff turn the house back over to us to finish, okay?" I offered.

"Okay," she replied, "sounds great." And with that she walked to the front door, gingerly opened it and waved goodbye.

Daily during the next week one of us, Ms. G, Tracy, Reid, Karen, Steve, or I, would fill an ice chest with frozen goodies or stop at the local convenience store and load up on bags of Takis then drop by for informal conversation with whomever was around when the busses arrived.

We usually started by sharing what was happening inside the house and then moved on to discuss the gardens and flower beds. Sometimes we'd bring landscape diagrams and pictures of the plants and shrubs we hoped to install.

Each of us had our favorite projects and almost always spent more time talking about those. Mine was the library, and I always managed to bring along a book or two that would be kept there when the house was finished.

No matter the person visiting the park on any given day, before leaving, there would be mention of the timeline for completion and details of the celebration that had been planned once *Sweet Grass Memories* was all dressed up and ready for guests. Some days were better than others, but at some point we noticed that several of the kids, to include the original porch crew, started to drift back by to see what was happening when everyone but one of us had left.

As the days passed we picked up several new visitors to the house; faces we had not known previously. One went to a different school and had joined us to improve his reading comprehension. He lived up the street in a different apartment complex and when his curiosity got the better of him he mustered the courage to walk down the road and introduce himself. Polite and easy-going I looked forward to his visits.

In addition to Rahim, there were three girls who were talented, dedicated workers and dreamers, with superb problem solving abilities, a keen sense of humor and a desire to be all that they could be.

I knew immediately that each would probably have succeeded without crossing paths with Sweet Grass Memories. But I also knew they had been drawn to us for some reason, and I was grateful. They brought a different perspective and a new sense of responsibility to us all. Clearly Rahim, Esi, Teru and Naki had very important roles to play on our story.

In early fall, we created and delivered individual invitations to the children with whom we had established the closest bonds. They included the original "porch crew" members who were still around as well as Rahim, Esi, Teru, Naki, and another new face Karina.

The invitation invited them to a special afternoon preview of the house one Saturday in early October after all of the projects had been substantially completed. Since the Habitat property was also being developed simultaneously alongside our house and construction traffic was heavy, the invitation read that we would pick them up promptly at 1:00 p.m. Ms. G shared that they were expecting a school bus and thought that stupid since the house was only across the road from where they lived.

She chuckled as she reported Jimar's comments, "Ain't no traffic ever bothered me."

I arrived at the apartment complex around twelve forty-five and together with Ms. Tracy and Ms. G began to gather the kids together near the front entrance. Surprised and heartened by how many had decided to accept our invitation, it was easy to fall back into sweet, excited conversation.

There were all sorts of conversations and multiple questions for us, the adults, "When is the bus gettin' here? What time will we be back? Can I just walk back across the road when I get ready? Are Mr. Reid and Mr. Steve comin? When we gonna start playin over there again? Is there a place to study? Are we gonna have tutors?"

And then the ultimate one we had anticipated, "Will we get anything to eat while we are at the house?" Robert inquired.

All eyes turned to me. I knew Ms. G and Ms. Tracy, both of whom had fallen in love with the huge kitchen, had been baking cookies and making homemade ice cream for a couple of days in anticipation of today's events. But before I could respond both smiled at Robert.

Ms. G enveloped him in a bear hug and responded, "Well, maybe, we'll just have to see. Didn't you eat your lunch?"

Robert grinned and nodded, yes, but it didn't matter since we all knew his propensity for cookie consumption.

I glanced up the hill just in time to see the three limousines Reid and Steve had booked for the event turning right onto Tremont. I pulled my iPad out just in time to capture some of the astounded facial expressions.

"Wow, Ms. Jamie, you see those limos? I wonder who they for? You think there is a funeral or wedding somewhere 'round here?" Jimar cried out.

With Jimar's comment everyone turned to watch the three shiny vehicles slowly glide past us, make a U-turn at the bottom of the hill and turn toward our parking lot. You could have cut the anticipation in the air with a knife.

Suddenly Justine, jumping up and down, shouted, "They comin here! They comin here!"

The kids were spell bound but giggly as the cars pulled into the parking lot and came to a stop. In disbelief each watched as Reid, Steve, and Karen slowly opened a door of each of the cars. I am not certain whom they expected to see, but once they knew the faces were familiar ones they squealed with delight ran to look inside all three open doors.

That October afternoon was like a rebirth for us all. When we arrived at the house, Reid gathered us all together in the newly paved circular driveway. He asked the kids to look up at the house, and then quietly reminded them that while a lot had happened in the past months, other than getting all spruced up, the house was still the same old place they had hung out and, more importantly, it still belonged to only them. As I listened I smiled inwardly at his uncanny ability to inject love into every situation and make each person involved feel so extraordinarily special.

He motioned for all of us to gather at the steps of the veranda. I watched him look into each of our children's faces and softly grant them permission to go inside, "The front door is unlocked and open just for you. You are free to explore every inch of the house on your own, but remember Ms. Blessing is watching over all of us today, and it would really be nice if each of us said a prayer of thanksgiving for her and Mr. Matthew before going inside.

I was touched to see that all of them bowed their heads. Some uttered a silent, individual prayer while others held hands and surprised us by praying openly and out loud. Most of their prayers were short, but all were sincere, I think. They were anxious to be turned loose, and as each child stepped onto the veranda and crossed the threshold of her front door Sweet Grass Memories seemed to ooze love and warmth.

We had decided to permit the kids to explore every room by themselves that day while each of us adults monitored a different section of the house and explained what would be happening in the specific areas. It took a while, but once they felt comfortable, laughter erupted on every level and footsteps reverberated above and below.

The excitement had returned, and I knew we had reached another milestone. Nothing would ever be the same. After exploring every room multiple times we all sat around on the dining room floor eating Ms. G and Ms. Tracy's cookies and slurping the ice cream as we talked about what each of us could do to prepare for the December Open House event. Decorating for Christmas was always special, but this time even more so, and everyone wanted to play a memorable part. The kids were "back," and it was like old times.

Before breaking the spell of our magical afternoon, I asked that everyone remain in the dining room for one last surprise. Motioning to Suhailah to follow me into the foyer I opened a closet door and retrieved her jar of treasured shells. She was puzzled when I asked her to share her story about how she discovered them, but when I told her it was time we all knew the whole story of the house and that she had discovered a very important piece of the story, she beamed with pride.

While I had yet to explain the rich history of Sweet Grass Memories to our beautiful children, primarily because I believed most of them too immature to understand, I wanted them to know we were in an exceptional place that enveloped them with love. I had already decided the whole story would be shared over time when the kids were curious and ready.

Chapter 55

Do All Stories Have Sequels?

I wanted a perfect ending. Now I've learned,
the hard way, that some poems don't rhyme, and
some stories don't have a clear beginning, middle
and end.

—Gilda Radner

Months later as winter melted into spring, and the beautiful Open
House event was little more than a warm, fuzzy memory, Karen and
I were sitting in comfortable lounge chairs on the back veranda sipping iced, sweet tea. We held up our glasses in a mock toast as we
listened to the laughter flowing from the kitchen window and once
again recalled Charlotte, Indigo, Matthew, and George's different
reactions to the house on that never to be forgotten day. The kids
were mesmerized by all of our South Carolina visitors but particularly clung to Indigo and George.

Several of the younger ones sat on George's lap and at his feet.
When I happened to walk past them to take yet another visitor to
meet Matthew and Charlotte, I overheard Jimar ask him to "talk
that other language from where he was from." Laughing unrestrained
George played along, and the kids had a blast trying to figure out
what he was saying. I think he was in heaven sharing stories about his
city, particularly as he shared how he took care of the carriage horses,
and I didn't miss the fact that he had packages of benne wafers in his
pocket for all of them to try.

It was Ms. Indigo, resplendent in her Gullah colors, however, who captured the attention of the older children as she told them story after story of Charleston, the plantation days and her heritage. I clearly saw the awe in their faces, particularly, Justine and Suhailah, as she closed her eyes and spoke of the marshes and the sea that were so much a part of her life.

Both Matthew and Ms. Charlotte were imposing figures in their formal attire and charmed our guests with many stories about Jillian and Thomas. Local dignitaries were taken aback that this beautiful story in their own back yard was just now coming to light. When several asked if we had any historical documents we could share, I glanced over at Karen, and we both smiled and winked at one another. Indeed, Charlotte was in her element and her southern charm was never more evident than that afternoon standing in the library of Sweet Grass Memories.

The smell of baking drifted through the windows of the kitchen, and we returned to the present. Ms. G, Ms. Tracy and several of our older kids were baking and decorating elaborately themed cakes for an auction the next evening to raise money for our upcoming summer mission trip. The generosity of one of our local churches was legendary, and, sometimes, individual cakes sold for $500 or more!

We'd come full circle with our children and now, radiating confidence and love, many were ready to pay it forward by participating in a second mission trip. In addition, both the house and grounds were resplendent with the vibrant colors and warmth of spring; as Ms. G would say, "the love that abounded all 'round was infectious."

For the most part things were good, and our original "porch crew" babies and their friends who had joined us were thriving. But time has a way of challenging us all, and now, some four years later, we were facing new, unexpected trials.

"Has it already been four years?" Karen turned to me and asked.

"Sometimes it feels like more than that," I suggested. We laughed out loud as close friends can easily do and sipped the icy tea Esi had made that afternoon. A breeze rustled the new leaves of surrounding trees, and I felt slightly uncomfortable, even uneasy, as I considered our journey and now wondered about its conclusion.

I glanced over at Karen and realized that she, too, was privately reminiscing. So much had happened since those idyllic first months of renovation that both good and bad memories flooded our thoughts. Our organizational objectives were on target, and, just as we had hoped, most of our local kids were improving their situations: some were even thriving.

We had marketed *Sweet Grass Memories* as a supportive academic, spiritual and character development center, and, in my opinion, we had been quite successful. All the local Dallas and Fort Worth television news programs had featured our story because it was (a) good, (b) slightly mystical, and (c) something different. All of us, including our kids and our Board, had beamed with pride.

Our after school and summer programs included community service opportunities that included the local Habitat for Humanity site, lessons in agronomy and horticulture, health, nutrition and cooking classes, and the proper care of animals. We also continued our daily scriptural devotionals for kids and teens.

Most programs were full, and some even had waiting lists. It was especially gratifying to realize that since introducing some of these programs to our little ones while they were still in upper elementary and middle school, they were now approaching high school with a better idea about what courses they wanted to take.

Finally, as we had promised our original "porch crew," we continued to offer daily tutoring programs, and had set aside a couple of rooms as a computer lab and library for anyone who needed those resources but was unable to access them after school.

There were days when I couldn't find a seat anywhere in the house: particularly in the library, the living room, and the kitchen, and it reminded me of a book I had read as a child, *Cheaper by the Dozen* by Frank Gilbreth.

Sweet Grass Memories resplendent and seemingly quite comfortable in its makeover had become known as a beacon of hope for the disenfranchised in our local, metropolitan community. As word of our success traveled, it did so quickly, and through all sorts of circles, even spilling onto the streets of south Dallas, and the Stop Six area of Fort Worth.

In an effort to encourage other organizations to duplicate our model we had vigorously shared the story using all forms of media. The message was that *Sweet Grass Memories* was a place of refuge, support and learning. More importantly, we stressed that it was also a model that could be replicated. Yet even the best intentions can have unintended consequences.

More often than not those who contacted us these days were less interested in replicating our model and more interested in immediate assistance. Never intending to take on the persona and responsibilities of a shelter, we now had come face to face with what can happen when people catch a glimpse of something that is working for the betterment of those in need and desperately want to be part of it.

We seemed to be adrift. The original "porch crew" wanted desperately to help those who came to see us for help and, as a result, seemed out of sorts. Yet our Board, the Blessing family and those of us closest to the kids all agreed that we needed to maintain our mission as originally designed.

As we referred those needing basic services to agencies more equipped to help them, it was an opportunity for us to show our children that while we would never let someone walk away from Sweet Grass Memories without hope, we were truly only equipped to do what Ms. Jillian had envisioned so many years before.

While our explanation seemed to pacify the children, the passion of our little family was slowly draining away like water seeping from a garden hose with a troublesome pinhole. We needed something to pull us together.

I looked over at Karen, and as if she could read my mind she commented, "How much have you talked with some of our newest additions lately?"

"Who in particular?" I inquired

"Well, these past few weeks I have been in the computer lab when the middle and high school kids came in from school. They are an amazing bunch, by the way, and probably think much more deeply than we realize."

She took a sip of tea, smiled sheepishly and then continued, "For example, did you know Naki, Karina, and Esi have been researching the possible connection of Michelle Obama to the Gullah people?

And then there's Suhailah. She never tires of telling the story of the Sweet Grass journey, and her eyes shine every time she shares the connection of the house to the Gullah people of Charleston, in particular, Ms. Indigo, George and Jillian." She is so skilled at story-telling and so passionate about her love for a place she has never seen, that she mesmerizes anyone who will listen almost every afternoon, and they promptly forget their homework assignments to dream about the possibility of going there. She has slowly planted a seed that maybe they need to raise enough money to surprise you with a trip back."

Truth be known long before there was some uneasiness on Blessing Path, I'd started dreaming about the pull of the salt marshes once again. Every so often I'd even imagine I could detect the smell of pluff mud when I'd open a window or door and feel a soft, evening breeze.

More pointedly, a couple of days this past week I'd awakened around 4:00 a.m. and in the darkness felt a strong urge to go back to Jim Isle; to go back and sit a spell amid the swaying Spanish moss tendrils with Indigo and George. My regular conversations with Charlotte and Matthew indicated that both were doing well, but I missed seeing them in person.

I wasn't concerned that I seemed no longer able to hear messages from the house yet the old addiction for Charleston that had subsided months earlier had returned, and it left me just as restless and confused as before. Was there more I needed to do? I couldn't imagine that there was, but I was back to being edgy. Was the house waiting for me to do something else?

I could barely wrap my head around Karen's next words as she whispered, "So, who are you thinking should go with you this time? Suhailah has grown up a lot and still wants to place her shells back on the beach, and then there are our wonderful mission trip kids. We've always dreamed of showing them the world. And after their mission trip experiences, why not expose them to the history of Charleston and Sweet Grass Memories?"

After another sip of tea she closed her eyes, smiled knowingly and let the spring breeze carry both of our thoughts into the sky. I sensed she thought that it was time for me to get to know some of the older kids a little better, especially those who came to us later on. After all, bridges work to cross many streams and many years.

Chapter 56

Embracing Diversity

"We should embrace our immigrant roots
and recognize that newcomers to our land are not
part of the problem, they are part of the solution."

—Roger Mahony

So was this the new challenge the house was communicating to me, albeit indirectly? Were we to help our children better internalize the beauty and possibilities of new comers to BridgesWork, to our state, and country overall?

The Gullah heritage of our southland and Sweet Grass Memories were certainly representative of our rich diversity. I pondered whether this was the new twist, something that would not only bring us back together but also equip our kids for the political and social climate to come. As I thought about that idea, I recalled Jillian's words in one of the letters she penned to Charlotte years ago:

"Quite honestly, I believe that God must surely have had a long-range plan when he united Thomas and me. Thomas has taken great pains to incorporate the best aspects of both Charleston and western architectural features in the design of the house, but we now realize that our real mission is to let the community know we believe that differences should be celebrated and embraced. We hope the house, in its uniqueness, will simply be a catalyst for that message."

When I observed the kids in our house on any given day, I saw a variety of shapes, sizes, colors, and personalities. Some came from places as far away as Mexico, the Republic of the Congo, Botswana, the island of Tonga, and the Sudan while others had never been out of the Dallas-Ft. Worth area.

Karen was right. It would be a good experience for some of the older kids to see Charleston. It might better solidify their understanding of the miracle that is Sweet Grass Memories. But selecting those who would go was another matter entirely.

There was no question that Suhailah would be a good choice. It was all she had dreamed of since the day she showed me the shells, but who else and how many? And how would we pay for the trip? I didn't want to make this complicated, but I wanted it to be fair.

I brought up the whole idea to Reid at dinner that evening. He shook his head and smiled, "The wheels never stop turning, do they? I must admit I'm not surprised, and I do like the idea that we should be sharing and modeling a respect for diversity with the kids . . ."

I interrupted, "I hear it in your voice, there's a "but" in there somewhere, isn't there?"

He grinned. "Well, actually a couple of them. First of all, I'm a little disappointed you don't want to return with just me. Secondly, and much more important, you have a Board you're gonna need to run this by, so I hope you haven't said anything to the kids yet."

I rolled my eyes at him and smirked. "No, I haven't said anything yet. I've learned a thing or two since we started. And of course I want you to go, especially if we take a boy."

He leaned back in his chair. "Speaking about who gets to go, how are you gonna decide that touchy issue?"

"I hadn't gotten that far yet. Any ideas?" How many do you think the Board might approve? Should I ask them to be part of the process? Should I ask one of them to go?"

Sipping his wine Reid suggested, "Well, how about an application and selection process? That might whittle the number down a bit, and I'd set an age limit. You know how squirrelly junior high kids can be, maybe you should only invite high school age kids to apply."

I grinned excitedly. "Great ideas, so you will go, right? You know it would have to be summer and it's really humid. I know we'd have to work around birthdays, but I can't imagine being there without you."

"I have a good idea every once in a while, you know"—he smiled smugly—"and as for going along, well, you'll have to let me think about it. Kids, humidity, and no down time, what kind of a vacation is that? Remember, I don't even go on mission trips."

Chapter 57

So Who Will Go This Time?

"Broad, wholesome, charitable views of men and things cannot be acquired by vegetating in one little corner of the earth all of one's lifetime."

—Mark Twain

It took a while but the Board approved the trip, and the money for the expenses for two adults and up to five students. We decided upon an application and interview process and had a house meeting one afternoon to share the news with the kids. As Reid explained everything, I watched their faces thinking I would be able to tell who was really interested, but I couldn't. When we shared the criteria for eligibility the little ones were disappointed, but I knew that would pass when Ms. G brought out the freshly baked cookies for snack time that afternoon.

The old excitement seemed to have resurfaced, and there was much chatter as several picked up applications. They questioned one another and me. "How far away is Charleston? Will we go on an airplane? I ain't never been on one. Where we gonna stay, in a hotel or at someone's house? Is there an ocean there?"

The first to the stack, as expected, was Suhailah. She grinned at me and asked if I would help her. I told her that I didn't think she would need my help and suggested she give it a try on her own. She smiled timidly and agreed.

As she started to walk away she looked back over her shoulder and said, "If I don't get picked will you put my shells back?"

It took a while, and I could see them engaged in a private conversation off to the side of the living room, but eventually, the students Karen had encouraged me to study, Esi, Teru, Naki, and Karina, secured copies as well. They had two weeks to complete the questions before the deadline.

Thinking about how far we had come I still couldn't help but be saddened by the loss of contact with many of the original "porch crew." Planning this trip caused me to wonder what it would have been like to introduce them to Charlotte, Matthew, George, and Indigo.

I remembered Ms. G's words when I was in Charleston with Ms. Blessing for the first time, and she explained that Abeo and her family were moving. That had been a turning point for me, and I tried to stop worrying about losing touch with individual kids. I had made a point since then to try to connect with each child as long as we could and be grateful for the time we had together, however short.

The void was still there, however. Chanté, Cassandra, Jimar, and Jalissa had long since moved away, and we had lost contact. Raven, Jessamy, Amber, Justine, Robert, and Sam were involved in athletics and other things and didn't come by very often. When I'd see them I'd gently invite them back but usually to no avail.

The morning of the fateful day when the applications were due, Ms. G and Ms. Tracy called to ask Karen and me to come by for tea. They were adamant that we needed to be there before the kids came in from school. I was curious and even a little concerned as I walked up the steps to the house and knocked at the door.

Karen was already there as I could hear her laughter coming from the kitchen through the screened front door.

When she heard the knock Tracy called out, "Come in, Ms. Jamie, we are in the kitchen gettin' ready for this afternoon's meetin'."

When I reached the kitchen, I could smell the delicious aroma of chocolate chip cookies wafting from the oven, "What's the occasion? What meeting? Did I forget something?"

Pulling a cookie sheet out of the oven, Ms. G grinned and said, "No, but the kids came to me and Tracy yesterday in mass asking if we could get you two here this afternoon promptly at four thirty for a special meeting. When I asked what it was about, they tried to be all serious and said it was a secret. The little ones, however, were grinning like Cheshire cats and bursting at the seams to talk. You know they can't keep no secrets."

Retrieving a spatula to remove the cookies from the baking sheet, she continued, "I decided to play along 'cause I figured someone would spill the beans. Sure enough when the older ones was out of sight, about five minutes later here come little Faith to see us."

Tracy picked up the story. "We acted surprised to see her and asked if she needed help with something. She slowly shook her head, made us promise not to tell anyone, and then whispered that they, meaning all of the kids, had been secretly meetin' together for a few days and had decided to 'elect' those who would go to Charleston themselves. She was so proud she grinned from ear to ear. Their plan is to meet with you today and give you the applications of the ones they elected."

Karen and I were more than a little stunned, and it took us a minute to respond. I had been dreading the fact there would be a review process, and, depending on the number of applications, knew someone would inevitably be disappointed. I had even toyed with removing myself from the committee, consisting of Karen, Steve, Ms. G, Ms. Tracy, Reid, myself and a Board member, but later realized I needed to be part of the decision since both Reid and I would be going with the kids. This was definitely a new wrinkle in the process.

"I don't know what to say but am definitely glad for the head's up," I finally commented, "but did either of you have any clue that this was going on? Whose idea was it anyway, do you think?"

Karen spoke up, "Well, it is a surprise, but think about it, our kids decided to make the decision for us. That's a pretty grown up, democratic thing to do. I just wonder if they factored in the criteria we set. That will be the only thing to check. Of course the applications themselves will still need to be read by the committee, and we had planned to interview the kids anyway so it sounds win-win to me!"

"I agree and am really proud of the group," I grinned, "but I am still really curious about how this all got started."

Looking somewhat sheepish Ms. G and Tracy began to laugh. "Now come on, you two," Tracy responded, "Who has been the ring leader in this Charleston dream all along?"

"We had an idea something was up last week," Ms. G chimed in, "when a whole group began to skip my snack time and gather in the library whispering quietly together. I'd pass by the door and ask what was goin' on, and they would hush and hide papers, saying they was workin' on a school project. I decided just to keep my eyes open for a spell."

Chuckling, I said, "Let me guess was Suhailah in the middle of everything? I'm surprised she didn't ask for chart paper and markers! How did they do the ballots, I wonder?"

"Oh, one more thing," Ms. G added, "I think they must have interviewed one another because I could hear what sounded like speeches a day or two ago. I thought maybe that was part of that same school project."

We all agreed not to mention anything about our little get together that morning and act as surprised as possible at four thirty. I called Reid on the way home to share the news. He sounded both proud and reflective, like a parent of a child who has done something unexpectedly full of character.

Chapter 58

Returning Home the Second Time

"Coming together is a beginning. Keeping together is progress. Working together is success."

—Henry Ford

Left to right top to bottom:
Karina, Naki
Justine, Esi, and Teru

Karen and I decided to drive together and arrived about four twenty-five. We walked through the door to cheers and chocolate chip cookie smudged faces while Ms. G whispered that everyone had been on pins and needles worrying if we'd come today.

Rahim, one of our middle school young men, spoke first, "Hey, Ms. Jamie and Ms. Karen, we have been waiting for you." Rahim had started behind the eight ball when he arrived in Texas from the Congo and enrolled in the third grade. He didn't have a foundation in either the nuances or the basics of the English language and soon gave up and started hanging out with other kids to whom failure was the norm.

Being raised by a grandmother who worked very long hours to support both he and his sister, he had few positive male role models in his life until the summer he joined our reading program. Now he is Reid's right-hand man and is developing some great leadership qualities.

"Hi, Rahim, we didn't know there was a house meeting today. What's it about?" I asked.

As he was helping some of the older kids restore order to the room, he looked over at us with his characteristic, captivating smile and said, "Just sit over here, and we will tell you."

About that time, Reid made a surprise appearance and pandemonium erupted. The kids always loved it when he dropped by because it was usually unannounced, and he never failed to make each one feel extra special.

Rahim was thrilled to see him, but I could also see that he was torn because he had a job to do and couldn't take time for a personal conversation. I was pleased that he chose to continue on with his responsibilities.

Reid winked as he took a seat across from Karen and me, and the kids began their presentation. There was obviously a script of sorts because those who spoke read from notes.

With stern looks from the older kids to the fidgeting young ones, Rahim began, "Ms. Jamie, Ms. Karen and Mr. Reid, we thank you for coming to our meeting today. All of us know the story of

Sweet Grass Memories and have wondered about this special place called Charleston where Ms. Jillian Blessing, its mother, was born."

"Sometimes Suhailah, who has been here from the very beginning, tells us stories about the house when it was sad. She tells us that many times she thought the house would be torn down, but God saved it for us. When we heard that some of us might get to visit where Ms. Jillian lived we were excited but scared. We knew that not everyone could go this time but hoped that each year more and more of us might have that chance. So I will let someone else tell you about our idea." With that, Rahim closed his notes to the applause of the kids.

A second young man, Pallav, picked up where Rahim left off. Another with potential who sorely needed male guidance and companionship to make the right choices, he had latched onto Reid and Steve like a clinging vine. He was more nervous than Rahim but the kids' whispers, smiles, and thumbs-up gestures gave him just the boost he needed.

After clearing his throat and opening his paper he began, "Okay, so here's what we all decided. Each year, we will pick four or five of us kids to go learn about Charleston and the history of the house. We will stick to the rules you all set and vote for only those who meet them. Now, Suhliah will tell you who we think should go this year."

There was more applause when sweet Ms. Suhailah slowly stood to speak. My heart swelled with memories as I recalled our early days together. One of the few remaining "porch crew" still with us pictures and conversations over the past five years glided slowly through my mind; the day she showed me her treasure of shells and honestly felt they should be mine to keep, the day she had the courage to come by and tell me the kids didn't feel part of the house anymore, her reaction to the house when we went on a private tour, and so many, many more. Who but this child, I mused, better represented the soul of Sweet Grass Memories?

The room was hushed as she unfolded her notes and then, just as suddenly, put them down. I looked across at Reid with tears welling in my eyes. I never had a tissue when I needed one.

She cleared her throat, looked straight at me and began, "Ms. Jamie, I knows that you know how much I have always loved this house. I knows that you know I want to go to Charleston, smell the ocean, and put my shells back on the beach that Ms. Jillian got them from. I've heard your stories so many times that I can almost see the place. But I want you to know that I didn't put my name on the list to go this year because I felt it would be not be right. When everyone voted we picked four of us: Naki, Teru, Karina, and Esi. After it was all over, Naki, in front of everyone, asked for a vote to make me the fifth person."

As her voice trained away she said, "I hope my application will be accepted too."

When she sat down all the kids ran over to hug her while we, the adults in the room, were overpowered with emotion pride and, most of all, love.

And so it was decided which applications would be sent for review to the committee. It was time to call Ms. Blessing and George to let them know we were beginning yet another chapter in the life of Sweet Grass Memories. I walked outside on the front veranda to compose myself when the breeze picked up, and I thought I heard a voice from the past,

"Nicely done, Jamie, nicely done. Say hello to George and Indigo for me."

I grinned openly as I tried to recall that special smell of pluff mud. On impulse, I looked at my phone contacts and found a number for George.

It rang several times but eventually he picked up. "George, hello, it's Ms. Jami, have you got a minute?"

Charleston Team 1

Esi

Esi, whose name means "born on a Sunday," is an exceptionally bright young woman who has an uncanny ability to communicate hope, love of learning, and/or innocence with most everything she meets. She is our ray of sunshine and is also quite beautiful and a natural in front of the camera. She arrived in Texas from Rwanda several years prior when her family was sponsored by a local Methodist

Church to be relocated to the United States. As a happy, curious child, she never appears to exhibit any transition issues and during our first mission trip she shared that being part of a team that actually helped someone meant a lot to her.

Naki

Definitely the most introspective and reflective of all of our kids, Naki, whose name means "firstborn girl," was a tough shell for me to crack. From day 1 in our programs, she and her mother have been an integral part of everything we do. She was the oldest in our group early on and demonstrated leadership tendencies well beyond her age from the very first time we met. While wise beyond her years and very private, she had to be coaxed into participating in everything we did, and I always wondered if we were connecting because we never talked much.

It was on that first mission trip that she reassured me that maybe we had crossed paths for a reason. Placing a handwritten note in my comments envelope, she shared that I was the grandmother she had never had and she loved being with me. A beautiful soul inside and out, I could only imagine the courage it must have required to write that, and I could easily envision great things for her future.

Teru

Teru, whose name means "good" tagged along to one of our programs with a younger brother. From the Sudan, her story is one I do not know well. Inseparable from Esi, they are a package deal. Teru appears a deep thinker but says very little, often allowing Esi to dominate the conversation. However, she is another beautiful, budding adolescent who is beginning to find her voice and her place in the world. When reflecting upon our first mission trip, she looked straight into the camera and said, "I was sad on the last day and wanted to keep on going helping people as a team member."

Karina

Gentle, caring Karina, whose name means "pure," is the antithesis of what I envision our influence on our children can accomplish. While a beauty in her own way, she is also studious, demure, innocent, full of hope, and always willing to sacrifice for others. She told me one evening as I was taking her home that because of our programs she now has a purpose in life and thinks she wants to go into service as a law enforcement officer.

Suhailah

Suhailah and Savannah

The child we know as Suhailah, whose name translates as "gentle," is and has always been the epitome of her name. From our very first days together, she was the one whose quiet eagerness never wavered in her quest to learn more: to be a part of our plan for the house, its future, and the future of the children of Oak Lakes whatever that might be.

In her book, *Gift from the Sea*, Anne Morrow Lindbergh, uses various shells to describe her reflections on life. She begins the chapter "Double Sunrise" with these words:

"One does not often come across such a perfect double-sunrise shell. Both halves of this delicate bivalve are exactly matched. Each side, like a wing of a butterfly, is marked with the same pattern; translucent white, except for three rosy rays that fan out from the golden hinge binding the two together. I hold the two sunrises between my thumb and finger. Smooth, whole, unblemished shell, I wonder how its fragile perfection survived the breakers on the beach." (Lindbergh, 2003)

I've come to think of Suhaliah as a Double Sunrise, until now unblemished, and always the same regardless of when and how one crosses her path. As I watch her grow, I wonder how her fragile perfection can continue to survive without the opportunities she so desperately seeks.

Maybe that's the mission for all of us who have invested our love in Sweet Grass Memories, to provide opportunities for all of our children as we continue to walk the road of life with them.

Isaiah 6:8

Then I heard the voice of the Lord saying,
"Whom shall I send? Who will go for us?
And I said, "Here I am. Send me."

References

Brown, Alphonso. 2008. www.historypress.net. Charleston, S.C.

Lindbergh, Ann Murrow, 2003. New York, New York. Pg. 55–56

www.beaufortcountylibrary.org/htdocs-sirsi/sweetgra.html

http://gullahtours.com/gullah/gullah-words

www.ccpl.org/content.asp?id=15762&catID=6044&action=detail

http://www.brainyquote.com/quotes/authors/m/
martin_luther_king_jr.html

http://www.brainyquote.com/quotes/authors/l/logan_p_smith.html

http://thinkexist.com/quotation/the_best_kind_of_friend_is_the_
kind_you_can_sit/12768.html

http://www.searchquotes.com/quotes/author/Angela_Bassett/

http://www.brainyquote.com/quotes/quotes/d/dhlawren188639.
html

http://www.quoteworld.org/quotes/10648

http://www.goodreads.com/author/show/476787.Tony_Dungy

http://www.great-quotes.com/quotes/author/Muhammad/Ali

http://www.brainyquote.com/quotes/authors/m/marian_wright_
edelman.html

http://www.brainyquote.com/quotes/authors/s/sai_baba.html

http://www.verybestquotes.com/in-a-good-bookroom-quotes/

http://www.brainyquote.com/quotes/authors/a/anais_nin.html

http://thinkexist.com/quotes/ruby_dee/

http://www.brainyquote.com/quotes/quotes/m/mayaangelo104542.html

http://www.brainyquote.com/quotes/authors/a/alice_walker_3.html

http://thinkexist.com/quotes/rachel_carson/

http://www.brainyquote.com/quotes/authors/e/emma_goldman.html

http://www.goodreads.com/work/quotes/16452470-beyond-sandy-ridge

http://www.goodreads.com/author/quotes/5818618.Kellie_Elmore?page=2

http://www.goodreads.com/quotes/tag/charleston\

http://southernafternoon.tumblr.com/post/795175042/there-was-a-land-of-cavaliers-and-cotton-fields

http://www.goodreads.com/quotes/14140-coincidence-is-god-s-way-of-remaining-anonymous

http://www.brainyquote.com/quotes/quotes/a/anaisnin133281.html

http://lovequotes.symphonyoflove.net/kahlil-gibran-love-quotes-and-love-sayings.html

http://thinkexist.com/quotation/when_you_put_faith-hope_and_love_together-you_can/145457.html

http://www.brainyquote.com/quotes/quotes/m/mahatma-gan135180.html

http://www.brainyquote.com/quotes/authors/s/sarah_orne_jewett.html

http://www.brainyquote.com/quotes/authors/m/mike_singletary.html

http://www.goodreads.com/work/quotes/82450-the-lords-of-discipline

http://www.quotationspage.com/quotes/Eleanor_Roosevelt

http://www.brainyquote.com/quotes/authors/l/leonardo_da_vinci.html

http://www.brainyquote.com/quotes/authors/j/johann_wolfgang_von_goeth_3.html

http://www.brainyquote.com/quotes/authors/m/morgan_freeman.html

http://www.brainyquote.com/quotes/authors/l/lord_chesterfield.html?vm=l

http://thinkexist.com/quotation/when_i_was_young_i_was_sure_of_everything-in_a/199076.html

http://www.goodreads.com/work/quotes/3244642-little-women-or-meg-jo-beth-and-amy

http://www.goodreads.com/work/quotes/3271379-a-thousand-splendid-suns

http://www.brainyquote.com/quotes/authors/s/sarah_ban_breathnach.html?vm=l

http://www.brainyquote.com/quotes/quotes/a/alicewalke446417.html

http://www.goodreads.com/author/quotes/6264.Elisabeth_Elliot?page=2

http://www.brainyquote.com/quotes/quotes/j/johnfkenn114922.html

http://www.brainyquote.com/quotes/authors/s/steve_jobs.html

http://www.famous-quotes.cc/authors/eden-ahbez

http://www.brainyquote.com/quotes/authors/p/peter_marshall.html

http://www.goodreads.com/author/quotes/1054.Beryl_Markham

http://www.goodreads.com/work/quotes/13014066-what-happened-to-goodbye

http://www.brainyquote.com/quotes/authors/g/gloria_steinem.html

http://www.brainyquote.com/quotes/authors/p/phylicia_rashad.html

http://www.goodreads.com/quotes/455537-ends-are-not-bad-things-they-just-mean-that-something

http://www.brainyquote.com/quotes/quotes/r/ronperlman467731.html

Glossary

A Glossary of Gullah Words taken from The Black Border by Ambrose E. Gonzales, and the vocabulary of Alphonso Brown.

"A">A	
ANUDDUH	Another
ANSUH	answer, answers, answered, answering Also used for message, especially for one requiring an answer; as: "Uh sen' uh ansuh to de gal fuh tell'um uh wan' hab'um fuh wife" I sent a message to the girl to tell her that I wanted to marry her
AP'UN	apron, aprons
ARUH	each, either
ASHISH	Ashes
ATTACKTID	Attacked (See "'tack"' and "'tacktid")
ATTUH	After
ATTHR'UM	after him, her, it, them
ATTUHW'ILE	after a while

AUGUS'	August
AXIL	axle, axles
AX'ME	ask, asks, asked, asking me
AX'UM	ask or asked him, her, it, them
"B">B	Return to top
BAA'BUH	barber, barbers
BAA'K -(n and v)	bark, barks, barked, barking
BAA'NYAA'D	barnyard, barnyards
BACTIZE	baptize, baptizes, baptized, baptizing
BAD MOUT'	bad mouth-a spell, a form of curse
BAID	beard, beards
BAIG	beg, begs, begged, begging
BAIG'UM	beg, begs, begged, begging him, her
BAIT'UM	bait, baits, baited, baiting him, her
BAKIEN	Bacon
BALMUHRALSKUUT	Balmoral skirt: a dark worsted underskirt with red stripes above the hem, of the time of Queen Victoria and named for her castle at Balmoral
BANDUN	abandon, abandons, abandoned, abandoning
BAPTIS'	Baptist, Baptists
BARRIL	barrel, barrels
BARRUH	barrow, a bacon hog
BAWN	Born
BAYRE	bare bares, bared, baring
BEABUH	beaver, beavers

BEAGLE	fox hound, fox hounds
B'DOUT	without, unless, except
BEEFU'T	Beaufort
BEEHIBE	beehive, beehives
B'FO'	before; as: "Befo' de wah"
B'FO' DAY	before day (See "crackuhday," and "'fo' day")
B'HABE	behave, behaves, behaved, behaving
B'HIN'	Behind
B'KAUSE	Because
BEHOL'	behold, beholds, beheld, beholding
BELLUH	bellow, bellows, bellowed, bellowing
BELLUS	bellows (blacksmith's)
BEMEAN	to be mean to any one, to slander, or abuse
BEN'	bend, bends, bent, bending
BERRY (sometimes "werry")	Very
BERITYWELL	very well
BERRYWELLDEN	very well then
BET'	Best
BETTUH	Better
BEX VEX	vexes, vexing; angry, anger, angers, angered
BIDNFSS	Business
B'GIN	begin, begins, begun, began
BIGGUH	Bigger
BIGHOUSE	the Master's house
BILE	boil, boils, boiled, boiling
BILIN	Boiling

BILLIGE	village, villages
BUMBYE	bye and bye
BIN	been, was
BINNUH	been, was, was a; as: "W'en uh binnuh boy "when I was a boy
BITTLE	victuals, food
BLACKBU'D	blackbird, blackbirds
B'LONG	belong, belongs, belonged, belonging; used redundantly as: "Da' gal him blan blonx to my Maussuh" That girl she belonged to belong, or used to belong, to my Master
B'LEEW	believe, believes, believed, believing
'BLEEGE	oblige, obliges, obliged, obliging
BLINE (n and v)	blind, blinds, blinded, blinding
B'LONG	belong, belongs, belonged, belonging
BOA'D (n and v)	board, boards, boarded, boarding
BODDUN	bother, bothers, bothered, bothering; worry, worries, worried, worrying
BODDUHR'UM	bother, bothers, bothered, or bothering him, her, it, them
BOFF	both (See "alltwo")
BOL'	Bold
BORRUH	borrow, borrows, borrowed, borrowing
'BOUT	About
BOWRE	bore, bores, bored, boring

BRAWTUS	Broadus
BREAS'	breast, breasts
BREDDUH (also brudduh)	brother, brethren (formal)
BREKWUS'	breakfast, breakfasts
BRESH	brush, brushwood; brush, brushes, brushed, brushing
BRESS	bless, blesses, blessed, blessing
BRE'T'	Breath
BRIAH	briar, briars
BRITCHIN'	breeching (harness)
BRITCHIS	breeches, trousers
BAUK'UP	break, breaks, broke, breaking, broken; "brukfoot man' a brokenlegged man
BRUKAA'M	broken arm
BRUKFOOT	broken foot, or leg
BRUK'UP	break up, broke up, broken up: "De meetin' done bruk'up"
BRURO	bureau, as "Feedmun' bruro"
BRUSTLE	bustle, bustles
BUBBUH (familiar)	Brother
BUCKRUH	A White person or persons; the white people
BUCKRUHBITTLE	white man's food
BUCKSLEY	Berkeley (county)
BUD	bud, buds, budded, budding
BU,D	bird, birds
BU'DCAGE	birdeage, birdcages
BUH	brother, as "Buh Rabbit"
BUHHIME	Behind
BUHR	burr, burrs

BULLYELLIN'	bullyearling, or yearlings
BU'N	burn, burns, burned, burning
BURRUH	burrow, burrows, burrowed, burrowing
BUS'	burst, bursts, bursting
BUTT'N	button, buttons, buttoned, buttoning
BURRUH	burrow, burrows, burrowed, burrowing
BUZZUM	bosom, bosoms
BUZZUT	buzzard, buzzards; vulture, vultures
"C">C	Return to top
'CAJUN	occasion, occasions
CALLICRO	Calico
CANNIBEL	cannibal, cannibals
CANTUH	canter, canters, cantered, cantering
CATT'RACK	cataract, cataracts (eye)
'CAUSE	because (See "bekase")
'CAWCH	scorch, scorches, scorched, scorching
CAWN	Corn
CAWNFIEL'	corn field, corn fields
CAWNSTALK	corn stalk, corn stalks
CAWNUH (n and v)	corner, corners, cornered, cornering
CAWPRUL	corporal, corporals
CAWPSE	corpse, corpses; coffin, coffins
CAWSS' (n and v)	cost, costs, costing
'CEEBIN'	Deceiving
'CEITFUL	Deceitful

'CEP'M	except, excepts, excepted, excepting; accept
CEP'N	accepts, accepted, accepting; unless
CHAA'GE	Charge, charges, charged, charging
CHAA'STUN	Charleston, S C (See "Town")
CHANY	china, chinaware
CHANYBERRY	Chinaberry, or Pride of India tree
CHAW	chew, chews, chewed, chewing; also noun, as of tobacco
CHEER	chair, chairs
CHIL'	child, children
CHILLUN	child, children
CHIMBLY	chimney, chimneys
CHINKYPEN	chinquapin, chinquapins
CHRIS'MUS	Christmas
CHRYCE	Christ
CHU'CH	church, churches
CHU'CHYAA'D	churchyard, churchyards
CHUESDAY	Tuesday
CHUNE (n and v)	tune, tunes; tune, tunes, tuned, tuning (up)
CHUNK (n and v)	chunk, chunks, chunked, chunking, throw
CHUPID	stupid
CLAWT'	cloth
'CLA'TO GAWD	declare to God a mild oath
COA'SE	coarse
COL'	cold

COLLUH	color, colors ("we colluh," our color, or Negroes)
COME'YUH	come here
CONKYWINE	concubine, concubines; used for masculine as well as for feminine affiliations
COONOO	canoe, canoes
CUNSAA'N (n and v)	concern, concerns, concerned, con
CUNSUMPSHUS	Consumption
CONTUHDIX	contradict, contradicts, contradicted, contradicting
CO'SE	course, courses, as of a stream
CO'T (n and v)	court, courts; court, courts, courted, courting
COULDN'	could not
COULD'UH	could have
COUNSTUBBLE	constable, constables
COW	cow, cows, bull, bulls, ox, oxen, cattle
CULLUD	colored, colored people, the dark race
CRACK 'E BRE'T'	crack his or her breath; same as "crack 'e teet"
CRACK 'E TEET	crack, cracks, cracked, cracking his, her or their teeth, meaning opened her or his mouth to speak; as: 'E yent crack 'e teet
CRACKUHDAY	crack or break of day
CRAP (n and v)	crop, crops; crops, cropped, cropping
'CRAPE (n and v)	scrape, scrapes, scraped, scraping

'CRATCH (n and v)	scratch, scratches, scratched, scratching
CREDENSHUL	credential, credentials
CREDIK (n and v)	credit, credits, credited, crediting
CREETUH	creature, creatures Commonly applied to a beast of burden
CRIK	creek, creeks
CROOKETY	crooked; also tricky, unreliable
CROSSROAD	the cross roads
CUMP'NY	company, companies
CUMPOSHASHUN	conversation
CUNWEENYUNT	convenient, conveniently, convenience
CUNWENSHUN	convention, conventions
CUSS (n and v)	curse, curses, cursed, cursing
CUT'DOWN, or TEK'DOWN	dejected, chagrined
CUZ,N	cousin, cousins (Shakespeare's "coz")
CYA'	carry, carries, carried, carrying
CYAA'	car, cars
CYAAF (n and v)	calf, calves; to calve, etc.
CYAAM	calm, calms; "uh cyaam sea"
CYAA'PENTUH	carpenter, carpenters
CYAARIDGE	carriage, carriages
CYAA'T	cart, carts
CYAN'	can't
CYAS'	cast, casts, casting
CYAS'NET	castnet used for taking shrimp and mullet from tidal creeks

CYA'UM	carry, carried, etc, him, her, it, them
CYO'	cure, cures, cured, curing
"D">D	Return to top
DAT	that
DAA'K	dark
DAA'KY	darken, darkens, darkened, darkening
DAA'TUH	daughter, daughters
DA' DEY	that there
DAINJUS	dangerous
DAMIDGE (n and v)	damage, damages, damaged, damaging
DAYBRUK	daybreak, day has broken
DAYCLEAN	broad daylight
DEBBLE'UB'UH	devil of a
DEEF	deaf
DEEPO'	depot, railway station
DEESTUNT	decent, respectable
DEM	them, they, those, their, theirs them," as "Sancho dem," meaning Sancho and his companions
DEM'OWN	theirs, their own
DEMSELF	them, they, themselves
DEN	then, than
'DENTICUL	identical
DESE	these
DESEYUH	these here
DISSO	just so
DE'T'	death
DEY	they

DEY	there
DEY DEY	there, there; right there; a repetition for greater emphasis
DEYFO'	therefore
DIBE	dive, dives, dived, dove, diving
DIFFUNCE	differ, difference
DIMMYCRACK	Democrat, Democrats, Democratic
DIS'	this; just
DISAPP'INT (n and v)	disappoint, disappoints, disappointed, disappointing, disappointment, disappointments
DISGUS'	disgust, disgusts, disgusted
DISHYUH	this, this here
DISTRUS'	distrust, distrusts, distrusted, distrusting
DISTRUSS	distress (See "deestruss")
DISTUNT	distant, distance
Do'	door, doors
'DO'	though, although
DOG (n and v)	dog, dogs, dogged, dogging
DON'	don't, doesn't
DONE DO' UM	did it, finished the job
DONE'UM	did it
DO'STEP	doorstep, doorsteps
DO'UM	do it, does it, did it, doing it
DRAP (n and v)	drop, drops, dropped, dropping
DREEN (n and v)	drain, drains, drained, draining
DRIBE	drives, drove, driven, driving
DROBE (n)	drove, droves, as of animals

DROWNDID	drown, drowns, drowned, drowning
DUB	dove, doves
DUH	do, does; in, to,
DUNKYUH	don't care, doesn't care, didn't care
DUNNO	don't know, doesn't know, didn't know
DU'T	dirt, earth
DU'TTY	dirty, soiled
"E">E	Return to top
'E	he, she, it
EART	earth, world, or soil, ground
EBBUH	ever
EBBUHLASTIN'	everlasting
EBE	Eve, woman's name; also eaves
EBENIN'	evening, evenings; "good evening," a salutation
EB'N	even
EB'NSO	even so
EB'RY	every
EB'RYT'ING	everything
EB'BYWEH	everywhere
ECKNOWLEDGE	knowledge, ability, understanding
EDDYCASHUN	education
EEDUH	either
EEDUHSO	either so, either, else, or
EEGNUNT	ignorant
EEN	in
EENBITE (also eenwite)	invite, invites, invited, inviting

EENFAWM	inform, informs, informed, informing
EENHABIT	inhabit, inhabits, inhabited, inhabiting
EENJINE	engine, engines
EENJY	enjoy, enjoys, enjoyed, enjoying; experience
EENSIDE	inside
EENSULT	(n and v) insult, insults, insulted, insulting
EENTITLE	entitle, entitles, entitled, entitling
EENTITLEMENT	entitlement, "title;
EENTRUSS	interest
EF	if
EH, EH!	an exclamation
ENNY	any
ENT	ain't, are not, is not, isn't
EN' T'ING	and things, and everything
ENTY	ain't it, isn't it, are they not, etc.
ENT WUT'	isn't worth, meaning totally worthless, of no account
EPPRULL	April
'ESE'F	himself, herself, itself
'E STAN'	So it, he or she, stands so, it is so, it looks so, etc.
EXCEED	succeed, succeeds, succeeded, succeeding
EXCUSIN'	excusing, except, excepting (See "'scusin")

EXWANCE	advance, advances, advanced, advancing
EXWANTIDGE	advantage, advantages
EDWICE	advice
EDWISE	advise, advises, advised, advising Ezas
"F">F	Return to top
FABUH (n and v)	favor, favors, favored, favoring
'F'AID	afraid, afraid of
FAIT'	faith
FAIT'FUL	faithful, earnest
FAITFULES'	faithfullest
FAMBLY	family, families; family's, families'
FANNUH	a wide, shallow basket used for winnowing beaten rice or separating the corn husks from grist after grinding.
FARRUH	father, fathers
FARRUHLAW	Father-in-law, fathers-in-law
FAS'	fast
FASHI'N	fashion, like, resemblance
FAST'N	fasten, fastens, fastened, fastening
FAU'T	fault, faults
FAWK	(n and v) fork, forks, forked, forking
FAWM	(n and v) form, forms, formed, forming
FAWTY	forty
FAWWU'D	forward
FIBBYWERRY	February

FEDDUH	feather, feathers
FEED'UM	feed, feeds, fed, feeding him, her, it, them
'FEN'	fend, defend
FIAH (n and v)	fire, fires, fired, firing
FIBE	five; "fibe dolluh en' seb'ntyfi' cent'"
FLABUH	(n and v) flavor, flavors, flavored, flavoring; as: "Da' buckruh' hogmeat flabuh me mout' 'tell uh done fuhgit uh hab sin fuhkill'um"That white man's pork flavored my mouth so that I forgot the sin I committed in killing the hog.
FLATFAWM	platform, platforms
FLO'	floor, floors, floored, flooring
FO'	four
'FO'	before (See "befo"')
FO'CE	force, forces, forced, forcing
FORRUD	forehead, foreheads
FO'TEEN	fourteen
FOWL	fowl, fowls; chicken, chickens
FREEDMUN	freedman, freedmen
FREEDUM	freedom
FREEHAN'	freehanded, generous, liberal
FREEMALE	female, females
FR'EN'	friend, friends
FRUM	from
FRYBAKIN	fried bacon
FUDDUH	far, farther, farthest; further
FUH	for, for to

FUHGIT	forget, forgets, forot, forgetting, forotten
FUH HAB	for have: "One dance bin fuh hab deepo' las' night a dance was to have been had at the depot last night.
FUHR'EBBUH	forever, always, all the time
FUH'UM	for him, her, it
FSUTT'N	for certain, sure
FUH TRUE	in truth, for truth, it is so
FULL'UP	filled up, as a hive with honey, or a lady with wrath
FLUN'RUL	funeral, funerals
FUS'	first
"G">G	Return to top
GABRULL	Aingel Gabrielhe
'GAGE	engage, engages, engaged, engaging; hire, hired, etc.
GAL	girl, girls; girl's, girls' Also used familiarly in addressing women
'GATUH	alligator, alligators
GAWD	God, Gods, God's
GEDDUH	gather, gathers, gathered, gathering
G'EM	give, gives, gave, giving him, her, it, them
'GEN	again
'GENSE	against
GIB' / GI	give, gives, gave, giving
GIMME	give me, gives me, gave me, giving me

GIN'NLLY	generally, in general
GIN'UL	general
GIT	get, gets, getting, got
GITTA	get a
GITT'RU	get through, got through; finish, finished
GITTUH	get a
GIT'WAY	get, gets, getting, got away
GI'WE	give us, gives us, gave us, giving us
'GLEC'	neglect, neglects, neglected, neglecting
GLUB	glove, gloves
GONE'WAY	go away, goes away, gone away, went away
GOODFASHI'N	good fashion well, thoroughly
GOT	get, gets, have, had; also, has got to
GO'WAY	go away! get out!
GRABBLE (n and v)	gravel, gravels, graveled, graveling
GRABE	grave, graves
GRAFF	grab, grabs, grabbed, grabbing; grasp, seize, seized
GRAMMA	grandmother
GRAN'	Grand, grandchild, grandson, or anyone in such relationships of "grand"
GRAN'MAAMY	grandmother

GRANNY	grandmother, but used for any old Negro woman, whether related or not
GRAN'PUH	grandfather
GREE	agree, agrees, agreed, agreeing
'GREEMENT	agreement, agreements
GREESE (n and v)	grease: "greese 'e mout'," to feed with fatness, as with bacon
GREESY	greasy
GROUN'	ground, land, piece of land
GRUMMA	grandma GRUM'PA grandpa
GRUNNUTS	groundnut, peanuts GUBNUH governor,
GWINE	going, going to
GWININ'	goings and goings on
GYAA'D (n and v)	guard, guards, guarded, guarding
GYAA'D'N	garden, gardens
GYAP	gap, gaps, as in a fence or hedge nebbuh gyap"she never opened her mouth
"H">H	Return to top
HAA'BIS'	harvest
HAA'D	hard
HAA'DHEAD	hardhead, hardheaded
HAA'KEE	hark you or ye, hear
HAA'NESS (n and v)	harness, harnesses, harnessed, harnessing
HAANT	haunt, haunts; apparition; ghost, ghosts
H'AA'T	heart, hearts
H'AA'T'	hearth, hearths

HAB	have, has, had, having
HAFFUH	have to, had to
HAIR RIZ'	hair rose (with fright)
HALFACRE	half acre 210 feet squarea measure of distance or area
HAN' (n and v)	hand, hands, handed, handing
HANKUH	hanker, long, longs, longed, longing for; desire,
HAPP'N	happed, happens, happened, happening
HARRICANE	hurricane, hurricanes; "hurricane tree," one thrown down by storm
HATCHITCH	hatchet, hatchets
HAWN	horn, horns
HAWSS	horse, horses
HEAD (n and v)	head, heads; head, heads, headed, heading off
HEAD'UM	get, gets, got, getting ahead of him, her, it, them
HEBBY	heavy, great; as: "uh hebby cumplain"'a great outcry
HE'LT'	health
HE'LT'Y	healthy
HENDUH	hinder, hinders, hindered, hindering
HENG	hang, hangs, hanged, hung, hanging
HENGKITCHUH	handkerchief, handkerchiefs
HICE	hoist, hoists, hoisted, hoisting
HICE DE CHUNE	raise or hoist a tune

HIM'OWN	his, hers, his own, her own, its own
HIN'	hind, behind; as, "hine foot" hind feet
HISTORICUSS	historic, historical
HITCH	hitch, hitches, hitched, hitching; also for marry, marrying
HOL' (n and v)	hold, holds, held, holding
HOL'FAS'	Hold Fasta favorite dog name
HOLLUH (n and v)	hollow, hollows, hollowed, hollowing
HOM'NY	hominy
HONGRY	hungry, hunger
HUCCOME	how come, how came;
HUND'UD	hundred, hundreds
HUNNUH	you (See "oonuh" "hoonuh!l and "wunnuh")
HU'T (n and v)	hurt, hurts, hurting
"I">I	Return to top
INFLUMMASHUN	information
INGINE	engines
INJUN	Indian, Indians
I'UN (n and v)	iron, irons, ironed, ironing
IZ	is
"J">J	Return to top
JALLUS	jealous, jealousy
JAYBU'D	jaybird, jaybirds
'JECK'	reject, rejects; object, objects, objected, objecting
'JECKSHUN	objection, objections
JEDGE (n and v)	judge, judges, judged, judging

JEDUS	Jesus
JESTUSS	justice
JINE	join, joins, joined, joining
JININ'	joining; adjoining
JINNYWERRY	January
JIS'	just
JISSO	just so
JOOK	jab, jabs, jabbed, jabbing
JOOKASS	jackass, jackasses
JUE	Due is due
JU'K	jerk, jerks, jerked, jerking
JUNTLEMUN	gentleman, gentlemen
"K">K	Return to top
'KACE	scarce
'KACELY	Scarcely, hardly
KETCH	catch, catches, caught, catching; took, take; as: "'E ketch 'e tex f'um de fus' chaptuh een Nickuhdemus."He took his text from the first chapter of Nicodemus Also for reach, reached; as: "Time uh ketch de ribbuh bank, de dog done gone"
KETCH'UM	catch, catches, caught, catching him, her, it
KI	an exclamation (Sometimes "kwi" or 'kwoy
KIBBUH (n and v)	cover, covers, covered, covering
KIBBUH'UM	cover, covers, covered, covering him, her, it
KIN	can

KIN	kin, kindred
KIN'	kind, kinds; sort, sorts
KIND'UH	kind of, sort of
KNOW'UM	know, knows, knew him, her, it, them
KYARRYSENE	kerosene
"L">L	Return to top
LAA'D	lard
LAA'GIN'	enlarging, swaggering, boastful
LAA'N	learn, learns, learned, learning
LAB'RUH	laborer, laborers
LANGWIDGE	language, talk
LAS'	last, lasts, lasted, lasting; last (adverb); shoemaker's last
LAS'YEAH	last year, last year's
LAUGH (n and v)	laugh, laughs, laughed, laughing
LAVUH (n and v)	labor, labors, labored, laboring
LAWFULLY LADY	Negro's legally married wife
LEABE	leaf, leaves
LEABE (n and v)	leave, leaves, left, leaving permit, permission
LEAN FUH	lean for set out for with haste and speed
'LEB'N	eleven
LEDDOWN	lay, lays, laid or lie, lies, lay, lying down
LEEK	lick, licks, licked, licking with the tongue
LEELY	little, in size or quantity
LEETLE	little, in size or quantity
LEF'	leave, leaves, left, leaving (See "leabe")

LEF' HAN'	left hand or left handed, "lef' ban' foot," or "lef' ban' feet" left foot or left leg
LEF'UM	leave, leaves, left or leaving him, her, it, them
LEGGO	let go, lets go, letting go
LEH	let, lets, letting
LEH WE	let us
LE'M	let them
LEM'LONE	let, lets him, her, it, them alone
LEMME	let me
LEN' (V)	lend, lends, loaned, lending
LENGK	length, lengths 'LESS (or onless) unless
LIA	Lie liar, liars
LIB	live, lives, lived, living
LIBBIN'	living '
LIBE	alive
LIBBUH	liver, livers
'LIBBUH	deliver, delivers, delivered, delivering
LICK (n and v)	a blow; to whip, whips, whipped
LICK BACK	turn, turns, turned, turning back, while moving rapidly
LICKIN' (n and v)	a licking, lickings, whipping, etc
LIGHT ON	light onmount, mounts, mounted, mounting
LIGHT'OOD	lightwood resinous pinewood
LIGHT OUT	to start, start off, or away
'LIJUN	religion on listens, listened, listening

LOCUS PASTUH	local pastor, or preacher
'LONG	along, along with
LONGIS'	longest
LONGMOUT'	Long mouth descriptive of the surly or contemptuous pushing out of the lips of an angry or discontented Negro
'LONGSIDE	alongside
LONGUH	longer
'LONG'UM	along with, or with him, her, it, them
'LOW'UM	allow, allows, allowed, allowing him, her, it, them
LUB (n and v)	love, loves, loved, loving; like, likes, liked
LUK	like, alike
LUKKUH	like, like unto, resembling
LUK'UM	like or resembling him, her, it, them
"M">M	Return to top
MAA'CH	March; march, marches, marched, marching
MAA'K (n and v)	mark, marks, marked, marking
MA'AM	madam
MAAMY	mother, mothers
MAA'SH	marsh, marshes
MANNUS	manners, politeness, courtesy
MANNUSSTUBBLE	Well-mannered, polite
MARRI'D	married, marry, marries, marrying
MASS	master when used with a name
MASTUH	Master used only for God

MATCH (n and v)	match, matches, matched, matchin Yet "matches" is sometimes used for the singular; as, "Gimme uh matches" give me a match
MAUM	same as "maumuh," when used with the name of the person spoken to or of, as "Maum Kate"
MAWNIN'	morning, mornings; also "good morning!"
MEAN	mean, meanness
MED'SIN	medicine, medicines, physic
MEDJUH (n and v)	measure, measures, measured, measuring
MEDJUHR'UM	measure, measures, measured, measuring him, her, it, them
MEK	make, makes, made, making
MEK'ACE	make haste
MEK ANSUH	make, makes, making, made reply
MEK FUH	make for; to go to, goes to, went to, going to
MEK OUT	make, makes, made, making out; a makeshift
MEK YO MANNUS	make your manners, your obeisance
MEMBUH	member, members as of a church or society
'MEMBUH	remember, remembers, remembered, remembering; remind, etc.
'MEMB'UNCE	remembrance, remembrances

MEN' 'E PACE	mend his, her, its, their pace; hurry, hurry up, etc.
MENS	Men
MUHSELF	myself I
MET'DIS'	Methodist, Methodists
METSIDGE	message, messages
MIDDLEDAY	midday, noon
MIDDLENIGHT	midnight
MIN'	mind, minds, minded, minding; heed, etc.; take care
MINE	of, protect, cherish, guard
'MIRATION	admiration, wonder, astonishment
MIS	Miss, Mrs., Mistress
MISTUH	Mr.
MO'	more
MOAN	moan, moans, moaned, moaning
MO' BETTUH	more better, better
MO' LONGUH	more longer, longer
MO'N	mourn, mourns, mourned, mourning
MO'NFUL	mournful
'MONG	among, amid
MONK'Y	monkey, monkeys
MONSTROSITY	monstrous
MO'NUH	mourner, mourners
MO'NUH	more than
MO'NUH DA'	more than that
MOOBE	move, moves, moved, moving
MO'OBUH	moreover

MO,RIS, MO'RES'	most
MOUT'	mouth, mouths
MUHLASSIS	molasses
MUKKLE	myrtle, myrtles; myrtle thickets
MUNT'	month, months
MURRUH	Mother, mothers
MURRUHLAW	Mother-in-law
MUS'BZ	,must be, must have, must have been
MUSKITTUH	mosquito, mosquitoes
MUSSIFUL	merciful
MUSSY	mercy, mercies
MUSTU'D	mustard
MY'OWN	mine, my
"N">N	Return to top
NAKID	naked
NARITY	naked, nakedness
'NARRUH	another (See "'nodduh" and "Inorruh")
NAVUH	neighbor, neighbors
NEBBUH	never
NEEDUH	neither
NEEDUHSO	neither so, neither, nor
NEMMIN'	Never mind
NES' (n and v)	nest, nests, nested, nesting
NEWNITED STATE	United States
NIGH	near, also draw near to
NIGH'UM	near, or nearing him, her, it, them
'N'INT	anoint, anoints, anointed, anointing (See "renoint")

NO'COUNT	no account, worthless
'NODDUH	another (See "'narruh" and "'norruh")
NOMANNUSSUBBLE	impolite, without manners, rude
NOMINASHUN	nominate, nominates, nominated, nominating
NOTUS (n and v)	notice, notices, noticed, noticing
NOWEMBUH	November
NUBBUH	never (See "nebbuh")
'NUF	enough, abundance
NUH	nor; also for and
'NURRUH	another
NUSS (n and v)	nurse, nurses, nursed, nursing
NUSSO	not so
NUTT'N'	nothing
NYAM	eat, eats, eating, ate; sometimes "nyamnyam," a epetition for emphasis
NYANKEE	Yankee, Yankees
NYOUNG	young
NYOUNGIS'	youngest (n and v) use, uses, used, using (See NYUZE (v) used, using
"O">O	Return to top
OAGLY	Ugly
OBJECK'	object
OBSERB'	observe, observes, observed, observing
OB'SHAY	overseer, overseers
OBUH	over, above

OBUHTEK	overtake, overtakes, overtook, overtaking
OBUH'SHROW	overthrow, overthrows, overthrew, overthrowing; overthrown
OCTOBUR	October
ODDUH	other, others
ODDUHRES	the other rest, the rest, remainder
OFF'UH	off, off of
OFFUH	offer, offers, offered, offering
OFF'UM	off, or off of him, her, it, them
ONBUTT'N	unbutton, unbuttons, unbuttoned, unbuttoning
ONCOMMUN	uncommon
ONDEESTUNT	indecent, indecency
ONDELICATE	indelicate, presumptuous
ONDUH	under
ONDUHNEET'	underneath
ONDUHSTAN'	understand, understands, understood, understanding
ONDUHTER	undertake, undertakes, undertook, undertaking
ONE	only; "me one," I only
ONE'NARRUH ONE'NODDUH	one another
ONETIME	once, once upon a time
ONHITCH	unhitch, unhitches, unhitched, unhitching; also marital separation
ONKIBBUH	uncover, uncovers, uncovered, uncovering

ONLOCK	Unlock, unlocks, unlocked, unlocking
ONMANNUSSUBBLE	unmannerly, impolite, rude
ONNUH (n and v)	honor, honors, honored, honoring
ONNUHRUBBLE	honorable
ONRABBLE	unravel, unraves, unrav
ONREASUNNUBBLE	unreasonable
ONSAA'T'N	uncertain
ONSATTIFY	unsatisfied, unsatisfying
ONTE'L	until
ONTIE	untie, unties, untied, untying
'OOD	wood, woods
OOMAN	woman, woman's; women, women's
OSIITUH	oyster, oysters
OUGHTUH	ought, ought to, ought to be
OUT'UH	out
"P">P	Return to top
PAA'D'N (n and v)	pardon, pardons, pardoned, pardoning
PAA'DNUH	partner, partners
PAA'KUH	Parker low-country family name
PAA'LUH	parlor, parlors
PAA'SIMONY	parsimony, also avarice or rapacity
PAA'S'N	parson, parsons
PAAT'	path, paths
PAA'T (n and v)	part, parts, parted, parting
PAA'TY	party
PAPUH (n and v)	paper, papers, papered, papering

PARRYSAWL	parasols
PASHUN	patience forbearing
PASSOBUH	Passover
PASS'UM	pass, passes, passed, passing him, her, it, them
PASTUH	pastor, pastors; pasture, pastures
'PORTUN'	important
'PAWTUNCE	importance
PEACEUBBLE	peaceable, peaceful
PEAWINE	peavine, peavines
PENITENSHUS	penitentiary
'PEN'PUN	depend, depends, depended, depending upon
PERUSE	to saunter, walk in a leisurely manner
PINCH'UM	pinch, pinches, pinched, pinching him, her, it
'PIN	Spill, spins, spun, spinning
PINDUH	pindar, peanut, peanuts
PINELAN'	pineland, pinelands
'PINION	opinion, opinions
P'INT (n and v)	point, points, pointed, pointing; direct
'P'INT	appoint, appoints, appointed, appointing
'P'INTMENT	appointment, appointments
'PISKUBBLE	Episcopal, Episcopalian
'PISTLE	Epistle, Epistles (Bible)
PITCHUH	pitcher, pitchers
PIT	put, Puts, Put, Putting
PIT'UM	put him, her, it, them

PIZEN	poison, poisons, poisoned, poisoning
PIZENOAK	poisonoak, or poison ivy
'PLASH (n and v)	splash; to splash, splashes, splashed, splashing
PLATEYE	A ghostly apparition
PLAY	'Possumto make believe, to fool, deceive
PLEASE KIN	please can – a redundancy; as: "please kin gimme"
PLEDJUH	pleasure, pleasures
PLEDJUHR'UM	please, give pleasure to him, her, it, them
PO'	poor, also thin, lean, low in flesh
PO'BUCKRUH	a poor white man, the poor whites
PO'BUCKRUHNIGGUH	a Negro who had formerly belonged to the poorer whites, or those not of the "quality"
PO'CH	porch, porches
POLITICUSS	political (See "cawpsus politicksus")
PO'LY	poorly, describing health
POOTY	pretty
PO'R	pour, pours, poured, pouring
PO'R'UM	pour, pours, poured, pouring it, that
POS' (n and v)	post, posts, posted, posting
POSITUBBLE	positive, positively
POSSIMMUN	persimmon, persimmons; the tree and fruit

PO'TRIAL	Port Royal
PRAISEMEETIN'	Prayer meeting
PRAY (n and v)	prayer, prayers; prays, prayed, praying
'PREAD	spread, spreads, spreading
PREECHUH	preacher, preachers; minister, ministers
PREECHUH ON DE SUKKUS	the circuit or traveling preacher
PREMUSBIZ	premises
PRESINCK	precinct
PRES'N'LY	presently
PREZZYDENT	president
PRIBLIDGE (n and v)	privilege, privileges, privileged
PRIZZUNT	present, presents, presented, presenting
PRIZZUNT AA'M	present arms
PROMMUS (n and v)	promise, promises, promised, promising
PUOOBE	prove, proves, proved, proving
PROPUTTY	property, wealth
'PUBLIKIN	Republican
PUSCEED	proceed, proceeds, proceeded, proceeding
PUHAPS	perhaps
P'UHJEC'	project, projected
PUHJUH	perjure, perjures, perjured, perjuring
PUHLICITUH	solicitor, solicitors
PUHLITE	polite, politely
PUHTEK	protect, protects, protected, protecting

PUHTEKSHUN	protection
PUHTETTUH	potato, potatoes usually sweet (See "tettuh")
PUHTICKLUH	particular, particularly
PUHWIDE	provide, provides, provided, providing
PUHWID'N	providing, also provided
PUHWIDUH	provider, providers
PUHWISHUN	provision, provisions; ration, rations
PUHWOKE	provoke, provokes, provoked, provoking
PUHWOKIN'	provoking
PUHZAC'LY	exactly, precisely
PUHZISHUN	position, positions
PULBLIC	public, the public
PUNKIN	pumpkin, pumpkins
PUNKINSKIN	pumpkin colored or mulatto Negro
PUNNOUNCE	pronounce, pronounces, pronounced, pronouncing
'PUNTOP	upon, on, on top of
'PUNTOP'UI	upon top Of, on top of, at
PUSSON	person, persons
PUSSONULLY	personally
PYAZZUH	piazza, piazzas; porch, porches; veranda
"Q">Q	Return to top
'QUAINTUN'	acquainted, acquainted with
'QUAINTUNCE	acquaintance, acquaintances
QUAWL	quarrel, quarrels

QUAWLMENT	quarrel, quarrels, quarreled, quarreling
QUAWT	quart, quarts
QUAWT'LY	quarterly
QUAWTUH (n and v)	quarter, quarters, quartered, quartering
'QUEEZE	squeeze, squeezes, squeezed squeezing
QUESCHUN SQUESCHUN (n and v)	question, questions, questioned
QUILE (n and v)	coil, coils, coiled, coiling
'QUIRE	require, requires, required, requiring
'QUIRE	inquire, inquires, inquired, inquiring
QUIZZIT	(quiz) ask, asks, asked, asking; to question, questions, questioned
"R">R	Return to top
RABBISH	ravish, ravishes, ravished, ravishing
RAB'N	raven, ravens; vulture, vultures; buzzard, buzzards
RAB'NEL	Ravenel, Ravenel family name
RACKTIFY	to break, breaks, broke, broken, breaking Confuse in mind
RAIN (n and v)	rain, rains, rained, raining
RALE	real, very, truly
RAPPIT	rapid, rapidly
RASHI'N (n and v) r	ration, rations, rationed, rationing
RAYBE	rear, rears, reared, rearing

'READY	already
REB'RENT	reverend used also as a noun, as "de reb'ren'"
RECISHUN	decision, decisions
REDDUH	rather
REFEN'	defend, defends, defended, defending
REINGE	reins
REMONIA	pneumonia
RENITE	unite, unites, united, uniting
RENOINT	anoint, anoints, anointed, anointing
RENOINTED	anointed
REPEAH	appear, appears, appeared, appearing
REPLOY (rare)	reply, replies, replied, replying
REPOSE	oppose, opposes, opposed, opposing
RESPLAIN	explain, explains, explained, explaining; elucidate
RETCH	reach, reaches, reached, reaching
'RIAH	Maria
RIBBUH	river, rivers
RIDICK'LUS	ridiculous, also outrageous, scandalous
ROAS'	roast, roasts, roasted, roasting
ROKKOON	raccoon, raccoons
ROOS' (n and v)	roost, roosts, roosted, roosting
ROOSTUH	rooster, roosters
RUBBIDGE	rubbish
RUCKUHNIZE	recognize, recognizes, recognized, recognizing

RUDDUH	rather
RUPPEZUNT	represent, represents, represented, representing
"S">S	Return to top
SAEB	serve, serves, served, serving
SAA'BINT (also "saa'bunt")	servant, servants
SAA'BIS (also sarbis)	service, services, use
SAA'CH	search, searches, searched, searching; also examine
SAA'F	soft
SAA'F'LY	softly
SAA'PUNT	serpent (biblical)
SAA'T'N	certain
SAWANNUH	Savannah
SABBIDGE	savage, savages
SABE	save, saves, saved, saving
SABEYUH	the Savior
SA'LEENUH	St. Helena Island, on the South Carolina coast
SAME LUKKUH(also sukkuh)	same like, like, resembling
SAN'	sand
SAT'D'Y	Saturday
SATTIFACKSHUN	satisfaction
SATTIFY	satisfy, satisfies, satisfied, satisfying
SAWT (n and v)	sort, sorts, sorted, sorting
SAWTUH	sort of after a fashion
SAY	say, says, said, saying
SCA'CE	scarce
SCA'CELY	scarcely, hardly (See "kacely")

SCATTUH	scatter, scatters, scattered, scattering
SCHEMY	scheming, tricky
SCOLE	scold, scolds, scolded, scolding
SCRIPTUH	Scripture the Bible
'SCUSE (noun)	excuse, excuses
'SCUSIN'	excusing, except
'SCUSSHUN	excursion, excursions
'SCUZE (verb)	excuse, excuses, excused, excusing
SEAZ'NIN'	seasoning
SEB'N	seven
SEB'NPUNCE	seven pence (See "fo'punce")
SEB'NTEEN	seventeen
SEB'NTY	seventy
SECKBITERRY	secretary, secretaries
SECTEMBTUH	September
SECUN'	second
SEDDOWN	Sit or set down, sits or sets down, sat or set down
SEE	See, sees, saw, seen, seeing
SEEGYAA'	cigar, cigars
SEEM	seem, seems, seemed, seeming
'SELF	himself, herself, itself, themselves
SENCE	since
SEN'UM	send, sends, sent, sending him, her, it, them
SESSO	say so, says so, said so, saying so (See "susso")
SET	sit, Sits, sat, sitting (See "seddown")

SETTLE'	settled, as: "settle' 'ooman," a settled woman, a Negro woman of a certain age, not a 'flapper
SETT'N'	Sitting
SETT'N'UP	sitting up a Negro wake; a small religious meeting
SEZZEE	says he, said he
SEZZI	says I, said I
SHAA'K	shark, sharks
SHAA'P	sharp
SHAA'P'N	sharpen, sharpens, sharpened, sharpening
SHABE	shave, shaves, shaved, shaving
SHADDUH (n and v)	shadow, shadows, shadowed, shadowing
SHAME (n and v)	shame, shames, shamed, shaming, ashamed
SHAWT	short, shawtpashunt," short patience or irritable, irritability
SHAYAYRE	share, shares, shared, sharing
SHAYRE'UM	share, shares, shared, sharing him, her, it, them
SHE'OWN	her own
SHEPU'D	shepherd, shepherds
SHE SHE TALK	woman's talk, gabble
SHET	shut, shuts, shut, shutting
SHISH	such
SHO'	sure, surely
SHO'LY	surely
SHOOT'UM	shoot, shoots, shot, shooting him, her, it, them

SHOULDUH	shoulder, shoulders, shouldered, shouldering
SHOULD'UH	should have
SHOUT (n and v)	shout, shouts; shout, shouts, shouted, shouting; frenzied outcries of a religious devotee A plantation dancing festival, frequently accompanied by beating sticks on the floor
SHOW	show, shows, showed, showing
SHOW'UM	show, shows, showed, showing him, her, it, them
SHROUD	shroud, shrouds; also surplice, surplices, as: "De 'Piskubble preechuh pit on 'e shroud"
SHUB	shove, shoves, shoved, shoving
SHUH	pshaw!
SHUM	see, sees, saw, seeing him, her, it, them
SHU'T	shirt, shirts
SIDE'UH	on the side of, alongside
SILBUH	silver
SILBY	Silvia
SILUNT	silent, silence, as "silunt een co't!'@silence in court I
SISTUH (formal)	sister, sisters
SKAY'D	scared
SKAYRE	scare, scares, scared, scaring
SKAYTODE'T'	scare or seared to death
SKU'T	skirt, skirts
SLABE	Slave, slaves
SLABERY	slavery

SLABERY TIME	slavery times before freedom
SLEEBE	sleeve, sleeves
SLIP'RY	slippery
SMAA'T	smart
'SMATTUH	what is the matter?
SNAWT	snort, snorts, snorted, snorting
SNOW'RE	snore, snores, snored, snoring
SOAD	sword, swords
SOBUH	Sober
SOBUHR'UM	sober, sobers, sobered, sobering him, her, them
SODUH (n and v)	soldier, soldiers; soldiering
SOMEBODY	somebody's, someone, some one's
SOMEBODY'OWN	somebody's own
SONNYLAW	son-in-law, sons-in-law
SOONMAN	A smart, alert, wide awake man
SPAA'K	Spark, sparks
SPANG	all the way, expressive of distance
SPARRUH	sparrow, sparrows
SPARRUHGRASS	Asparagus
SPEC	expect, expects, expected, expecting; suspect, suspects, suspected, suspecting
SPECIFY	from specify, but greatly extended to include almost all meanings of "specifications" proving inadequate, not coming up to expectations, etc.
SPECKLY	speckled
SPEN'	spend, spends, spent, spending

SPERRITUAL	Spiritual, spirituals, the Negro religious songs
'SPERIUNCE	experience, experiences, experienced, experiencing
SPESHLY	specially, especially
SPIDUH	spider, spiders
SPILE	spoil, spoils, spoiled, spoiling
'SPISHUN	suspicion, suspicions
'SPISHUS	suspicious, suspiciously
'SPIZE	despise, despises, despised, despising
'SPLAIN	explain, explains, explained, explaining
SPLOTCH	blot, blots; stain, stains
'SPON	respond, responds, responded, responding
'SPONSUBBLE	responsible, also used emphatically or specifically; as: "Tell'um 'sponsubble fuh do da' t'ing"
'SPOSE	expose, exposes, exposed, exposing
S'POSE	suppose, supposes, supposed, supposing
SPO'T	sport, sports; also sporting man
SPOT'N' (n and v)	sport, sports, sported, sporting
SPO'TY	Sporty
'SPUTE (n and v)	dispute, disputes, disputed, disputing; contest with
'SPUTE'N	disputing

SQUESCHUN	question sometimes used for the more common "quizzit," which see
STAA'CH (n and v)	starch, starches, starched, starching
STAAR	star, stars
STAA'T	Start, starts, started, starting
STAA'T NAKID	stark naked
'STABLISH	establish, establishes, established, establishing
STAN'	stand, stands, stood, standing; look, looks, looked, looking
STAN'	A stand, stands; deer stands, etc.
STAN'LUKKUH	stand, stands, stood, standing like; to look like, etc.
'STEAD'UH (also 'stidduh)	instead of STEAL steal, steals, stole, stealing
STO'	store, stores; shop, shops
'STONISH	astonish, astonishes, astonished, astonishing
STRAIGHT'N FUH	made for, making for; run quickly or swiftly
STRENGK	Strength
STRETCHOUT	stretch out extend
'STROY'D	destroy, destroys, destroyed, destroying
'STRUCKSHUN	destruction
'STRUCKSHUN	construction
STRUCTID	struck, striking
STUBB'N	stubborn
STUDY	think, plan, ponder
STUHR	stir, stirs, stirred, stirring

STUHSTIFFIKIT	Certificate
STYLISH	stylish, meaning also appropriate, dignified, suitable, as: "uh stylish grabe," being a grave ornately decorated with broken china or glass
'SUADE	persuade, persuades, persuaded, persuading
SUCKAIG SUCK	egg as: "uh suckaig dog"
SUCK ME TEET'	and "suck 'e teet"a contemptuous gesture, frequently indulged in by the fair sex
SUDD'NT	sudden, suddenly
SUFFUHRATE	separate, separates, separated, separating; also divorce, divorcing, etc.
SUH	Sir
SUH	that, say
SUHCIETY	society, societies
SUKKLE (n and v)	circle, circles, circled, circling
SUKKUH	same, same like, resembling
SUKKUHR'UM	same like, or like him, her, it, them
SUKKUS	circus, circuses
SUKKUS-PREECHUH	circuit preacher
SUMMUCH	so much, so many
SUMMUH	summer, summers, summertime
SUMP'N'	something
SUMP'N'NURRUH	something or other
SUNDOWN	Sunset

SUNHIGH	late morning, about the middle of the forenoon
SUNHOT	sunshine, heat of sun
SUNLEAN	period of the day when the sun begins to decline, and its declining: "sunlean fuh down"
SUN'UP	Sunrise
SUPPLOY	supply, supplies, supplied, supplying
SUPPUH	Supper
SUPSHUN	substance, sustenance, strength of food, as of a juicy roast: "Da' meat hab supshun een'um" that meat has much nourishment
SUSSO	say so, says so, said so, saying so (See "sesso")
SUH	So
SUTT'N	certain, certainly
SUTTINLY	certainly
SWALLUH	swallow, swallows, swallowed, swallowing
SWALLUHB'UM	swallow, swallows, swallowed, swallowing him, her, it, them
SWAWM	swarm, swarms, swarmed, swarming
SWAY,	swear, swears, swore, swearing
I SWAYTOGAWD	swear to God
SWEETH'AA'T	sweetheart, sweethearts
SWEETMOUT'	sweet mouth blarney, flattery
SWEETMOUT' TALK	soft talk of a philanderer with the gentler sex

SWELLUP	swelled, swollen up, puffed up with anger, importance or authority
SWEET'N	sweeten, sweetens, sweetened, sweetening
SWEET'NIN'	"sweetening"
SWIF'	swift, fast Swimp shrimp, shrimps
SWINGE	Singe, singes, singed, singeing
SWINK	shrink, shrinks, shrunk, shrinking
SWONGUH	"swank," swagger, swaggering, boastful
"T">T	Return to top
TAAR (n and v)	tar, tars, tarred, tarring
'TACK (n and v)	attack, attacks, attacked, attacking
'TACKTID	attacked (See "attacktid")
TACKLE (n and v)	tackle, tackles, tackled, tackling; arraign, hold accountable
'TAGUHNIZE	antagonize, antagonizes, antagonized, antagonizing; arraign, arraigned, etc.
'TAIL (n and v)	entail, entails, entailed, entailing
'TAKE (n and v)	stake, stakes, staked staking
TALK'UM	talk, talks, talked, talking; talking it, speak out, etc.
TALLUH	Tallow
TALLYGRAF (n and v)	telegraph, telegraphs, telegraphed, telegraphing; telegram, telegrams
'TAN'	stand, stands, stood, standing

'TAN'UP	stand, stands, stood, standing up
'TARRYGATE	interrogate, interrogates, interrogated, interrogating; question, questioned, etc.
TARRYPIN	terrapin, terrapins
TARRIFY	terrify, terrifies, terrified, terrifying
TARRUH	t'other, the other
TAS'	task a measure of distance as well as of area: 105 feet or 105 feet square
TAS'E	taste, tastes, tasted, tasting
TAS'E 'E MOUT'	put a taste in his, her or their mouth or mouths; meaning something appetizing to eat
T'AW'T (n and v)	thought, thoughts
'TAY	stay, stays, stayed, staying
TAYRE	tear, tears, tore, tearing
TAYRE'UM	tear, tears, tore, tearing him, her, it, them
TEDAY	Today
TEET'	tooth, teeth
TEET'ACHE	toothache
TEK	take, takes, took, taken, faking
TEK'CARE	Take care
TEK'ESELF	take, takes, took, taking himself, herself, itself, themselves
TEK ME FOOT EEN ME HAN'	"tek him foot een 'e han'"Took my foot in my hand, took his or her foot or their feet in his, her, or their hand or hands meaning hastened, hurried, speeded up

TEK'UM	take, took, taken him, it, them
TEK'WAY	take, takes, took, taking away
TEK WID'UM	taken with, pleased with him, her, it, them
'TELL	till, until
TELL'UM	tell, tells, telling, told him, her, it, them
'TEN'	attend, attends, attended, attending; intend, intends, etc.
TENDUH	Tender
T'ENGKFUL	thankful
T'ENGK'GAWD	thank God! thank, thanks, thanked, thanking God
T'ENGKY	thank you
T'NIGHT	Tonight
'TENSHUN	attention
'TENSHUN	intention
TEP (n and v)	step, steps, stepped, stepping
TETCH (n and v)	touch, touches, touched, touching Also a remnant, as: "T'engk Gawd, 'e lef' uh leetle tetch een de bottle"
TETCH'UM	touch, touches, touched, touching him, her, it, them
'TETTUH	potato, potatoes usually sweet
T'ICK	Thick
'TICK (n and v)	stick, sticks, stuck, sticking
T'ICKIT	thicket, thickets
'TICKLUH (n and v)	particular, particulars
T'ICKNESS	thickness, thicknesses
'TICKY	Sticky

T'IEF (n and v)	thief, thieves; steal, steals, stole, stolen, stealing "T'ief iz bad, but t'ief en' ketch iz de debble" It is bad to steal, but to steal and be caught is worse
T'IEFIN'	thieving
TIE'UM	tie, ties, tied, tying him, her, it, them
TIE UP 'E MOUT'	tie, ties, tied, tying up his, her, or their mouth or mouths; meaning held his, her, or their speech
T'ING	thing, things
'TING	stirig, stings, stung, stinging
T'INK	think, thinks, thought, thinking
T'IRTEEN	thirteen
T'IRTY	Thirty
T'ISTLE	thistle, thistles
TITTUH	sister, sisters (informal)
TODDUH	the other, t'other, the others
'TOOP	stoop, stoops, stooped, stooping
TOOT'	tooth, teeth
'TOP	stop, stops, stopped, stopping
'TOOPUH	on, on top of
'T'ORUHTY	authority
TOTE	"tote" carry, carries, carried, carrying
T'OUZ'N	thousand
TOWN	Charleston, "the City" (See "Chaa'stun")
TRABBLE	travel, travels, traveled, traveling
'TRAIGHT	straight

'TRAIGHT'N	straighten, straightens, straightened, straightening "'Traight'n fuh" straighten for, to hurry or extend oneself for a certain point
'TRANGLE	strangle, strangles, strangled, strangling
T'RASH	thrash, thrashes, thrashed, thrashing; thresh, threshed, etc.
T'RASHUH	thrasher, thrashers; thresher, threshers
TREDJUH	treasure, treasures
TREDJURUH	treasurer, treasurers
TREE (V)	tree, trees, treed, treeing
T'REE	rarely "stree" three
T'REETIME	three times
'TRETCH	stretch, stretches, stretched, stretching"
T'RETCHOUT	Streten out
'TRIKE	strike, strikes, struck, striking
TRIMBLE	tremble, trembles, trembled
'TRING	string, strings, strling, stringing; "tringbean" string or snapbeans
T'ROAT	throat, throats
T'ROW	throw, throws, threw, thrown, throwing
T'ROWBONE	throw "bones" (dice) play craps
T'HOW'D	threw, thrown
T'ROW WAY	throw, throws, threw, throwing, thrown away
TRUBBLE (n and v)	trouble, troubles, troubled, troubling

TRUS' (n and v)	trust, trusts, trusted, trusting
TRUTE	Truth
TRUTEMOUT'	truthmouthone who will not lie
TRYBUNUL	tribunal, tribunals
TUCKREY	turkey, turkeys
TUHBACKUH	tobacco
TUH DAT	to that
TUHGEDDUH	together
TUHRECKLY	directly
TUHR'UM	to him, her, it, them
TUK	Took
TUMMUCH	too much, intensely, ardently, fervently
'TUMP (n and v)	stump, stumps; stump, stumps, stumped, stumping
'TUMPSUCKUH	stumpsiicker, a cribsucking horse or mule
TU'N (n and v)	turn, turns, turned, turning
T'UNDUH (n and v)	thunder, thunders, thundered, thundering
TU'NFLOUR	turned flour, scalded corn meal, mush or porridge; same as Italian polenta
TU'NUP	turnip, turnips
TU'N UP	turn, turns, turned, turning up
TUP'NTINE	turpentine
T'URSD'Y	Thursday
TWELB'	Twelve
TWIS' (n and v)	twist, twists, twisted, twisting
TWIS'MOUT'	twist mouth twistmouthed
TWIS'UP	twist or twisted up

TOW CHUESDAY, Two T'URSDAY, etc.	the second Tuesday or the second Thursday in the month
TWO PLACE	second place, in the second place
TWO TIME	two times, twice
TWOT'REE	two or three
"U">U	Return to top
UHHEAD	Ahead
UHHEAD'UH	ahead of
UHLLY	early UM him, her, it, them
UP TUH DE NOTCH	Up to the notch to the Queen's taste, perfect
US	we, our
USE'N	used to be, in the habit of
USETUH!	used to, accustomed to
"W">W	Return to top
WAAGIN	wagon, wagons
WAA'MENT	"varniint, varmints," destructive animals or birds
WADMUHLAW	Wadmalaw: an island of the Carolina coast
WAH	War
WAIS'	waist, waists
WANTUH	want to, wants to, wanted to, wanting to
WARRUH	what, what is that
W'ARY	weary
WAS'E	waste, wastes, wasted, wasting
WASHUP	worship (religious)
WATUHMILYUN	watermeloia, watermelons
WAWN (n and v)	warn, warns, warned, warning
WAWSS'	wasp, wasps

WAWSS'NES'	wasp nest
WE	our, us
W'EAT	wheat
W'EATFLOUR	flour, wheat flour
W'EDDUH	whether
WEDDUH	weather, weather; to rain or storm
WEDD'N'	wedding, weddings
WEEKDAY	a week day
W'EEL (n and v)	wheel, wheels, wheeled, wheeling
W'EELBARRUH	wheelbarrow, wheelbarrows
WEGITUBBLE	vegetable, vegetables
WEH	where
WEHR'AS	whereas
WEHREBBUH	wherever
W'ENEBBUH	whenever
W'ENSD'Y	Wednesday
WE'OWN	our own, our;
WERRY	very
WE'SELF	ourselves
WESKIT	waistcoat, waistcoats
WHOEBBUN	whoever
WICTORIA	Victoria also victorious
'WICE	advice, advices
W'ICH, N	which
W'ICH EN W'Y	which and why as: "W'ich en' w'y talk' contradictory talk
WICKIT	wicked, wickedness
WID	with
WIDDUH	widow, widows

WIDT'	width, widths
W'ILE	while, awhile
WIL'CAT	wild cat, the baylynx of the Southern swamps
WIN' (n and v)	wind, winds; wind, winded winding
WIN' (n and v)	wind, winds, wound, winded
WINE	vine
WINEGUH	vinegar
'WISE	advise, advises
WISH DE TIME UH DAY	pass de time uh day a salutation, greeting
WISIT (n and v)	visit, visits, visited, visiting
W'ISKEY	whiskey
WITCH	witch, witches
'WITCH	bewitch, bewitches, bewitched, bewitching
W'ITE	white
WOICE	voice, voices
WU'D	word, words
WUDDUH DA'	what is that
WUFFUH	what for, why
WUH	what, that
WUHEBBUH	whatever
WU'K (n and v)	work, works, worked, working
WU'LL'	world, worlds
WUNDUH (n and v)	wonder, wonders, wondered, wondering
WUNT	won't, will not
WURRUM	worm, worms
WUS'DEN'EBBUH	worse than ever Wuss worse, worst

WUSSUH	worse
WUT'	worth, is worth, was worth, etc "Ent wut"a disparaging characterization Wuz was
W'YMEKSO	what makes it so, why
"Y">Y	Return to top
YAA'D	yard, yards
YAA'N	yarn, yarns
YAAS	yes
YAAS'SUH	yessir
YALLUH	yellow
YALLUH YAM	yellow yam a variety of sweet potato
YANDUH	yonder
YEAH	ear, ears (corn or other grain) ; also year, years
YEARIN'	hearing
YEDDY	hear, hears, heard, hearing
YERRY YEDDY'UM	hear, hears, heard, or hearing him, her, it, them
YELLIN'	yearling, yearlings
YENT	(ent) ain't, is not, are not; so pronounced when preceded by a soft vowel sound
YEYE	eye, eyes; so pronounced when preceded by a soft vowel sound "E yeye red" his or her eyes are bloodshot with anger
YEZ	ear, ears (human or animal)
YISTIDDY	yesterday Yiz is; so pronounced when preceded by a soft vowel sound

YO	your, yours
YOU'OWN	your own, yours
YUH	here
YUH HIM	here he, she, it is, or they are
"Z">Z	Return to top
'ZACKLY	exactly (See "puhzackly")
'ZAMMIN'	examine, examines, examined, examining; question, questioned, etc.
'ZYD'N	presiding; as: "'Zyd'n' elduh'presiding elder.

Brown, Alphonso. 2008. www.historypress.net. Charleston, S.C.

Jhanelle Brown

Jhanelle Brown, a budding artist, illustrator, and a self-taught intermediate Korean speaker, is a senior of Trinity High School and was born in Long Island, New York on September 21, 2001. Although she was born in the United States, she was raised in Kingston, Jamaica and lived with her parents and her younger sister who are Jamaican born. As she lived in her childhood home, her influence was her aunt, who inspired her to pursue art by drawing portraits of people in the family or creating colored-pencil pieces of her favorite characters at the time. In 2011, she moved to Dallas, Texas to continue her education. Her illustrations and portrait pieces have gained recognition from fellow scholars and beloved art teacher, Carolyn Allen. Her interests include but are not limited to studying the arts, international languages and culture, with the intention of becoming an interpreter as well. Her first professional piece was commissioned in 2015 and since then, she has been commissioned to do more paintings and illustrations. At the moment, she has also shown an interest in illustrating semi-realistic anime and has created her own characters. She aspires to owning her own businesses/studios here in the United States and abroad. Jhanelle has thoroughly enjoyed her contribution to this body of work and looks forward to participating in others.

About the Author

Jan Morgan is a retired school administrator living with her husband and two Scottish terriers in Bedford, Texas. She enjoyed over thirty years of service in public schools working as a teacher, a campus administrator, and finally a central office administrator. In addition, she had the privilege of working as an adjunct professor with both graduate and undergraduate students at Texas A&M University, the University of Texas at Arlington, the University of North Texas, and Concordia University Texas.

In 2012, she and her husband, Randy, founded BridgesWork, a 501(c)(3) entity that epitomizes their lasting commitment to children who grow up steeped in a culture of poverty. BridgesWork continues to thrive and grow in the Dallas Ft. Worth area today, and the Morgans persist in their dream to ensure that, despite obstacles of poverty, the children whose lives are touched by BridgesWork know they are valued, loved, and can succeed in today's world.

Dr. Morgan attended the College of Charleston, Clemson University, the Ohio State University, and the University of North Texas. *Sweet Grass Memories* exemplifies her love for the people and culture of low-country South Carolina, the magic of Wymen Meinzer's Texas, and her steadfast belief that when people come together with a shared yearning anything is possible.

CPSIA information can be obtained
at www.ICGtesting.com
Printed in the USA
FFOW03n0429300318
46082354-47039FF